Copyright 20~~ ~~

Editor: Jodi McDermitt

Cover: Tyler Bertrand

Published By: Glory Days Press

*To Alaina,*
*choose wisely!*

*Roy Wendt*

# Pick-A-Path: Apocalypse

## Book 2

You wake in a hospital after a car accident tossed you through the windshield. You were rushed to the hospital, where you had an MRI to check for fractures to your skull. Your arm was broken and is now in a cast. Bandages cover much of your head from the lacerations from the shattered windshield and the contact with the ground. Abrasions all over your body have been cleaned and bandaged. In truth, you're a mess, but at least you're alive. The damage could have been much worse.

You're not sure how long you've been out, but you vaguely remember the accident. You were unconscious when they brought you in and have spent much of the time recovering, so you aren't even sure how long you've been there. You need rest and would like to get more sleep if only the nurse would respond to your call. The IV bag is almost empty. You need pain meds bad. The button either doesn't work, she was too busy, or she was ignoring you. The throbbing in your head is getting stronger. If she doesn't come in soon, you are going to get out of bed and go find pain pills on your own.

You check the time and see it's nearly nine in the morning. Where is your partner? She/he was supposed to be there by now. In one of your lucid moments, you remember hearing that. *Wasn't it?* Or was it a dream?

A loud crash comes from the hall, like someone has overturned a large cart or a gurney. You wince at the thought. That would be painful.

Then someone screams, and you wonder what's going on. Perhaps the staff is dealing with a violent patient. Wasn't breakfast supposed to come around eight? Maybe you slept through it. But they would have left it for you, wouldn't they? You glance around the room. No tray.

Another crash, and this time, glass shatters.

"Damn!" you say, then shout out, "Lucky you're in a hospital. Although I'm not sure they can fix that."

An eerie silence, more complete than you'd think possible in a hospital, fills the hall. It is broken moments later by something else crashing. You are caught between curiosity and fear.

Do you:

1A) stay in bed? Read on.

1B) get up and check the hall? Go to page 71

1C) slide out of bed and hide behind it? Go to page 74

1A) You continue pressing the call button, but no nurse enters to check on you. Frustrated, you shout, "Hey, is there anyone out there? Somebody…please, I need meds. Anyone at all. Anyone alive out there?"

Still, no one comes. Then something bangs against your door. The sudden impact startles you. You jump, sending instant pain to your head. "What the heck was that?" you mumble. Then, to your relief, the door opens, but the drawn curtain prevents you from seeing who entered. For a moment, nothing happens. "Hello? Is that my lovely nurse?" You hasten to add, "Or my beautiful girlfriend/boyfriend?" Just in case.

You get no response but hear the scraping of feet along the tiled floor. You mind suddenly fills with every scene from every horror movie ever made in a hospital. Then, the curtains are ripped back, and you realize the movies have become reality.

You want to scream as the horrifying visage stares at you like it has no clue what you are. A sudden thought penetrates your building fear and you begin to relax. It's almost Halloween. This must be a gag.

"Ha! Good one. You had me going there for a minute." Yet you can't shake the willies. Something about this…what, creature?… doesn't feel right. "Whoever did your makeup is a genius. You look great."

The bulging red eyes study you. The wild hair reminds you of the old depictions of mad scientists. The teeth seem a little too long for the mouth, and the face too long for the body, but it's the realistic-looking blood that still appears wet that adds that final scary touch.

"Ah, I know you're having fun, and I really do like your costume, but can you get me some more pain meds? This bag is nearly empty." You point at the IV bag and the crazy looking man follows the motion.

"Okay. Maybe not. I think you're carrying this a little far, don't you? I'm a patient whose patience is running out."

The creature ambles forward.

"Okay. Cool. I'll be happy to play along once I'm properly numbed."

The man reaches the bed and lifts his hands. The nails are long and brown and look like they're full of fungus. Bits of something red are under several of them. You marvel at how real everything looks and how far he has gone to make the costume authentic. You are about to comment when one of the clawed hands swipes at you, raking deep furrows across your chest.

You cry out and swear. "What the hell are you doing?" The pain is intensified by your own injuries. The hand rises again, but before it can strike, you shift your body and lash out with a foot. It hits the creature in the midsection and propels it backward.

*Can this be real?* You glance down at your bloody chest. *Hell yeah, it's real.*

The creature advances again

You roll out of bed on the opposite side. The pain is sharp, and you collapse to one knee. As the creature comes around the bed, you unlock the wheels and pull the bed in front of you. The temporary barrier confuses the beast for a moment, giving you time to regroup your thoughts. You must get out of here before it's too late.

You search for a weapon but find nothing. The creature leans across the bed and swipes at you. You jump back, avoiding contact. You pull the bed with you. You are now pressed against the wall with no room to move.

The creature presses forward. The bed pins you to the wall. Your only defense has now become a tool for the creature. It lifts an arm again, readying another attack. You are out of time.

Do you:

1A1) try to reason with the creature? Go to page—no, don't bother; why waste a page? Go watch a horror movie. How has reasoning with the monster ever worked? This is right up there with hiding in the cemetery or trying to get out through a locked door without at least trying to unlock it. While you're pleading your case, the creature thrusts its claws through your eyeballs and into your brain. As death closes in, you're aware of a popping sound. The creature has pulled out your eyes and is eating them. Gruesome? With a choice like this, it deserves to be. Next!

1A2) find a way to escape? Read on.

1A3) go on the attack? Go to page 59

1A2) As the arm descends, you duck behind the bed. The claws swipe overhead. To your right is open space. You crawl away from the bed, get up, and run. A sharp pain rips at the back of your hand. You cry out and stumble backward. You glance down and see blood coming from the insertion site of the IV needle.

You yank it out and run, but the brief delay has given your attacker a chance to catch you. Strong hands grab you from behind and yank you off your feet. You fall back, landing with a solid thud on the floor. The wind is knocked out of you and your already concussed head throbs with a steady drumbeat, leaving you stunned.

Your vision clears in time for you to see large teeth closing on you. You raise your arm and the teeth sink into your cast. That gives you an idea. You pull your arm back, and with all the force you can muster from your position, you slam it into the creature's mouth. It howls in pain as blood drips onto you and a tooth falls from the cast.

The creature rears up and clutches at its wounded maw. You make a break for it, scampering to your feet, but the creature reacts in time to grab an ankle and trip you up. You stumble but catch your weight on your hands. A piercing pain shoots up the arm with the cast, but you push it aside.

Before the creature can drag you back, you lift a leg and slam your foot into its mouth. This time, the force sends it toppling backwards. Legs free, you take a few steps on hands and feet before righting yourself and sprinting out the door.

Once in the hall, you freeze in shock. The place looks like a war zone. Everything has been overturned or cast about. The halls are littered with trays, gurneys, supplies, and blood. Lots of blood.

A howl from your room raises the hairs on the back of your neck. You sprint down the hall, hearing the door open behind you. Your body protests, but fear is a great motivator. You push harder. You glance around for anyone who might help, but all you see are bodies…bodies whose flesh has been bitten and torn.

You reach the gap that connects to the parallel hallway. Between the two halls are the elevators. You press the button, but nothing happens. You don't have time to wait. The footfalls and howls are getting closer. Spying a sign for the stairs, you bolt for them. You reach the door, push through, and guide the door closed as as possible. Once it is shut, you run down the stairs.

You are only on the third floor, but by the time you reach the ground floor, you are gasping for air. You open the door and race out but stop after a few steps. The lobby is full of people. Dead people. There must be thirty bloody and mangled bodies strewn around the floor. This must be a drug-induced nightmare.

The outer doors are to the right. You start that way, but hear a scream coming from one of the shops to the left. Behind you, a howl echoes in the stairwell.

Do you:

1A2a) continue out the doors? Read on.

1A2b) go see who needs help? Go to page 29

1A2c) search for someone who can help? Go to page 49

1A2a) In spite of the screams for help, you decide to get free of the madness. You sprint for the door, your butt hanging out of the hospital gown. You burst through the doors and freeze in utter disbelief. It looks like there was a war outside and you slept through it.

The streets are in chaos. Car crashes are everywhere, vacant and scattered like a massive junk yard. Smoldering remains of several fires still spew black smoke into the air, like a city of factories in the early 1900s. Several bodies are strewn about in various stages of destruction. Some look as if they died of fright. Others had missing body parts or huge gaps in their flesh, making cause of death obvious.

In the distance, you hear alternating screams and car horns. Multiple gun shots make you cringe and duck. You turn to run back into the hospital, but through the glass, you see the wild man who attacked you prowling the hall. *Is he searching for you?* You don't want to find out, but where can you go?

You move away from the door. As you reach the end of the building, the parking lot comes into view. Maybe you can find a car to steal. You jog that way, aware of your assorted injuries nagging for your attention. You stop at the curb and stare over the lot. You have no skill at hotwiring cars, but you do know that newer cars are harder to boost, so you scan the lot for something older.

Just then, a woman screams, and you pivot toward the emergency room doors. You see another wild creature-like man attacking her. You take an involuntary step in her direction, thinking to help, but when you see the man rip a huge chunk of flesh from her neck, you blanch and freeze. Seeing the blood jet into the air like some fountain from hell, you retch.

A car horn makes you jump out of your skin. You back away, the desire to flee the only thing on your mind. You turn to run, but a woman calls to you. "Hurry, get in before it sees you."

You stop and turn, not sure if you're more surprised an avenue of escape has presented itself, or that she referred to the man as an it.

"I'm not waiting. Either get in or take your chances, but I'm going."

One glance at the man-thing ripping more flesh from the woman's body is all the motivation you need. You run for the car and hop in the back seat. The driver barely waits for the door to shut before racing away. You peer out the rear window in disbelief at landscape of the horror spread out around you.

You glimpse the man-thing once before the car turns a corner. It holds the lifeless body in one hand, tilts its head back and howls like a wolf. No, not a wolf, a werewolf. You sink low into the back seat and curl up into a ball. Your mind threatens to run and hide. If not for the sound of the woman's voice, you would have gladly let it go.

"Are you injured?"

"Ah, yeah. I was in an accident."

"No, I mean, did any of those things attack you? Do you have any bites or scratches?"

You look yourself over, even though you already know the answer. "No," you lie, ignoring the gouges in your chest. "Just what I had from the accident. What the hell's going on?"

"You don't know? Where have you been?"

"Ah, in the hospital," you say as if it should be obvious.

"But for how long? This has been going on for three days now."

"I think I was unconscious. I only woke up an hour ago. What's happened?"

"No one's sure. At least not completely. The popular theory is that the flu shots were either tainted or tampered with. You know the huge push this year for getting the flu shot because of the killer strain coming from Asia, right?" She continues before you can answer. "Anyway, the thinking is it was all a ruse to get as many people infected as possible. The first reported cases had people going crazy, tearing at their own skin. A few assaults and lots of destruction came next. But within hours, there were so many cases no one could keep up with them, and law enforcement was stretched too thin to handle them all."

She makes a series of quick turns, throwing you from door to door on the back seat.

"When the police became overwhelmed, the National Guard was called in, but so many of them had the shots, it became a civil war. Now only pockets of uninfected Guardsmen remain."

You are unable to respond. The entire story is so full of madness that you have trouble absorbing it. How could this happen? "Is someone behind the tainted vaccines?"

"That's the thinking, but everything fell apart before they found an answer. Hell, we could be under attack by foreign forces by now and don't even know it."

"Where are we going?"

"I'm going to my house. I need to check on my family. My husband got the shot, but not the kids. I'm worried ..." She can't finish the sentence, but you understand her concern. If the husband turned into a crazed killer, the kids might be in trouble. You straighten to a sitting position and watch out the front windshield.

Death and destruction surround you. Something hits the car and bounces away. You look back to see what it was and see two wild things giving chase. You shiver violently. The pain is building. You wish you had time to grab some drugs.

"You okay?"

You look up to meet her gaze in the mirror. "The pain is getting bad."

"I should have something you can take at the house. It should only be a few minutes." She adds under her breath, "If we get that far."

She turns into a residential community. A house is on fire. Bodies litter the yards. A man hangs out a car window. His arm is missing. Up ahead, a head on collision blocks the road. Without pause, she angles up a driveway, across the front lawn, and down the next driveway. Another right turn, and she screeches to a stop in front of an older vinyl-sided two-story house.

"Oh God," she says. You see why instantly. The front door is open, and a chair is on the front lawn, having been thrown through the picture window.

She jumps from the car and runs up the front steps.

Not sure what you should do, you look from the house and the disappearing figure of the woman running through the open door to the keys dangling in the ignition.

Do you:

1A2a1) go after her? Read on.

1A2a2) wait in the car? Go to page 13

1A2a3) take the car? Go to page 14

1A2a1) You hear a scream come from the house, but it's not the sound of fear, but more one of complete devastation. As it morphs into an anguished wail, you open the door and start up the stairs. You peek into the house. The furniture in the front room is a pile of wreckage. You hesitate, but the keening draws you in.

You glance to the right to find the kitchen equally destroyed. Following the crying, you enter a hallway. A few broken pictures litter the path, but otherwise it has escaped with little damage. You come to the first room on the right, a bathroom. It is empty. The next room, a bedroom, is a scene of nightmares. The woman is on the floor, arms wrapped tightly around the small bodies of a boy and a girl. Mangled is the only term that describes their condition.

The woman sobs into their limp bodies. She is covered in their blood. You stand there helpless, unsure what to do, or what you can do. While she completes her grief, you backtrack to the bathroom and search the cabinet for any kind of pain pills. You don't even find aspirin, but that could be because she wanted to keep them out of the children's reach. Where would she hide them? It comes to you then. The kitchen—high in one of the cabinets.

You move in that direction. The floor is covered with broken tableware and glasses. You try to step around the mess since you are barefoot. That's all you need—to get glass in your feet so you can't even run. You manage to place your feet in the clearest areas and stand in front of the first row of cabinets. There is nothing on the first two shelves. A few seldom-used items are on the upper two.

You check each one with similar results. No drugs. *Damn!* You close your eyes and rub your temples, but the soft motion does no good. Opening your eyes, you glimpse a pill bottle under the wreckage on the floor. A crumb of hope ignites. You squat and scoop it up. Vitamin C. Where there was one, there might be more.

You scatter the shards and rummage through the mess. You find calcium, fish oil, children's multi-vitamins, and a probiotic, but nothing for pain. The disappointment amplifies your agony. You sigh and are about to give up, when you spy three more bottles near the back wall under the kitchen table, which remarkably is the only piece of furniture you've seen so far that has not been upended or broken.

The desire for the bottles and the relief their contents might hold leads you to move quicker than is prudent. Sure enough, sharp pain spears you. You howl and hop, clutching your injured foot. You lean back against the counter and lift your foot to examine the damage. A small bead of blood dots the sole. Rubbing a finger over it, you wince, finding a small piece of glass protruding.

You reach for it, but before you can get up the nerve to yank it out, a voice says, "I'll do it."

You jump high enough to land in a sitting position on the counter. She is a demon visage. Her green scrubs are covered in blood. Red smears and black eyeliner streak her face. She walks through the detritus, stops in front of you, and grabs your foot. "Hold still."

She locates the glass and plucks it free. You wince, but she has no sympathy. She frowns at your display and you feel foolish. She scans the floor, moves a few things aside, then bends to grab a tube. A disinfectant cream, which she applies and a band-aid.

"I didn't see any pain pills, but it looks like there's a few bottles over there."

She retrieves them. "Yeah, here's Motrin and Tylenol." She hands you the bottles. "I've got some more powerful stuff in the bedroom. Maybe you can find some clothes and shoes to wear, too."

Just then, you hear a howl from the backyard. You look through the window and see a man on his knees, tearing at his hair.

"Is that...?" you ask.

She nods. "My husband." She watches him for a few moments, then says, "We'd better get you fixed up before he comes back." She turns and exits the kitchen. You slide off the counter, putting weight on your foot in increments. It hurts, and you hope no glass slivers were left behind. As you step, your eyes stop on the handle of a large utensil. You squat and pull it free. It's a chef's knife. The howling comes again. You decide to keep the knife and follow the woman.

You enter the bedroom to the right, avoiding looking into the room on the left. She is sliding into a clean t-shirt when you enter. Without looking in your direction, she says, "Clothes are in those drawers. Shoes in the closet. Hopefully something fits." She steps out of her scrub bottoms, kicks them aside, and grabs a pair of jeans.

You go through the clothes until you find some that fit reasonably well. Regardless of fit, it's better than running around in a hospital gown. Shoes are snug but doable until something better comes along.

Dressed, she rummages through a nightstand drawer and gives you two medicine bottles, then she leads you back through the hall to the front room. You want to say something comforting about her children, but in truth, there are no words to ease the pain and sorrow of losing your family. She looks over her shoulder at you. "Let's gather anything useful and get out of here."

A figure bursts from the kitchen, kicking up fragments of glass like water off grass. It plows into the woman and they crash to the floor. You recognize the husband and freeze for a moment. They wrestle and roll, but the man clearly has the advantage. You step forward to help, but realize you set the knife down in the bedroom when you were trying on shoes. You run back for it. By the time you return, the man-thing has his hands around her throat. Her eyes are bulging, her face bright red, and the fight has left her.

In a flash of anger, you advance toward the creature, but it sees you and rears up. It charges and impales itself more than you stab it, however, it shows no signs of recognizing the injury or the pain. Its momentum forces you back. Its hands encircle your neck. You slam into the wall with a thud that drives your already low air supply from your lungs. Fear grips your heart and squeezes your chest. You feel the life slowly ebbing from you.

A distant thought fights its way through the deepening haze in your mind. *The knife.* The thought brightens to a flash and with both hands, you lift the knife. You slice through muscle and organs until the blade stops at the bottom rib.

The beast howls in agony. Its grip lessens on your throat. A rush of air invigorates you. Strength returning, you twist the blade and pull it hard to the right. The light fades from the man, and for the briefest of moments, his face relaxes, showing signs of the human he had once been. Then, he slides to the floor, hands tracing a bloody line down the clean shirt. He pools at your feet, the huge gaping wound rises and deflates, then stills.

You stand breathing hard, the bloody knife still in your hands. Then you remember the woman, and rush to her side. She is not moving, and you see no rise and fall of her chest. You check for a pulse, then listen for a heartbeat, but both are absent. You sit back with a sigh.

*Now what?* You look around the destruction and death. You're not sure how long you sit staring, but a crash in the distance snaps you from your fugue. You stand and peek out the broken window. You don't see anyone, but that may change fast. You try to think of a plan, then remember your boyfriend/girlfriend and wonder if he's/she's still alive.

You go to the woman's bedroom, change your shirt again, then dump a pillow from its case. You search the room for anything useful, ignoring clothes. You can get your own at home. You take all the medical supplies and food you can fit in the pillow case, then step to the front door. You take a long scan of the neighborhood, then with a backward glance at the woman, you race for the car.

As you drive off, you wonder what you'll find at home. "Please God, let her/him be all right."

Go to Chapter 2 on page 93

1A2a2) You sink down in the seat, so no one can see you. Seconds later, a nerve-shattering wail rises from within the house. You sit up to look but don't see anything. You wait, trying to decide if you should go inside or get out and run. It's obvious from the cries of anguish that the children are dead. You look around with concern. What if her cries draw the attention of another one of those crazy killers?

After an eternity, the crying stops. You sit, waiting impatiently for her to return, flipping a mental coin over whether you should go in and entice her to hurry.

A few minutes later, still undecided, you catch sight of her walking through the front room. Then, a flash of movement and she disappears. Something has attacked her. Should you help her or drive off? Leaving would be cowardly, considering she rescued you.

Finally, guilt wins out and you get out, aware of how little you have on. You move toward the front door. At first, you don't hear anything. Then, a gasp and a cry of pain reaches you. You need to hurry. You make it to the top of the stairs and all noise ceases. You stop and listen. A strange sound comes next. You can't place it, but something about it sends an eerie chill racing through your veins. Then, it comes to you. It's the sound of chewing. The blood flushes from your face and you feel faint.

Slowly, you take a backward step down the stairs, aware the fearful moan you hear is coming from you. You are about to turn and run for the car when a man, or what once was a man, appears in the doorway, fresh blood dripping from its mouth. It snarls at you, bits of flesh and bloody spittle spraying.

You scream as the creature launches off the porch at you. You raise your hands to deflect it, but it smashes through your paltry defenses and bowls you over. Your head smacks hard against the concrete walkway. Darkness descends over you. The last sight before unconsciousness mercifully takes you is of lips curling back, revealing bloody teeth angling toward your neck.

End

1A2a3) You aren't sure what the woman is going to find inside, but when you hear the blood-curdling wail erupt from the house, it makes up your mind for you. It's time to go.

You slide into the driver's seat and though guilt assails you for abandoning her, you shift and drive off. You think about your own girlfriend/boyfriend and wonder if a similar fate awaits you upon your arrival home.

You live on the opposite end of town. Will the way be clear, or will you have to dodge other crazies? You reach the main street and try to decide the best route. You opt for the highway and turn right. The entry ramp is a quarter of a mile down the road.

When you reach the top, you realize it is a mistake. Everyone attempted to get out of town at the same time. The highway is an endless traffic jam. You drive along the shoulder for a long way before being forced to find another route. You change lanes onto the highway, and for the next half mile move in and out of traffic.

In the distance, you see another vehicle doing the same. It's good to see someone else alive. Guilt returns about leaving the woman. You think about going back for her, but quickly push the notion aside.

Soon, the highway is completely blocked, and you are forced off the road again. The car scrapes against the guardrail on the right, but you keep moving. You keep a watchful eye on the other vehicle, an SUV, to get an idea of what lies ahead. It climbs a rise and disappears down the opposite side. Almost a full minute later, you reach the rise. Immediately, you hit the brakes. Below, not more than a quarter mile, the SUV is under assault.

A mob of creatures is rocking the SUV. A wall of stopped vehicles prevents forward movement. As you watch, the SUV shoots backward and crashes into a pickup truck. The short burst breaks free from the mob, but it doesn't travel far enough. The mob attacks again. The driver works hard to get clear but has little room to maneuver. The driver's side window is shattered. Hands reach through. A struggle ensues. Though the driver struggles fiercely, it's clear the battle will not last long.

Do you:

1A2a3a) drive down to help? Read on.

1A2a3b) honk your horn to distract the mob? Go to page 17

1A2a3c) decide you can't help without being caught yourself, so you turn around? Go to page 18

1A2a3a) You argue with yourself about helping or running, but in the end, you come to the conclusion that if you were in that SUV, you'd pray for someone to come to the rescue.

You feed the gas and move down the hill. As you watch, the SUV races forward, but the wild, out-of-control mob has a grip on the driver and are not shaken off. Several others cling to the hood, obscuring the driver's view. It smashes into another car.

You increase speed, but with limited clearance, you are forced to whip the wheel from side to side in order to get through. By the time you make the turn to face the mob, they have the driver halfway out the window.

If you don't do something fast, the driver is dead. You push the pedal down and aim for the mob. The sound of the approaching car draws the mob's attention. For the moment, the driver is forgotten. Though still in their hands, he is no longer being dragged out.

You plow directly into the crowd, bowling over some, sending others flying, and a few become speed bumps. You brake, reverse, and hit them again. With the mob dispersed, you scream to the driver. "Get in!"

The man falls out the window and staggers toward the car. A few of the mob who have avoided your car advance toward him. He is moving too slow. You open your door and smack a few of them back. However, your attempt to close the door meets resistance. Panic sprouts in your gut.

"Get in the car!" you shout.

He reaches for the rear door, but hands grab him. The contact seems to bring him into focus. He pushes them back, opens the door, and jumps in. You don't wait for him to shut the door. You whip the wheel around and make a sharp turn. You run out of room. Several of the crazed mob are still chasing. Their hands reach for you through your still-open door.

Reversing allows you to use the door to clear some away. You ram into another car and hear a scream. A glance in the mirror shows one of the mob pinned. You work the wheel hard again and manage to get clear. You push the pedal down hard and in seconds are clear of the attackers.

You make the sharp turn and head back up the hill. You're so excited and let out a whoop of joy. "We made it," you say with equal parts relief and surprise. You get no response and look over your shoulder. The back seat is empty. The rear door is still open. He is gone.

You look back at the mob. They are occupied with something on the ground. Although you can't see, you have a good idea what it is.

Your elation plummets, and you get a queasy feeling in your gut. You park, get out, and shut the back door, then drive off to find another route home.

Go to Chapter 2 on page 93

1A2a3b) You are unsure what to do, yet you feel the need to do something. You lay on the horn. It blares loud and sharp. You watch the mob for any change, but they are too involved in their task to be distracted by something so distant.

Regardless, you honk several more times and stop when you see the mob turn the SUV on its side. They break the windows and climb in. The vehicle sways. You should have had done something different. Honking the horn was as worthless as the idea was stupid. It was the equivalent of honking the horn at a grocery store shopping cart as it rolls toward your car.

You back away and search for an alternate route home.

Go to Chapter 2 on page 93

1A2a3c) You wait too long. The mob has the driver out of the SUV and are tearing him apart. You watch in disbelief and shock. What could have possibly affected those people so much they would devolve into cannibalism? You can't watch any longer. Before they notice you, it's time to retreat.

You back the car up but maneuvering in reverse through the maze of abandoned cars proves difficult and slow. You bump into several vehicles along the route and must pull forward and adjust angles too often. It might be quicker to get out and walk; to find a car with its keys in the ignition near the back of the jam. That would be the smart move, but the memory of those creatures ripping their prey apart sends a violent shudder through your body. Fear prevents you from leaving the car.

You make a turn and think you see the way out when another car comes up behind you, blocking your way. You can't move backward and sure aren't going forward. You roll the window down and motion the driver to go back. The driver of the other car leans out and motions you forward.

With some mild curses under your breath, you lean out and shout, "I can't go forward. There's a crazed mob over that rise. They just pulled a guy from his vehicle and I think—" you choke on the words. "I think they ate him."

The driver, a woman, gasps. "B-but, I have to get home. My family's there."

"I understand. I'm doing the same, but we can't go that way."

You wait for her to respond or reverse, but as you watch, her eyes grow big enough to pop. The hairs on the back of your neck rise, and you turn to where she's looking. Your eyes bulge as well. Several of the mob are working their way through the jumble of cars in your direction. You are trapped.

Do you:

1A2a3c1) get out and run? Read on.

1A2a3c2) slide to the floor and hide? Go to page 21

1A2a3c3) get out and run to her car? Go to page 26

1A2a3c1) You press your foot down and the car jumps backward. However, with the other car in your way, you have no place to go unless she moves. In her haste to escape, she rams into an RV and gets the bumper trapped. Your only hope of escape is to get out and run.

You fling the door open and get out. The wild bunch, having heard the crash, are moving in your direction. You run. You catch a glimpse of the woman as you burst past. She is shocked as you run by, leaving her to face the mob. You don't want any harm to befall her, but as you dodge between stopped cars, you think of the old adage, *I don't have to be faster than the bear—just faster than you.*

You run hard. Your legs grow fatigued and heavy. Your chest hurts, as does your head. You look back. The wild bunch are still advances. They pass your car and approach the woman's. You notice she is no longer inside. You scan the area but do not find her.

You notice, with alarm, your pursers run past her car and zero in on you. With the realization the woman was playing her own adage, *if they can't see me they can't catch me,* you explode into a run again. You push as hard as you can, but your energy fades fast. Unless an avenue of escape presents itself soon, they will catch you. A sob sticks in your chest, robbing you of more breath.

You are too afraid to look behind you, but they are not quiet in their pursuit. Several times, you hear sounds indicating they are closing in. The thought spurs you on.

You reach an intersection. A car races toward you. You wave your hands to get the driver's attention. For an instant, you think you're safe. Then, whether he didn't see you or saw what was chasing you, the car whizzes past. All hope fades. Then, like a heaven-sent angel, a woman yells, "Hurry! Over here."

You scan and find her. She's in the doorway of a building forty yards away. Safety is a short, hard sprint away. You call on your last reserves and race toward her. The distance evaporates fast. Twenty yards. Ten. Then, to your shock, her face takes on a look of horror and she slams the door with you still five yards away.

"No!" you shout. Then, the first animal is on you. You sprawl on the walkway and roll. Before you can get to your feet, two others leap on you. As others arrive and the pain intensifies, you catch a glimpse of the woman watching from a front window, a hand to her mouth as she takes in the horrifying and agonizing manner of your death.


End

1A2a3c2) You button the window up and turn the car off, hoping they haven't marked your location yet. You slide to the floor and wedge yourself under the dash. A prayer forms on your lips. You wait with intense focus on the external sounds.

You hear a crash and think the woman must be trying to back away. You hope she makes it and that the mob of cannibals chases her long enough for you to make your escape.

You slap a hand over your mouth to prevent the scream from escaping as crazed and bloody figures parade past your window. Several of them glance inside, but you don't think any notice you. The woman hits something else, then for long, agonizing moments you hear nothing. Not knowing what is going on drives your anxiety levels higher. You want to look, just a quick peek, but are too afraid to move. Then, a shrill scream fills your head. It pierces your mind, heart, and soul. You close your eyes tight and put palms over your ears, but the anguished cry refuses to diminish within your mind.

The screams come one after the other. Her pleas are desperate. You want to help; wish you had the power to do so, but you don't. To attempt a rescue would only result in your death, too. Despite the closed eyes, tears escape and flow over your face. *Please let it be over fast*, you pray, and as if in answer, her cries cease.

*How can this be happening?*

You want to curl up in the fetal position. In panic, you realize your knee hit the brake pedal. *Did the brake lights blink on?* Had the mob seen them? Of all the stupid things to do. With growing trepidation, you wait, expecting the car to be attacked any second.

Minutes later, no one has appeared at the windows. Unable to contain your angst, you slide your legs from under the steering wheel so as not to bump the brakes again. You inch your back up the side of the well on the passenger's side and lean against the door. You can't hear anything outside. You are still hidden, unless someone walks by the driver's side. Your entire body vibrates like an electric current is coursing through you. You search for the cause, only to discover you are shaking from fear.

*Could they be gone?* Only one way to know for sure. You force

21

yourself to stay hidden another five minutes. While you do, a myriad of gruesome thoughts fill your mind. How long does it take for the creatures to devour a person? How much of the body do they eat? If they just fed, are they too full to eat you?

In small increments and as slow as you can, you stretch your body upward until your eyes are high enough to peer out. From that vantage point, you see nothing, only stranded cars. As much as you hate to do it, you must climb up on the seat to see anything. With a whimper, you pull your body up and set your knees on the seat facing backward so you can look out the rear window.

The woman's car is forty feet behind you. The door is open, but no one, human or otherwise, is in sight. Jumpy, expecting one of whatever those things are to appear at your window at any second, you swing your head nervously from side to side. Still nothing moving. You begin to relax, thinking you are safe for the moment.

You rise up to better see the street. The first creature stands up, blood dripping from its mouth. You start and drop lower into the seat. You don't think it saw you, but you fear the sudden movement may have made the car bounce.

Afraid to move again, you sit, but staying still is impossible, as your body vibrates at an even higher frequency. Several moments later, nothing has happened. You want to risk another peek but have to force courage into your body before it agrees to move. You place your head in the space between the front seats. Nothing is looking back at you.

You lift your head up and catch sight of two other man-things as they stand bloody and panting from their efforts. Icy fingers crawl up your spine and with a jolt, you get the sickening feeling you are being watched. With slow, forced effort, you pull your head back and glance toward the passenger window. The face of a creature is pressed against the glass, a grotesque and bloody image. The blood on its mouth smears the glass like an artist's abstract painting.

You let out an ear-piercing shriek and crawl backward. The creature answers with a howl. You swing into the driver's seat, start the engine, and as other howls join in an eerie symphony, you shift into reverse and floor the pedal. You hear rather than see the thumps. You smash into the woman's car, swinging the wheel as you move forward, and pin the first creature between your bumper and a minivan. It leans across the hood, red-rimmed eyes glaring, and attempts to claw its way to you.

You have never been more frightened, yet some still-sane portion of your brain tells you to drive. Though you can't take your eyes from the being, you whip the wheel and reverse. Its body falls, and as you shift forward again, it rises slowly in front of you and bares its unnaturally long teeth.

Breathing becomes difficult you've used up all the air in the car. You pull forward, aiming straight for the man-thing. However, this time it is prepared and leaps up onto the hood. You continue moving but press back hard into the seat as if getting like that would give you distance from it.

As the car speeds forward and impacts the minivan, the creature is propelled into the windshield. Its head smacks the glass with a sickening thud, indenting the glass. You scream and put the car into reverse again. Looking over your shoulder, you see two more creatures moving your way. You peel backward, but both are too agile and move to either side of the car to avoid being hit.

You smash into another car, spin the wheel and shift. Looking up, you think this next turn will get clear of the minivan. From there, however, it's only guesswork and prayer. To your disbelief, the creature on the hood opens its eyes and fixes them on you.

Pushing the pedal down hard, the car leaps forward. The car clips the bumper of the minivan, but powers through. You now have a clear lane for as long as it lasts. However, the view disappears as the creature on the hood fills the windshield. It raises a clawed fist and pounds it into the indention its head created.

A thump from the back and you look to see one of the others has jumped on the trunk. The third one is running alongside the car, attempting to smash the back window. You drive blind, spinning the wheel from side to side to dislodge the creature. It has a hold on the lip of the hood and pulls a huge fist back to strike again. This time, the blow plows through the glass. Streaks of blood flow down its arm as it shoves through to grasp you.

You dodge to the side. With your eyes focused on the creature, you have no idea where you're going until you make contact with a car. The impact throws the man-thing backward. Its arm is wrenched from the hole, but before it is dislodged, it closes its strong fingers around the glass.

The momentum, together with its uncanny strength, yanks the entire windshield out.

It tumbles off the hood, but you have come to a stop. Reversing, you see the one alongside just before it smashes through the back window. Thuds on the roof tell you where the second one is. You shift again and drive forward. The one on the side clings to the window frame as you accelerate away.

You work the wheel in a frenzy, maneuvering through the abandoned vehicles. The one on the side is powering its way inside the car. If it makes it, you won't survive. You spy a delivery truck and angle toward it. Before the creature realizes what you are doing, you sideswipe the truck and scrape the man-thing's body off the car with a sickening wet plop.

Two down, one to go. You break free of the jam and turn left. A hand hits the driver's window. You see the fingers gripping the rain channel above the door. It gives you an idea. A risky one, but you have to do something.

You open the door a crack and as the fingers fill the space, you pull the door shut as hard as you can. You hear a snap as the fingers break. A pained howl follows. Up ahead, you see a cross street. You make a high-speed left turn and open the door, releasing the fingers. You are rewarded by the sight of the creature flying off the roof and bouncing on the street. You are free.

Air returns to your lungs. You slump in the seat as the adrenaline subsides. Then, a hand slaps the hood and the first man-thing reappears. Its head rises like a summoned demon from the depths of hell. Its eyes narrow with determined hatred.

With all its amazing strength, it pulls itself upward, driving its claws into the metal for grip. No matter what you try, you can't shake it loose. With no windshield to protect you, your time is limited.

Up ahead, you see what you hope is salvation and head straight for it at high speed. Just before impact as the creature gets a grip on the windshield frame, you hit the underside of the semi- trailer. The car slows as the upper section of the car is ripped from the chassis. Blood soaks the interior of the car, covering you. The engine continues to whine as the car inches forward.

You look up at the undercarriage of the trailer and estimate you need another eight feet to get clear. You urge the car on. Six feet. "Go, you bastard, go." Four feet. Then, the car shudders and stops. "No!" You shift into reverse and floor it. The tires spin, but the car does not move. You rock the car back and forth several times like you do when you're stuck in snow, but the car refuses to budge.

You open what's left of the door and crawl out. Duckwalking, you come out on the far side. You are free, but on foot, which makes you an easy target for anything hunting. You look around for a second to make sure you're safe, then walk. You are still a good five miles from home. Maybe you can find another car along the way.

Go to Chapter 2 on page 204

1A2a3c3) You shake yourself from your frightened immobility and look back, searching for an avenue to escape. To your dismay, you find none. Your only chance is to run. You open the door and jump out. The woman is watching you, a confused look on her face. You point behind you as you run. She doesn't seem to understand and as you go by, hear the whir of a window descending. You glance inside.

"What's going on?" she asks.

"They're coming," you reply, keeping your voice low.

She glances forward, fear etched on her face. As she searches for the danger, you decide to run toward her car. Reaching through the open window, you unlock the door and jump in. She cowers against the door, staring at you. As you button the window up, you say, "Hurry up and drive, or they'll be on us."

Still fear freezes her. "Snap out of it." You slap the wheel. "Drive or die. That's our choices."

That sinks in. She turns the wheel and feeds the gas. She is moving too slow. She has no idea of the need for urgency. You want to take the wheel from her, but that would waste time. You encourage her. "Go. Go. Go."

She eases toward a stopped car and stops. She shifts and looks over her shoulder just as she'd been taught years before in driver's education. You want to explode. Then, the creatures come into view. They hear the car, then spot you. She stops the car again before it hits the one behind her, afraid of damaging her car. She has no concept of the danger she's in.

You scream in frustration and jump across the console and into her lap. She screams and beats on your back, but you have control of the wheel. You shove the pedal down. The car whines as you turn the wheel as far as it will go. You ram the car in front of you, reverse sharply, hit the one in back, and go forward again.

The woman is shouting at you to stop destroying her car.

"Look, you fool. Look out the window." You hit the car in front and reverse fast. "It's either your car or your body. They will rip you apart." Crash. "And eat you." Crash. "Is that what you want?" Crash. The first of the mob reaches the car then and pounds on the driver's window. She cringes, and you hear her sobbing.

The car bangs into the fender of the front and clears it. Two more things join the first. One jumps on the trunk while the other tries to smash its way inside. You work the wheel hard and find the path back. You sideswipe one car, but that also wipes away one of the creatures. However, the one at your window manages to slam an elbow through the glass, imploding shards over both of you.

You turn left at the first intersection and have enough straight, unimpeded road to get the car up to eighty. The creature hangs to the door, legs flapping and banging against it like a flag.

"Peel its fingers back," you say.

She is still crying, frozen. Sitting on her puts you too far forward to do it yourself. You're moving at too great a speed to look back. You risk a glance, note the position of the fingers, and fire your elbow back. Pain shoots up your arm, but a second glance shows only one hand hanging on.

Then he woman shakes from her fear-induced hysteria and grips a finger. You hear her grunt as she peels a finger back. She works on, then says in a shrill voice, "Every time I get one free and work on the next, he puts the first one back on."

"You're gonna have to break each one."

"Oh God!"

"Listen, it comes down to him or us. We have to get him off, or we can't stop."

"Ahh!"

You aren't sure if she's crying, moaning, or meditating, but a few seconds later, you hear a snap and a howl. Now you know she's crying. "Oh God! Oh God! I think I'm going to be sick."

You cringe at her words, knowing where her vomit will end up.

"That's okay, but don't stop. Break another finger."

"Ohhh!"

She grunts again, and another bone cracks. The howling increases, but still it holds on.

"Keep going."

She does, and this time, the resulting howl decreases with distance as the creature falls away. You look in the side mirror and see it bouncing along the roadside. You relax, then you hear "Ugh!" and the spew wets your back.

The smell hits and makes you want to join her. Suddenly, a hand reaches through the window and grabs your ear. It yanks, and you yelp. Your ear feels like it's being ripped from your head. Something warm runs down your neck, but you aren't sure if it's her vomit or your blood.

You slam on the brakes and the thing slides off on the driver's side. It's clutching the door frame and your ear. The grip pulls you toward the window. You are forced to go with it or lose the ear. From your periphery, you see movement. The woman has leaned forward. If she's going to do something, you wish she'd hurry. You're not sure how much longer your ear will stay attached. The nails dig deeper into your skin.

A howl proceeds the creature releases its hold on you. You turn as it falls away and see the woman's mouth bloody. You are shocked, thinking her incapable of biting anyone, let alone such a horrid, filthy thing, but you're thankful she did.

You pull over and stop. You climb out, your body sticky with puke and blood.

"Wow! That was close," you say. "Thanks for saving me."

You look down at her face. She is traumatized by her ordeal. You bend to look at her. There is something in her eyes you don't recognize but it brings you up short.

"I'm sorry," she says and puts the car in drive. She speeds off.

You sigh and curse under your breath. You look around, hoping you're alone, and start walking the five miles toward home.

Go to Chapter 2 on page 204

1A2b) You glance toward the doors and know safety is only a few steps away, but can you abandon someone who needs help? The scream, more shrill and desperate this time, makes the decision for you. You pivot toward the shout and move that direction. This section of the hospital is lined with flower and gift shops and coffee and sandwich eateries.

You stand in the hall between them, unsure which one has the person in need. Then something crashes to the floor inside the flower shop. You step to the doorway and scan the space. Assorted floral arrangements fill the room. Coolers full of flowers line the wall to the left. A counter stands in front of you. To the right behind the counter is a doorway to the back room. You find yourself standing there with no memory of moving forward.

Something pounds into a door to the back left. You see a heavyset woman, arms raised to strike again. You guess it's the bathroom. From inside, a female voice shouts, "Leave me alone." If the attacking woman heard, she gave no indication. Her fists land against the door again, causing it to shake in its frame.

Crouching, you enter the room and work your way toward the woman. She continues to attack the door. You hear a crack and know the door has reached its limits. As you close in, you observe the woman. She's big, but you think you can take her down and hold her until whoever's inside can escape. Then she snarls and grunts at the door like an animal. But it isn't her noises that bring you to a stop, it's the expression on her face. The contorted, rage-filled features look more demonic than a human. The idea of taking her down flees your mind. You are about to flee as well when the door splinters.

The scream rises several octaves. No, you can't go. The reason you came in was to help the person trapped in that room. You must find the courage. You find strength in a heavy glass vase standing on a work table with a bunch of assorted flowers inside. You grab it, dump the flowers, and advance.

The large woman reaches through the remains of the door, but her bulk prevents her from entering. Her growls increase in volume. Spittle flies like that of an overheated dog. You creep up behind her, the vase in both hands. You step closer on wobbly legs. You can't believe you're about to hit another person. It's against everything you've been raised to believe. But, is this really a person?

You raise the vase over your head as another concern enters your mind. What about the consequences of your actions? Will you be arrested for assault? What if she dies? Your step falters. Then, the trapped woman cries out, "Someone help me, please!"

Her desperate plea steadies your resolve. You take the last step and are about to strike when the woman turns her face and glares at you with a snarl that freezes your lungs, preventing breaths. Her eyes are so hard, so full of hatred, so evil, that any fear of causing her severe injury dissipates in a flash.

She turns to come at you, but her bulk is caught in the cracked opening of the door. It won't hold her long. You push all fears and doubts aside and bring the vase down on her head as hard as you can. The vase shatters in your hands. The blow staggers her, but other than a brief wobble of her legs, it has no other effect.

You back away, scanning the room for a weapon. Your eyes light on a pair of shears you hasten to them as she pulls free of the door. One long splinter is impaled in her chest below her breast. She thunders toward you. You dodge behind the work table, the shears in front of you, hoping the sight will give her pause. If she notices, she shows no hesitation. She snarls and rushes toward you.

You back away and stab at the air in front of you. The idea of sticking her with the shears causes bile to rise up your throat.

The trapped woman yells out to you, "Kill her! Stab her!"

Her words only increase your angst. "Help me!" you call to her. From your periphery, you see her step out of the bathroom. You are hopeful that help is on the way, but when she glances to her left down a narrow hall, you realize she's about to bolt out the back door. "No! Help me. I came for you."

You continue around the table, but the woman picks up speed. She barrels into you, unphased by the stab her momentum caused. She gets her hands around your neck, her fingers digging into your skin, and prevent your scream from escaping. Her weight pins you and bends you backward over the table. Her face lowers toward you, her teeth gnashing like a starved beast. You put your hands between the two of you and push with everything you've got, but it barely holds her at bay.

Wild thoughts flash through your mind. You can't believe this is happening. You can't believe you're going to die this way. It's like watching a zombie show on TV.

Your arm brushes something hard. You reach for it, desperate for anything that might help. Your hand wraps around the long wooden fragment from the door. Evidently, it has pierced her skin because it feels wet. Instinctively, your hand wraps around it, and as her weight wins out over your strength, you shove the wood upward. It slides into her flesh, but you can't see that it's having any effect on her.

Her jaws snap together, the sound like a bear trap. She inches closer. Her breath makes your eyes water. Drool plops on your cheek. She emits a snarl of frustration. You are seconds away from being ripped apart.

A metallic clang resonates above your head. The woman stops pushing forward and a blank look appears on her face. Above her, a fire extinguisher hovers like possessed by some spirit. It descends, landing with another ringing sound on the top of your attackers head. Blood colors her hair. She stands erect and staggers in her effort to turn and face her new attacker.

Air floods your lungs, leaving you dizzy. A third clang lands on the side of the woman's head. You push up and though your legs feel weak, you yank the shears from the woman and drive them with all your might into her back. She stumbles, reaching in vain for the shears.

The butt end of the extinguisher strikes her face and her head snaps back. You get out of the way as her body falls back into the table. The impact forces the shears deeper. Her eyes roll up, a trickle of blood traces a jagged path from the corner of her lips.

She rolls and drops to the floor. You stare down at her, nauseated, then remember the other woman. You turn her way, but she backpedals and raises the extinguisher, ready to strike you. Her eyes are wide and her breathing short and raspy.

You raise your hands to show you're no threat. "Hey, it's all right. I won't hurt you. I came to rescue you, remember?"

Her lips tremble and tears fill her eyes. "Who-what-I don't understand. Why did she attack me? What happened to her? She acted like a rabid animal."

"I don't know. I was attacked by a man upstairs. I've been unconscious for, heck, what day is it? I don't know how long I was out. What has happened?"

"I'm not sure. I came in to work today, shocked at how little traffic there was. I've been off the past two days, staying at a friend's cottage. If something happened, I wasn't around to hear about it. I came into work, saw the usual people, then came back here to work. Then this crazy lady came in, growling like she was a dog, and attacked me."

"Is it just in the hospital or is this happening everywhere?"

"I don't know."

"Maybe they got injected with something that drove them crazy?"

She shrugs.

"We need to find out. Do you have a phone?"

She nods and walks to a desk. She rummages through a purse and pulls the phone out. She checks the screen. Her face scrunches up as she reads something. "It's a text from my boyfriend. He wants to know if I'm someplace safe and warns me to stay off the streets." She quickly types and sends a reply, then stares at the screen, waiting for an answer.

"Can you Google?"

"Yeah," she twists her mouth as she watches the screen. "I guess he'll get back to me when he can."

While she taps her phone, you walk to the door and peer out into the hall. You hear more commotion, but not voices or screams. As far as you know, you may be the only two left alive in the hospital.

"I, uh, I can't get a signal."

"Is that normal?"

"No, I mean, some places in the hospital you can't get a signal, but I've always been able to get one here."

"Maybe we need to go outside?"

"We can try, I suppose. Let's go out the back door."

You follow her. She leads down the narrow hall and stops at the door. "What if there's others like," she motions with her chin, "her?"

"Guess we won't know until we check." She makes to open the door. You stop her. "Just open it enough to look outside. If anyone's out there, we may have to close it fast."

She nods and cracks the door. She hesitates a moment, then opens it only far enough to slip her head out. You want to see, too, but don't want to crowd her.

"Well?"

"I see the parking lot, but even though there's cars, the place has the feel of being deserted."

"Can I look?"

She steps back, and you poke your head out. A car careens out of an aisle, smacking into a parked car. It continues moving and turns toward the exit. You catch a quick look at the terrified woman driving. A few seconds later, you see the reason for the terror. Two men are chasing her. They move fast in predatory fashion, but the car is faster. They soon stop. One of them howls like a wolf. Maybe that's it; a few people have been bitten by a wolf, and now they're werewolves.

You scoff at that notion. It's pure fantasy. Werewolves and vampires and zombies don't exist. There has to be another explanation. More like, it has something to do with drugs. That makes more sense. Whatever the mystery drug is reverts people to a more animalistic nature. Whatever the cause, this is insane. There has to be others alive and working on a solution, right?

Another howl snaps you from your thoughts and brings your focus on the two animals. One is staring right at you. Your heart skips a beat. You close the door and pull on it to make sure it locks.

"There's two of them out there and they saw me. We have to get someplace safe."

"Where's that?"

"I don't know, but if this is centered on the hospital, then we have to get as far from here as possible. Do you have a car?"

"Yeah. It's out front."

"We should take it and drive away."

"Where?"

You think for a moment and realize you are still in your hospital gown. "First, to my house so I can get some clothes." And hopefully find your girlfriend/boyfriend. "We can figure out where from there."

"How far do you live?"

"Not too far. Less than ten miles."

She looks around the table and picks up a knife. She holds it in front of her in both hands. "Sorry. We don't have another one."

"That's all right." You pick up the fire extinguisher. "This'll work."

You lead through the shop and creep up on the open doorway. You hear crashes and banging in the hall somewhere to the left. The outer door is on the right. Something howls; something else snarls. A muscle-freezing cold leaves you unable to move until the woman nudges you.

You spring to the right. The doors are in front of you, but as you near, you slow. Directly beyond the doors stand the two man-things you saw in the rear parking lot. She plows into you from behind.

"I think they're coming. Why are you stopping?"

"'cause there's two in front of us, too."

She sweeps her gaze from the front doors to down the hall. "Shit!"

"Yep. We're trapped."


Do you:

1A2b1) take your chances and go outside? Read on.

1A2b2) go back to face the unknown? Go to page 40

1A2b3) search for another way out? Go to page 45

1A2b1) "We can't just stand here," you say. "Sooner or later we're going to be discovered by one group or another. Maybe both."

"What can we do?"

"We either stand and face what's coming or go out and attack those two."

She's thinking, but you understand her hesitation. Neither choice is appealing. "Let's go out. Maybe we can take them by surprise. Where's your car?"

"Straight out the door, but it's in the last row." She points. "That light blue one there."

You nod and calculate the distance and the odds of being able to outrun those things. The howling down the hall sounds closer. It's now or never. "Okay, let's go. Follow me. I'll try to knock them down with the extinguisher. You stab them if you can. We have to strike fast and hamper their pursuit. Once past them, run as fast as you can." A thought hits you. "You do have the keys, right?"

"Yeah." She pats a jean pocket.

You suck in a breath as if hoping to find courage floating there. Then, you push through the first door. You pause at the second door as one of the two creatures turns. It is looking at something in the parking lot. As soon as it swings its head away, you exit.

Your first few steps are gentle and tentative. You close to within fifteen feet before one of them tilts its head upward and sniffs. Afraid it has caught your scent, you rush forward, extinguisher held over your shoulder.

They both turn as you get within five feet, but by then, you are already in full swing. The metal canister smashes into the first one's head, sending it flying. The second one leaps for you, but flies past, only grazing you with a gash down your flank. You glance at the woman. She stands frozen, staring at the bloody knife.

Behind you, the doors open. You grab her arm and pull as you take off running. "Get to the car!" you shout. You have a narrow lead and will need more to be able to make it to the car. As she runs on, you take three more steps then turn to face your pursuers.

One is a small black man, the other a large woman. The man leaps like a wild cat. You swing the extinguisher and connect with a solid, ringing blow. The man flips over backward and slams into the ground. The woman runs straight at you. You don't have time to use the extinguisher. She barrels you over.

You are stunned by the tackle and cry out from the contact with the parking lot. Skin is scraped from your back and buttocks. An elbow smacks hard, sending pain up your arm. The woman face plants and stops with a wet plop. Her face is a bloody mess when she rises.

You scramble to your feet, aware that you are bleeding from several places. Racing toward you are the first two creatures you knocked down. You lift the extinguisher to defend yourself but have another thought. You pull the pin, give the canister a quick shake, then depress the button. A white, foamy stream jets out, soaking the first one's face. You quickly alter your aim and drench the second. Both of them stop and wipe at their faces. The foam smears.

The woman begins to rise, and you drive the butt of the extinguisher down on her head. Her face smashes into the blacktop again. Without waiting for another rush, you pivot and race for the car. She is backing out as you arrive, leaving you to wonder if she was going to wait for you. You bang on the door's window. She jumps, stares at you as if she's never seen you before, then something in her eyes softens and she unlocks the door. It's a two-door, and you hop in and toss the extinguisher into the back seat. She is moving before you get the door closed.

Neither of you speak for the first few minutes. You stare, unseeing, out the window, still in shock from what just happened. Her gasp of surprise shakes you alert.

"It's like one of those post-apocalyptic movies. Abandoned cars are everywhere, and no one is around. It's like we're the only two people left in the world."

You scan the streets as she maneuvers through the maze of stopped vehicles. The desolation is eerie. She's right. It's like one of those catastrophe movies come to life.

"Where to?"

"Ah, turn left at the light."

Driving takes forever. The going is slow. After three miles, she is forced to go over the curb and drive along the sidewalk before the street is passable again. A few minutes later, one of the creatures bounces off the passenger door. You flinch, and she jerks the wheel. The car slams into a parked truck.

The creature pounds on the window. Its face is contorted as if surgically altered. She reverses. The thing snaps its maw at you, its nose pressed to the glass. She pulls forward but is unable to get up enough speed to pull away from it. Finally, the cars clear and she jams the pedal down. In seconds, the beast is left howling at you.

"My God! How are we going to survive?"

You wish you had an answer for her. "One step, one plan, and one day at a time. Let's see what awaits us at our homes. Maybe it's not as bad, the farther we get away from the city."

She is too shocked to respond. You lean back in the seat and ponder her words. *How will you survive?*


Read on to Chapter 2.

Chapter 2

You arrive at the house and stop in front. The curtains are drawn, and it looks deserted.

The woman asks, "Is this it?"

"Yeah."

"Are you going in?"

"Yeah. But if no one's home, I don't have a key to get in."

You open the door, glance up and down the street, then get out. You run up the front steps, aware the hospital gown is flapping open. The door is locked. You knock and listen. Nothing. You knock again and call your partner's name. Moving to the side door you try again. Still no reply. Concern for your partner grows, but you are standing there in the open.

The woman honks the horn. You move to the front. She is motioning for you to come, a mixed expression of desperation and fear on her face. A howl to the right is all the explanation you need. You run for the car and hop in. Ahead are three creatures.

"What should I do?"

"They can't get to us if we're inside the car and moving. Drive past them. But fast."

She peels out leaving them behind without incident. "Now what?"

You think. "What about your house?"

I live with my folks, but it's a forty-minute drive."

"Well, we've got nothing else."

You drive fifteen minutes before running into the next problem. An overturned delivery truck blocks the road. A man is trying to pull himself out the door. He is stuck. He sees the car and calls out for help. You hesitate, look around, and seeing no creatures, get out. "I'll be right back."

You run to the truck and look for a way to climb up. Your bare feet touch something hot. It takes several attempts before finding safe footholds. You reach the door, but before you can ask what's wrong, a beast's head appears on the other side of the man. Before he can react to your shocked expression, the creature launches at him. They disappear inside the truck. It rocks from the conflict. The man screams.

Before you can decide on a course of action, sounds draw your gaze to the car. Two creatures have jumped on the hood. The woman is in full-blown panic. She reverses and drives away, the beasts still attached, and leaving you stranded.

You jump down, scan for a safe haven, then run for the nearest car. It's locked. You move down the street, car to car, knowing time is running out. A distant howl puts extra pep in your step. The next car's door is open. You dive inside, lock the door, and hide on the floor.

Your gaze swings from window to window, then lights on an unexpected sight. The keys are dangling from the ignition. You scramble to the driver's seat as a creature walks past. It sees you, snarls, and launches at the window. You start the engine and speed away. The beast gives chase, but you lose it quickly. With no place else to go, you head home again.

Continue Chapter 2 on page 214

1A2b2) "I don't know about you," you say, "but I'd rather avoid any more fights with those things. Is there another way out? Maybe we can slip past whatever's behind us."

"There's a side entrance, but we have to reach another hallway. We might run into more trouble going that way."

You look at the two in front of the doors. If only they'd move on, but how long can you wait before being discovered? You reach out, grab the woman's arm, and pull her back to the wall. You press into the wall as if trying to become part of it. "We have to decide now. How far is it?"

"Just past the elevators on the right."

"Okay, let's at least check that way. Maybe we can get through without a fight."

You don't wait for her to respond. Keeping to the wall, you creep back the way you came, past the shops, until you reach a long information desk in the lobby. Behind it is the elevators and to the far side, the opening for the side hallway.

The ceiling rises to the third floor, where balconies surround the three interior walls on both the second and third floors. In the middle of the open lobby, you see three altered humans squatting over something. Two men and a woman. They crouch over a body. The white lab coat, now splattered with gore, tells you it was a medical staff member.

They are preoccupied for the moment, feasting. You glance at the desk and estimate the distance. Dash or creep? You step out in a crouch and move slow enough not to make noise, but quick enough to prevent your fear from taking control and run screaming down the hall.

You reach the desk and the breath you didn't realize you'd been holding bursts from your lungs louder than you intended. The two of you stay there for several long minutes. The only sounds are the low growls of the diners and the rending of flesh. You feel sickened, but you take deep breaths to keep from vomiting.

Crawling to the far side of the desk, you peer around the corner.

One of the men stands and sniffs at the air. *My God! Can they actually smell our presence?* It follows its nose, edging ever closer to you. You duck back, making every effort to remain calm, but you're losing the battle fast.

The woman's expression forms a question mark. You answer with a finger to your lips. Your eyes fall on the serrated steak knife she still holds in both hands like it's a magic wand. For a second, you wonder what they needed a steak knife for in a flower shop, then realize how stupid the question is.

Something bumps the desk. You can hear the creature sniffing, drawn ever closer by your scent. You must make a move and fast, before it sees you and sounds the alarm. It scrapes along the front of the desk as it comes your way. You have seconds to decide on a course of action.

In a blur, you rip the knife from her hands, spin, and almost freeze as you come face to face with a grossly deformed face that is more animal than human. As it draws a deep breath to emit its howl, with all your strength, you drive the blade up through the jaw and deep into the roof of its mouth. The howl is contained, but the thrashing begins. You yank it down to the floor and press your body over it. Its claws tear at the knife. You realize then that you have created a temporary stalemate. The blade hasn't penetrated far enough to kill, and you have nothing else to finish the job without making enough noise to draw the other two.

With one hand, you press its head down. The woman throws herself across its legs to prevent them from kicking. You rip the knife down, but you don't have the room or leverage to dislodge it from your position. You shift, allowing the creature freedom. It tosses you aside, and the knife tears out. The creature howls in pain and one hand clutches its wound. Blood flows down its arm, covering you. Before it can attack, you plunge the blade through an eye socket and end its cry. It stares at you until the light dies in its good eye. It falls, and you extricate yourself from under it.

You lay there, breathing hard, until you hear *sniff sniff sniff.* The others have caught your scent. You give the knife back to her and say, "Run! Now!"

You sprint away from the desk and reach the hallway before you know for sure she is following. Multiple howls fill the lobby, the echoes making it sound like there are ten instead of two. It spurs you faster. The outer doors are thirty yards ahead. You push harder, knowing you have reached your maximum speed in bare feet.

The doors grow bigger before you and success looms seconds away. Then you remember you still have to go around to the front of the building and to the last row of the parking lot to have any hope of safety.

You hit the first door hard and plow through. The second passes just as fast. Outside, you feel the rough concrete wearing away the skin on your soles. Still, your legs churn, the extinguisher under an arm like a football.

Behind you, the doors burst open and you feel a chill up your spine like you've just entered an air-conditioned building with sweat running down your back. You reach the roadway in front of the hospital. You hear screams at your back. Afraid of what you'll see, you look over your shoulder. The woman had tripped and fell in the street. She is pushing to her feet when the first creature launches at her.

You come to a painful stop as your feet drag across the concrete. You run back as the female creature arrives. She pays you no mind, focusing on the meal in front of her.

The woman kicks, flailing and screaming. The man presses his bulk down on her and edges closer to her throat with bared teeth. The female snags a leg and is close to snapping her jaws down.

Pulling the pin from the extinguisher, you aim the nozzle and fire. A stream of foam shoots out, striking the male in the face. It leaps backward, more from surprise than actual pain. While your partner is free for the moment, you switch aim and douse the female just as her mouth opens. The jet fills her mouth and she falls back, gagging.

Stepping forward, you grab the woman's hand and help her to her feet. "Get to the car and start it. I'll buy you some time."

She takes off without a word. The male recovers and charges you. The foam won't stop him this time, so you reverse the canister and drive it into its face. It howls and goes down. At its feet you see the steak knife. You scoop it up and stand just as the female comes at you with a vicious snarl. Her teeth snap shut, missing your arm by a fraction.

You lunge with the knife and impale her gut. Her eyes widen, and her hands wrap around the knife. You try to pull it out, but her hands hamper you. The male surges forward again and you must defend, so you release the knife. The female drops to her knees as you pivot the face the male.

It attacks in a berserk frenzy but has enough control to avoid your attack. With the extinguisher away from your body and slightly off balance, it strikes and knocks you down. You hit the ground hard. Stunned, you are defenseless to stop the creature from climbing your body and sitting on your chest. It raises its face to the sky and lets out a victorious howl that freezes the blood in your veins.

Answering cries pop up from several places around the grounds. It presses its face toward you and opens its maw wide enough to swallow your head. With one hand braced under its chin, the other drags the nozzle of the extinguisher closer. You hear your own whimpers as you see your death in the creature's eyes. With no other option and needing both hands, you release its chin and pull the canister closer. As its teeth touch the skin of your neck, you jam the nozzle into its mouth and trigger the foam. Its mouth fills and it jumps back, looking like a rabid dog.

Frantically, it wipes the foam from its mouth. Flaming red eyes glare and it takes a step toward you just as a car rams into it, sending it flying.

The woman looks down and says, "Hurry! Get in."

You need no further invitation. You speed around the car, rip the door open, and jump in. However, before you can close the door, a hand grabs your leg. You look to see the female has crawled to you, giving up on removing the knife from her belly.

You kick your leg free and slam the door, hearing a howl of pain. Looking out the window, you see the female being dragged. You take an unnatural joy from the sight, then open the door and let her roll away. As you close it, the woman says, "Where to?"

"I need to get some clothes. Let's go to my house first. We can decide where after that." Your thoughts turn to your girlfriend/boyfriend and wonder if he/she is all right. If not, you pray he/she is dead rather than one of those creatures.

You sit back in the seat and close your eyes. What has happened to the world? More importantly, how will you survive whatever it is?

Go to Chapter 2 on page 217

1A2b3) You step away from the door and press against the wall, praying the two creatures outside don't turn. Sounds of movement and more destruction come from down the hall. You are about to be trapped. Your mind races for a solution. Scanning the hall for a possible way out, you stop at the entrance to the coffee shop.

The woman is hyperventilating. She looks like she's on the verge of panic and about to do something stupid, like scream or run. You grab her arm and shake her. She looks at you like you have two heads. "Hey! Stay with me. Is there a back exit from the coffee shop?"

She doesn't seem to hear you. You try again. "We have to go now. Can we get out through the coffee shop?"

"I-I think so."

"Okay. Follow me. And stay quiet."

You take her hand and lead her toward the entry. It is not a doorway, but an arch that is wide open, making barring the way impossible. You slide between the tables, angling for the counter. Her head sweeps every direction at once. She bumps into a chair and knocks it over. For a moment, you freeze, then the first howl reaches you, followed by several others.

You release her hand and run for the counter and the open doorway behind. You are in a small kitchen and prep area. As you pass through, you snatch up a knife, carrying the extinguisher under an arm. A slight jog to the left leads you to a storage room. To the right is the door. You hit the panic bar and burst through to the outside. The sunlight blinds you for an instant, causing you to throw up a shielding arm and stop. The woman crashes into you, knocking you forward.

Regrouping, you say, "Which way to your car?"

She gets her bearings. "This way."

You follow, aware that her path will lead you in view of the two creatures in front of the hospital. Hopefully, by the time they see you, you have enough lead to make it to the car safely. In bare feet, it's difficult to keep up with her. She passes the corner, and almost immediately the howls begin. The sound makes you hesitate for an instant. They are already on the move toward her by the time you come into view.

You squeeze the knife tighter and prepare for a fight. If it comes, you are determined to get in the first attack. You crouch but keep running. The concrete rips at the soles of your feet. You wince when you step on a small stone. It slows you, but you keep going.

She runs on, dodging through the first row of cars, unaware of the closeness of the pursuit. You push harder, realizing they haven't seen you yet, and are zeroing in on her. If they take her down, it might be enough of a distraction for you to slip away. You quickly erase that idea from your mind. You couldn't live with yourself if you left her. But as your run continues, you see she's going to be taken down and there's nothing you can do to stop it.

She passes through the second row of cars and angles to the right —a move that puts her closer to the things chasing her. You push harder, but you hear a scream and she disappears as the two creatures pounce on her.

You arrive seconds later. She is attempting to roll away from her attackers and kicks. One grabs her hair and yanks her head back. Her screams turn shrill. You pause, not sure what to do, but your hesitation only means she will die. You swallow the lump in your throat, and as they gain control of her body, you race forward and bury the knife deep into the back of the one holding her legs.

The creature arches backward and lets out its own shriek of pain. Its hands grope for the knife but cannot reach it. Burning bile rises in your throat. You can't lose it now; the woman is in trouble. With one creatures writhing on the ground, you lift the extinguisher over your shoulder and slam in down on the second one's skull, just as its teeth close around the woman's arm.

The force of the strike propels the head down, where it face plants into the parking lot. It lets out an almost human moan. The sound stops you from slamming it again. Did the blow knock the animal out of him? *Maybe physical pain reverts them to human nature.*

As you watch, hopeful you won't have to strike again, the being shakes its head, then turns its malevolent glare at you. The sight is so frightening, you feel like your spirit has fled your body. Your legs wobble and you almost collapse. The beast rises, eyes only for you. Your mouth has gone arid. As it advances with a deep snarl, you back away, the fear leaving you inactive.

As it reaches its claws for your neck, its eyes suddenly go wide, and it stops. The eyes roll back, and it drops to its knees where it stares off like it's confused.

Behind it, you see the woman, face and arms bloody, her hand still clutching the knife. She lets out a scream, and in a violent rage, plunges the knife into the creature over and over until it falls in a bloody heap. You both stare at the body until a howl snaps you from your fugue.

"Come on," you say. "Let's get out of here before we have others to contend with."

She moves but keeps looking back at the body she made into a corpse.

"Which one?"

"Huh?"

"Snap out of it. You did what you had to do. They would have killed both of us if we didn't kill them first. Now, show me where your car is."

"Over there." She runs, stopping at a few years old Chevy Cruze. She hands the key to you. "You drive. I don't think I can."

That's a good idea, judging by how much her hand shakes.

You unlock it with the fob and pull the door open. Not caring that the seat is too close to the wheel, you force your body in, insert the key, and start the engine just as more beasts reach the car. In a flash, you press the button to lock the doors and throw the stick into reverse. The car leaps back, dislodging the three creatures from their holds.

The speed is too fast and your reactions too slow to prevent the collision with a car in the next row. The shock snaps your heads forward and back into the headrests. You are relieved the airbags don't deploy. Shifting again, you shoot forward, connecting with one of the beings. The car bounces over the thing and outruns the other two.

Whipping the wheel, you work your way out of the lot and onto the street. Stopped cars dot the road in front of you. You maneuver through and turn left at the first intersection. You have about ten miles to go to get to your house.

Next to you, the woman covers her face and sobs, the bloody knife still clutched in her hand.

You turn your attention to the road and the devastation surrounding you. How did this happen? A better question is, how will you survive?

Go to Chapter 2 on page 214

1A2c) Unsure of what to do or what's going on, you decide you need to find someone who has answers. You move back into the hospital. One hand holding the back of the hospital gown closed, you head toward the information desk, just around the corner.

Reaching the intersection, you turn left and within four strides, you determine no answers will be coming from anyone there. The floor is strewn with ripped-apart bodies. Blood runs in streams, pooling in lower places, then filling up and flowing again.

In the center of the lobby, three creatures squat around the body of a woman wearing scrubs. You back away and lean against the wall. Where else can you find help? Where is the security office?

You glance at the information desk, thinking a list of departments might be there. You edge forward. The three creatures are still absorbed in their task. You suck in a deep breath and move. Staying low, you advance toward the large desk. Arriving, you collapse, working hard to keep your breathing under control. Your heart pounds hard, loud enough to be heard on the fourth floor.

You scoot backward and focus your hearing. Nothing has changed, at least that you're aware of. The desk has three cushioned rolling chairs. Each side has three drawers. Rising high enough to see, you scour the desktops for a map or roster of departments. Pinned between the first two sections is a piece of paper that reads *Security*, followed by a phone number. There is no room number. You look at the phone. Will it make too much noise? You decide to search further.

A strange sound draws your attention. You freeze, trying to identify the origin. It comes to you and with it, the horror of understanding what you're hearing. Someone is sniffing at the air. *My God! Can they smell me?*

Grunts and groans come in rapid succession. *Is that how they communicate?* The sniffing is closer. You have nowhere to escape to without them seeing you. Your only chance is to hide. With agonizing slowness, you roll the middle chair back and crawl under the desk and pull the chair back in place behind you.

Something bumps the other side of the desk. A second later, the desktop over you creaks. Whatever it is has climbed on top of the desk. You hold your breath. The sniffing grows louder. A footstep lands right above your head. You put a hand over your mouth to prevent the whimper building in your throat from escaping.

A foot comes into view. It dangles for a moment before the second one appears. The creature pushes off the desk and lands on the floor right in front of your hiding place. It sniffs the air. It has your scent. It bends over the chair. You've been caught. Its twisted face is four feet away. It will attack in a moment, and there won't be anything you can do to prevent it.

Its nose twitches as it lowers over the chair. It will see you any second. You brace to explode outward. It might have you, but you vow to go down fighting.

Then, to your great surprise, the creature focuses on the purse hanging over the back of the chair. Its nose disappears inside the large bag, followed by its entire face. It rummages through the bag and comes out with a spray bottle of perfume. It sniffs at the nozzle, then sprays it. Inserting its head in the middle of the mist, it inhales deeply. It lets out a chuffing sound that sounds like a laugh.

It repeats the process, then climbs back over the desk. A commotion ensues. You decide it's time to get away from there. You crawl to the far edge of the desk. The elevators are to the right, but you dare not use them. There's no guarantee they still operate. Beyond them is another hall. You calculate the odds of making it unseen but staying gives you no options. You peek around the desk and see the three creatures fighting over the perfume bottle. Their actions and behavior remind you of chimps at the zoo.

You crawl away from cover as far as you dare, then get up and bolt down the hall. Within seconds, the wolf-like howls follow you. Ahead is an exterior door. To the left, you notice a small hallway. The signs above say executive offices. You turn that way, hoping security is among them.

You pass by several doors with lettering spelling out *Administration*, *HR*, and *Purchasing*, but they are all dark and look empty. The hallway dead ends. The last door on the right says *Security*. You twist the knob but find it locked. The door across the hall is also locked.

Panic increases. If they find you down here, you'll be trapped. You run for the next set of doors, but they are all locked. Four more doors line the hallway before you reach the main hall. The howling grows louder. Pursuit is closing in. You must find someplace to hide. You hurry toward the next doors. Each of those is locked as well.

As the creatures draw closer, you backtrack, hoping the distance will help hide you. You press into the door of the security office. The few inches give scant cover, but it's all you have. The glass is cold against your bare butt. You wonder if you'll be able to break it. The sound of shattering glass will tell them where you are.

The first of the creatures comes into view. It passes by without a glance. You breathe a sigh of relief. The second one also passes, but the third, the one who found the perfume, stops and sniffs the entry to the hall. You press against the door harder and suck in your breath to make yourself smaller.

The thing stands there, scanning the hall. You pray that if they've become animals, their eyesight has remained human. Your lungs strain for air. Holding your breath had been a mistake. Your vision clouds, and a black border forms, narrowing your view. Lungs about to burst, the creature moves on. You let the air out in what you hope is a silent, controlled hiss.

You take several quick breaths, thinking you are safe, then the creature pokes it head around the corner and sniffs again. Sweat pops from your every pore. It advances into the hall. It can't help but see you. Your hand finds the knob and you twist it hard in both directions. The creature moves even with the first set of doors. It is then that it spots you and tilts its head back, releasing a long howl. It is answered, and you know you are out of time.

As it runs toward you, you pound on the door, hoping to break the glass. It is too thick. A scream forms deep in your core and is slow to release. You turn to face your attacker, balling your hands into fists that you know will have little effect on the beast. It gets to within ten feet of you, and your scream reaches full volume.

You bring your arm back, thinking to strike it with your cast, but just as it launches, the door opens behind you. You are pushed to the floor and a man steps out, gun in hand, and fires four times, point-blank into the creature. It slams into the wall, falling on top of you.

"Quick," the man says extending a hand. "Get inside."

He grips your hand and yanks you from the floor. You fly past him, landing in a squat inside the office. He closes the door as quietly as he can, then with a finger to his lips, motions you farther inside. He guides you around a corner and takes up a position that allows him to see the door. You slump to the floor, shaking at your close call.

You hear a howl from the hall and a scuffling sound. Your savior watches without moving. Five minutes later, he turns to you and says, "I think they're gone now. You can get up."

You rise, staying against the wall for balance. "Thank you. You saved my life."

"Yep. You were lucky. I try not to open that door, but I can't imagine there's too many people left alive in here."

"Can you tell me what happened?"

"You don't know?"

You shake your head. "I woke up a short time ago in a hospital bed. The chaos had already begun."

He looks you over. "Let's get you some clothes and some water. Then we'll sit down and talk."

He enters an internal office and goes to a closet. He pulls out a pair of sneakers, sweat pants, and a t-shirt. The fit isn't perfect, but certainly better than what you had. You sit down to lace up the shoes and he places a paper cup of water on the desk.

"Well, as you can see, the world has gone crazy."

Just then, something crashes against the outer door, halting his explanation. He motions for quiet, then slips from the office with his gun drawn. You stand and watch as he edges down the interior hallway, stopping where he watched the door before. In a burst, he disappears around the corner. Panicked by his sudden move, you move down the hall.

The door opens, and you hear a cacophony of sounds. Cries from a woman, howls from creatures, and gunshots all happen at the same time. "Quick! Get inside," he says. You reach the corner in time to see a woman in midair land hard on the floor at your feet.

Gunshots erupt, barking one after the other, then nothing. The man swears. He steps for the door and is almost through when a blur slams him into the wall. He tries to turn and fight, but another creature lands on him, pinning him to the floor.

You run forward to help, but one of the beasts sinks his teeth into the back of the man's neck and tears out a bloody hunk. He screams. The creature turns its face toward you, the hunk of flesh hanging from its mouth as it chomps.

You make a hasty decision and slam the door. You turn the lock and back away from the gory scene. The woman sits up, sees the dying man and screams. You hug her to you and cover her view.

He's gone," you say. "We can't help him. Let's get back inside."

You enter the office you were in before, close the door, and slump to the floor. The woman paces. She's wearing green scrubs. You assume she's a staff member.

"What are we going to do?" she asks. "We can't stay here forever." She stops pacing and looks down at you expectantly. "Well, do you have a plan or what?"

You are surprised by her tone. "Why would I have I plan? Why would anyone have a plan for this?"

"You're security. I thought you had a way to deal with everything, or at least a way out of here."

You realize her mistaken assumption. "I'm not security. I came looking for help, too. He was the only one here."

She stares open mouthed, then begins pacing again. She glances down periodically then stops. "You were a patient?" she asks, pointing at your cast.

"Yes. I woke up today. I'm not sure how long I've been here. I have no idea what's going on."

She paces again. A sudden heavy thump against the exterior door makes you both freeze.

"Oh my God! Are they getting in?"

"I don't know."

"Well, go see!" she orders, near hysteria.

You want to tell her to go see, but one of you has to, and clearly, she's not capable. You stand and exit the office. She closes the door behind you, but you stick a foot in to block it. "Don't even think about locking me out."

She steps back, and you swing the door all the way open.

There's nothing to prevent her from shutting it once you walk away. If she does, you vow to yourself to kick it in and toss her out. You reach the end of the hall and peer around the corner. The number of creatures has increased. Three are feasting on the man's body while another attempts to get inside. Its eyes meet yours and it lets out an excited howl. One of the others stands and joins it at the door.

You duck back, but the sound of them pounding on the door has you sweating. You jog back to the room. The door is ajar. You enter, shut and lock it, then go to the desk. You put your weight into moving the large metal desk, but your hand makes getting a grip on it difficult.

The woman panics. "Oh my God! Oh my God! They're coming, aren't they?"

"Not yet, but I want to be ready in case they do. Help me."

She doesn't move and continues to rant. You shout. "Hey! Help me push this against the door!"

She stays where she is, but at least she's no longer talking. The desk inches forward. It is heavier than you anticipated, but if you can get it against the door, it should be beneficial. You turn and press your back to it, pushing hard with your legs. The desk slides.

To your surprise, the woman joins you. She doesn't add much strength, but at least she's trying. You manage to advance the desk flush against the door. Then, you scan the room for weapons. Nothing other than a lamp. You heft it. It has a wooden base and ample weight to cause damage. It gives you an idea.

"Do you have a car?"

"What?"

"A car. Do you have one?"

"Yes."

"Where is it?"

"In the employee parking lot."

"Which direction from here."

She goes to the window to get her bearings. "That way." She points left. "Around the back. Why?"

"If we get out of here, we're going to need it to escape. Can you run?"

"Yes."

"Do you have your keys?"

She pats her pockets and her body sags. "They're in my purse."

"And where's that?"

She flops into the desk chair. "Upstairs at my work station. On the fourth floor."

You slump, too. With the room quiet, the sound of pounding is louder. You pray the glass will hold out. You lean against the wall and let your mind go blank. Thoughts come unbidden. *If only the security guard made it back inside. If only he had an extra gun. If only the woman hadn't forgotten her keys. If only you had a car here.*

The process ignites a thought. You hurry to the desk and rifle through the drawers. Papers fly like confetti. You search each drawer. Nothing. Did that mean they were on the man? You look at the locker. One last hope. You attack the door, ripping it open. There, on the shelf at the top of the locker are keys. You snatch them up, holding them in the air with pride like you'd just netted a trophy bass.

"We have keys."

Her eyes widen with hope. "Do you know which car it belongs to?"

"No, but there is a fob. We can find it by pressing the button."

She stands, excited for at least a chance.

"How do you plan on getting out of here?"

"The window." Without further explanation, you pick up the lamp and smash the base into the glass. It spiderwebs. You hit it twice more before the lamp falls apart in your hands. Lifting your leg as high as you can, you kick the damaged shatterproof glass. Exhausted from the effort, you give it one more good kick and your leg plows through.

You're stuck.

You pull but are unable to free it.

"Help me."

She steps forward and grabs your leg.

"Push on the glass."

With the two of you working together, you manage to free your foot. You have several small cuts around your ankle. You study the glass to find the best place to work, then you begin to methodically pound the glass from the frame with the wooden lamp base.

You finish one corner when the woman says, "Will this help?" She holds up a pair of scissors.

"Put it right here against edge and drag it against the frame."

Again, the teamwork pays off. You clear two corners and have the glass sheet folding

downward when you hear the glass door shatter.

"We're out of time. We have to get out now. Quick, get the chair."

She drags it over.

"Climb up and put your legs through the opening. I'll support you from here."

"What about you?"

"I'll follow once you're out, but I might need some help, so stay there." She steps up and you direct her. Her feet balance on the narrow external ledge while you keep your casted arm on her abdomen, your good hand bracing both of hers.

Outside, the main office is being destroyed. It won't be long before they move down the hall.

"I can't reach the ground."

"They're coming. You'll have to jump down."

She hesitates, but you push her body out, forcing her to jump. Her body clears, but her arms smack into the glass. She cries out and disappears below the frame. You step up on the chair and stick one foot out. Bending, you place your hands on the inside ledge, then lift your other leg through. The glass presses against your stomach. If you don't do this right, you risk eviscerating yourself.

Noise outside the door hurries you. You push up and back, clearing your torso, but slam your head into the top part of the frame. Pain ignites and a blinding light flashes inside your head. You fall to the ground, clutching your already banged up head.

"The woman shouts, what are you doing? We have to go!"

The pain is too severe for you to reply. She's next to you, but instead of helping you, she's going through your pockets, looking for the key. Finding it, she runs.

"Wait," you try to say, but the word has little volume.

From inside the building, you hear someone pounding on the inner office door. Fear replaces pain and you get to your feet. You run on unsteady legs toward the parking lot, not sure where the woman went. Then, you hear the honk. She has found the car.

With a renewed sense of urgency, you race through the lot searching for her. An engine roars to life a few rows ahead. You increase your speed and reach the row as she pulls out of the parking spot. You place yourself directly in her path. If she doesn't allow you in the car, she might as well run you over.

The look on her face leads you to believe she is not going to stop. You brace for impact, but at the last second, you alter the plan and jump on the hood. You land hard, knocking the breath from your lungs. You manage a hand hold at the hood's edge. The impact startles her enough to stop the car. You slide off on the driver's side. Keeping one hand on the hood, you look her in the eyes, only glass between you, and say, "Open this door."

She shakes her head.

You slam a palm into the window, and she screams and presses down on the pedal. However, she loses control and plows into the rear end of a parked car. You run up, slam your elbow into the rear window, and shatter the glass despite your pain. She screams again and shifts into reverse. You reach in and open the rear door as the car shoots backward.

You are flung away from the car, left hanging onto the door with one arm. As she brakes to shift again, you dive through the window and land face first on the rear seat with your legs hanging outside. You crawl in and lay there panting and in pain.

The woman drives like a maniac, but you don't move, trying to control the pain. After what feels like twenty minutes, you rise, snake an arm around her neck, and pull back. She gasps.

"Stop the car. Do it now, or I'll choke you out."

She sobs but does as instructed.

"Put it in park and get out."

She shifts to park but doesn't make a move to get out. "Please, don't leave me," she manages between sobs. "I'm sorry. I'm just so scared."

"Why shouldn't I leave you? You were going to leave me."

"Please." She leans over and cries hard.

You reach over her and withdraw the key from the ignition. Then, you get out and open the driver's door. You want to yank her from the car and leave her, but something about her crying, defenseless form keeps you from acting on it.

Instead, you slide in and push her to the passenger side. She curls in a heap, crying softer.

You get your bearings and drive, deciding to go to your home first to get clothes and find a weapon, then figure out how to survive in this crazy new world.

Go to Chapter 2 on page 214

1A3) The creature swipes at you. You duck back. It lunges across the bed, its hand swatting you to the side. The force of the blow almost knocks you down. You brace with your hand then swing your left arm at the attacker, forgetting about the cast. It strikes the creature on the side of the head. You both howl in pain.

Its formerly human eyes narrow, alive with rage and burning. You doubt whatever stands before you now could ever be mistaken for human. As it lets out a fierce roar, you launch a right-handed punch into the center of its face. Human or not, the solid contact results in a geyser of blood.

It staggers back, and feeling more confident, you shove the bed forward, driving it back. You increase speed and the power behind your push. When the bed hits the opposite wall, it slams the creature, stunning it. With it dazed, you unleash a series of punches to its face that soon renders it unconscious.

You lock the wheels, keeping it pinned and move toward the door. *What the hell is going on? Where did this deranged man escape from?* There must be a mental ward on one of the floors. You need to find someone and report the attack. You stand in the hall and your jaw falls open. It looks like a tornado has gone through. Everything in its path has been destroyed and lies in wreckage on the floor.

You advance toward the nurses' station, hoping to find help, or at least someone who can explain what's going on. You hear a moan coming from behind the large semi-circular desk. Peering over the top, you see legs splayed out on the floor. Smears of blood coat the floor around the legs. A wave of nausea sweeps over you. You take short, rapid breaths to gain control before spewing everywhere.

Concerned, you race around the desk to find a nurse with her throat ripped out and large chunks of her torso missing. You can't help but gasp in shock. Your thoughts turn to the creature and the gashes it put in your chest. You could have ended up the same way the nurse had.

You don't bother checking for a pulse. Instead, you go to the desk, locate a landline phone, and pick it up. You are relieved to hear a dial tone, but after dialing 911, all you get is a busy signal.

Disconnecting, you try several more times with the same result. Confused, you stare at the phone as if it's to blame. Then, you hear the moan. It startles you. You whip around, ready to defend, but see no one.

Advancing deeper into the station, you hear the moan again. It sounds eerie, raising goose bumps on your arms. You pray that whoever is moaning is human. You continue on. Finding a pair of scissors, you snatch them up, thankful for a weapon. At the far end of a series of cabinets, another set of legs stick out. You continue forward, but angle away from the legs.

As the body is revealed, you raise the scissors, ready to strike. A woman comes into view, a nasty gash on her forehead. Her eyes are closed, but you see the rise and fall of her chest. She is alive, but is she human? What if this is like every zombie movie you've ever seen, and once you're bitten or scratched, you're infected, destined to become one of them? Then you look down at your own bloody chest and pray the movies got it wrong.

Afraid to get too close, you call to her. "Hey! Hey lady, you all right?" A stupid question, considering the blood. She doesn't respond. You call again, but this time, nudge a leg with your bare foot. Her eyes flutter open. She's calm for a moment, but as her vision and mind clear, she sees you standing there with scissors and tries to climb the wall as her shrill screams make you wince.

Backing away, hands up, you say, "Easy, I'm not that crazy guy. I won't hurt you. I just wanted to make sure you were all right." You're not sure how many of your words penetrate her screams, but after several seconds, she calms. Her eyes are wide with fright.

You stay back, but say, "Your head is bleeding. Can I do something for you?"

"No! No. Just stay away." She is terrified.

"Okay." You step away again. "One of the other nurses is dead. I tried to call the police, but the line's busy. Can you call hospital security?"

She doesn't reply to your question, but a look of concern crosses her face. "Dead? Who's dead?"

"I don't know. She's by the front desk. She's wearing green scrubs, so I just guessed she's a nurse."

The woman steps forward with a hand up in front of her. "Back away so I can see."

"Okay. It's pretty gory. I guess you're used to seeing this stuff, but that's no way for a person to die."

Your words confuse her, but you move to the front side of the desk. She gasps at the sight and collapses back against the wall. "Oh my God! It's Debbie." She glances at you, more fearful now.

"It wasn't me. I swear. I'm a patient. I was in that room," you point before realizing she can't see which room you mean from where she stands.

"Some deranged man attacked me. I left him unconscious in my room."

"He-he's in there now?"

"Yeah. I didn't know what to do or what was going on. I came out here to find out."

She relaxes a bit and moves to the desk. She disappears for a moment. When she stands, she has a purse over her shoulder and a stun gun in her hand. "Stay away from me, or I swear I'll use this."

You believe her and back away. "Hey, I'm not the threat here. I was attacked, too. What's going on?"

"I don't know, but I'm getting out of here." She walks around the desk but backs away so she can keep an eye on you. "Don't follow me."

"Can you tell me what I should do?"

"Run. Find someplace safe to hide." With that, she reaches the stairs and disappears through the fire door.

Stunned, you spin to look around for options. The first thing you should do is care for the wounds on your chest. You rummage through the cabinets until you find gauze pads, tape, and antibacterial cream. At the sink, you wet a paper towel and dab at the scratches. They burn, and you wince. As the pain subsides, you wash the wounds with soap, rinse them, and apply the cream. You place the pads over the scratches and tape them down.

That accomplished, your next task is to get your clothes. You hesitate to enter the room, for fear the wild man has awakened and is ready to attack again. Inching the door open, you peek in. The man is still slumped over the bed. You creep in and open the small closet. Your clothes are there. You grab everything and exit. After taking another long look down the hall, you get dressed, tossing what's left of your hospital gown behind the desk.

Scissors in hand, you advance down the hall. You haven't gone two steps when you hear a snarl and rush of movement behind you. The man-thing from your room leaps at you, its claws poised for another strike.

Without thought, you duck and push your hand forward. The creature lands on you, but its own weight and force impale it on the scissors. It howls like a wounded dog. Jumping away from you, it rips the scissors from your hand. The twin blades are buried deep in its chest. It claws at the implement to pull it free.

It stumbles backward and bumps into the wall. You watch in shock, then decide it's time to leave. You pivot and race for the stairs, leaving the wounded man-creature behind.

At the bottom, you burst through the fire door and come out in the lobby. Bodies are strewn all over the floor. The tiles are slick with blood. To the right, you hear a scream. You pause for a moment, then run that way.

You pass the information desk and the elevators, turning right down a side hallway. At the end of the hall near the outside doors, you see two more creatures bent over a green-clad bloody body. They appear to be ripping chunks of flesh away and eating it. You stop and stare in utter disbelief. You recognize the victim. It's the female nurse from upstairs.

Her purse is lying ten feet from the deadly duo, and the stun gun another five from that. You can't stand there forever. Sooner or later, they will notice and come for you. You have to move but are undecided what to do.

Do you:

1A3a) run forward and try for the purse and/or stun gun? Read on.

1A3b) retreat and look for another exit? Go to page 67

1A3c) find a weapon and attack the creatures? Go to page 68

1A3a) With the two creatures busy, you take a chance they won't come after you. You creep forward and inch through the doors until you're ten feet away. The gruesome sight leaves you stunned. It's like something from a movie, but this is real and happening right in front of you. Bile rises your throat, burning and leaving you nauseous. You shake it off as best you can and make a break for the purse. You manage to scoop it up before being noticed, but before you reach the stun gun, they spot you.

One turns, but the other is more intent on the current meal. You take a swipe at the stun gun as you race past but miss it. You shift into high gear and sprint away, moving into the parking lot. With your good hand, you fumble through the purse, searching for the key, and praying she didn't have it in her hand.

You hear running steps and the huffing of breath behind you. Risking a glance, you see one of the men is after you and closing fast. The look on its face is horrifying and spurs you to move faster. You fling items out of the purse, cursing its size, weight, and state of disorganization. As the being gains on you, it's clear you will not make the car, even if you knew where it was.

The purse does have one redeeming quality though, and you put it to use. Stopping, you pivot and swing the purse by its strap with all your might. It connects with the creature's head with enough force to stagger it. You move forward and deliver a vicious kick to the creature's balls, hoping nothing there has changed. Its eyes light up and a squeak replaces the snarl.

It clutches its groin and sags to its knees. With a backhand swing, you connect with the purse again and the creature rolls to its side. You don't hesitate and take off deeper into the lot. You reach the third row and duck behind a minivan to better search the purse. You still have trouble finding the keys and dump the contents on the pavement. You rifle through the pile. No key, but you do find pepper spray. You pick it up, thankful the woman was defense-minded. About to give up, you take a last glance inside the purse. Hanging from a clip is the key. You snatch it off the clip and press the button. You hear and see nothing that helps locate the vehicle.

The emblem on the key says it's a Ford, which helps somewhat. You stand and try again, pushing the button, then turning in another direction and trying again. After trying each direction twice, you decide must be too far away. You scan the lot, still full of cars and wonder where all their owners are. Are they inside hiding, or have they all turned into these creatures? The third is that they're dead.

Your eyes stop on a sign that gives you a new hope. *Employee Parking.* You move toward the rear of the hospital. As you round the corner, you press the button again, saying a silent prayer. A flash of lights and a honk draw your attention to what looks like a red Taurus in the third row. However, it also draws unwanted attention.

Two heads with blood-streaked faces pop up from the second row. They look behind them, giving you a chance to duck. You take a second to gather your thoughts, then work your way to the back of the lot, then around the outside to the employee lot, hoping to come up behind the car and the creatures.

As you come to the back row, you notice the two creatures wandering through the lot in search of the source of the honk. You wait them out. They separate and go in different directions. The one on the right is four cars away; the other, three. You can't wait any longer. You crouch and work your way toward the red Taurus.

It is right in front of you, but you must cross the open space between the rows. You peek around the car and scan the area in both directions. You don't see anything, but a sudden howl from the right ices your blood. Too scared to wait any longer, you dart toward the car, choosing not to button the doors open for fear of bringing the creatures down on you. Instead, you squat outside the driver's door and insert the key. The door unlocks at the same time one of the creatures appears at the end of the row. You freeze, afraid to move. It sniffs at the air, then turns its face toward you.

Your bowels threaten to release. You yank the door open and lift the pepper spray. As it closes, you release the entire canister into its face and mouth. It howls in a painful tone, but its momentum continues forward, bowling you over.

As it rolls on the ground wiping at its face, you get to your feet, jump over it, and dive into the car. You insert the key, but before you can shut the door, it is ripped from your hand. The second creature snarls and leans inside.

Panic steals your breath. As the car roars to life, you shift and bend as far away from the being as possible. Shifting into reverse, you floor the pedal. The car leaps backward, the open door catching and lifting the creature. Unable to control the vehicle, it slams hard into the car behind you. The crash propels the creature in the opposite direction, the door slamming into its head. It drops, but you are stunned and whiplashed. You clear your mind as both creatures rise in front of you.

In simultaneous movements, you close the door and shift, then slam the pedal down once more. The car lurches forward, striking them both. You whip the wheel into a turn, but the cast on your left hand makes quickness difficult. You impact the car in front, but brake before it hits hard enough to deploy the airbags.

However, the collision forces you to reverse again. As you do, both creatures pound on the driver's window. Shifting again, the window implodes, showering you with glass shards. You flinch, delaying your escape. One of them reaches through the window and grabs your head. You drive off with it hanging in through the window, trying to bite you.

Reaching the end of the row, you turn hard and close to the last car, sideswiping it and scraping your attacker off with a crunch of bone and spray of blood. It slowly slides from the window.

Breathing so hard you risk hyperventilating, you exit the hospital grounds. With no other options and a desperate desire to see if your girlfriend/boyfriend is all right, you head for home. The road is littered with abandoned cars and torn-apart bodies. Along the route, you see a few creatures loping along the roads. You avoid them, although several give chase.

You have ten miles to go to get home, but what do you do from there?

Go to Chapter 2 on page 93

1A3b) You stop and back away from the door until you are once again in the lobby. You do a three-sixty pivot, scanning for someplace that will offer refuge. You hear a howl and your heart stops for a beat. Looking up, you see a creature leap the second-floor balcony. It lands on the floor not ten feet from you. A loud snap sends the creature into a roll, clutching at its lower leg and howling in pain.

The bone juts through the skin. The sight bends you, ready to spew. You fight back the urge and run to the left toward the front exit. The creature lunges for you as you pass. It misses, but your speed increases and you run blindly down hall.

You run so hard and in such a panic that you burst out the front doors without looking. In front of you are two creatures taken as much by surprise as you are. They back away as if under attack. You hesitate, but then take off for the parking lot, aware that in your haste, you have no plan other than to outrun them. That lasts for all of two minutes before the first one leaps on your back. You can take three more steps before the extra weight bears you down.

You crash to the ground and the beast releases its hold. You are free for the moment, but before you can get to your feet, the second one barrels you over. Your head snaps backward and cracks against the pavement, stunning you and sending bright lights flashing inside your head.

As unconsciousness closes over you, you are aware of a pain in your neck. Warmth spreads over you and you feel like you're floating. Soon, there is no pain.


End

1A3c) The sight enrages you. Never one to back down from a fight, the thought that these creatures might also feast on you doesn't enter your mind. You search for a weapon, finding a fire extinguisher on the wall. You heft it, but rational thought prevails. You set it down, realizing how dangerous attacking the two creatures might be.

You are about to give up the notion when you look outside again. The woman left you, but she didn't deserve this. You have no idea what's going on, but you are determined to survive it. You spy her purse lying on the ground ten feet from where she died. Her car key might be inside. The only way to find out, though, is to take out the two beasts.

Working yourself up to a fighting rage, you exit the hospital, carrying the extinguisher. Yanking the pin, you ready the extinguisher. You approach at a run, lifting the canister over your shoulder. With luck, you can crush one of their skulls before they know what hit them.

Their heads turn as you approach. One dives to the side, but the second is too slow. You smash the extinguisher into its face, indenting the features. Blood sprays the air. Your momentum carries you too far, and you trip over the slumped body, landing on the bloody corpse of the woman. You land with a squish and fight down the urge to vomit.

The first creature is on its feet and advancing at you for the kill. Unable to regain your feet in time, you lift the nozzle and press the trigger as the beast launches. You hit it in the face with a stream of white foam. It tries to veer away in midair, and lands a glancing blow off your shoulder. However, the impact is enough to dislodge the extinguisher from your grasp.

The second one tries to rise, its bloody, ruined face making it look even more sinister. You kick it in the face and send it sprawling over backward. Getting to your feet, you reach for the extinguisher as the other beast lands on your back, driving you to the ground. You crash face first, scraping a long patch of skin from your cheek.

It claws at you. Pain shoots up you back like it's been set on fire. You gasp and throw an elbow. It connects, but not with enough force to knock it off. It snarls and nips the back of your neck. Panic sends you into a desperate frenzy. You flail wildly and become disentangled for a second. You flip on your back and kick as it lunges for you again. Your foot plants into its stomach and drives it back. For the moment, it is at bay but circling for an opening.

As it moves, you spin to keep your legs in front of it. You hand brushes something hard. The extinguisher. It rolls away from it, but you twist and manage to snag it. However, the move leaves an opening for the creature. It dives on top of you, blasting the air from your lungs. It lowers its bloody mouth toward you with steady progress against your weakening arm. Just as it opens its mouth to bite, you jam the nozzle in its mouth, slide your hand down to find the trigger, and press it. Foam fills its mouth. It rolls away, spitting and wiping.

With its weight no longer on you, you get to your knees, lift the extinguisher in both hands over your head, and bring it down as hard as you can. It slams into the creature's head knocking it to the ground. You smash repeatedly. By the time you are too tired to raise it again, the head is a disgusting mess of bone, blood, and brain matter.

You stumble to your feet and scoop up the purse. Walking as you rummage through it, you eventually find the key clipped to a ring on the side of the bag. You walk through the parking lot pressing the button until you see the headlights of a red Ford Taurus blink on.

With relief, you climb inside, lock the doors, and slump in the seat. Your body is humming with fear and adrenaline. A thump on the door startles you. You jump and notice another creature at your door. It is then you realize you were in such a hurry, you forgot to pick up the stun gun. Too late now. You slip the key in the ignition, start the car and back away, ignoring its repeated attempts at smashing in the window. As you drive away, you watch it chase you until you round the hospital and head for the street.

Once there, you are shocked by the number of abandoned cars and-ripped apart bodies that litter the streets. Several creatures lope toward you. It's time to put some distance between them and you. You have a driving desire to go home and see your boyfriend/girlfriend. You pray he/she hasn't fallen prey to any of the creatures.

As you drive, you wonder what has happened to the world since you went into the hospital. More importantly, how will you survive whatever it is?

Go to Chapter 2 on page 93

1B) After waiting more than five minutes for anyone to answer your call, you give up pressing the button and decide to go out into the hall to track someone down. You slide out of bed carefully, grabbing the IV stand and wheeling it with you to the door.

The nurses' station is almost directly across from your room. To your surprise, no one is there. Briefly, the idea that budget cuts may have limited the amount of staff crosses your mind. A hospital is a bad place to cut personnel.

You look down the hall in both directions and again are amazed at the lack of people. Were they all in rooms checking on patients? It could happen, you suppose, but it just feels so empty. Turning to the right, you walk to the next room. The door is closed, so you move on. The next room's door is open. You peer in, searching for a nurse, but the room is empty. You are about to move on when you see something on the floor on the far side of the bed.

You glance around the hall. Still no one in sight. You enter to see what is on the floor. You reach the end of the bed and freeze, shocked at the sight. The patient has fallen out of bed. Blood has pooled and begun to coagulate. That means the patient has been there for a while. You step forward to help, then decide that might not be the smartest thing to do. You back away, amazed by the amount of blood. Would a fall cause an injury that bled so much?

You exit the room and make your way toward the nurses' station. It is still unattended. You're baffled. This is a hospital. A place where they handle medical emergencies. How can they be dealt with if no one is there to help?

Something crashes hard in one of the rooms down the hall in the opposite direction. You are both relieved to know someone is here and concerned about the amount of crashes. You wonder if a patient went psycho and it's taking the entire staff to subdue him.

A man wearing scrubs comes out of a room near the end of the hall. Head down and walking slow, you get the feeling he's been through a war. He places his hands on a portable computer cart and leans as if exhausted. He is disheveled, and from where you stand, his clothes look torn and stained. With a jolt, you realize the stain is blood. *His or the patient's?*

You take a few steps, then call out, "Hey! A patient needs your help down here."

The man's head snaps up and he glares at you. You can feel the heat from his gaze. The ordeal of dealing with the crazed patient must have eroded his patience. He doesn't look in the mood to deal with another problem at the moment.

As the man starts forward, you try to explain. "It's not me." You turn and point at the room. "The patient in that room fell out of bed and looks to be hurt bad." You turn back to see the man is now running. You think he understands that there's an emergency. Then, you notice the red-rimmed eyes and the bloody face and grow curious. Did the patient he restrained bite him?

It isn't until he's twenty feet away that you realize the blood is in his mouth, on his clothes, and his hands. He snarls, and you understand he is not coming to help you, but he's coming for you. You hasten to your room and shut the door, leaning against it with all your weight and strength.

The man slams into it with such force, it knocks you back and off balance. The door opens, and you lunge to close it. You hit and drive the man back, but he howls like a wild animal and shoves back. It is clear he is stronger. You push with everything you have while searching the room for defensive options, then your brain for ideas. You soon conclude your best hope may be someone to come to your rescue, but that may be too much to wish for. What if this crazy man has already killed everyone on the floor?

The door edges inward as your feet slide across the floor. You are quickly losing ground. You flip and press your back against the door while pulling the IV from your arm. A hand reaches around the door and grabs your hair. The touch shocks you and you pull off the door for a second. But that second is enough for the man the gain entry. You back away. "What are you doing? What do you want?"

But the man, who looks more like a beast now that you see him up close, only snarls. As he reaches for you, you jab his arm with the IV needle. It sticks, and he yanks the hand back. The action rips the IV out. He howls and his eyes narrow with determination.

You tip the IV stand and jab at the man again to keep him back. It works the first three times, but the frustration level drives him crazy. He charges and swats the stand aside. His hands claw at you, leaving long scratches on your arms. You kick, but it has little effect on him.

His hands close around your throat. You kick again, trying to connect with his balls, but if you hit your mark, it doesn't stop him. He drives you backward and slams you into the wall. The air explodes from your lungs and your head strikes hard. Your already-concussed head flares with blinding light and searing pain. A black circle forms around your vision, closing in by the second.

You make a feeble attempt to break his hold, then strike out at his eyes. You make slight contact, which only serves to anger the man more. He pulls you away from the wall and slams you back again. Your vision narrows and you brain numbs. Once more, he bounces you back. Blackness surrounds you just as you feel the teeth bury into your neck and the lights blink out for good.


End

1C) You try the call button a few more times before giving up. Exasperated, you toss the control down on the bed and pound the sheets with your fist. Outside, you hear glass shatter. Something is wrong. Maybe all the nurses were needed to deescalate a psycho patient's tirade.

You wait a few more minutes and press the button again. A howl echoes through the hall. Not a human one. This one is more animal and it chills you. You burrow deeper under the covers. Another howl sounds closer. You look around for a weapon in case there's a crazed madman roaming around.

Finding nothing, your best option is to hide. You slide out of bed on the side away from the door. Instantly, you see the IV is going to be a problem. You grip the tape and peel it back, wincing at the pulled hair, then you slowly withdraw the needle. A small droplet of blood beads.

A noise near the door draws you up short, halting your breath in mid-exhale. You slide backward and try to become one with the wall. Through a gap under the bed, you watch as feet enter and stop. You picture whoever it is scanning the room. The shoes are rubber-soled, and by the size, you guess it's a man. He's wearing green scrubs. One pant leg is stained dark red, and you realize with a start it is blood.

Then you hear something strange. It sounds like crying, or perhaps someone has a severe runny nose. Then it dawns on you. It's sniffing the air as if searching for a scent. *My God! Maybe it is an animal.*

You hunker lower, trying to sink into the floor. So far, it hasn't advanced farther into the room. You want to change your angle to get a look at the face, but if you can see him, he can see you. So, you sit and wait, praying your fear and sweat don't become a scent he can pick up.

The feet move a quarter turn, perhaps scanning the room closer. Can't he see the room is empty? What's keeping him here?

With relief, you see the feet turn heel and move toward the door. As they disappear, you release a long breath. You wait a few seconds before standing, but as you press on the floor, pain shoots up your left arm. You forgot about the cast. You lift and clutch the arm to your chest, but the move sends you off balance. You topple toward the IV stand, causing an audible clatter. You freeze. A snarl rises from the hall.

You drop back down and pray he doesn't reenter. Seconds later, the feet are back and standing in almost the same spot, again sniffing. He takes a step forward and stops. You can almost feel his eyes boring through the bed and into your skull. The tension mounts and you want to scream. Then you sense a change and wonder what he has discovered.

You glance around. To your horror, you see what. The IV bag is swinging. With a sudden burst, the bed is pulled to the side, a difficult task with the wheels locked. But this person has little trouble moving it, leaving you in the open.

Reluctantly, you look up. What you see only resembles a man in form, but his head is slightly elongated, and the eyes are sunken, red-rimmed, and wild. It raises its hands, revealing two claw-like appendages. But what really sets you to screaming is the blood-soaked beard.

It leaps at you. Though filled with terror, you lift your legs, catch the man-thing, and propel it backward. It hits the wall, stumbles for balance, and releases an angry roar at you.

You are on your feet before it comes at you again. Your hands wrap around the only instrument you have close, the IV stand. You lift it, turning the bottom toward him and ignoring the pain in your left hand. That's not going to matter much if this thing manages to get his hands or teeth—you shudder with revulsion—into you.

It leaps, as if not seeing or perhaps, not caring about the slim metal pole in your hands. It slams into the base, driving it backward. The top hits the wall and serves to set the blunt end spear. The pole stops him short and with a *woof*! His legs fly up from under him and he slams to the floor. He lays stunned, but you don't give him a chance to recover. You drive the now-bent pole into his face. The nose explodes and blood flows everywhere, covering him in a red mask. This time, the howl is one of pain.

You lift the stand for another strike, but it catches the end in its hands before the blow lands. You battle for control as he rolls to his knees. You fear if he stands you will lose, so you kick him in the ribs, knocking him back down, but not before it manages to swipe at you. The hideous yellow and red nails create three long lines across your chest. They are not deep, but blood wells and seeps.

The stand comes free and you spear him again, hitting him in the chest. He scoots under the bed for protection. If he gets out the opposite side, you fear he'll have the advantage. You need something more substantial to hit with, but nothing presents itself. Then an idea hits. You lift the pole in both hands horizontal with the floor, then bring it down over your knee. The pole bends but doesn't break.

The man-thing pulls himself up on the other side of the bed. You whip the pole down on its hands and it releases its hold and falls back to the floor. Turning the stand over so the bend is to your knee, you repeat the action. The pole bends the other way. You work the metal back and forth until the crack is complete and the two ends separate.

You examine the ends. They will have to do.

The creature howls in rage. Then, it leaps up on the bed and launches toward you. With all your strength, you spear upward. The creature hits and the jagged end pierces the chest. It cries out like a wounded dog and lands on the floor, writhing. Its hands clutch the metal rod and pull it free. It hadn't penetrated deeply enough. Before it can rise or defend, you slam the second half down at its face. One hand deflects the strike, and the sharp end rips a furrow down the side of its face and into the ear.

It howls louder and rolls away. You can't let it get to its feet. You follow and jab repeatedly but can't make an incapacitating hit. It rolls to one knee and catches the pole in its hands. With brutish strength, it rips the pole, bringing you closer to it. If you lose the pole, you have no chance. With its weight back and trying to rest the pole away, you plant a kick to its face and send it toppling over backward.

The pole is yours to control for the moment. You take advantage of the freedom and jab down with your entire weight. The pole enters the eye and continues its path with a sickening wet sound until it hits something solid.

The creature isn't moving now. Your breathing comes in such large gulps that it hurts your chest. You glance down at the gore and immediately vomit all over the creature. You back away and stare in disgust and disbelief at what you have done.

From the hall, you hear another howl. This one is faint, leaving you to think it's still a distance away. The thought of others like him still roaming the halls sends urgency into your body. You run to the door and peer in both directions. The nurses' station is across from you, but it is vacant.

Ducking back into the room, you grab your clothes from the closet and step into the bathroom to dress and wash the blood, vomit, and sweat from your body. Dressed and somewhat refreshed, you open the door slowly, afraid the body has reanimated, but to your relief, the bloody form is still on the floor.

You sit on the bed for a moment to regroup your thoughts. You have no idea what's happened, but you have to decide what to do.

Do you:

1C1) Search for anyone who can help? Read on.

1C2) Leave the hospital? Go to page 82

1C1) You leave the room and advance toward the nurses' station, hoping to find help, or at least someone who can explain what's going on. You hear a moan coming from behind the large semi-circular desk. Peering over the top, you see legs splayed out on the floor. Smears of blood coat the floor around the legs. A wave a nausea sweeps over you. You take short, rapid breaths to gain control before spewing everywhere.

Concerned, you race around the desk to find a nurse with her throat ripped out and large chunks of her torso missing. You can't help but gasp in shock. Your thoughts turn to the creature and the gashes it put in your chest. You might have ended up the same way.

You don't bother checking for a pulse. Instead, you go to the desk and pick up a landline phone. You are relieved to hear a dial tone, but after dialing 911, all you get is a busy signal. Disconnecting, you try several more times with the same result. Confused, you stare at the phone as if it's to blame. Then, you hear the moan again. It startles you. You whip around, ready to defend, but see no one.

Advancing deeper into the station, you track the moans. The eerie sound raises goosebumps on your arms. You pray whoever is moaning is human. Finding a pair of scissors, you snatch them up, thankful for the weapon. At the far end of a series of cabinets, another pair of legs sticks out. You continue forward, but angle away from the legs.

As the body is revealed, you raise the scissors, ready to strike. A woman comes into view, a nasty gash on her forehead. Her eyes are closed, but you see the rise and fall of her chest. She is alive, but is she human? What if this is like every zombie movie you've ever seen, and once you're bitten or scratched, you're infected, destined to become one of them? Then you look down at your own bloody body and pray the movies got it wrong.

Afraid to get too close, you call to her. "Hey! Hey lady, you all right?" A stupid question, considering the blood. She doesn't respond. You call again and nudge a leg with your foot. This time, her eyes flutter open. She's calm for a moment, but as her vision and mind clear, she sees you standing there with scissors and tries to climb the wall as her shrill screams make you wince.

Backing away, hands up, you say, "Easy, I'm not that crazy guy. I won't hurt you. I just wanted to make sure you were all right." You're not sure how many of your words get through her screams, but after several seconds, she calms. Her eyes are wide with fright.

You stay back, but say, "Your head is bleeding. Can I do something for you?"

"No! No. Just stay away." She is terrified.

"Okay." You step away again. "One of the other nurses is dead. I tried to call the police, but the line's busy. Can you call hospital security?"

She doesn't reply to your question, but a look of concern crosses her face. "Dead? Who's dead?"

"I don't know. She's by the front desk. She's wearing green scrubs, so I guess she's a nurse."

The woman steps forward with a hand in front of her. "Back away so I can see."

"It's pretty gory. I guess you're used to seeing this stuff, but that's no way for a person to die."

You move to the front side of the desk. She gasps at the sight and collapses back against the wall. "Oh my God! It's Debbie." She glances at you, more fearful now.

"It wasn't me. I swear. I'm a patient. I was in that room." You point before realizing she can't see which room from where she stands.

"Some deranged man attacked me. I left him in there."

"He-he's in there now?"

"Yeah. Don't worry, I'm sure he's dead. I didn't know what to do or what was going on. I came out here to find out."

She relaxes a bit and moves to the desk where she removes a purse. She pulls out a stun gun. "Stay away from me, or I swear I'll use this."

You believe her and back away. "Hey, I'm not the threat here. I was attacked, too. What's going on?"

"I don't know, but I'm getting out of here." She walks around the desk, backing away so she can keep an eye on you. "Don't follow me."

"Can you tell me what I should do?"

"Run. Find someplace safe to hide." With that, she reaches the stairs and disappears through the fire door.

Stunned, you spin to look around for options. The first thing you should do is care for your wounds. You rummage through the cabinets until you find gauze pads, tape, and antibacterial cream. At the sink, you wet a paper towel and dab at the scratches. They burn, and you wince. As the pain subsides, you wash the wounds with soap, rinse them, and then apply the cream. You place the pads over the scratches and tape them down.

Scissors in hand, you advance down the hall. You haven't gone two steps when you hear a snarl and rush of movement behind you. Another man-thing leaps at you, its claw-like hand poised to strike.

Without thought, you duck and push your hand forward. The creature lands on you, but its own weight and force impale it on the scissors. It howls like a wounded dog. Jumping away from you, it rips the scissors from your hand. The twin blades are buried deep in its chest. It claws at the implement in an attempt to pull it free.

It stumbles backward and bumps into the wall. You watch in shock, then decide it's time to leave. You pivot and race for the stairs, leaving the wounded man-creature behind.

At the bottom, you burst through the fire door and come out in the lobby. Bodies are strewn all over the floor. The tiles are slick with blood. To the right, you hear a scream. You pause for a moment, then run that way.

You pass the information desk and the elevators, turning right down a side hallway. At the end of the hall near the outside doors, you see two more creatures bent over a green-clad bloody body. They appear to be ripping chunks of flesh away and eating it. You stop and stare in utter disbelief. You recognize the victim. It's the nurse from upstairs.

Her purse is lying ten feet from the deadly duo; the stun gun another five from that. You can't stand there forever. Sooner or later, they will notice and come for you. You have to move but are undecided what to do.

Do you:

1C1a) run forward and try for the purse and/or stun gun? Go to 1A3a on page 63

1C1b) retreat and look for another exit? Go to 1A3b on page 67

1C1c) find a weapon and attack the creatures? Go to 1A3c on page 68

1C2) You exit the room, check the halls, then advance toward the nurses' station. Peering over the top, you see legs splayed out on the floor. Smears of blood coat the floor around the legs. A wave of nausea sweeps over you. You take short, rapid breaths to gain control before spewing everywhere.

Concerned, you race around the desk to find a nurse with her throat ripped out and large chunks of her torso missing. You can't help but gasp in shock. Your thoughts turn to the creature and the gashes it put in your chest. You might have ended up the same way.

You don't bother checking for a pulse. Instead, you go to the desk and locate a landline phone. You are relieved to hear a dial tone, but after dialing 911, all you get is a busy signal. Disconnecting, you try several more times with the same result.

Now what? Picking up a pair of scissors from the desk, you move with caution down the hall. Broken equipment clutters the floor. Smears of blood add accent to the scene. You pass by each room with the scissors in front of you, expecting someone or something to jump out at you. You reach the end of the hall without incident.

You glance at the elevators but choose the stairs. Pushing the fire door open slowly, you peek inside the stairwell to make sure you're alone. Though no one is there, the tension ratchets up. Making your legs obey your commands takes great effort. You reach the next floor and decide to check it. Maybe the chaos is only on your floor.

As if cued by opening the fire door, a scream fills the hall, followed by several howls. The eerie sound shakes you to your core, but the scream continues. Whoever is in danger is still alive, but for how long?

Do you:

1C2a) try to help? Read on.

1C2b) continue down the stairs? Go to page 89

1C2a) Whoever is screaming needs your help. You don't feel brave, but knowing you have the scissors as a weapon gives you more confidence. That is, until you glance down and see how bad your hand is shaking.

You falter halfway through the door. Then, the scream comes again. It fills you with guilt, then strengthens your resolve. You step forward to search for the victim, praying you get there in time and that your newfound courage doesn't get you killed.

If anything, the destruction on this floor is worse. You peer into one room and freeze at the blood and gore. Your resolve begins to erode. The amount of violence it took to destroy a human body like that is unthinkable.

"No! Stay away!" The voice screams. Someone is still fighting for their life. Wouldn't you want someone to come to your rescue if the situation was reversed? You tighten the grip on the scissors and move forward.

You reach a point where the hall branches. The left, passes the elevators and connects with the parallel hall; the other goes straight. You choose straight, but you're not sure why; maybe because you believe the scream came from the other hall.

You don't want to look in any other rooms for fear the accumulative bloody scenes will cause you to turn and flee, but you have to look to make sure nothing jumps out at you. You are midway down the hall when you hear the sounds of a struggle. Grunts, smacks, and snarls mix together in a symphony of death.

The nurses' station is to your left. A connecting walkway leads to the other hall. You walk that way, knowing the fight is close. Sweat rolls down your face in steady rivulets. You wipe at your eyes with a sleeve. You work hard to control your breathing, but there is an intense urge to hyperventilate.

At the end of the walkway, you pause and sneak a look around the corner.

"No!"

The voice comes from a room across from you. You hasten across the hall and glide along the wall until you reach the door. With a quick peek, you are filled with actionable information.

A man is pinned in the far corner. He is almost on his back, fighting to keep a male and female creature away from him. You see blood but can't be sure if it's his or theirs. You take several courage-enhancing breaths, then step into the room.

As if in a trance, you advance toward the struggle. The man is losing the battle. The strain has his face bright red. The male creature presses his weight down on the man, whose arms tremble and bend at the elbows. He only has seconds left.

The woman creature slips her head under the man's arms and snaps at his neck.

You force your feet to keep moving and raise the scissors high over your head. An imaginary target appears on the male creature's back. Just as the man's arms give way and the creature emits a howl of victory, you plunge the blades into its back. It arches backward, head tilted upward, the horrid features contorted in pain.

His quick movement pulls the scissors from your hand. They are still embedded in its back, out of its reach. With no other weapon and the creature still a danger, you swing your hand down as hard as you can across the throat. Something gives inside. The beast's head snaps forward and a gagging sound emerges. You hope you've crushed its larynx and that it suffocates.

The female, having made contact with the side of the man's neck, worries her teeth back and forth, trying to tear at the skin. She seems unaware her partner is no longer aiding in the battle. The man places both hands on the woman's chest and pushes. She is forced away, but not before piercing the neck. She comes away with a small portion of skin.

You step forward and backhand her across the face, knocking her into the wall. She snarls and gnashes her teeth at you. Even though not close enough to bite, you jump back. The move gives her the room she needs to get to her feet and attack you.

The man lashes his foot out, catching her ankles. She trips and comes headlong at you. Sidestepping, you bring your fist down on her back, dropping her to her hands and knees. You kick her in the ribs, flipping her on her back, then lift a foot and stomp on her face. It is only a glancing blow. Before you can try again, the man pushes you aside and goes into a berserker rage. He pounds his foot down on her head so many times that it is nothing more than a puddle of gore and pieces of bone when he loses steam.

He steps back, out of breath. The male creature attempts to rise and you deliver a kick to its face, sending it down and out.

The two of you stand catching your breath and unable to speak. Finally, the man straightens, groans, and places a hand on his neck. The wound is bleeding profusely, but at least it's not jetting.

"Come on," you say. "We need to stop that bleeding."

You leave the room, but not before checking the hall. You move to the nurse's station and rummage through drawers and cabinets searching for supplies. You step over two nurses who have been partially devoured, trying not to look too closely.

Finding what you need, you call the man over. Using paper towels, you blot the wound. It is raw where the skin has been removed. The jagged edges show teeth marks. Not sure if you can stop the bleeding, you press a gauze pad to it. "Hold that in place."

You open a tube of ointment that's supposed to kill bacteria and aid healing. Smearing it over another pad, you say, "Okay, let go." You remove the first pad, now soaked, and replace it with the ointment-covered one. Then you secure it, using enough tape to wrap a Christmas present.

"I don't know if it will stop the bleeding, but it will have to do until we can get somewhere safe."

He nods. Tears well. Shock must be setting in. "Thank you."

You nod. "No problem. We should find a bag and fill it with medical supplies." You look at him and realize he's wearing a hospital gown. "You're a patient?"

He nods. "Yeah."

"You should get dressed. I'll gather the supplies. Go."

He leaves in a hurry; perhaps afraid you'll leave him alone as soon as he's gone. You find a purse big enough to be a duffel bag in one of the cabinets. Inside it, you find a key ring. That gives you an idea how to get out of there. Attached to the key ring is a pepper spray. Not the best of weapons, but better than none. Tossing out everything you don't need, you fill the purse with gauze, tape, ointment, and a random assortment of pills.

The man returns. The pad is already soaked with blood. Nothing you can do for it now. "Let's get out of here."

"No argument here," he says.

You reach the stairs, check them, then descend to the main floor. You peek out and see movement down the hall on the right. To the left about thirty yards is an exterior doorway. You lead that way. Trying not to make noise, you creep, but the pace gets faster with each step. By the time you get halfway to the doors, you're both running.

You burst through without looking, as if the outside was an official safety zone of sorts. You come to a momentary stop to catch your breath and plan.

"Do you have a car?" you ask.

"No, I was dropped off. You?"

"No, it was wrecked. I do have these keys, however. We just have to find the right car."

You walk into the parking lot and press the unlock button. You don't see or hear anything. "Let's move left." Hopefully, you don't have to go completely around the hospital grounds to find the car.

Finishing the front with no luck, you turn left and go up the side. Halfway through you see movement in your periphery. Instinctively, you duck, not sure if it's human or creature. Your new friend is to your right and ahead of your position. You want to warn him, but calling out will give you away.

Duckwalking, you move through the cars until you enter the row where he is. "Psst! Hey!" you call in a whisper. He hears and turns. You motion for him to get down. He ducks just as the creature bursts from between cars and tackles him. They roll across the pavement snarling and thrashing.

You run to help. The two hit the rear end of a car. Your friend ends up on the bottom. The creature swipes a hand and slashes deep gouges across the side of the man's face. Blood and bits of flesh go flying. You arrive and kick at the creature, but it is unaffected by the blow.

You think about putting an arm around its neck, pulling it back and choking it out, but you hesitate, afraid of putting your arm so close to those savage teeth. Instead, you get behind it and drive your foot into its back, sending it forward, head striking the bumper. Stunned, it gives its head a violent shake.

With a momentary respite, your friend twists beneath the creature, toppling it off to the side. He skitters away, and you step forward to deliver a kick to its face. The head snaps backward and something cracks. The eyes roll up and the beast collapses.

"I can't take much more of this," he says. "We need to find a car now."

You agree and continue through the lot at a jog, much more aware of your surroundings. You find the vehicle in the back lot. It's a black Dodge Charger. You hop in the driver's seat and as your friend settles in the passenger seat, you fire up the engine. Without discussion as to destination, you pull out and speed through the lot.

You make a turn onto the service road leading to the main street in front of the hospital. Twenty yards in front of you stands four creatures. Having heard your approach, they turn in unison. Their faces contort, and they tilt their heads back and howl.

As they advance to meet you, a thought enters your mind. You're in an appropriately-named car. You shove the pedal to the floor and feel the power of the engine. The car leaps forward like a jousting horse. The creatures show no fear, or perhaps in their warped minds don't understand the danger. No matter. You plow into them, sending bodies flying in all directions.

You whip the wheel without touching the brakes and turn right onto the street on protesting tires. The car swerves as you right the wheel. Gaining control, you speed toward the intersection, dodging around abandoned vehicles and discarded bodies. Well, almost all the bodies. At the speed you travel, it's difficult to avoid them all.

As you make another high-speed turn at the intersection, you say, "Where to?"

"I don't know. Someplace safe. If that exists."

You think about your girlfriend/boyfriend and wonder if she's/he's all right. "I live about ten miles away. Let's start there."

"Sounds good to me."

"Do you have family or anyone you want to check on?"

"No. No one local. I'm from Cleveland. I was here for a conference when I got sick."

"Let's go to my place and decide what to do from there."

He merely nods his approval.

You wonder what you'll find there and pray he/she is all right. But somewhere along the way, you have to find out what's happening. Maybe then you can figure out how to survive.

Go to Chapter 2 on page 242

1C2b) You want to help, but your body refuses to respond. Your hand shakes so badly that you are surprised you can still hold the scissors. Another scream comes. Conflicted, you stare without seeing anything. Then, you release the door and let it close, the guilt assaulting you like a physical attack.

You want to help, you really do, but what good would it be if you got killed, too? The image of that beast attacking strengthens your desire to get out of the hospital as fast as you can.

You run down the stairs until you reach the bottom. There, you catch your breath and try to block your mind from hearing the screams over and over. Not sure how long you stand there, a noise from somewhere above snaps you from your fugue.

You peek out the door and see movement in the lobby to the right. You're not sure if it's human or creatures but decide not to chance it. To the left are the outer doors. You go that way.

Keeping close to the wall, you walk toward the doors. Every fiber in your being screams for you to run, but you manage to keep control, barely. You advance with caution, not wanting to run into unseen trouble. Stopping at the inner doors, you peer out. It looks like a normal day. The parking lot is full, the sun is shining, it looks…peaceful. Then, you realize nothing is moving. Not people, not cars, not anything. Even the vehicles in the street in front of the hospital are at a standstill. It's like a science fiction novel you read as a kid. The memory of that story still makes you shudder.

You push through the door and pause at the outer doors before exiting. An eerie silence fills your mind. No sound of car engines. No honking horns, people talking, children laughing, or ambulance sirens announcing their arrival. You scan the grounds and feel completely alone. *Now what?*

You have no car and no way of contacting your girlfriend/boyfriend to come and get you. Whatever you do, it will be on you own. Weighing your options leaves you still standing there undecided. Then you hear the howl, and the decision is made for you. *Run!*

You take off to the left at a sprint, since the howl came from the right. You angle through the parking lot, darting through the parked cars, and aim for the street. An idea forms as you run. If the cars have stopped on the street for whatever reason, they may have keys in them.

You zero in on a red Impala closest to you. Ten feet from it, you realize with a jolt of fear that you are not alone. You glance back to see one of the creatures bounding toward you at high speed. The sight kicks you into an all-out sprint. You reach the car in plenty of time, but for some strange reason, the doors are locked. You don't have time to wonder why. You pivot and run for the next one, knowing you have lost precious seconds.

The next car has no keys. You move on, aware the creature has reached the street. The third car is also keyless. Judging you have time for one more before facing the monster, you jump on the hood of a Chrysler 300 and slide down the other side. You grip the door and look up to see the wild eyes locked on you like a guided missile. Your hand touches the handle, and without looking, you pull it open and jump into the car.

The creature manages to grasp the frame before you shut the door. It rips backward with incredible strength, almost pulling it from your grasp. With one hand hampered by the cast, you're unsure how long you can maintain a hold, but one thing is sure; he's stronger than you are even with both hands healthy. If you don't get the door closed fast, you will lose, and not just the battle for the door.

Leaning back, putting all your weight into holding the door at least where it is, you lift a foot and stomp it down on the creature's fingers. Once, twice. One hand lets go, but the other hangs on and is still almost too strong for you.

You kick the other hand, and it releases the door before you connect. The door slams shut, and you fly backward, slamming into the passenger door. Neither of you have control of the door. For a second, you lock eyes. Then, as if hearing the starter's gun, you both lunge for the door. Just as he grips the handle, you slap the lock down, then push the button on the panel to make sure all the doors are locked.

You breathe a brief sigh of relief before the pounding begins. The creature slams a balled fist into the driver's window, rattling both it and you to the core. The glass will not take much more abuse before imploding.

You glance at the steering column, wondering if you can hotwire the engine, even though you have no idea how. You open the console and then the glove box, searching for anything to help.

"Here, use these," a voice says from behind you. You jump so high that you bounce your head off the roof. Your vision clouds with tears. Pushing the shock and pain aside, you slide away, pressing into the dashboard, ready to fight. Your eyes clear and focus on the frightened face of a young woman. She is dangling keys in front of you. Tears run down her cheeks, flowing over the tracks of previously dried ones. Her eyes are wide with fear. She looks at the creature outside the car. It is no longer striking the glass, but now looking at the woman with what appears to be curiosity.

"Hurry," she says, the desperation evident in her cracked voice. "Take the keys and get us out of here."

Heart pounding, you grab the keys and insert them, starting the car from the passenger's seat, one leg over the console, barely touching the gas pedal. As the engine grinds for a few horrifying seconds before catching, the creature resumes its assault on the window. Fearing it will implode on you if you move into the driver's seat, you shift from where you are and pull away. The awkward position and too much gas causes the car to lurch forward and slam into the car in front of it before you can gain control.

The woman screams, and you are thrown sideways into the dash, sending pain up your shoulder. The creature runs to catch up. You jump into the driver's seat, reverse, and move past the creature in the opposite direction. You brake shift and pause, as once again you lock eyes with the creature. You press the pedal and aim for him. He leaps on the hood and impacts the window with a shoulder. The glass spiderwebs but holds.

You turn fast to avoid hitting the car in front. The creature slides but catches the hood edge with one hand. You swing the wheel in the other direction and weave your way through the maze of abandoned vehicles.

The creature rolls with the car's movements, sliding from side to side on the hood, keeping its one-armed grip. Reaching a stretch of road that's relatively clear, you speed toward the intersection. The speedometer rises fast. Fifty. Sixty. Just shy of seventy, you yell, "Hold on!" and stand on the brakes.

The tires squeal and grip the pavement. The back end rears up. The front end nosedives, and the creature shoots off the hood like a plane catapulted off an aircraft carrier. It hit the street and rolls. As you turn, it is already getting to its feet. You watch the distance increase, but note the creature is still chasing you. How far will it go? Can it smell the scent of the car and follow it anywhere? *Those are crazy thoughts,* you decide, and shake them off. But just to make sure, once you lose sight of him, you make a series of turns to further throw him off track.

"Is it safe yet?" the woman says.

You look in the mirror, but do not see her. Then, her head pokes up from behind the seat, rising to a point where only her eyes are in view. "Is he gone?"

"Yes," you mumble, "I hope."

She sits up and leans on the seat backs. "What are we going to do?"

Good question. You hadn't really given a destination any thought. An image of your boyfriend/girlfriend forms in your mind's eye. Is he/she all right? You have a sudden need to know.

"I live about ten miles from here. Why don't we start there? We can make further plans then."

"I only live a few minutes that way. Let's go there first."

You meet her eyes in the mirror. "Do you have someone there you want to check on?"

She nods. "Yeah—that, and I want to get my gun."

Now, that sounds like a plan.

You turn where she directs.

Go to Chapter 2 on page 214

Chapter 2 (1A2a1, 1A2a3a, 1A2a3b, 1A3a, 1A3c)

You arrive at your house, a vinyl-sided two-story in an older section of town, and park at the curb rather than the driveway, figuring it will be easier to get away if the need arises. You study the house for any movement or anything out of the ordinary.

The house looks asleep, and in fact, so does the entire street. You scan the neighborhood, making sure none of the creatures are sneaking up on you. You decide to leave the pillowcase full of medicines on the floor of the passenger side and get out. As an afterthought, you reach in and take out the prescription bottle. Its oxy. You tap one out and put the container back in the case. You lock the door and move toward the front steps, keeping your head on a swivel.

On the porch, you look through the windows, moving from one to another. Nothing is moving inside. You move to the door and try the knob. Locked. You don't have any keys. Do you risk knocking? You opt to try to side door.

You trot down the stairs and up the driveway, stopping at the old wooden door you'd always meant to paint, but never got around to it. Through the window, you see the stairs leading to the basement and the short section up to the main floor. The door at the top of the stairs is closed.

You debate whether to break the glass or pry the door. The door has two locks, the door lock and a deadbolt. Breaking the window is the easier choice, but that also means once broken, anyone can gain entry. Of course, that's only important if you plan on staying there.

You step back and examine the lock area. There's a little give, but you don't have anything to use as a pry tool, and if you ruin the lock or door frame you have the same security problem. After thinking it over for a few minutes, you opt to break the window.

You go out front and pick up a decorative stone from the border you made in the spring. Controlling the strike, you hold onto the stone rather than throw it, aiming for the bottom corner above the lock. The glass breaks and falls inside the house. The shatter is amplified in your head. You glance around to see if anyone responds, then realize how stupid that is since you're standing in the open. You reach through the jagged hole, careful not to cut yourself, and unlock the dead bolt. However, the door latch is out of reach.

You are forced to lean in as far as you can. Your fingers brush the latch. As you push beyond your limits, a shard of glass pierces you. You wince but push in farther. The latch releases and you withdraw your arm to find a trail of blood dripping down your arm. Just another thing to have to deal with. You enter, closing and locking the door behind you.

You climb the three steps to the closed door and press an ear to it. No sounds penetrate the wood. You close your hand around the knob and turn slowly. Pushing the door open, you step up to the kitchen. Before you can take another step, a blur flashes in front of you and pain explodes in your chest. You are propelled back down the stairs, tumbling and slamming into the floor. Only your quick reactions prevent you from falling all the way down the stairs to the basement.

Through the haze, you hear, "Oh my God!" Footsteps descend, and you fear a follow up attack. But your assailant squats next to you and places an arm around you. "I'm so sorry. I thought you were one of those things."

You look up to see your girlfriend/boyfriend looking down at you, a baseball bat in hand.

You struggle to your feet. As if you didn't have enough injuries, now you have to worry about cracked ribs. You stand for a few moments to make sure you can breathe without pain, then climb the stairs. As soon as you reach the top, you are embraced, creating more pain.

"What the hell's going on?" you ask. "What's happened since I've been out?"

"You don't know?"

"How would I?"

"What the news said before it all went dark was that someone developed some sort of biological weapon, combining rabies and something else. I think the idea was to create some sort of super warrior. However, it went horribly wrong. The test subjects became more animal than human and broke out of the facility. I guess they were highly contagious. If you get bit and don't die, you become one of them."

"Rabies?"

"Oh, I don't know. Something like that. What does it matter? You get bit, you die."

"Must be a lot of people bit, then, because I saw a lot more of those creatures then I do humans."

"That's why I'm in the house. One of the last broadcasts said to lock ourselves in our homes. I'm sorry I didn't come back to the hospital, but we were supposed to stay off the streets."

"Is there anyone in authority handling the situation?"

"If there is, I haven't seen them. I've seen a few of those things roaming the street, but never any police or National Guard or anything."

You walk to the kitchen table and sit down.

"What are we going to do?" your significant other asks.

*Good question.* You give it some thought. What choices do you have?

Do you:

2A) stay in the house? Read on.

2B) leave in search of other survivors? Go to page 182

2A) "I think for the moment, we should stay here. At least we know we're safe."

You change clothes and begin collecting weapons. The sad array on the kitchen table does not fill you with confidence. You have several steak knives, a chef's knife, a hammer, a small hand hatchet, and two baseball bats. Now you wish you hadn't been against having a gun in the house.

You fold some cardboard and wrap it with duct tape. Sliding one of the steak knives in the homemade sheath, you hand one to your partner. "Carry that with you at all times."

You do the same for the remaining steak knife and the chef's knife. You slide the steak knife in your belt and hand the chef's knife to your partner. You take the hatchet and put it in your belt opposite the knife. You place the hammer on the kitchen counter in easy reach, then set the bats near the front and side doors. It's not much, but better than you had on your trip home.

You go around the house, making sure the drapes are drawn. The room is dark. Your partner switches on the kitchen light. "I think we should leave the house dark for now, at least until we know what we're dealing with or if there's any help coming."

The light goes off. The silence that follows is deep and foreboding. You go to your partner and hug him/her, trying as best you can to pass confidence you don't feel through your touch. Then you step into the kitchen and grab the flashlight from the catch-all drawer. "We'll use this when we need it."

"So, what, are we just going to stay here until we die?" he/she asks.

"I hope not, but we need more information about what we're facing. Do you want to take a chance going out there, having to face those things? Believe me, that's not something you want to do. I've done it. I was lucky. But luck only goes so far."

You settle down at the kitchen table and discuss what you know so far. While you try to puzzle things out, your partner uses the phone to contact someone…anyone. 911 is constantly busy, but the fact there is still a steady tone gives you hope that the system is still working.

A howl rises from outside your house, chilling your blood. You freeze, eyes staring at the front drapes as if you had x-ray vision. Your partner comes to the kitchen door, the phone pressed to his/her ear and a look of concern on his/her face.

Your hand squeezes the chair arm so tight that your fingers have lost color.

Another howl arises. Was it the same one, or was it an answering call? How many of those things are there? Surely, there has to be more people than those animals. Maybe everyone is hiding, like you are.

A gasp from you partner draws a scared look from you.

"What?"

"One of those things is in the backyard."

You stand and join your partner in the doorway. "Where? How can you see through the curtains?"

"Through the gap between them. It walked into view and paused for a second, sniffing the air like trying to catch a scent, then moved out of sight."

You creep past and stop at the back kitchen window, moving the curtain back a fraction to reveal the yard. A quick glance shows nothing. The part of the yard you can see is vacant of any life form.

Moving the curtain farther and pressing your head forward against the glass, you see the rest of the yard. Still nothing. The head jumps into view, glaring at you through the window. You shout and jump. The curtain falls back but leaves enough gap for you to see the animal.

It tilts its head back and howls. It sounds like a victory cry. However, seconds later, you hear two other howls and realize it was calling to the others. Panic ensues. You snatch up the hammer and stand next to your partner, breathing hard, yet unable to get enough air.

Your partner picks up a bat and faces the front door. His/her nervous energy is contagious. Your sweat flows, running into your eyes and stinging. You wipe it away.

Something pounds against the back window hard enough to rattle the glass. You step forward, deciding it's better to meet the beast before it gets in the house. As you approach, the glass is struck again, this time exploding inward, the curtain catching the shards. You jump back as the creature leaps and grabs the inside sill.

Seconds after the window crashes, something thumps against the front door. You turn, distracted for a moment. By the time you look back, the beast is almost inside the window. Though fear clutches your heart, you force yourself to rush forward. The beast gets one leg inside, sees you coming, and snarls. You lift the hammer and swing with every bit of strength you possess. The beast ducks the attack, but it lands with a solid connection to its shoulder. It howls in pain and falls back but catches itself before tumbling outside.

You step forward to attack again. It snarls and snaps its abnormally long teeth at you. The miss clacks the teeth together as loud as a gunshot. The hammer descends, but the beast lifts a claw-like hand and catches your wrist, preventing it from landing. You struggle in its grip for control of the hammer.

The beast is stronger than you are. It bends your wrist back. It doesn't take long before realizing you are going to lose it. Sliding your left hand to your belt, you remove the knife just as the hammer is wrenched from your grip, you drive the steak knife into the beast's side. It yelps in pain, leaning away from you. With its balance in the window shifted, you lift a foot and kick it back outside. It falls from view.

Gasping, you bend at the waist, sucking air. You reach for the dislodged hammer, just as the front door bursts open.

Your partner screams as two beasts race through the doorway. Still screaming, he/she swings the bat in a violent arc, smashing the first creature's face in. The blow lifts the thing horizontal and slams it to the floor.

The second creature comes too quick for the backhand strike to connect. It hits and plows your partner over. They roll across the floor and your partner shrieks. You leap forward and bring the hammer down on the back of the creature's head. It rolls off your partner. You don't wait to see if it is still alive. You're not going to give it a chance to attack again. You slam the hammer into the creature over and over until you're too tired to raise it again.

Chest heaving, arms on fire, you look down at the bloody mess you've created. Behind, you hear a scraping sound. You turn to see the other beast getting to its feet. You plunge the steak knife into its body. It straightens and wraps both hands around your hand, holding the knife in place.

Unable to remove or slide it upward and slice through organs, you release the knife, step back, and taking a baseball-type swing, impact the side of the beast's head with the hammer. The skull caves in. The creature staggers back, drops to its knees, and stares blankly at you. You strike twice more before it falls. With several raspy breaths, the air leaves its lungs for the last time.

You stare in shock at the deaths you caused. Despite knowing they were wild and dangerous and would have torn you apart without hesitation, a wave of nausea sweeps through you. They were once people, no different than you. For them to die as animals was too much to accept. But in the end, better they died than you.

Your partner lets out a sob. You glance down to see him/her rolled in a ball, bloody hands pressed to his/her face. Panic and concern assault you. You drop the hammer and squat to see the problem.

"It bit my face. That thing, ripped open my cheek."

You force his/her hands apart to get a look. There's too much blood. "I have to clean it. Can you get up?"

"I don't know. Oh, it hurts."

"Stay there. I'll be right back."

You run to the bathroom and gather items you'll need. Washcloths, gauze pads, bandages, tape, disinfectant. You wet one of the towels, ring it out and go back to your partner. You wipe and wash the wound. As soon as you clear the blood, it refills. However, you have revealed enough to see a horrid, jagged, wound. A large portion of the cheek is gone, leaving raw flesh. In one small spot, there's a hole through to the mouth. The sight makes you sick to your stomach, but you continue with your task as much for yourself as your partner.

You disinfect the area and place some antibacterial cream over the wound before pressing two gauze pads down. After taping the pads in place, you help her/him sit up.

"It's bad, isn't it?"

"It's not that bad," you lie. "But I should get you to a doctor." The hospital is out of the question. You think about where the closest urgent care is. Maybe a mile away."

"I'm afraid to go outside. What if there's more of those things?"

You're pretty certain, there are more of them. A lot more. "We can't stay here anymore. The door's broken. We can't protect ourselves. Even if we don't find a doctor, we have to get someplace safe. "Come on," you help her/him up and wrap an arm around her/him.

"I don't want to go. I need to sit down."

You guide him/her to a sofa.

"You rest while I gather things we might need."

You get no response but run around the house and fill large bags with food and medical supplies. Then you fill two suitcases with clothes for you both. By the time you rejoin him/her in the front room, he/she is curled up on the sofa sleeping.

Do you:

2A1) wake him/her? Read on.

2A2) load up the car and wait for her/him to wake? Go to page 122

2A3) pack the car and leave? Go to page 125

2A1) Your partner wakes, but only after much effort on your part. He/she is groggy and can only walk with your support. You are concerned with the lack of energy and muscle response. Once outside and down the steps, you pick her/him up and carry them the rest of the way to the car.

You get him/her situated in the back seat, lying down, then run back inside to get the belongings you collected. As you run back outside, overburdened with bags and suitcases, you hear a distant howl. It is answered by several others. You have a horrible feeling you are surrounded and it's too late to escape.

Throwing everything in the trunk, you run to the driver's seat and jump in. Just as the engine roars to life, you see two creatures enter the street in front of you. They stop and stare at you. They take turns howling as if announcing to others they found fresh food. Again, multiple answering calls fill the area and send ice shards through your veins. A glance in the rearview mirror shows two more loping toward you.

"Oh God, babe, hold on. I'll get you out of here."

You take one more look in front and back and shift.

Do you:

2A1a) go forward? Read on.

2A1b) go backward? Go to page 119

2A1a) The car jumps forward. The two in front race toward you. You accelerate eating up the distance in a hurry.

Do you:

2A1a1) aim for them? Read on.

2A1a2) avoid them? Go to page 117

2A1a1) You hunch over the wheel and aim the car right at them. They don't seem to take notice or fear being run over. Just before contact, they both leap in the air, landing on the hood and impacting with the windshield. One is thrown over the roof and bounces on the ground behind you. It does not get up. The other hits the glass butt first and is stuck halfway through. It's head whips back connecting with the roof. It hangs motionless from the cracked glass. You're not sure if it's alive or just knocked out.

You speed around the corner, tires protesting, and cry out in shock as another one you hadn't seen slams into the passenger side door. It hangs there for a moment, eyes locked on you, then slides off unable to find a handhold.

You sweep glances from the creature stuck in the windshield, to the one rolling on the street, and from to the two turning the corner still in pursuit to the road in front of you. Fear escalates as you begin to feel your efforts at escaping and maybe even survival, are futile.

You speed down two more streets, before turning again. The two chasing you are mere dots, but they haven't stopped their pursuit. Once out of sight, you stop, place the car in park and slide over into the passenger seat. Placing both feet on the creature's butt, you push hard to dislodge it. You're still not sure if it's alive or dead, you just know you'll feel better with it gone.

The body lifts and rolls but stays on the hood. You pause, trying to decide the best choice.

Do you:

2A1a1a) get out and remove the creature before driving on? Read on.

2A1a1b) drive on? Go to page 104

2A1a1a) *Seriously?* Why? You're about to crap a brick as it is, you want to leave safety? Oh well. You open the passenger door, hop out, and grab the creature by the shoulders and pull. It slides, but before it hits the ground, you hear a howl from behind you. Another beast has spotted you.

Your breath catches, and you give the creature on the hood one more tug. But as you do, its eyes open. It snarls, and you release it like it's a contaminate. You reach the door, but it leaps on you, grasping your head, and yanking you down. You fall, roll, and come up swinging. You land three straight, hard shots to its face and it is no longer moving.

You get up just as the other creature arrives and plows into you. You slam into the open car door. It creaks from the impact, hyper-extending the door like a knee.

A claw rakes at your face. Blood flies; pain rips through you. You manage to control the next swipe and knock it off you. You roll on top and pummel the beast until it barely moves. Once more, you try for the car, but as you stand, another weight lands on your back and knocks you down. Then another. The two giving pursuit have caught up.

As your energy drains and more and more of your skin is flayed away, you realize the end has come. You continue to fight, but your efforts have little to no effect. As one sinks its teeth into your arm, you scream and use the last of your adrenaline to dislodge it. You claw up the side of the car, desperate to get inside and shut the door. As your face reaches the height of the back window, you come face to face with your partner.

Your heart freezes. Your partner claws at the glass to get to you. The last thing you hear before one of the creatures sinks teeth into the back of your neck is your partner's howl. The end comes, but it is neither quick nor painless.

Choices! Choices! Choices!

As you stand in front of the Pearly Gates, St. Peter says, "Not such a smart choice, was it?"

Do you:

A) hang your head in shame and accept the rebuke?

B) flip him off?

Careful, now. This could be a Hell of a choice.

2A1a1b) Quickly, you scramble back into the driver's seat and floor the pedal, just as another creature reaches the car. You race from its reach. The body rolls back against the windshield and stays there as if glued.

You drive two more blocks. Then, to your shock, the creature opens its eyes. You stifle a cry of shock and race around the next corner. The force sends the beast flying before it can get a grip on the broken windshield. However, you made the turn at such a high speed, you lose control and slam into a parked car. The airbag punches into your face leaving you stunned.

You're not sure how long you sit there, but as your vision clears, you see nothing. The moment's panic passes as you realize it's the airbag. Taking the knife, you puncture the bag. A puff of putrid air fills the car, making it difficult to catch your breath.

The car has stalled. You pray it will start again. The engine grinds but doesn't catch.

"Oh God! Please."

You try it twice more before it coughs and starts. You roll the window down to clear the chemical smell, then back up. Behind you, two beasts are loping toward you. You shift and move forward. A loud grinding comes from the front end. You recognize the sound. The quarter panel has been crushed and now rests against the tire. You know you should pull it away, but with creatures so close, you decide to drive as far as you can before you fix it.

The car hobbles along. You extend your lead by two blocks before chancing getting out. You grip the crumpled metal and pull as hard as you can. It bends back enough and no longer touches the tire, however, it has already cut a deep groove all the way around the sidewall. The tire may not last long. Regardless, you must drive it until you get somewhere safe.

Back in the car, you check the back seat. To your surprise, it's empty. Your partner is not there. Panic strikes at your heart. Where could he/she be? Then, you lean back further and discover her/him wedged on the floor. Evidently, the crash tossed him/her off the seat. What bothers you now is the lack of movement. You focus on his/her chest and are rewarded by the sight of it rising and falling, however, the breaths look shallow. You have to get to a doctor fast.

You drive at a slower speed for fear the tire will blow. A few minutes later, you arrive at the urgent care. It looks deserted. You stop and study the building. There are few cars in the lot and no movement from within.

Do you:

2A1a1b1) wait until you see someone? Read on.

2A1a1b2) check to see if the door is open? Go to page 108

2A1a1b3) search for another medical center? Go to page 113

2A1a1b1) With the engine running, you stay inside the car and continue to watch, praying either someone will move inside, or another car will show up looking for help, too. If something doesn't happen soon, you'll either have to get out or move on.

You glance over the seat at your unconscious partner. He/she can't wait much longer. You have to do something.

Your attention is drawn to the rearview mirror as you see a car drive by on the street. For a moment you want to give chase. Maybe whoever is driving knows something that will help. You're about to shift when you think it's stupid to be here and not at least check the door. Maybe someone is in there, but they're keeping out of sight to prevent being seen by the creatures.

You reach for the door, when the car that passed by a few seconds before swings into the driveway. It coasts to a stop in front of the urgent care. A lone driver leans out the window to scan the building.

You watch, waiting to see if anyone gets out and checks the door. Whoever it is must also have someone in need of care. Nothing happens for a minute, so you decide to get out and approach them. You take a survey of the parking lot. Nothing is moving. You open the door and step out. However, before you can take two steps, the car drives off. You shout and wave your hands. The driver, a woman, looks around, but doesn't see you. The shouting frightens her to speed up.

You look at the building then at the receding car. You run for the door, pull on it. It's locked. Watching the other car leave the parking lot, you pound on the door. Nothing happens, and you can't wait any longer. You don't want to lose sight of the other car.

Sprinting back to your car, you jump in, shift into park and drive. You turn the wheel and hear a scraping sound, then an explosion. The car leans to the left. Without looking, you know the tire has blown.

You slam the steering wheel in anger and watch as the car drives out of view.

While you sit contemplating your options, a hand reaches over the driver's seat and grabs your head. You jump so high that you smack your head on the roof. Pulling back, you see your partner crawling over the seat, but you have no joy in their recovery. The face glaring at you has morphed into a hideous version of your partner.

*Oh no!* Your heart sinks, knowing he/she is lost to you.

You slap the hands away and scoot toward the door. One of his/her flailing hands rips furrows into your cheek. It burns like it was set ablaze. You reach and open the door, but as you turn to step out, he/she gets an arm around your neck and pulls you back.

You feel the hot breath on the back of your neck. A few weeks ago, that sensation would have aroused you and perhaps led to something much more enjoyable. You grab the arm and peel it from your throat, but although you have control over the arm and make progress toward escaping, you have no control over the mouth.

A snarl rings in your ear before the teeth bite deep into the side of your neck. You scream and slam a palm into its forehead to dislodge it, but it tears and whips its head back like a dog. In seconds, it rends a large chunk of meat from your neck. However, the bite is pushed aside, having been replaced by the gout of blood that strikes the windshield.

As the blood rolls down the glass, coating it like paint, you slap a palm to the wound in hopes of keeping as much of your life force inside.

You manage to get free and out of the car as it chews on your flesh. The entire scene nauseates you. You take several steps on ever-weakening legs before one gives out and you fall. You land on your knees but do not feel the pain.

You get one foot beneath you and push to stand. A howl ices your spurting blood, even more so knowing it's your partner. Someone you've shared so much with. Laughs. Tears. Hopes. Plans. Your bed. Your life.

As your love pounces on you, driving your face into the blacktop, you think with a maniacal laugh, *and now, we share a last meal.* The light dims and you don't feel the next bite.


End

2A1a1b2) "Hang tight. I'm going to see if it's open." You get no response. Your concern heightens. Scanning the area, you decide it's safe to leave the car, or as safe as it can be. You run to the front door and find it locked.

You take another look around, then pound on the door. No one responds. You bang louder. "Is anyone in there? We need help."

You knock once more, beating with both fists. "Help us. Please!"

You give up and back away. Just before you turn, a corner of the blind on the nearest window is peeled back and an eye peers out. You step forward, cautious not to spook them. You paste a forced smile on your face. "Hi. We need medical help. Can you let us in?" The corner folds back. "Please," you say louder.

A different eye comes to look, higher up the shade and bigger. "Help us. Please. My partner needs medical attention."

Someone pulls the shade to the side on the front door. It's a woman wearing a white lab coat. You step in front of her, so she can see you're not a threat. She studies you for a long minute, then says, "Where's your partner?"

"In the car. Can I bring him/her in? Will you help us?"

She turns and speaks to someone out of sight. Then to you, "Do you have any food or water?"

You hesitate, not wanting to give away what you have.

"That's the price for treating your partner. Otherwise we can't let you in. We don't have enough for more people."

"Yes, I have both food and water."

"Okay. Get it and we'll let you in."

You jog back to the car. Your mind whirls with thoughts. They may try to take you out and steal the food. They may let you in but refuse to treat your partner. Or, they may try to strong arm you at the door, take the items, and keep you out.

You open the back door, pull your partner out, and lift her/him in your arms. She/he looks more dead than alive. You hurry back the building. The woman is watching and opens the door but blocks the way.

"Where-where's the food?"

"I'll get it next, but he/she needs help now."

She looks at the patient. You lose patience and push past her. Inside, you see two others standing in the lobby; a man, and a woman.

The second woman says, "What's wrong with him/her?"

You set her down on the counter and say, "She got bit by one of those things."

A hand flies to the second woman's face. "But-but, we can't—"

"Yes, we can," the man says. "You go get your supplies and we'll take him/her in the back and get started."

You pause, feeling like something's wrong, but your partner can't wait for treatment. "Okay. He's/She's bad. I'll get the stuff and be right back. But if you haven't started by the time I get back, you get nothing."

You leave and run for the car. From the front seat, you take the axe and slide it into your belt behind your back. Then, you open the trunk and pull out one bag of food. You slam the trunk shut, then slip the knife out, holding it concealed behind the bag.

You enter and see your partner is no longer on the counter. The only person in the lobby is the first woman. You hope that's a good sign.

"He's/She's through there," she says, pointing to a door. You head that way and glance behind you. The woman stands at the door, but she's nervous about something. When she turns and sees you watching, she averts her eyes. Something is up. You glance at the door.

The woman walks closer. "Is that the food?"

She can't take her eyes off the bag. She reaches for it. You pull it away. A frightened look flits across her face, but her eyes do not budge from the bag. They are desperate for food. Desperate people do desperate things. You sneak another look at the door, then hold the bag out for her to take. Her face brightens. She reaches for it, then looks at you and freezes. Your plan must show on your face.

She steps back, but not far enough. You grab an arm, whip her in front of you, and shove her through the door. She tries to speak, but you hear a thump followed by a cut off shriek and a thud.

You step through with the knife up and ready to strike. The man you saw in the lobby is holding a fire extinguisher and staring down at the woman. Blood pools under her head. He sees you and rage flushes his face. Knowing what will come next, you slash his arm as he lifts the extinguisher for an attack. He screams, and the canister falls to the floor at his feet with a loud clang.

Others scream, and a second man rushes you. Before he closes, you wave the knife to show you're ready to take him on, too. He stops.

The second woman cries out. "Please don't hurt us! We didn't mean any harm. We don't know you and were afraid you'd try to hurt us."

"So, you decided to hurt me first, eh?"

A third woman says, "We're just scared and hungry. You've been out there. You know what's going on. We were just trying to protect ourselves."

"At another person's life? What's wrong with you? Survivors need to stand together. I haven't seen many as it is, but you want to eliminate the competition for food. You people are crazy and deserve to be killed."

The second woman covers her face and sobs.

You look around and a stab of panic hits you. "Where's my partner?"

They exchange glances, but no one speaks.

You grab the wounded man and place the blade to his throat. "Somebody better talk to me, and fast."

The third woman steps forward. "Please. I'm begging you. Don't hurt him." From the impassioned plea, you judge there's a connection between them.

"Then where is she/he?"

"She's/He's gone. She/he can't be saved. You've been out there. You know how it is. Once you're bitten, you either die or become one of them. There's nothing you can do."

Her words assault you like a physical blow. You wobble on your feet. The wounded man takes advantage and fires an elbow at you. You dodge it, but it strikes your shoulder with enough force to knock you back. The second man jumps in, punches you, and tears the knife from your grasp. You stagger, and as he lunges, you reach back, pull the axe out, and bury it in his skull.

He drops at your feet, his body twitching. The second woman faints. The wounded man stares down at the body, mouth agape. The third woman rushes into his good arm and sobs.

"It didn't have to be this way. You could've just been human. Instead, you're no different than the monsters roaming the streets. What's wrong with you? We could've all worked together…to-to survive or figure things out. I would've been happy to share the food with you. His death is on you. Now, somebody tell me where my partner is or someone else is gonna die."

The third woman points to a back door.

You head towards it, picking up the knife on your way. You back toward the door, which leads outside. You push it open and look around but don't see your partner. "Where?"

With a defiant glare, the woman says, "In the dumpster."

The word sends a boiling rage through your core. You grab a rolling chair and wedge it in the door to keep it open, then you walk to the dumpster. You slide the side door open, and there on top, is the body of your love, face smashed in from what you assume was the fire extinguisher.

Your anger is uncontrollable. You run toward the door with intent to do serious damage. The wounded man is there clearing the chair away and yanking as hard as he can on the door. It slams shut before you arrive.

You pound on it, then kick it until your rage subsides. "I hope you all starve to death. I hope when the first one of you dies, you are forced to eat them. Then you can all sit around and wonder who's gonna die next."

You give the door one more kick, then walk around the building. You get in the car, tears falling, and drive to the far end of the lot. There, you get out and search the vehicles for one with keys. You find an SUV and transfer everything from the car.

As you drive away, no thought to where you are going, your mind is full of memories. After a while, you clear your head. The only memories to be made now will be those of nightmares.

Go to Chapter 3 page 246

2A1a1b3 The place is deserted. You look in the back seat. Your partner is still unconscious and getting weaker. You must find someplace that can help. You remember another medical facility not far from there. It's not a hospital or urgent care, but the building houses an assortment of doctor's offices. One of them has to be open.

You fly through the parking lot and bounce hard onto the street. Your mind whirls with concern, fear, and disbelief. This can't be happening.

The building comes into view in the distance, the red brick standing several stories taller than any surrounding structure. You focus on it with hope and do not see the figure dart at you until just before you slam into him. The body goes airborne, skimming off the roof, deflecting off the trunk, and bouncing along the street.

The car comes to a stop long before the body does.

Heart pounding, you watch in the mirror for any signs of life. Was it human or monster? It doesn't matter now. You pray it was one of the creatures, because the guilt will overwhelm you otherwise. Two creatures appear in front of you. They stop in the street twenty yards away, as if positioning for a duel. You don't have time for this. Your partner doesn't have time for this.

You press the gas pedal down and rocket forward. They are either going to have to move or be run over. The choice is theirs. You hunch over the wheel, bracing for impact, but before that happens, the two beings leap to the sides. You race past, watching them in the mirror.

They rise, tilt their heads back and you can imagine the howls. Then, to your dismay, they give chase. *I can't get a break.*

Though the medical center is a straight shot down the road, you take preventative measures by making multiple turns. You can no longer see them as you whip into the parking lot. Again, you see cars, but no signs of life. You skid to a stop in front of the building and lean across the seat to scan the lobby. Nobody is inside.

You jump out of the car and run to the front doors. They do not open. *Damn!* Now what? You do a slow scan of the area, searching for other options. There has to be someplace open.

Rather than stand in the open, you climb back in the SUV and try to think. You are surprised when you feel the tears on your cheeks. The frustration at not being able to help your love is taking its toll on your emotional state.

An arm circles your shoulder. You are ecstatic to find your partner is awake and pray it bodes well for recovery. You wipe the tears with one hand while taking your partner's fingers in the other. You turn to face him/her just as the teeth come at you. You jump back as they snap shut, missing your nose by a fraction.

The arm wraps tighter around your neck and you pull back. He/she snarls, and you no longer recognize your partner in the face. Instead, it is that of a wild animal with only facial similarities of the person you loved. It leans over the seat, trying to get at you. "No!" Ducking your head, you manage to slip free of the chokehold, but it does not stop the attack.

It is halfway over the seat when your hand brushes the door handle. You open the door and fall out more than step. You kick the door shut and backpedal in a crabwalk. It pounds fists on the window. The snarl comes through loud and clear. The person you once loved is long gone, leaving behind this monstrosity.

You stand in shock and near an almost full emotional melt down. The door opens. You step forward and kick it shut. The beast inside goes berserk, slamming hands and head into the glass until it explodes in a shower of shards.

You step back as the beast pushes through the frame. Your fingers brush the knife in your belt. In slow motion, you withdraw it. Your once lover leans out of the frame and swipes elongated fingers at you. You step back. It emits a constant snarl like an animal battle cry.

Hanging out of the car, its hands now touching the ground, you take short, quick breaths to build up your courage, then run forward and bury the knife in its back. It rears upward, howling in agony. You yank the knife free and repeat the attack. More howls. It swipes at you, connecting with your leg. The swipe has enough power to knock you off balance, making you lose your grip on the knife.

It crawls out the window, the knife still embedded. On all fours, it eyes you with feral hatred. As it rises, you step forward and deliver a kick to the wolf-like face. The blow drives it up and back, slamming into the car. It shrieks, both hands reaching behind it. It slides down the car, leaving a bloody streak, and collapses on all fours. The knife has been driven deeper.

In the distance, another series of howls rises and makes its way through the streets to your ears. The hairs rise on your neck and arms. Reinforcements are coming. You have to get out of there, now.

The creature tries to crawl toward you, determined to feast on your flesh. You back away, trying to make a plan, but are too scared and distraught to latch onto anything. However, the next series of howls are closer. You risk a glance away from the creature and spy two loping shapes coming your way at high speed.

Your ex-partner lunges. Hands wrap around your ankles and pull tight like a defensive back holding desperately to a running back waiting for teammates to finish the tackle.

Panic sets in again. You can't give in or you'll die. Looking down at the beast inching its open maw toward your leg, you squat, shove the head into the ground, and yank hard to free a leg. Once out of its grip, you stomp down, smashing the face into the blacktop. Your other foot comes loose, and you sprint for the SUV.

You are pulling away as the other two beasts arrive. One manages to get its hands inside the car's broken window. Fingers drag across your shoulder, but are too short to dig in. The accelerating car knocks the hands from the window and you speed off.

The car bounces into the street, careens off a parked car, and continues on. With adrenaline fueling you, it feels like you are running rather than driving.

The scene disappears from the rearview mirror and you settle into an unknown course. *What the hell do you do now?* First thing is to find a new vehicle. You try several parking lots before finding an SUV with the keys in the ignition. You look around for any clue where the owner is, but decide your need is greater than whoever it belongs to.

In a few short minutes, you transfer everything to the SUV and are on your way. However, a destination still eludes you. You keep driving, hoping for a brainstorm. Something will come to you. It has to.

Go to Chapter 3 on page 246

2A1a2) As you close the distance, you make a last-second decision to avoid hitting them. You angle the car up a driveway, across two front lawns, and back down the next driveway. As you hit the street and turn, you realize the speed is too great. You hit the brakes to bleed off the speed, but the car skids sideways, hitting a parked car.

The crash jars you. Your head snaps to the side and bounces off the window. Stunned, you try to shake the fog from your brain. The pounding on the car is what finally clears your head. The two creatures you avoided are now climbing on the car. Behind them, two more race to join the festivities.

You press the pedal down, but no matter how much gas you feed, the car refuses to budge. You're locked up somewhere. If you don't get free fast, the creatures will smash their way inside the car. Feeling the panic grip you and the acidic bile rise in your throat, you shift into reverse. The car jerks back, but still won't move. You begin a series of rocking moves, like the car was caught in deep snow. Back and forth you go. With each attempt, you feed more gas until you can smell the burning rubber.

After half a dozen tries, the car moves about a foot in both directions. Then, the other two creatures arrive and jump on the car. One jumps on the roof. The center section has already gone concave. One is on the hood pounding the windshield, while the other two are slamming the two passenger side windows.

There doesn't seem to be enough air in the car as your breaths become raspy. Your throat constricts, making breathing even more difficult. Unable to keep your eyes off the assaulting beasts, you work the steering wheel with each gear shift. The moves create more space. You begin to think escape may be possible.

Then, the rear passenger window implodes, and the beast jumps in.

Immediately, you fear for your partner. You glance back and discover he/she is no longer on the seat. A quick glance shows he/she is on the floor, evidently thrown there after the crash. You have to get away from here to deal with the intruding beast before it tears into your partner.

You press the pedal down and scream at the top of your lungs. The tires screech. The smell of burnt tires is nauseating. As the beast climbs into the back seat, you shift again and turn the wheel. With a loud metallic shriek, the car breaks free and shoots forward.

The beast at the front passenger window is left behind. The one on the roof topples down the trunk and hits the street. The beast on the hood pitches into the windshield, leaving a dent where its head hits. It is either dead or stunned, but either way, it's no longer trying to gain entry. The creature inside, after being thrown back into the seat on takeoff, is now scrambling to get at you. You brake hard, sending it head first into the front seat. Sliding the knife out, you jab at it while trying to drive. The blows are ineffectual, giving the creature the chance to right itself and come at you.

You can't drive and defend, so you hit the brakes again. The beast is thrown into the dashboard. You whip the knife forward, impaling the beast in the neck with such force that it embeds the blade into the dash, pinning the beast there. It claws at the knife desperately and gags on its own blood.

You drive away, leaving the others well behind. Once you're safely out of sight, you throw the car into park, flick the unlock button, and race around the car. You open the passenger door and reach inside. The creature is still trying to pull the blade out, but its efforts are weak.

You shiver violently at the thought of touching it but need to get it out of the car. You grab the knife and its eyes lock on yours. You hesitate. Then, on a mental count of three, you yank it out. In one motion, you grab the creature's legs and pull. It tries to kick out of your grasp, but you are determined.

The beast comes out of the car, bouncing head first on the frame, then on the pavement. You shut the door and run back to the driver's seat. You have the car moving well before the door closes.

You look in the back seat. Your partner is not moving and barely breathing. He/she is almost out of time. You race to the urgent care.

Go to page 113

2A1b) The two behind are farther away. You throw the car into reverse and spin in the seat to look out the back window. You shove the pedal down, whip the wheel around to back up the neighbor's driveway, but cut the turn to sharp. The car bounces up the curb and smacks into the mailbox. The post snaps, the metal mail box, crashes into the back window, smashing and hanging in the hole it created.

You forget about the approaching creatures for a moment, reaching back to wipe glass shards off your partner. Your concern grows, seeing the lack of response to both the crash and the glass. You shake him/her. "Hey! You all right?" No response other than a low moan. "Stay with me. I'm getting help."

A thump jolts you in your seat. You see the two from in front have arrived. The two behind are within twenty yards. A creature pounds on the passenger side window while the other jumps on the hood and attacks the windshield. You shake from your initial shock and shift into drive. The car lurches forward, pitching the one on the hood into the glass. As you turn onto the street, it rolls off. You leave those two behind and now face the second pair. They stand in your path as if they think their bodies will prevent you from going past.

You increase speed. Just before contact, they both leap in the air, unconcerned for their own safety. One misses, and the front end clips its legs, flipping it face first into the hood. A gout of blood erupts, and it bounces off the car.

The second one slams into the windshield, its body leaving an imprint in the glass. is shattered all the way across, but still holds in one piece. You round a corner at high speed, trying to dislodge your unwanted passenger. Several more sharp turns in the opposite direction still do not remove the beast. It is stuck, and the force of the high speed keeps it pinned back. Its arms flail wildly and its legs kick at the air, but it is unable to move.

Changing tactics, you slam on the brakes. The creature rolls free from the glass, but instead of getting off, it launches at the windshield, punching an arm through the glass. You jump back and scream. It reaches for you, pressing its shoulder to the glass. Not sure how much longer the windshield will hold, you floor the pedal. The car jumps, throwing the creature into the window. The sudden weight and pressure is all it takes. In a downpour of glass, the window implodes, and the beast is inside.

Without thought or hesitation, you pummel the creature with your right hand while still trying to drive. It flails as it tries to right itself. You land punch after punch, but from a sitting position and striking sideways, you can't do any real damage.

As it gains a better position, it attacks. You jam your foot down on the brake, sending it into the dashboard and off balance. You fumble for the knife as it snarls at you. Before it can resume its assault, you jab the knife into its arm. It howls. You withdraw and stab again. You make two more small wounds before it slashes its claw at you. A fiery pain shoots up your arm as the knife falls from your grasp.

It closes on you with inhuman strength. It's a struggle you know from the onset that you cannot win. Its twisted, wolf-like face inches closer to you. Teeth larger than a man's should be close the space between the two of you. With each snap, you feel the bite, but each time, it falls short.

You get your cast under its chin and push. For a moment, you gain some distance, but it increases its efforts with a wild howl, and you know the battle is over. As it closes, its horrid, foul breath melts your face, and you scream and put all your remaining effort into prolonging the inevitable. Just as you feel its face press to yours and its mouth opens for the first bite and rending of your flesh, it rears back and howls in pain.

As it arcs back, its hands reaching behind it, you see your partner, a ghostly white, as if his/her spirit had risen and attacked. For an instant, your eyes lock. The wisp of a smile touches his/her face, then his/her eyes roll back, and he/she falls from view in the back seat.

With the creature thrashing next to you, you search for the discarded knife. Your hand brushes it. The beast swipes a hand at you, knocking you back. You dive forward, as if clearing a path for a running back, and knock it against the door. Your hand wraps around the knife. Holding the beast in place with one hand, you lift and plunge the knife through the beast's eye. It kicks and snarls, arms sweeping back and forth at your hand, trying to knock it away.

You continue to push and then twist the blade until the beast's death throes cease. You back away, coated in blood, breaths bursting from your lungs. You watch the beast as you recover, fearing it may come back to life and attack again, but when nothing happens a minute later, you lean over the seat to check on your partner.

He/she is slumped on the floor, unconscious and barely breathing. You have to get him/her to a doctor right now. Leaving the beast where it is, you jump in the seat and drive off at high speed. As you drive, you choke back sobs, trying not to think about what might have happened, had your partner not wakened in time to save you. You race down the street and make the turns to the urgent care center.

You skid to stop in front of the door and hop out. The doors are locked, and no amount of pounding brings anyone to open them. You try to remember another location and recall a medical facility housing multiple doctors not far away.

You climb back in the car and head that way, praying someone will be there who can help.

Go to page 113

2A2) You gather items you think you will need and load the car one bag at a time. With each trip past your partner, you bend to make sure he/she is still breathing. Once the task is completed, you block the door closed and sit in the chair opposite the couch and stare, wishing he/she would wake, and pray he/she will be all right.

Your mind wanders, memories rushing to fill your thoughts. With each pleasant remembrance, one of horror invades your brain, pushing them aside. How had the city fallen so fast? Did whatever happened here spread elsewhere? How were you going to survive? There has to be someplace safe. Someplace where other "normal" people have gone.

You stand and pace. How long should you wait before waking him/her? You stop at the front window and pull the curtain aside. For the moment the street is vacant. In fact, if you didn't know better, it would look like a typical day in the neighborhood.

Just as you begin to believe everything is all right, you hear a howl somewhere down the street. The sound chills you. You take a step back and narrow the curtain gap, but you can't take your eyes off the street. The howl is louder when you hear it next, but what is more frightening is the two answering calls.

Several minutes and many howls later, three of the strange creatures meet in front of the house. One is a woman. From behind, they look like anyone you might meet on the street. However, you would never mistake them for normal once they turned around. Their faces are elongated, and eyes sunken, red-rimmed, and feral. They look like a Hollywood makeup artist had worked on them to be extras in a horror flick.

The woman whips her head around and looks at the house. You have the terrifying feeling she is looking right at you. You back away. Sweat pops from your pores, beading on your forehead. The female curls up her lips and you imagine the animal snarl she releases in your direction.

A band of panic tightens across your chest. For a moment, you struggle for air. She can't possibly see you, can she? You inch the tiny gap closed. Right until it closes, you feel her eyes locked on yours. It's a relief when the curtain breaks the contact. You still have a desperate need to see what they are doing, so you hurry to the bedroom and kneel at the window. You pull the corner of the curtain back and unconsciously hold your breath.

The air bursts from your lungs a second later when the three are no longer in sight. You widen the gap and press your face to the glass. They are no longer in front of the house. Anxiety steals away your breath.

You run to the front room and to the picture window. You take a deep breath and release it to gain control over your shaking hands, then gap the curtain again. Still no one. Where did they go? A thought strikes more fear into your heart. You race to the kitchen and advance with caution to the window. With full expectation that the three creatures are trying to find a way in, you part the curtain. At first, you can't believe your eyes. You blink and look again. The yard is empty.

You feel your shoulders sag, releasing some of their tension. Evidently, the creatures have moved on. Suddenly, breathing is less labored. You take one more look before returning to the front room. You check again, but the street is vacant. Relieved, you step back, then you leap so high you fear slamming into the ceiling as someone touches your shoulder.

You land, spin, and clutch at your heart, to find your partner has risen from the couch.

"Oh my God! You scared me half to death. You feeling better?"

She/he doesn't respond. You finally look at her/him with more focus and realize something is wrong. "What's the matter? Are you sick? You look pale." Then you realize the change in her/him is much more drastic than you first realized. When you understand why, it is already too late to stop the attack. She/he launches at you with a horrifying snarl.

You get your hands up in time to prevent the suddenly longer and sharper teeth from closing around your throat, but the force of the attack drives you backward. You slam into the window. The curtains are torn from the rod and pool over you.

As you fight, your body twists. At the window are three sets of sharp teeth snapping and snarling at you from the other side of the glass. You manage to push your partner away and run for the bedroom but are tackled from behind. You fall face first into the wall, sending blinding pain through your body. You fight to clear your head, but the claws dig into your skin and tear long furrows down your back. You scream and kick wildly.

The sound of an explosion comes from the front room. You realize the picture window has been broken, which also means the other three creatures will be coming in soon. You have precious few seconds to get away from your partner and to the safety of the bedroom.

You turn and punch your partner in the face, snapping its head back. The grip on your legs is loosened. You scramble backward and spin to get to your feet, just as the woman from outside rounds the corner. She steps on your partner's back and leaps at you as you reach for the bedroom door.

You are driven to the floor. You deliver a punch and see your partner crawling toward you, blood mixing with the foaming spittle around the lips. The two others arrive at the same time and pinball off each other as they try to get to you.

You gain freedom for a moment, but before you can rise, you feel a sharp pain in your calf. You look to see your partner gnawing at your leg. The fear and pain swirl around your head. You vomit all over the woman, who doesn't appear to notice.

As the four descend on you, bite after bite tears into you. You feel each one and scream as you flail, but the end is inevitable. The blood loss weakens you. Your eyes blur. Memories come and sweep through your mind. The battle is short, and thankfully, the pain lessens. You lock eyes with your partner, a chunk of your body in its mouth. As the blackness closes around your vision, your brain takes you to the first time you ever met. My, how things have changed.


End

2A3) You pack the car with as much as you can, then go back to see how your partner is doing. You get no response. You fear if she/he doesn't get medical attention soon, they will die. But where can you go? The hospital is out. The urgent care is not far, but will you be able to get your partner into the car in this condition?

You think about it for several minutes then decide the best and quickest solution is to go to the urgent care yourself and make sure it's open and there's someone there who can treat her/him.

You block the door shut and exit through the side door. As you drive away, several creatures lope into the street in front of you. The sight freezes you with fear that sucks the air from the car. Then, in unison, they howl. The sound pierces through your immobility. You shift into reverse as the creatures close the distance. You back all the way down the street until you reach the intersection. There, you whip the wheel hard, cutting the turn too sharp, and bounce up the curb.

The contact throws you forward, striking your head on the steering wheel. It stuns you for a second. You shake it off and see the trio of creatures still in pursuit. You shift and drive away. Soon, you've created enough distance and the creatures are no longer in sight. That should relax you, but instead your hands are white-knuckled on the wheel. You sweep glances in all directions, expecting to see more creatures any second.

By the time you reach the urgent care, you are exhausted and sweating as if you ran there instead. You stop at the front door. You find the building is dark and deserted. There are plenty of cars in the lot, but no people. They couldn't all have turned into those things. Someone must be holed up inside one of the businesses.

You get out and check the doors. Locked. You rap on the glass loud enough to be heard if someone was inside and chose to look. After several attempts, you turn and scan the area. You're at a loss, but you can't just stand there.

Do you:

2A3a) get in the car and find another medical facility? Read on.

2A3b) walk down the line of businesses to see if any are open? Go to page 162

2A3c) break into the urgent care? Go to page 169

2A3a) You recall a doctor's office complex not far from there. You hop in the car and speed through the parking lot. Twice you are forced to retreat and find an alternate route because the number of abandoned vehicles make passing impossible.

Finally, you see the building. It stands several stories above any other structure in the vicinity. You zero in and never see the creature before it leaps at the car. It bounces off, but its sudden appearance startles you into braking. It hit so fast, for a moment you aren't sure if it was human or the other.

Then, it stands. One arm dangles at its side. Blood oozes from a cut on its cheek. It snarls and runs at the car. You emit a squeak of despair and jam the pedal down. The car jumps forward, leaving the injured creature far behind.

You reach the building and race up the drive, stopping with a squeal of rubber in front of the main entrance. You jump out and run to the doors. To your shock and great relief, they open. You start to enter, then go back and lock the car doors.

From inside the building, you scan the parking lot to ensure no one is stalking you. You are standing in a large lobby that runs the entire length of the building. In the middle is a semi-circular information and security desk with no one manning it.

Beyond the desk, a hallway runs left and right. Just beyond are two banks of elevators, three to a side. You doubt they are running but push the button just the same. It does not light up, nor do you hear the whirring of machinery. Two sets of stairs are past the elevators. Before you go up, you decide to check the two halls.

You stand in the intersection and take a long look down each direction. You see four doors each way. You choose right and hurry. Footsteps echo off the walls, giving you the sinking feeling you're alone.

The first doors on both the right and left are locked. Each has a translucent curtain hanging over the long, narrow windows on either side of the solid door. You press close to peer inside each one. The interior lights are off, but you get a good look at the reception area. They are both empty. You move on.

The last two offices are the same. You go the other direction. If you have to search the entire building, you're determined to find someone who can help. You reach the lobby and catch movement in your periphery. You duck back and peer around the corner. Two creatures are sniffing around your car.

Your hand slides to the steak knife, but you change your mind and pull the hatchet out. The two beasts sniff at your door, as if picking up your scent. One howls. Though you've heard the eerie sound before, it still chills you to your soul.

They turn toward the building's doors. You inhale a deep breath to force calm over yourself. It does little to help, but it does keep you from panicking. If these things can pick up a faint smell, how can you ever hope to get away from them?

As they start for the doors, you pivot and sprint down the hall for the far stairs. You push through the fire door and take the stairs, two at a time. At the second-floor landing, you pause at the door. You need to search the building but staying safe is of more immediate concern. Is it better to search each floor as you go, or get to the top, farther away from the creatures and work down?

Do you:

2A3a1) check the second floor? Read on.

2A3a2) continue up? Go to page 153

2A3a1) You whip open the door to the second floor and step through. As you look down the long hallway, you hold the door until it closes softly. You move down the hall, checking each door. They are all similar design; the only difference is the window treatment in the windows next to the doors. Most offer a view inside, but a few have heavier curtains that block everything.

You don't spend as much time as you'd like checking each office, fearing the creatures will arrive on the floor any second. That thought drives you to move faster. You run between doors until something nudges a memory of high school and how the students on the first floor could hear when students on the second floor moved. Are the running steps a beacon for the monsters below to zero in on your position? You slow to a fast walk.

Three doors from the end of the hall, you heard a noise from behind. You turn to see one of the creatures stepping into the hall. You freeze for a second, then race toward the opposite stairs. Once it sees you, it tilts its head back and howls, signaling others.

You don't wait for others to arrive. You slam the fire door open and pause. Up or down? Knowing they have entered the building, you don't want to get trapped by going further up. You choose down.

Reaching the bottom, you inch the door open and peer out. You don't see anything, but they might be around the corner. You allow the door to close softly, then creep down the hall, hugging the left side wall. At the corner, you squat and peek. The lobby appears empty. You switch your gaze to the front doors. No one. You don't want to face the creatures inside, so decide to make a break for the car. Just as you make a move, a van pulls up next to your car and two men hop out.

They run to your car, scan the interior, then one lifts a crow bar and smashes the rear passenger side window. You pause in shock, then a spark of anger ignites. By the time you reach the front doors, it has exploded into full rage. You burst through the doors as each man lifts a bag of stuff—*your* stuff—out of the car and move toward the van.

You roar like one of the creatures and run at them. They freeze, then run when you roar. One drops his bag and the other disappears around the van. You manage to catch the second man and tackle him. His body scrapes across the black top with you riding him. His face loses skin; his nose erupts in blood.

You press his face down and look at the man hanging out of the sliding door. His face is a mix of panic and fear. He fumbles for something on the seat. You realize its a gun before he can grip and aim. You yank your victim's head up and duck behind him.

A woman screams. "It's gonna bite him!"

They think you're one of the creatures.

The gunman yells, "Joe, you gotta move! I can't shoot him. You're in the way."

Joe is too stunned to move or respond.

"Throw my stuff out and I'll let him go."

The sound of your voice startles them. The man stammers. "You-you're not one of them." He steadies his gun again. You wrap an arm around Joe's throat, pull him close, and squeeze.

"Toss that bag of stuff out and you can have your friend back."

"Don't trust him," the woman says. You see she is the driver.

You tighten your grip and pull him higher to cover more of your body. Joe groans from the strain you're putting his body through.

"I'll shoot you. I will." The gunman sounds more like he's trying to convince himself, rather than you.

"Throw my bag out. It's as simple as that. You'd better hurry, though, cause there's creatures inside the building. They might come out anytime."

He hesitates, visibly unsure what to do. The gun shakes in his hand. The woman is talking to him, but you can't hear the words. The gunman shushes her. "Let me think," he says.

You think about the absurdity of the situation: humans fighting each other with a much deadlier common foe lurking nearby. You try to remember what you put in the bags. Is it really anything you're willing to kill for—or to be killed for, for that matter?

"Look," you say, "this is ridiculous. We shouldn't be fighting each other. We need to band together to fight those creatures. What's in that bag can't be so important that you are willing to kill or be killed for it. What if I come with you and we take all the bags? Isn't it better to have more people than fewer?"

"He's trying to trick you into lowering your gun," the paranoid woman says.

The gunman wipes sweat from his brow. "So, you're saying we join forces?"

"Exactly."

The woman says something else, but he cuts her off. "Quiet, Dee." Then to you, "How do I know I can trust you? We could take you in, then you kill us and take our stuff."

"That works both ways. How do I know you won't strike a deal, then kill me some night while I'm sleeping? We either trust each other or we don't, but whatever you decide, we need to do it now. Either toss out the bag or join forces. Your choice."

Joe stirs beneath you, drawing a quick look from you.

The gunman says, "There's third option. I can just shoot you." He steadies the gun and aims.

The woman screams. It draws the gunman's attention. He turns his head. It's enough of a distraction for you to make your move. You release Joe. His head bounces once off the blacktop. You run at the gunman. To your surprise, he has forgotten about you and turning toward the driver.

As you reach him, you see why. The woman is being dragged out of the window by one of the creatures who was chasing you.

"Dee!" he shouts and aims the gun.

The woman is clinging desperately to the steering wheel and screaming at the top of her lungs. A cry of pain from behind has you spinning. The second creature has jumped on Joe and tries to rip a hunk of flesh from the back of his neck.

You turn, undecided on a direction, then Joe screams as the teeth dig in. Knife in hand, you run back to Joe. Behind you, the gun barks. You don't feel pain, so you assume the bullet was directed elsewhere. You leap at the creature. Its head is down, attending to its task. It is more interested in the meal in front of it than in you.

You hit, leading with the knife. It carves a long slice across the creature's back. It howls in pain as you drive it off Joe. Contact with the blacktop sends a spike of pain through your knee, but you can't let it slow you. You spin on the ground and push up, but the creature reacts faster. It jumps on you, landing on your chest with a victorious roar.

As it lowers its already bloody maw to your face, you punch it in the side with the knife. It hits bone and skids off. The beast barely reacts to the cut. You manage to get your cast up under its neck and push to gain leverage. The distance between you widens, but only for a moment. Still, it's enough to strike at the chest with the knife.

The blow is enhanced by the creature's own weight as it forces its body down. The blade penetrates. Its eyes widen almost as much as the open jaw. It still tries to get at you, but the effort has slackened. You pull the knife to the side, keeping it buried in the creature's body. As its jaw touches your face, the light in its eyes blink out and it collapses in dead weight on your chest.

Grunting, you shove it off and sit up. Joe is rolling on the ground, clutching at the back of his neck. Inside the van, the gun fires again. The gunman opens the driver's door and steps out. "No!" you hear. You stand, waiting for your legs to steady, then walk around the van.

The gunman is kneeling next to the woman, her lifeless body cradled in his arms. The beast lies dead next to her. The gun is on the ground by the man's side. Using his anguish to cover your movement, you slide close, bend, and take the gun. You back away. If the man has noticed, he gives no indication.

You go around the van, retrieve your bag and return it to the car. You pick up the discarded bag and do the same.

Do you:

2A3a1a) get in the car and leave? Read on.

2A3a1b) go back inside and continue looking for medical help? Go to page 144

2A3a1c) see if you can help the survivors? Go to page 151


2A3a1a) You want to go back inside. Your partner still needs medical attention. With the window broke out in the car, leaving it will make it easy for the gunman to strip the car bare. You get in and drive down the street and around the building to the front drive. You pull in and park on the side of the front entry.

Gun drawn, you enter the lobby. Through the glass on the far side, you see Joe on his feet and standing behind the gunman and the woman's body. You crouch, using the front desk for cover. Once at the intersection of hallways, you veer right. Out of sight from the front doors, you sprint down the hall to the stairs. This time, you go all the way upstairs to the sixth floor and work your way down.

At the fourth-floor landing, you run into a barrier. Someone has moved office furniture on the landing to block anyone from continuing further. Desks, file cabinets, sofas, and other heavy and large pieces are jammed together from front to back and floor to ceiling, preventing passage. The fourth-floor door is not accessible.

At first, it makes you mad. You need to get upstairs. The frustration at yet another obstacle to overcome has you ready to rage again. But the more you think about it, the less angry you are. A barricade means there are people somewhere above. You just have to figure out how to get to them.

You wonder if the other stairways have barriers as well. You decide that if one is blocked, it didn't make much sense not to do the same with the other ones.

You study the mound, searching for the best way to get beyond it without having to disassemble the furniture wall. Although the collection covers the entire landing, only a few pieces have been placed on the first and second steps of the next flight. There is a small space starting at the third step. If you climb over the railing, you might be able to angle and twist your body in a way to slide through.

You step up and over the lower rail and reach for the upper one. You glance down. Between the rails, the open space leads all the way down to the main floor. A fall guarantees pain and serious damage. One foot fits securely on the step, but there is little room for the second.

Your body is too long to roll over the bar. Gripping the rail tight to your chest, you slide the left leg over the bar. Balancing on the rail, you extend the foot to the step and follow it with the right. Your feet have solid footing, but your torso is wedged between the rail and the bottom of the ascending flight. You slide down the rail like a child sliding down a banister. From there, you squeeze your frame through. You made it. Now, to see what waits above.

Gun leading, you climb to the fifth floor. You stop at the fire door. There is no window, so you press your ear to the metal door. Either no one is there, no one is speaking, or the door is too thick for you to hear anything. Although it opens toward you, something holds it closed. Someone has to be there.

For a moment, you contemplate knocking, then decide to see what's on the sixth floor first. The sixth-floor fire door is rigged the same as the fifth. You try to puzzle out how the door was fixed. Since you don't see anything under or above the door to hold it back, the only way you can think of is to attach something to the door knob.

You turn the knob slowly. It moves, but grudgingly. Putting a foot on the frame for leverage and added power, you tuck the gun under your arm and grip the knob with both hands. You pull and push. The door budges, but not much. You release it and take out the hatchet and repeat the process, holding the hatchet in your left hand. As soon as the gap appears, you smack the blade between the door and frame. It takes three attempts before you can seat it. With the door wedged open, you bend to the level of the knob and peer through the gap. Although it's hard to see, you believe the door is tied with rope.

You slide the knife through the gap an inch above the hatchet and saw back and forth. The angle is not good. You can't see but feel the knife in contact with the rope. You continue for several minutes before stopping.

You pull the knife out to look at your progress, if any. As your eye focuses, something on the other side moves. You watch for a second, about to call out, when a hand appears above your head. Not a fraction too soon, you pull back as the long knife is shoved through the gap, aimed at your eye.

Someone hammers on the other side of the door and seconds later, the hatchet falls to the floor. You slam a palm on the door. "Hey! I'm not one of those creatures. Let me in." You wait, but nothing.

"Please! I'm in need of medical attention. There's no place else to go."

If anyone is listening, there is no response. You pound several times. "Come on. We're all human. Let's help each other. Don't turn me away." Then an idea forms. "I have a car full of food. I'm happy to share it with you. Just…" you sigh, "open the door."

You lean against it, discouraged and ready to give up. "I hope you're never in a situation that you need someone else's help. If we don't help each other now, all hope is lost."

You stand, not looking forward to the return climb down. A muffled voice room behind the door says, "How do we know we can trust you?"

Your heart leaps. Hope returns. Her words are a repeat of the previous situation. She said *we*, meaning she is not alone. "I'm alone. I have no other agenda. I have several bags of food and will share it for entry. I'm not one of those beasts. As far as I know, they don't speak, other than to howl."

"Have you been bitten?"

"No." Your thoughts go to your partner and their condition. What did being bit have to do with anything? Did that mean you'd become one of them. A deep heartache fills you. What will you find when you return home?

"Step back away from the door. Go down a few steps and stand where we can see you."

You move backward and slide the gun behind your back. You do the same with the hatchet and slip the knife back in the homemade sheath. Seconds later, the door opens a crack and two sets of eyes peer out, one above the other. You guess one of them is a woman and the other, a man.

You try to give an encouraging smile, but the tension won't let it spread across your face.

"Toss the knife over here by the door," a male voice says.

"I'll toss it down, but I'm not going to toss it to you and leave myself defenseless. I understand your hesitation, but I won't attack you. I'd much rather have allies than enemies. There's enough of them wandering the streets. I guess it comes down to trust. I have to trust you as much as you trust me."

The door closes, and you hear murmuring. It reopens. The man sticks his head out. He's about fifty with short black hair and a salt and pepper beard. "Where's this food you were talking about?"

"It's downstairs in the car. But let me be clear: I'm perfectly willing to share, but if you try to take it from me, we're gonna have a problem. Understood?"

The door closes again. It takes a few minutes this time before it opens. The man steps out. He is lean and looks fit. His eyes are hard. If you have to guess, you'd bet on him being a doctor.

"I'll help you bring it up."

Suddenly, you're not so sure this is what you want to do. Once they have your bargaining chips, they'll have no reason to admit you. Still, what choice do you have? The thought of going back outside alone to face those creatures again is enough to convince you. However, you have another problem. Once you turn, he will see the hatchet and the gun. You doubt he will to trust you enough to go first. If the positions were reversed, you wouldn't trust him.

You back away toward the steps and try to engage him in conversation. "It might take two or three trips. There's quite a few bags—but, it will be worth it." He doesn't reply. You take a few more backward steps, then turn sideways keeping your back toward the wall. Making it look like an afterthought, you turn toward him. "How many people are in there?"

This time he scowls. "Don't worry about it."

That's when you know this isn't going to go well for one of you. You force a happy tone to your voice. "Okay, I just wondered. You know, strength in numbers…that sort of thing. It's tough to survive out here alone."

He must sense your discomfort. His next words are lighter.

"When we get everything inside, I'll introduce you to everyone." He offers a strained smile that never reaches his hard eyes.

You create an opening in the barricade and trot down the stairs side by side without further conversation. As you descend, you take note of the man. He's in shape and barely breathing hard from the steady pace. You, on the other hand, started sucking air by the third flight. You also wonder why he's wearing a lab coat. What purpose did it serve? Then it comes to you. It's covering something up. Like a weapon.

Your mind whirls as the steps pass quickly beneath your feet. What kind of weapons might they have in a doctor's office? Scalpels. Needles. Drugs. Those small reflex mallets. You form a plan. You need to act before you open the car. Once he sees it, he'll make his move.

Reaching the main floor, he allows you to push through the door. You press your back to it in pretense of checking the hall and inch the door open. After taking a look, you slide out, holding the door for him. You catch movement from your periphery. His hand is now in the pocket of the lab coat. That tells you three things: where the weapon is, that he is right-handed, and he is ready to strike.

You need to get out ahead of his movements and, in fact, get out ahead of him. "This way," you say and take off running. You are down the hall and around the corner into the lobby before he can close. You feel him almost on your back.

"Is that it?" he says.

It's the only car by the front door, so he knows it has to be. The van and Joe are gone. Before he can make a move, you duck and spin away. Your hand reaches for your weapon. As you stand to confront him, gun in hand, you catch him with the needle held high, ready to plunge.

At the sight of the gun, he freezes, his once hard eyes showing nothing but fear.

Do you:

2A3a1a1) shoot him? Read on.

2A3a1a2) talk to him? Go to page 140

2A3a1a3) drive away? Go to page 142

2A3a1a1) You level the gun. He holds up his hands in a defensive position, the needle now pointed upward.

"Please, don't," he pleads.

"Why shouldn't I? I came to you in peace. I offered to share the food I had. All you had to do was let me join your group. But that wasn't good enough. Sharing wasn't what you wanted. You wanted to kill me and steal my stuff."

"I wasn't going to kill you. I swear. It's a sedative. It just would have put you to sleep. That's all."

"Then what? You would've left me here, defenseless against anything that came through the door?"

He stammers searching for a reply. "No, no. I would have dragged you into one of the offices, so you'd be safe."

"Yeah. Sure, you would have."

"Please. Don't shoot me." His eyes tear up. "I don't want to die. My wife is upstairs. Just let me go back to her."

His tears have the desired effect. You waver. You've never shot anyone before. It'd be different if he was one of those creatures. You lower the gun, and as soon as you do, he lunges. With a grunt, he stabs at you with the needle.

You manage to swat his arm to the side with the gun, but his body hits yours and bears you to the floor. You hit hard but maintain control of the gun. As he tries to get on top, you angle the gun and pull the trigger. The gun bucks, and because of the awkward position, skitters from your grasp.

Your attacker screams as the round burrows into his hip. He rolls off, clutching the wound. You crawl away and pick up the gun. Realizing what you are doing, he scrambles after you. His hand closes on your ankle and pulls you back. You snag the gun and roll onto your back. He still has the needle poised to plunge.

In a panic, you fire before you get on target. The round buzzes past his face and he flinches, giving you time to aim and shoot again. This time, the bullet punches through his eye, exploding out the back of his skull in a spray of bone fragments and brain matter and a mist of blood. He collapses on you, the needle sticking into your leg.

You cry out and yank it from your leg. You are about to throw it, but at the last second decide it might come in handy at some point.

Rolling the body off, you search his pockets and find another needle and a scalpel. You stand. Your leg aches. Hopefully, none of the sedative was injected, but in case it did, you want to get someplace safe.

You get into the car and drive home. You failed to find medical help for your partner, but maybe there's something you can do at home.

\* \* \*

You park in the driveway and climb the stairs. The front door is open. Pulling the gun, you advance inside with caution, fearful you will discover your partner torn to shreds on the couch. However, once inside, the couch is empty. You call out but get no response. Slowly, you check the house, but your partner is not there.

Confused and concerned, you stand on the small porch and scan the area. Nothing. Was she/he carried away or chased? You have to find her/him. You are trying to decide whether to search on foot or by car when she/he comes around the side of your house.

Your heart lightens with relief. You call out her/his name and start down the steps. The howl startles you. You freeze in your tracks and your heart sinks. The face is not looking at you with love, but like you're a meal. *Oh, no!* A sob catches in your throat. With a snarl, the creature now possessing the person you love charges at you.

You lift the gun, hesitate, and pull the trigger three times. As the body crumples to the ground, you break down, drop to your knees, and cry. Other howls are raised, and there is no time to morn. It will have to come later. Much later. For now, you must find a safe place to hide, if one exists.

You reach out to touch your partner one last time, but your hand stops inches from the face. It is no longer that of the one you love. The face is grotesque; she/he is long gone. You pull back, get in the car, and drive away.

Go to Chapter 3 on page 148

2A3a1a2) "I don't understand," you say. "Why would you want to hurt me? I came in peace and bearing gifts. What would have been so hard about accepting me into your little group? I might have been of great value to you. Besides, there doesn't appear to be many of us left. You're willing to kill another human for what? Food? Then, what happens once it ran out? Eventually, you'd have to go out searching for more."

"I'm sorry. It's just that, well, we don't know if we can trust you."

"So, you were willing to kill me, 'cause you have trust issues? Why shouldn't I just shoot you?"

He stammers, "No, no…not kill you. I swear. It's just a sedative. I just wanted to put you to sleep. That's all. Honest."

"And why should I believe you?"

His body deflates. "I guess you have no reason to believe me. Can we start over? My name's Jason. Upstairs is Beth, Deb, and Mick. If you'll accept my apology, I'd like to invite you to join us."

He seems sincere, but then, he just tried to drug and rob you, too.

"Set the needle down and back away."

He does, and you pick it up. You wonder how much you can trust him. Once you get the food upstairs, how safe will you be? One less mouth to feed makes a great motivator.

He senses your unease. "Let's go back upstairs so I can introduce you to the others. You'll see we're good people. We're just cautious."

*More like paranoid*, you think. Two can play at that game, though. You decide to go with him and then, once inside the office, you'll take whatever medical supplies they have. "Okay, lead the way." You motion with the gun.

He nods and leads the way you came. He opens the fire door and holds it for you, but you motion for him to go through first. He does and trots up the stairs. You follow. You're winded by the time you reach the floor. He keeps going while you lag behind. At the office door, he knocks.

"It's me. We're back."

There's a pause and some murmuring from inside.

"Just open up."

The door opens, revealing the first woman you saw. She glances from you to him. Her eyes widen as they drift down and notice the gun.

"This is Deb," he says. "This is…ah…" He pauses, waiting for you to fill in your name. When you don't, he continues. "We had a talk and I decided to invite him/her to join us." His hand sweeps back in a gesture of acceptance and admittance.

You take a step forward and realize your mistake too late. He had a second needle. The pain registers. You jerk to the side and hear the snap of the needle. The tube is empty. You swing the gun toward him, but Deb grabs your arm. The man throws a punch into your gut. Unprepared, the blow doubles you over. Your finger pulses and the gun fires and is then ripped from your hand.

As the drug takes effect, your limbs feel heavy. You become drowsy. Jason leans over and guides you to the floor. "Oh," he says, "I guess I lied. "It is a sedative, but it's a lethal dose."

His words register, but you cannot longer react. He drags you to the end of the hall and through the fire door. There he lifts your dead weight up over the rail. Your feet dangle in the space between the rails that goes all the way down to the main floor. You have a brief sensation of falling before your head strikes a rail and sends you into darkness, long before you hit the floor.

End

2A3a1a3) "You're a fool. You should see how much food I have in the car. Enough for at least a week. We could have shared it, but you had to have it all." You shake your head. "I should just shoot you."

"Please, I'm begging!"

"Oh, shut up. You were gonna kill me. In cold blood. Don't beg for your life."

"It's just a sedative. I wasn't going to kill you. I swear."

"No. Just rob me and leave me here, unconscious and defenseless if one of those creatures come in."

He puts his hands together as if praying. "Please, don't ..."

Annoyed, you shout, "Shut up!" You try to contain your rage. Though he deserves to be shot, you know you won't do it unless he forces you. "Set the needle down."

He does.

"You stay here until I leave."

"Can't we make a deal for some of the food?"

"You had your chance."

You back away until you reach the door. Once through, you turn and walk to the car. You sense more than hear his approach. He rushes at you from behind, the needle poised and ready to strike. You whip around and slam the gun across his face. The syringe goes flying. You drop a knee into his gut and press the muzzle to his forehead. A red veil descends over your vision. You want to pull the trigger so bad, but something inside prevents you from taking his life. Humanity? Fear? You're not sure, but you don't, and it makes you angrier.

You pat him down and find another syringe and a scalpel. You take both and stand up, gun still aimed at his face. He sobs for mercy. You pick up the discarded syringe and back toward the car.

A howl from close by startles you and you almost pull the trigger. You look up and see two of the creatures loping toward you. You fumble your key out and unlock the door. The doctor gets to his knees, glancing fearfully from you to the fast-approaching creatures.

You give him a last look and duck inside the car. As the engine turns over, you see him scramble to his feet and bolt for the door. One of the creatures goes after him. The other gives chase to you as the car pulls away. By the time you reach the driveway, it has stopped following and joined its partner.

You drive home. You have failed to get medical help for your partner, but maybe there's something you can do at home.

Go to *** on page 138

2A3a1b) You move to the driver's door and stick the gun through the window. "I'm sorry for your loss." It sounds false, but you mean it. "You shouldn't have tried to rob me. You need to get in the driver's seat and leave, or I'm going to be forced to shoot you."

He looks at you through tearful eyes. Then, without a word, he lays her body down and slides into the seat. He shifts and pulls away. You watch as the van disappears. You back away and enter the building still in need of finding medical assistance.

As you climb the stairs, you wonder how much of your stuff, if any of it, will still be there when you return. You climb to the next floor and over the next hour, check each one. On the fourth floor, someone gasps behind the door of an optometrist's office. You press an ear to the door and can barely make out whispers. At least two people are inside. Unless, of course, one person is talking to themselves.

You knock again. Nothing.

"Hello? I'm not here to hurt you. I'm looking for some medical help for my partner." Still, no answer. "I'm not one of those creatures. As far as I know, they don't speak. Please. Open the door. Do you want to be alone with all those beasts running around?"

You wait several minutes before giving up. You continue down the hall knocking on doors, bothered that humans are too scared to open the door to other humans. As you near the end of the hall, a sound makes you spin fast, ready to defend.

A woman's head pokes out the optometrist's door. You lower the gun and hold up your hands in a peaceful gesture. You take a step forward, but she flinches, and you fear she'll retreat inside. Lowering your hands, you tuck the gun in your belt out of sight.

"Honest, I won't hurt you. Is it okay to come closer?"

She squeaks something unintelligible.

"I'll just stay put. Do you know if any others are in here? My partner got bit by one of those creatures and I'm trying to locate someone who can help."

"Have-have you been bit?"

It's a strange question. "No, just her."

"Is she here?"

"No, I didn't think she could travel. I didn't want to drag her around until I found a doctor."

"I'm an optometrist. I can't help her."

"No, I guess not. Are there any doctors still here?"

"No. I've stayed in my office for days. I'm afraid to leave. Tried to leave once, but several of those creatures came after me. I just made it back inside. Did you see any of them?"

"Yes, quite a few."

"Are any in the building?'

"Not to my knowledge. It's just me."

Silence.

"Well, stay safe. I need to keep looking."

"You-you're leaving?"

"Yeah. I have to find a doctor."

"How long ago was your partner bitten?"

"A few hours."

"You should have just killed her/him."

That stuns you. "Why would I do that? I just need to find a doctor to treat her/his wounds."

"No doctor can save her/him once bitten. She/he'll turn into one of those creatures and there's nothing you can do to stop it. Would have been better for both of you to kill her/him before she/he turns."

You are dumbstruck by the callousness of the statement. A fearful chill races down your spine. A quick glimpse of your partner, now one of those beasts, flashes before your eyes.

"How do you know? If you haven't left your office in days, how can you know what happens?"

"It was on the news before they stopped broadcasting."

She sounds scared and defensive. You realize your words were loud and full of emotion and anger. You temper the tone. "Is there nothing anyone can do?"

"Not that I'm aware of."

"Is there no one to call or contact who has answers?"

"I'm sorry. I'm not trying to be mean. That's just what I heard."

"I should go to home and see for myself."

"Maybe."

"Before I go, do you want me to leave you some food? I filled the car before I left the house."

"You have food?" The idea is so alluring, she steps from the safety of the door without realizing it. She is short, plump, and perhaps forty. She pushes her glasses up on her nose.

"Yes. I'll leave you some. Or, if you want, you can come with me."

She glances at the open door. "I'm not sure that's a good idea. It's safer in here."

"What happens when you run out of food and no one comes knocking at your door with a refill?"

"I don't know. I'm just too afraid to go out there."

You nod. "I understand. I'll get you some food, then I have to go home and check on my partner."

"You-you won't forget me, will you?"

"No. I'll knock on your door when I come back."

"Okay. Th-thanks."

You go down to the car, and to your relief and astonishment, it is untouched. You rifle through a bag and take out some apples, a banana, granola bars, two cans of pop, and two cans of soup with pull top lids. Back upstairs, you set the food down and knock on the door. You walk away, thinking about your partner. As you push through the fire door, you hear, "Thank you." You don't reply. If what the woman said is true, you may no longer have need for a doctor. You think about your partner and what you might find when you get home.

You get into the car and drive home. You did not get medical help, but maybe there's something you can do at home.

Go to *** on page 157

## Chapter 3 (2A3a1a1, 2A3a1a3, 2A3b3)

A few miles later, you spy an SUV with its door open. You stop next to it, hoping its owner is close. You wait several minutes, but no one appears. You decide it is in better shape than your car, so you transfer everything. Minutes later, you are back on the road, trying to decide where to go that might offer safety...if such a place exists anymore.

The roads are littered with obstacles of all sorts, including bodies. You zigzag through, but the drive is slow. There must be someplace you can go, but after the stress and emotional pain of the past hour, you can't think clearly.

Up ahead, you see movement. Slowing, you focus on the area. Nothing. You start to think you're seeing things, but as you speed up, a woman and a girl of about five years old dash from behind a car. They run thirty feet and duck behind a car.

*Where are they trying to go?* More importantly, who or what are they running from? The answer comes fast. From around a building, three creatures bound. One lifts its head and sniffs the air. A second one howls. They are trailing the woman and child by scent.

Do you:

3A) go to the rescue? Read on.

3B) drive away? Go to page 150


3A) You pick up the gun and inch closer. The woman and girl dart to the next car. This time, the creatures spot them and emit a bone-chilling howl. They race after them. The woman rises, sees the pursuit, and runs, pulling the girl behind her. The girl cannot keep up and soon trips and falls. The woman continues to run, dragging the wailing girl.

You have to do something and soon. A quick plan forms with little thought. You roll down your window and speed toward the woman and child. Once they pass, you swerve in the creatures' path. They are coming fast and show no signs of slowing or altering their course. You have become their main focus.

You lift the gun and fire into the lead beast. It yelps and goes down. The next two hurdle it, unconcerned with its death. You switch aim and shoot again. That one takes three shots to put down. The third closes to within ten feet. You pull the trigger. The bullet leaves the barrel and the slide locks back. You never thought to check how many rounds you had.

Looking up, you see the bullet has struck an arm and spun the beast around, but it maintains its balance and renews its charge. Panic builds. You slam your foot down and the SUV leaps forward. However, the beast leaps and manages to get one claw inside the window.

You use the gun to slam down on the digits. One by one they release until the beast falls and you are free. You reach the intersection and stop. Looking over your shoulder, you search for the mother and child, but they are nowhere to be seen.

A car engine roars to life and you swing your gaze. Across the street, a car shoots down the driveway of an auto parts store and races in the opposite direction. At first, you are tempted to follow, but as the last beast rises and snarls, you decide to continue on.

Continue Chapter 3 on page 245

3B) You drive away, leaving them to their fate. You say a silent prayer, but the guilt of leaving them, is too great. You swing the SUV around. The woman is now carrying the girl. She is running as hard as she can, but she will never outrun her pursuers.

You move closer, get out, and stand behind the door. You aim the gun, wondering if you're too far to hit anything. You decide you don't care. You only want to distract them from the woman and give her a chance to escape.

The first beast crosses your line of sight and you pull the trigger. The gun bucks, and the bullet smacks into a car that is a good ten feet behind your target. Hitting a moving target was harder than it was in the video games you play.

You aim again. This time, you squeeze the trigger. The bullet misses but comes close enough to cause one of the beasts to stop and look your way. It bares its teeth. You shoot again. The bullet hits hard enough to knock the beast back, but not down. It looks at the wound in its chest as if it were a curiosity.

The first and third beasts still chase the woman. You aim for the first one. Three shots later, a lucky shot takes it down. The third beast stops and whirls in your directions. It lets loose a blood-curdling howl and charges. You glance back at the second one. It is moving toward you on rubbery legs—not much of a threat.

You take careful aim at the charging creature. You fire twice, both misses, and then the slide locks back. *Uh-oh!* You hear a car start and look up in time to see the woman drive away. That's a good idea. You jump in the SUV, back away from the oncoming beast, and drive off. You saved the woman and girl. That makes you feel good. Too bad it cost the rest of the bullets. Hopefully, you won't have need for it again.

As the thought finishes, you know it's folly.

Continue to Chapter 3 on page 245

2A3a1c) You put the gun in your belt and check on Joe. He is bleeding badly. Though not spurting, the jagged, puckered wound is as wide as a mouth. You run to the van and find a bag of clothes. You press a t-shirt to Joe's wound and place his hands over the shirt. "Hold it tight. I'm gonna try and find some bandages."

You go around the van. The other man is still cradling Dee on his lap, rocking back and forth like he's putting a child to sleep.

"Excuse me." He's lost in a trance. "Hey!" you shout. He turns his tear-streaked face toward you. It takes a few seconds for him to focus. "Do you have any medical supplies in the van? I need to stop Joe from bleeding out."

His anguished face transforms into a look of pure hatred and rage. "You!" He bellows. "This is your fault. You killed Dee."

He plants a kiss on her forehead and lowers her to the ground. He jumps to his feet and you retreat a step, hand reaching behind you for the gun. "Why couldn't you just let it go?" He leans into the van and fumbles for something. You have a feeling you're not going to like what he comes out with.

As he turns, you see he has a rifle. You rip the gun free and aim it at him. It becomes a race between who can get their barrel on target first. Adrenaline pumping, heart pounding, you both fire prematurely. You get your weapon on target first and pump three rounds into him. He is already falling before you can stop pulling the trigger.

You stand in shock, staring at his body. "It didn't have to be like this," you tell him. "No one had to die here. We could've been friends and helped each other. Why?" But no answer comes.

A sound from behind the van reminds you that Joe still needs help. You find him writhing on the ground. The blood-soaked t-shirt has been discarded. Joe is clutching his gut. Something strange is happening to his face. It is altered somehow. His eyes are sunken and dark circles surround them. The iris looks elongated and red.

You are frozen by awe and fear. *My God! Is he becoming one of those creatures?* Then a thought breaks through. Does that mean your partner will change, too? You have a sudden urge to get home as fast as you can. You turn toward your car and hear a familiar snarl. You spin to find Joe is now glaring at you and trying to rise.

You lift the gun and put a bullet through his head.

You open the car door and see the glass shards covering the seat. You transfer everything to the van, pick up the rifle, and drive your new ride toward home. Your mind is filled with wonderful memories of yourself and your partner. You don't want to think about what you might find when you get home.

Go to *** on page 138

2A3a2) You decide to get more distance between you and the creatures. The higher you go, the less likely they'll find you…or so you hope. Your best bet is to find other survivors. You run up the stairs. By the third flight, you have settled into a light jog, taking each step. At the fifth-floor landing, you slow to walk. By the time you reach the top floor your chest is heaving. You stop at the door and lean against it to get air.

You hear a sound from below. *No!* It can't be. You inch the door open and step through with as much stealth as you can muster. In the hall, you try to think of a way to secure the door, but since it opens outward, there is no handle to rig.

You hasten down the hall knocking on doors. Behind one, you hear a sound like an exclamation of surprise. You stop and press an ear to the door. You hear an excited voice say, "Someone's out there."

You knock again, this time with more urgency. "Please. I'm not one of the monsters. I need help."

Gripping the door knob, you give it a violent shake and knock again. "I know you're in there. I'm not gonna hurt you. Please let me in."

If anyone is listening, they do not respond. You pound several times. "Come on. We're all human. Let's help each other. Don't turn me away." Then an idea forms. "I have a car full of food. I'm happy to share it with you. Just…" you sigh, "open the door."

You lean against it, discouraged and ready to give up. "I hope you're never in a situation that you need someone else's help. If we don't help each other now, all hope is lost."

You stand, not looking forward to the return climb down. A muffled voice room behind the door says, "How do we know we can trust you?"

Your heart leaps. Hope returns. She said *we*, meaning she is not alone. "I'm alone. I have no other agenda. I do have several bags of food and will share it for entry. I'm not one of those beasts. As far as

I know, they don't speak, other than to howl."

"Have you been bitten?"

"No." Your thoughts go to your partner and his/her condition. What did you being bit have to do with anything? Did that mean you'd become one of them? A deep heartache fills you. What would he find when he returned home?

"Step back away from the door. Go down a few steps and stand where we can see you."

You do as instructed, then slide the hatchet behind your back and slip the knife in the homemade sheath. Seconds later, the door opens a crack and two sets of eyes peer out, one above the other. You guess one is a woman, and the other, a man.

You try to give an encouraging smile, but the tension refuses to allow it to spread across your face.

"Toss the knife over here by the door," a male voice says.

"I'll toss it down, but I'm not going to toss it to you and leave myself defenseless. I understand your hesitation, but I'm not going to attack you. I'd much rather have allies than enemies. There's enough of them wandering the streets. I guess it comes down to trust. I have to trust you as much as you trust me."

The door closes, and you hear murmuring. It reopens. The man sticks his head out. He's about fifty with short black hair and a salt and pepper beard. "Where's this food you were talking about?"

"It's downstairs in the car. But let me be clear: I'm perfectly willing to share, but if you try to take it from me, we're gonna have a problem. Understood?"

The door closes again. It is a few minutes this time before it opens. The man steps out. He is lean and looks fit. His eyes are hard. If you had to guess, you'd bet on him being a doctor.

"I'll help you bring it up."

Suddenly, you're not so sure this is what you want to do. Once they have your bargaining chips, they'll have no reason to admit you. Still, what choice do you have? The thought of facing those creatures alone is enough to convince you. However, you have another problem. Once you turn, he will see the hatchet. You doubt he's going to trust you enough to go first. If the positions were reversed, you wouldn't.

You back away toward the opposite steps you came up and try to engage him in conversation. "It might take two or three trips. There's quite a few bags, but it will be worth it." He doesn't reply. You take a few more backward steps, then turn sideways, keeping your back toward the wall. Making it look like an afterthought, you turn toward him. "How many people are in there?"

This time, he scowls. "Don't worry about it."

You now know this isn't going to go well for one of you. You force a happy tone into your voice. "Okay, I just wondered. You know, strength in numbers. That sort of thing. It's tough to survive out here alone."

He must sense your discomfort. His next words are lighter. "When we get everything inside, I'll introduce you." He offers a strained smile that never reaches his hard eyes.

You enter the stairway and slide to the side. You trot down the stairs side by side without further conversation. As you descend, you take note of the man. He is in shape and barely breathing hard from the steady pace. You, on the other hand, started sucking air by the third flight. You also wonder why he's wearing his lab coat. What purpose did it serve? Then it comes to you. Nothing, other than cover something up, like a weapon.

Your mind whirls as the stairs pass quickly beneath your feet. What kind of weapons might they have in a doctor's office? Scalpels. Syringes. Drugs. Those small reflex mallets. You make your plan. You need to act before you open the car. Once he sees it, he'll make his move.

You reach the main floor and inch the door open. You don't see any creatures and hope that means they left. As you start out the door, the hatchet is ripped from your belt.

"What's this? We're you going to take me by surprise? Hit me on the head with this?"

You back away. "No. I wasn't going to attack you, but I had to protect myself if you attacked me."

"So you say."

Anger rises, pushing aside any anxiety. "That's right," you snap. "So I say. I wouldn't have done anything to you, so long as you followed through with our agreement. All I want it some medical help for my partner. I'd gladly trade food for that."

"What's wrong with her/him?'

"She's/he's been bitten by one of those things."

He scoffs. "There's no amount of medical help you can get for that. Might as well write them off."

The words hit you like a blow from the hatchet. How did he know that for sure?

He advances, holding the hatchet in a threatening manner. You continue backing away until you reach the lobby. You turn toward the front doors. He glances over your shoulder. "Is that your car?"

You don't reply and keep moving. Your mind whirls, seeking a way to turn the tables. If you take him down, the others will never open the door for you. Somehow, you have to convince him you're not a threat.

You reach the glass doors. Movement to the left draws your attention. He reacts to the look on your face and pauses for an instant.

"Watch behind you."

"You're not getting me to fall for that."

You pivot and push through the doors. He follows, still unaware of the danger behind him. You fumble for your keys. You press the unlock button and reach for the door as he closes on you. He grabs your arm and spins you around. The hatchet is held high, ready to split your head in half. Before the blow can land, the creatures jump on his back and drag him down. The hatchet falls to the ground. You snatch it up and hesitate.

Do you:

2A3a2a) run? Read on.

2A3a2b) fight? Go to page 159

2A3a2a) You take a look at the rolling jumble of bodies and decide the best thing to do is run. After all, you don't owe him anything. He would've killed you for the food. You open the door, but before you can get in, one of the creatures disentangles and lunges for you. Its claw snags your leg and almost yanks you off your feet with a powerful pull.

You fall back against the car. The creature has one hand on your ankle, and the other stretches for a higher hold on your body. You swing the hatchet down on the extended hand, batting it away. Then, as it snarls in pain, you pound it down across the wrist at your ankle.

The blade isn't as sharp as it should be. Although it bites into the flesh, it more pummels the hand into the sidewalk than cuts it. The blow is enough to break the grasp. Without hesitation, you jump into the car. Just before the door closes, you hear the man cry out. "Help me! Please!" His hand is stretched toward you. A wave of guilt sweeps over you as the creature buries its teeth into the man's face. You shudder violently and close the door.

As you insert the key, the second creature slams into the driver's window. You jump in your seat and drop the keys. Amidst a torrid of curses, you fumble on the floor for the keys while reaching back to make sure the door is locked.

The beast strikes over and over, each blow harder than the previous one. With each, you fear the window will implode. Your hand brushes and snags the key. A whimper escapes you. You insert the key and start the engine. Your last view is of the man's bloody body twitching from another savage bite.

You drive home. You have failed to get medical help for your partner, but maybe there's something you can do at home. You try not to think about the doctor's words. They can't be true. You want to believe your partner will be all right.

\* \* \*

You park in the driveway and climb the stairs. The front door is open. Pulling the hatchet, you advance inside with caution, fearful you will discover your partner torn to shreds on the couch. However, once inside, you see the couch is empty. You call out but get no response. Slowly, you check the house, but your partner is not there.

Confused and concerned, you stand on the small porch and scan the area. Nothing. Was she/he carried away, or was she/he chased? You have to find her/him. You try to decide whether to search on foot or by car, when she/he comes around the side of the house.

Your heart lightens with relief. You call out her/his name and start down the steps. The howl startles you. You freeze in your tracks and your heart sinks. The face is not looking at you with love, but like you're a meal. *Oh, no!* A sob catches in your throat. With a snarl, the creature now possessing the person you love charges at you.

You lift the hatchet. It is as heavy as your heart. From your elevated position on the porch, you strike down with a crushing blow. The hatchet blade plows deep into the skull. As the body crumples to the ground, you break down, drop to your knees, and cry. Other howls are raised, and you have no time to morn. That will have to come later. For now, you must find a safe place to hide...if one still exists.

You reach out to touch your partner one last time, but your hand stops inches from the grotesque face. It is no longer that of the one you love. She/he is gone. You get in the car and drive away.

Go to Chapter 3 on page 245

2A3a2b) You hear the man cry out for help. You doubt he would answer a similar call from you if your positions were reversed, but you still possess enough humanity to help another person, even if they don't deserve it.

You stride forward, and with every bit of strength you possess, you bring the hatchet down on top of the top creature's skull. The head splits like an unripe melon, though the insides are a much more grotesque color than the fruit. Lifting your foot, you shove the body off and reposition for a second strike.

Aware of your presence, the second creature lashes out with a clawed hand, catching the back of your leg and sweeping your feet out from under you. You topple and lose the hatchet. As soon as you crash to the cement, you bounce to hands and feet and crawl from its reach.

You find and retrieve the hatchet. The man screams in pain. The creature is gnawing at his neck, trying to rend flesh from his body. You run up and slam the hatchet down, but it is squirming so much that the blade bites into the shoulder. It howls and flings an arm out, knocking you away again. This time, the hatchet is embedded in the beast.

Again, you crawl away as it eyes with you savage intent. You slide the knife from its sheath and prepare to defend, but to your surprise, it reverts to attacking the doctor. You notice the man's efforts are waning. He may only have seconds to live. You steel your resolve and run at the pile. Diving on the creatures back, you dig your free hand into its scalp and yank back the head. As it snarls and snaps at your arm, you drag the steak knife across its throat. It scrapes but doesn't cut.

Desperate to end the fight without getting bit just in case the doctor is right, you saw the blade back and forth until you are rewarded with a spurt of blood. You shove the creature's head down and prevent it from rising. It thrashes violently, but you press your weight down until it ceases to move.

You wait an extra minute to be sure it doesn't rise again, then drag it off the doctor. He is still alive but did not escape damage. His face and neck are bleeding, although you can't be sure how much of it is his and how much is the creature's. Not knowing what to say, you go to the fall back, "You all right?'

The doctor stares at the sky. You repeat the question and his eyes shift towards you. "No. I'm not all right. The damn thing bit me," he sobs. "I'm going to become one of them." His hand ensnares yours. "You have to kill me."

"What?" You pull free. "No way. I'll get you upstairs and your friends can take care of you."

"No. You have to kill me. Please. If you take me upstairs, I'll be a threat to them," he cries. Tears mingle with the blood, leaving reddish streaks down his cheeks. "One of them is my wife. I don't want to hurt her, and I don't want her to see me like this. Please."

"She'll think I killed you and left you here."

"No. If they check, they'll see the bites. I'm sorry for the way I treated you. We should have just accepted you."

"It's all right. I understand. It's difficult to know who to trust."

"No, you don't understand. We decided we had to kill you, so you wouldn't make trouble for us. In my pocket is a syringe loaded with an overdose of a sedative. It would have killed you. Inject me with it. I'll-I'll just go to sleep. It will be peaceful." He cramps up and clutches his gut. His face contorts in pain and something else, but you can't be sure what.

"It's already happening. I'm changing." A shaky hand reaches into his lab coat and withdraws the syringe. He hands it to you. "I don't deserve any kindness, but please. If not for me, do it for my wife."

His eyes hold yours pleadingly, then he convulses again.

You push up his sleeve and say, "I've never done this before. What should I do? Don't I have to flick it or something."

He coughs up a spittle of blood. "Just try to inject it as close to a vein as possible."

You place the needle over a blue line and hesitate. The idea of killing him makes you nauseous. His hand takes yours and steadies it against his skin. He groans long and loud. When it passes, he says, "Hurry. I can feel my body changing."

Sure enough, his face has undergone some magical transformation. It looks longer. The eyes have sunken. The sight shocks you into motion. You jab the needle in and push the plunger. When the tube is empty, you retract it and stick it back in his coat pocket.

"Yes. Thank you. Will you tell my wife I love her?"

"Sure." Your eyes well.

You sit with him until he loses consciousness, then you go upstairs and knock on the door. "You don't have to answer, but I wanted you to know the creatures got your friend. He's dead. He wanted me to tell his wife he loves her. I'm sorry."

You return to the car. You can't be sure, but you think the doctor is dead. You climb in the car and pray he was wrong about your partner becoming one of those creatures.

You drive home. You have failed to get medical help for your partner, but maybe there's something you can do at home. You try not to think about the doctor's words. They can't be true. You want to believe your partner will be all right.

Go to *** on page 157

2A3b) Unable to get a response at the urgent care, you walk down the strip mall and check each building for survivors or an open door. You pass a phone store and a dog grooming business. Both doors are locked. Next comes is a sub shop. The door is open, but the inside looks like a tornado hit it.

You hesitate before entering. If what you think is the cause for the destruction, they may still be in there. It'd be nice to have the food, but not worth the risk if you must face another one of those creatures. You let the door close softly and move to the last business, a convenience store.

That holds the most promise. They will have an assortment of drugs, bandages, and ointments that may help your partner. The door is locked. You press your face to the glass and scan inside. It doesn't appear as though anyone has been through it, since everything looks to be in order. You pull hard on the door, gauging the amount of give. Not enough to do anything with. The only alternative is to break a window.

You look around for something you can use and walk toward a retaining pond off the side of the property. The downward slope is covered in rocks of assorted sizes. You pick one up, heft it, and turn back to the store.

From somewhere behind the building, a puff of smoke curls upward and is taken away by the breeze. It takes a moment to register it must be someone smoking. You jog to the side wall of the building and creep toward the back. At the corner, you squat and take a quick peek.

An Indian man is sitting on an overturned plastic crate, smoking. He seems weary and in a daze. In robotic fashion, he places the cigarette between his lips, inhales deeply, then tilts his head back and blows the smoke out.

You pull back and try to decide your best approach. Talk or attack? You don't want to hurt him, but you want to get inside.

Do you:

2A3b1) step out and talk to him? Read on.

2A3b2) rush to subdue him? Go to page 166

2A3b3) race to get inside before he does? Go to page 167

2A3b1) You set the rock down to appear less threatening. You practice in your head what you want to say, then step out. He doesn't see you at first. "Excuse me, sir." Before you get any further, the man shouts, "You go away." He sprints toward the door. He has a thirty-foot lead on you. You break into a run. "Sir, I'm not going to hurt you. I need some supplies."

He grabs the outer door and swings it closed. You reach the door and try to catch the frame with your fingers, but he gives it a final yank and you let go, fearing your fingers will get pinched.

You slap the door. "Sir, I just need to get some medical supplies. My girlfriend/boyfriend is hurt and needs some help. Please. I won't harm you. I'll pay for what I need."

You pound with your fist this time. Inside, you hear him say, "You go away. We're closed."

"Come on. You gonna sit on that stuff and lose money? People still need stuff."

"Go away."

*No!* you think. Your anger grows. "I will not leave here empty handed." You jog around the building and retrieve the rock. In front of the store, you bang on the front door. The man peers out from the door leading to the back room. You hold up the rock and point to it. It is dark in the store, but you think you see the man's eyes widen.

"Let me in, or I swear I'll throw this through your front window. Good luck trying to keep people out then. Or, maybe one of those creatures will come by. How you gonna stop them from getting in?"

The man stands in the doorway but doesn't move.

"Okay. Your choice."

You step back, heft the rock several times, then wind up. The man races through the store waving his arms. He stops at the door. You stop and wait.

"You go away. I call police."

You laugh. "Go ahead. I doubt anyone will respond. Let me in, or I'm breaking the window."

"Go away."

"Last chance."

You start your windup again.

The man unlocks the door and runs. You set the rock down so that he won't be frightened of you and enter the store. Once inside, you see he has picked up a baseball bat. You hold up your hands. "Hey, I just want to get some supplies. I promise, I'll be out of here in a few minutes." You step sideways down an aisle. The man follows but stops at the end of the aisle, watching you with disdain.

You find medical supplies and grab everything you might need. Setting them on the counter, you go back and get two bottles of water and two candy bars. You take out a credit card and hand it to the man.

He stares at you like you're crazy.

"What?"

"No credit card. It does not work."

"Doesn't work," you repeat. Checking your pockets, you find five dollars and some change. There might be more in the car's ashtray, but if you leave, he may not let you back in. You push the water and candy aside and mentally total what you have left. You eliminate the bandages, figuring you can find something at home. You end up with a triple antibiotic ointment and a bottle of hydrogen peroxide. It's still more than what you have, but you push the money toward the man with a hopeful expression.

He looks from the items to you and shakes his head.

"Please. I'll come back with money. You won't even have to let me in. I'll set it at the door and leave."

He takes your money and says. "Don't come back. It's good."

You scoop up your items and head for the door. "Thank you."

He nods and before you're three steps away, you hear the lock engage. You didn't get what you wanted, but it's time to head home. You're worried about your partner.

Go to *** on page 157

2A3b2) You set the rock down, take a deep breath, then bust around the corner like a linebacker targeting a quarterback. The man sees you, freezes for an instant, then bolts for the door. He snags the knob and pulls the door, but you arrive before it closes and yank it open.

The man cries out, turns, and runs. You tackle him from behind. The two of you hit hard and roll. The man goes limp. You get up, ready to wrestle him into submission, but he doesn't move. For an instant, you're afraid you killed him. You find a pulse and breathe a sigh of relief. As long as he's out, you get up and go through the store. You grab a handful of medical items, then go behind the counter and find a bag. You load it up and take a second bag, which you fill with bottled water, chips, and candy bars.

You go through the back room to make sure the guy is still breathing, but he's gone. Puzzled, then concerned, you whirl around just as the man swings the baseball bat. A white flash goes off in your head, then the lights go out.

A sharp pain wakes you. Your eyes take a moment to register. You're outside and it's dark. The pain continues vying for what's already pounding in your head. You feel a heavy weight on your body. A face appears in front of yours. It's not a friendly face. Something warm drips from its mouth onto your cheek. You realize it's your blood. Panic sends waves of adrenaline through your veins, but it is too late to prevent the creature from diving at your throat for another mouthful of your flesh.

The pain subsides, and soon you are drifting peacefully toward a white light.


End

2A3b3) You race around the corner. The man sees you, lets out a strangled squeak, and bolts for the door. He has a lead on you, and you judge he'll make it before you get there. On the run, you whip the rock at him. It drills him in the side, knocking him off balance and into the door. By the time he stands, you're on him.

You blast him backward and he falls. While he struggles to his feet, you regain the rock. As he rises, you bring the rock down on his head, bashing it in. He drops. You lean over him and crush his head once more. The gray ooze is all the evidence you need. He's dead.

You stand and enter the convenience store, closing the door behind you. As the adrenaline ebbs, you feel light-headed. You step to the side and vomit. You killed an innocent man just to get access to medical supplies. You have no idea if he would've let you in or not, but you didn't want to take a chance. Now, you're a murderer.

Entering the store, you figure you might as well make your crime worthwhile. You fill up as many bags as you can carry, then exit the way you entered, trying not to look at the carnage you caused. In the car, you replay your assault. You hate that you resorted to violence rather than using reason. Forcing the images from your mind, at least for the moment, you drive home.

You park in the driveway and climb the stairs. The front door is open. Pulling the hatchet, you advance inside with caution, fearful you will discover your partner torn to shreds on the couch. However, once inside, you find the couch is empty. You call out but get no response. Slowly, you check the house. Your partner is not there.

Confused and concerned, you stand on the small porch and scan the area. Nothing. Was she/he carried away or was she/he chased? You have to find her/him. You try to decide whether to search on foot or by car as she/he comes around the side of the house.

Your heart lightens with relief. You call out her/his name and start down the steps. The howl startles you. You freeze in your tracks and your heart sinks. The face is not looking at you with love, but like you're a meal. *Oh, no!* A sob catches in your throat. With a snarl, the creature now possessing the person you love charges at you.

You lift the hatchet. It is as heavy as your heart. From your elevated position on the porch, you strike down with a crushing blow. The hatchet blade plows deep into the skull. As the body crumples to the ground, you break down, drop to your knees, and cry. Other howls are raised, and you have no time to morn. That will have to come later. For now, you have to find a safe place to hide…if one still exists.

You reach out to touch your partner one last time, but your hand stops inches from the grotesque face. It is no longer that of the one you love. She/he is long gone. You pull back, get in the car, and drive away.

You killed an innocent man for nothing. How will you justify your actions now? You force your mind blank and drive, unaware of anything going on around you or with any destination in mind.

Go to Chapter 3 on page 148

2A3c) Desperate and alone, you dig through the trunk until you find the tire iron. The small folding tool doesn't have the weight of its predecessors, but it's what you have. You step up to the glass front doors and swing. The tool bounces off. You swing hard twice more with only sweat for your efforts.

There must be another way. You search the area and find a fist-sized rock half buried in the dirt. You pry it out with the tire iron. It has good weight and should penetrate the glass. Taking several running steps toward the building like a javelin thrower, you launch the rock. It soars through the air and impacts the door frame inches to the right of the glass.

"You've got to be frigging kidding me!"

Irritated by the constant delays, you retrieve the rock, back up a few feet, and hurl it dead center into the glass just as you see a woman running inside from the back of the building, waving her hands. Too late to stop the throw, the rock punches a large jagged hole through the glass. The woman jumps back, placing both hands on her face.

Once the shards stop falling, she glares at you. You step toward the door and notice two other people join her, a man and another woman. They are gesticulating wildly and talking all at once. You reach the door and slip your hand through the hole with care. The three of them charge at you as they notice your movement. The first woman grabs your hand and tries to push it back. The man puts his hand on top of yours and forces it down on the glass. You are unable to prevent the move and a lance of pain races up your arm.

You drag it back, but only manage to slice a long furrow up your arm. Placing the cast under the other arm, you lift and pull at the same time and manage to get free.

"Are you crazy?" you scream. "What the hell was that for?"

"Look what you did, you asshole!" the first woman shouts. "How are we going to stay safe with a hole in the door?"

The man bends and speaks through the hole as if ordering food at a drive thru. "Get the hell away from here. We're not letting you in."

Enraged, and blood dripping from your arm, you advance toward them. As one, they jump back. "Then you should've just opened the door when I knocked. How was I to know you were cowering inside? Look what you did. I just came here to find medical help for my girlfriend/boyfriend. Would it have been so hard to just let me in? If you could help, fine. If not, you might have been able to tell me what to do. Have you lost all humanity, just because we have a crisis to deal with?"

The first woman, short with dark hair, said, "We will never let you in now. Go away."

"Not until you give me something to wrap this cut."

The man says something to the taller red-haired woman, and she disappears into the back room. No one speaks for several moments, then she returns, carrying what looks like a roll of gauze. She shows it to the man who nods toward the door. She walks over with tentative steps and drops the gauze and roll of medical tape through the hole. It lands on the ground near the door.

A vein throbs in your head. You walk forward and bend to pick them up, mumbling, "Yeah, thanks for your humanitarian gesture."

As you stand, you toss an angry glare toward the trio, but notice they are no longer looking at you, but at something behind you. From the terrified looks, it is not something you're going to like. You whip around to see two creatures, a male and female, running toward you. They are forty feet away and closing fast.

Do you:

2A3c1) run for the car? Read on.

2A3c2) try to gain access to the building? Go to page 175

2A3c3) Stand and face them? Go to page 179

2A3c1) With eyes bulging from your head, you make a break for the car. Since you parked in front opposite traffic patterns, the driver's door is close for you. You jump in and lock the door as the two beasts arrive on the passenger side and slam their hands on the glass.

Hand shaking, blood still running down your arm, you struggle to seat the key. Just as you do and turn the engine over, the side window implodes. The male beast dives inside head first. You press the pedal down and the car shoots forward. The beast has its legs hanging out the window and its head on the seat, yet still it tries to claw at you.

You reach the end of the parking lot in a panic. The car flies down the drive, bottoms out, and bounces. The jolt rips the wheel from your slippery grasp, preventing you from making the turn. You slam on the brakes inches before the car crashes into a pole.

With no time to put on your seat belt, you are flung into the wheel. The collision knocks the wind from your lungs. The creature is thrown into the well. Recovering, you slide the knife out and jab repeatedly. It howls and slashes at you. The strikes cause pain, but not much damage. It's hard to stab without risking being bitten.

You think about getting out and running around the car to attack from a superior position, but a glance in the mirror shows the female creature giving chase. It's bad enough dealing with one. You don't want to face her, too.

You throw the car in reverse and floor the accelerator. The car flies back up the drive and bounces again. This time, you manage to keep control of the wheel. However, the beast uses the time to scamper up on the seat. Just as the car slams into the woman, he launches, pinning you against the door.

In your panic, you keep your foot down and the car continues to move backward. Your hands are occupied with fending off the attack, so the car goes where it wants. It hits the walkway in front of the line of stores and goes airborne.

Your desperate struggles weaken. Each time the beast snaps its absurdly long teeth down, they are closer to your face. Then, the car crashes into the corner building and you are thrown backward into your seat, and you contact the headrest with enough force to see stars. The beast, however, is between seats, and the impact sends it flying into the back seat.

You shake off the effects, but your mind remains cloudy. You feel like you're moving in slow motion. The creature, too, has a recovery period as it rights itself. As your senses refocus, you grip the knife tighter. The creature comes back into the front seat face first, giving you a great target. With as much force as you can muster from the awkward position and angle, you drive the blade into his ear canal. The handle slips in your bloody grip, but you keep pushing until it is sticking into its brain as far as it will go.

The creature looks confused. The hostility fades as it tries to puzzle out what it's feeling. You press backward into the door, your hand searching for the door handle. It glances at you, then shakes its head as if clearing away sleep. It snarls, but not at you. Your hand finds the handle and you open the door. As you fall out, the space gives you enough room to pull in your leg and fire a kick. It lands squarely on the handle driving it deeper. The beast's eyes light like you rang the bell at a carnival, then dim, fade, and close. The head drops to the console.

You exhale a long, extended breath and feel the weight of fear fall from your shoulders. You climb out on shaky legs and notice the female lying in a heap on the pavement. Going around the car, you open the door and haul the dead beast out. You check out the car. The rear end is crumpled, but the tires don't look impeded. It may still run, but if you're going to protect your belongings, you'll need to find another ride.

You move the car and park next to an abandoned car. Getting out, you check the vehicles and find keys in an SUV. You transfer the bags and notice you are leaving a trail of blood. You need to bind the wound before you lose too much. You dropped the gauze and tape back at the urgent care.

Weary from your fight and loss of blood, you drive back. The trio in the urgent care attempt to patch the broken window with a board that looks like a shelf. They stop as you approach. The dark-haired woman presses her weight against the board to prevent you from gaining access.

You smirk at her and pick up the gauze and tape. You lock eyes with her and see the depths of her hatred. You pity her. She must have been a horrible person to live with. You break the gaze and look at the man. He shows no emotion.

"The only way to do the job so it holds is to put a board on both sides and screw them together."

He looks at the board, and a light clicks on. He nods and says, "Thank you."

You give him a salute and begin wrapping the wound. You have trouble keeping it tight enough to be of benefit. You are only vaguely aware of a discussion occurring inside. Then, to your surprise, the door opens, and the redhead emerges with a handful of items.

The door quickly closes behind her. She gives a quick, fearful look, then forces a smile. "I'm sorry. We're just a bit freaked by what's going on out here. Let me do that for you."

You lift your arm. She wipes the six-inch cut with a disinfectant wipe, then spreads an anti-biotic cream over the wound. "Put your hand on my shoulder." You do. She wraps your arm and tapes the gauze in place.

"That should do it."

You lower your arm. "Thanks. I appreciate the help."

"Take these." She hands you the gauze, tape, and cream. "You should change the bandage at least once a day. Keep it clean. If it looks infected, come back." She glances behind her. "I can't guarantee we'll be here or that the others will be accepting, but if we are, I'll take care of it."

You nod. "I hate to bother you for something else, but my girlfriend/boyfriend has been bitten and I need something to help her. Do you have any antibiotics she/he can take, or anything to clean the wound with?

She gets a sad look on her face.

"Okay. Never mind, if it's too much to ask." Your tone is abrasive.

"No, it's not that. Really. It's just that when the outbreak first occurred and we began seeing patients with bites, we found there is nothing you can do for them. The bite secretes something in the blood. If they don't die, they become one of them. If your girlfriend/boyfriend has been bitten, she's/he's going to turn. I'm sorry. If she/he hasn't already turned, the best thing you can do is put her/him out of her/his misery. If it's too late, don't try to talk to her/him, because she/he won't recognize you. Your best bet is to end her/him, before she/he hurts someone else. If you can't do it, I advise you to get back in your vehicle and leave. If you try to save her/him, you may end up the same way." She places a gentle hand on your arm. "I'm truly sorry."

Her words shock you. You're too numb to think straight, but you have an urgent need to get home.

"Thank you." Back in the SUV, you head home at high speed. If her words are true, you want to get there before the change to say goodbye.

You park in the driveway and climb the stairs. The front door is open. Pulling the hatchet, you advance inside with caution, fearful you will discover your partner torn to shreds on the couch. However, once inside, you see the couch is empty. You call out but get no response. Slowly, you check the house. Your partner is not there.

Confused and concerned, you stand on the small porch and scan the area. Nothing. Was she/he carried away or was she/he chased? You have to find her/him. You try to decide whether to search on foot or by car, when she/he comes around the side of the house.

Your heart lightens with relief. You call out her/his name and start down the steps. The howl startles you. You freeze in your tracks and your heart sinks. The face is not looking at you with love, but like you're a meal. *Oh, no!* A sob catches in your throat. With a snarl, the creature now possessing the person you love charges at you.

You lift the hatchet. It is as heavy as your heart. From your elevated position on the porch, you strike down with a crushing blow. The hatchet blade plows deep into the skull. As the body crumples to the ground, you drop to your knees, and cry. Other howls are raised, and you have no time to morn. It will have to come later. Much later. For now, you have to find a safe place to hide…if one still exists.

You reach out to touch your partner one last time, but your hand stops inches from the grotesque face. It is no longer that of the one you love. She/he is long gone. You pull back, get in the car, and drive away.

Go to Chapter 3 on page 245

2A3c2) Before panic takes over, you whirl on the door and say, "Let me in."

They look from the creatures to you, but no one moves. You grab the handle and give it several hard pulls. "Open the door."

The redhaired woman makes a move toward the door, but the shorter woman blocks her. They have words, but the panic has risen to a point the blood pulsing through your head is all you can hear. You look over your shoulder and see the creatures closing fast. You jab your arm through the hole, and the dark-haired woman lunges to prevent you from snaking your arm inside.

While she's occupied, the taller woman reaches around her and flicks the lock. You pull the door open and step in, closing it just as the two arrive. You hold the door while the redhead snaps the lock. You back away, your heart racing.

For a few seconds, they bang on the glass door, then the woman finds the hole and snakes an arm through. You pull the knife and stab into her wrist. She howls and retracts the arm.

"See what you did!" the shorter woman snaps.

"Now's not the time, Meg," the taller woman says.

Meg turns and runs to the back room.

Clearly frightened, the man says to you, "What are we going to do?"

"We have to keep them out, but we are still going to have to deal with them, which means going outside."

The man pales and looks as if he might faint. He'll be of no help. The redhead, however, doesn't look as rattled. She continues to slap at the beast's hands. The extended hand gives you an idea. "Can you grab one of their hands?"

She gives you a *wha chu talkin 'bout, Willis* look.

"Just hold it for a few seconds. Go for the woman's."

She focuses on the hands and makes a few attempts, but each time she makes contact, she cringes away. You stab at the male's hand until sticking it once deep enough to make it think twice about returning. This gives the redhead a better chance, and soon she snags and pulls it through the opening.

You place the serrated blade across the wrist and saw. The beast howls and pulls, but the man steps up and lends a hand. Between the two of them they hold the arm long enough for you to severe the vein. As a gout of blood shoots into the air, you say, "Okay. Let her go."

The beast holds her pulsing arm and runs in circles on the sidewalk. The male beast watches as if intrigued, but it no longer sticks its claw-like hand through the hole.

"We're going to have to entice the other one," you say.

"What did you have in mind?" she says in a tone that suggests she really doesn't want to know. She's wiping her hand vigorously on her pants as if wiping off cooties.

You give the question some thought, then bend and place your face at the hole. The male is still watching the woman dance, but her efforts are slowing. You call, "Hey!" It jerks its head and eyes you warily. You press your face into the hole, trying not to cut yourself. It watches you. You pull away from the hole slowly. You repeat the process twice more before it snarls and lunges at you. The hand scrapes the glass next to the hole, knocking another shard to the floor. You move close to the hole again. It grabs at you, this time coming through the hole. You barely avoid him. Keeping your face level with the hole, you howl at it. Confused, it tilts its head back and answers, then squats and sniffs at the hole.

You tighten the grip on the knife, lean closer and howl again. This time, it snarls and jams its face through the hole in an attempt to bite you. As fast as you can move, you drive the knife deep into the beast's eye. It howls in anguish and pulls back, taking the knife with it. For a moment, you watch stunned, then you yank the hatchet out and unlock the door. Before the redhead can stop you, you step outside.

The creature looks at you through one good eye, snarls, and slashes at you. You jump back, then stride forward, slamming the hatchet down on its head. Once. Twice. It falls. Then, a third time to be sure. Stepping back, you look at the woman. She is on her knees and fading fast.

You stand prepared, then her eyes roll up and she collapses. A minute later, she stops breathing.

Behind you, the door opens and the redhead steps out. She has a few medical supplies. "I'm sorry for this, but they're afraid to let you back in. Meg is having a meltdown and Bill…well, Meg's his girlfriend."

You nod, as if that makes everything all right.

"I want to wrap that cut on your arm. Is that okay?"

You lift your arm. She wipes the six-inch cut with a disinfectant wipe, then spreads an antibiotic cream over the wound. "Put your hand on my shoulder." You do. She wraps your arm and tapes the gauze in place. "That should do it."

You lower your arm. "Thanks. I appreciate the help."

"Take these." She hands you the gauze, tape, and cream. "You should change the bandage at least once a day. Keep it clean. If it looks infected, come back." She glances behind her. "I can't guarantee we'll be here or that the others will be accepting, but if we are, I'll take care of it."

You nod. "I hate to bother you for something else, but my girlfriend/boyfriend has been bitten and I need something to help her/him. Do you have any antibiotics she/he can take, or anything to clean the wound with?

She gets a sad look on her face.

"Okay. Never mind, if it's too much to ask." Your tone is abrasive.

"No, it's not that. Really. It's just that when the outbreak first happened and we began seeing patients with bites, we found there is nothing you can do for them. The bite secrets something in the blood. If they don't die, they become one of them. If your girlfriend/boyfriend has been bitten, she's/he's going to turn. I'm sorry. The best thing you can do is to put her/him out of her/his misery if she hasn't already turned. If it's too late, don't try to talk to her/him. She/He won't recognize you. Your best bet is to end her/him before she/he hurts someone else. If you can't do it, I advise you to get back in your vehicle and leave. If you try to save her/him, you may end up the same way." She places a gentle hand on your arm. "I'm truly sorry."

Her words shock you. You're too numb to think straight but have an urgent need to get home.

"Thank you," you mutter as you get back in the car and head toward home at high speed. If her words are true, you want to get there before the change to say goodbye.

Go to *** on page 157

2A3c3) You turn toward the door, but the three people inside are backing away. One after the other they turn and disappear behind the door leading to the offices. You turn to face them, knife in one hand, hatchet in the other.

The beasts approach at a run. You bolster your confidence and as they close with vicious snarls, you emit one of your own and step forward to meet them. Holding the knife out, you raise the hatchet high. You swing downward at the woman and try to stab the male. Though you score a hit on both, their combined momentum drives you backward. You slam hard into the glass door, knocking the breath out of your lungs.

Blood is everywhere, though you're not sure whose it is. You twist from the grasp of the man and stab the woman in the face. She screams and backs away. The man slashes you across the back. You arch away and cry your own anguished howl.

You spin and swing the hatchet, but the angle is wrong. It bounces off the male's back. He takes you down and your head smacks on the cement, sending white stars dancing before your eyes. You shake the effects off, knowing a moment's hesitation might mean your life.

As the beast opens its inhumanly wide mouth to bite you, you push the hatchet's handle between its teeth. It snaps down and tries to rip it from your grasp. In the meantime, your other hand stabs with the knife. It bites into soft flesh but doesn't appear to deter the beast's attack.

You push up with the hatchet and twist the blade. The pain infuriates the creature, who doubles its efforts to rip your face off. Digging its teeth deep into the wooden handle, it twists its head and yanks the hatchet away. It spits it out and you desperately jab and twist the knife again.

Something small and silver comes into view. It moves in front of the creature, then whips back. A fine line of red appears on its neck a fraction before the gush of blood covers you. You gag as some of the blood lands in your mouth and eyes.

The weight is lifted from you and you sit up. You're soaked in blood and unable to see through the blurry mess.

A hand touches you, causing you to swing the knife.

"Easy. I'm from inside. Here to help you. Can you stand?"

"I think so."

She helps you up. She is only a shadow, but from her height, you guess it's the taller redheaded woman. She wipes at your eyes, but that only manages to smear the blood more.

"Come. Let's go inside so I can clean you up and get a look at your wounds." She takes your arm and then you hear, "Meg, you open this door now, or I swear, I'll break it down myself."

After a slight delay, you hear the lock snap and you are moving again.

Meg says, "This is a huge mistake. We don't know anything about him. You should have left him outside."

"Shut up, Meg."

You say, "Yeah, shut up, Meg."

"Bill, give me a hand."

Another hand grips your other arm and you are led through an inner door and into a seat. A few seconds later, the redhead comes into view as she washes the veil from your eyes. She gives you a thorough once over, and not finding anything more serious than the cut on your arm, she sets about cleansing and dressing the wound.

"There. I think that will fix you up. You'll need to change out the bandage at least once a day. If it gets infected, come back. I'm not sure we'll be here, but you can check."

"Thanks for doing this and for saving my life. Would it be too much to ask for something to help my girlfriend/boyfriend? She's/he's been bitten by one of those things. I only left to find medical help or supplies. I have to get back."

She gets a sad look on her face.

"Okay. Never mind, if it's too much to ask." Your tone is abrasive.

"No, it's not that. Really. It's just that when the outbreak first happened and we began seeing patients with bites, we found there is nothing you can do for them. The bite secretes something in the blood. If they don't die, they become one of them. If your girlfriend/boyfriend has been bitten, she's/he's going to turn. I'm sorry. The best thing you can do is put her/him out of her/his misery if she/he hasn't already turned. If it's too late, don't try to talk to her/him. They she/he won't recognize you. Your best bet is to end her/him before she/he hurts someone else. If you can't do it, I advise you to get back in your vehicle and leave. If you try to save her/him, you may end up the same way." She places a gentle hand on your arm. "I'm truly sorry."

Her words shock you. You're too numb to think straight but have an urgent need to get home.

"Thank you," you mutter as you get back in the car and head toward home at high speed. If her words are true, you want to get there before the change to say goodbye.

Go to *** on page 157

2B) "Well," you say, "we can either stay here, or go find others. Maybe if we find enough survivors, we'll be safe."

Your partner glances around the room. "Wouldn't it be better just to stay here? I mean, we're safe now."

"Yeah, but for how long? What happens when we run out of food? We'll have to leave the house, and who knows how much worse it might be then?"

"Don't you think they'll get the problem under control in a few days?"

"And what if they don't? We might be trapped here and forced out rather than go out now, when we still have a chance to get someplace."

"So, what are you suggesting? We drive around with no plan, just see what happens? If we're attacked out there, we'll have less chance to survive than if we stay."

You sigh. He/she has a point. Then, you say, "Why don't we go to your sister's?" That gets the response you hoped for. "We can start out, and if it's too hard to get through, come back. But if we go there, you'll have family around you. Plus, Frank will have a ton of stuff stored in the basement. You know what a prepper he is." The word *prepper* gives you pause. "Huh! Who knew that goofy guy would actually be right about something?"

"It's ten miles. Can we make it?"

"Only one way to know for sure." You shrug.  "Up to you."

"Yeah, thanks."

A few moments of silence pass, then he/she says, "Okay. Should we take stuff?"

"Yeah. Load up some clothes for each of us. I'll grab all the food, medicine, and whatever else we can find. It'll be better if we don't show up to your sister's empty handed."

"Why? You think they won't let us in?"

"Your sister will, but if Frank has the place locked down, you know how paranoid he is. He may not let us in." What you don't say is that he may shoot you both for trespassing.

You busy yourself with loading a few boxes and some large garbage bags with anything you think will have some use or value. You deposit each bag at the front door. Once you have everything you need, you take one last look around. A thought strikes.

You go back into the kitchen and grab the chef's knife and a steak knife. Ripping the flap from one of the cardboard boxes, you cut it in half, fold each half in half, then wrap each with layers of duct tape to create a sheath for each knife. You hand your partner the chef's knife and you slide the steak knife into your belt. Then you go downstairs and grab the hammer and the hatchet. They're not the greatest weapons, but at least you won't leave the house unarmed.

After checking the street, you load the car and climb in. However, before you can start the engine, a series of howls drifts down the street. Your partner gives you a tentative look. "Are you sure we're doing the right thing?"

*No*, you think, but force a smile to your face and pat his/her leg. "We'll be all right."

You drive away feeling less secure than you had a few minutes ago.

The route is hampered by abandoned vehicles, but you manage to make steady progress. On another road, you see a car moving at high speed. Twice creatures make a run at your car, but you leave them behind with no problem. Another time, a herd of creatures stops and eyes you as the car goes by. They are half a block away, and you're surprised they don't give pursuit. The sight of so many of them together is unnerving. If they organize and attack as a band, surviving will be more difficult.

You reach the halfway point on your journey and leave the city. Your partner's sister, Carol, lives in a more rural area. You make a turn on a two-lane road and find a semi lying on its side, blocking the path. A bloody heap that you assume was the driver is on the ground near the cab. You stop well short of the obstruction.

"Now what?" your partner asks.

Good question.

Do you:

2B1) try to find a way around? Read on.

2B2) find an alternate route? Go to page 200

2B3) call 911 to report an accident? Sorry, I just wanted to give you a third choice. If this worked, the story would've ended on page two.

2B1) You inch forward, keeping one eye on the rig in case any creatures are lurking behind it, and one on the road. The trailer blocks both lanes and hangs over the drainage ditches on either side of the road.

You move toward the ditch on the right. It has a steep downward slope, but you try it anyway. The car angles, dangerously close to rolling. You stop, deciding there is little chance you'll get past. You throw it into reverse, but the wheels just spin. You have lost traction in the grassy slope.

After several minutes of spinning the wheels, you decide there's only one option left. You turn the tires and move straight down into the ditch. As you near the bottom, you turn to run horizontal. The car leans precariously and every time you hit a rock, the car threatens to flip.

You crawl along, but each time you try to climb back up the slope, the wheels spin. You opt to angle upwards a few feet at a time and maintain forward motion. You drive that way a hundred yards and are about to the halfway point. Ahead, the ditch ends, narrowing at a pipe that runs under the crossroad.

You are forced to angle faster than you want. The tires bite, and the climb goes well. The wheels begin to slide, but you catch a section of rocks and the car jolts upward. You crest the rise, elated to have made it, but your relief is short-lived as you come face to face with a mob of six creatures, all watching your progress with interest.

You stomp on the brake. The creatures eye you for a few more seconds before one tilts its face to the sky and howls. The others join in the chorus. An eerie chill descends over the car. You push the pedal down, but the car refuses to climb the final few feet. In panic you press the pedal down to the floor, but that only digs the wheels in further.

The creatures attack as one. Your partner screams. You join her/him a second later. The beasts slam into the car. They pound on the windows and climb onto the hood. With sudden awareness, you realize the car is moving. You discover if you feed the gas slowly, the added weight on the hood aids traction. You level off just as the passenger window implodes, sending glass shards through the interior. You feel pieces bite into your flesh, but you ignore them, concentrating on gaining momentum.

Still screaming, one arm covering her/ his head, your partner flails wildly with the chef's knife. The creature is joined by a second set of hands as they try to grab her/him.

The car increases speed. Once the front wheels touch pavement, you jam the pedal down and the car leaps forward. Those on the hood are thrown into the windshield. One rolls over the roof, dropping to the ground after bouncing off the trunk. One at the window falls away, but the second has a grip on the door frame and is hanging tough.

Swinging the wheel sharply from side to side dislodges the beast on the hood. Your partner slices the beast's fingers with the knife, and with a fading howl, the beast falls away. Keeping at a steady eighty miles per hour, you leave them behind in seconds.

Minutes later, you stamp on the brakes to make the turn onto the turn road leading to your destination. You barely miss a wire fence and two trees but manage to get back on the road. The surface is rough enough and you are forced to slow down to thirty.

The old farmhouse comes into view and you begin to relax. However, when you pull into the drive, you slow to a crawl. The place looks deserted. You stop in the large open area in front of the house.

"What do you think?" you ask.

"I'm scared. What if something has happened to them?" He/She spins fast and clutches your arm.

You sit silent for several minutes studying the house, barn, garage, and grounds. Nothing is moving.

"I'm getting out," your partner says. "I have to know."

You don't try to stop her/him. You leave the car running, but you get out, too. You can't shake the feeling someone is watching. You grip the hatchet, ready to fight if necessary. Your partner climbs the stairs and knocks on the front door. No one answers.

She/He moves along the wraparound porch, peering into each window. You stand watch. You don't see anyone, but for some reason, you are more nervous than before. The hairs on the back of your neck go up as if someone breathed on you from behind.

"We need to either get inside or back in the car," you say.

"Why? Do you see something?"

You don't answer.

"Well, do you?"

"It's not so much what I see as what I feel. I don't think we can linger here long."

She/He disappears around the far side of the house. Having her/him out of sight increases your anxiety to a level you didn't know existed.

Something moves in your periphery. You snap your head in that direction. Nothing. Was it your heightened angst, or did you see something? You stare at the spot for a moment, then something else draws your attention in the opposite direction. Again, nothing. Now, you think you're losing your mind.

You whip your head back to the first location and see a shape duck down fast. *Damn!* You run to the side of the house to warn your partner, but when you get there, she/he is gone. "What the ..."

You sprint across the ground along the side of the house. "Hey! Where are you? Something's coming. We have to go." Silence greets you. Panic takes on a new degree. Looking back, you see several forms lumbering through the fields. You have to find your partner as fast as possible. Racing hard to the end of the house, you round the back and still don't see her/him.

You scream her/his name. Unable to think, you decide you have to reach the car before the creatures arrive. Keeping them in sight as you go, you jump in the car while the beasts are still fifty yards away.

You drive around the house and cut behind it. You glance at the garage, then the house. She/He had to go inside one or the other.

Do you:

2B1a) stay in the car? Read on.

2B1b) go to the house? Go to page 192

2B1c) go to the garage? Go to page 196

2B1a) You have no idea where your partner went, which only adds to your level of anxiety. The beasts were closing in fast. If you don't find him/her fast, it might be too late. You stare at the back door. Was it open? Did she/he go inside? It's the only explanation you can come up with. Before you try the door, you want to be sure you're not leaving her/him outside. You move the car forward to view the far side of the house. Nothing.

You reverse and are about to get out and try the door, when you think, did she/he have enough time to get back to the front? Maybe she's/he's on the front porch? Do you dare take a chance? You know you can't. You could never live with yourself if something happened to her/him because you didn't check.

You decide to circle the entire house to be double sure. You drive forward, make the turn, reach the front, and turn again. Four creatures are running up the drive, less than twenty yards away. You drive slowly past the porch, roll down the passenger window and shout her/his name. No reply.

The creatures enter the open space as you go around the side of the house and drive toward the back. Hatchet in hand, you jump out of the car. Before you reach the door, the creatures burst around the house. You can't take a chance that the door is locked, so you sprint back to the car. You have it moving before the door closes.

Your first thought is to speed away, but you ease down on the brake and allow them to catch up. Wherever your partner is, it's better to lead the beasts away rather than leave them behind to find her/him.

They reach the car. One slams a hand on to the trunk. You move away, keeping a steady pace and allowing them to run next to you. Each time they close enough to touch the car, you pull away.

You turn down the long driveway and they follow. It's a long slow process, but eventually you reach the dirt road. You estimate you've gone a little more than a mile before they start to lose interest. They're still too close to the house, so you stop and let them make contact. One of them hops on the trunk. Two come up the driver's side and the fourth moves along the opposite side.

They snarl and pound on the glass. The one on the trunk climbs to the roof and bangs above your head. Fearing one will hit the window hard enough to shatter it, you drive on fast enough to avoid a solid shot to the glass, but not so fast it dislodges the rider on the roof.

You manage to string them along for another two miles before deciding you've had enough of their company. You punch the pedal. The car leaps, and the rider tumbles off. You increase speed gradually as they give chase, but in a few seconds, they are almost out of sight.

In another mile, you turn down a dirt road. Though unfamiliar with the area, you are going to come at the farmhouse from the opposite direction. It feels like you drive forever before reaching an intersection. You turn right. The road rises, then dips. As you come to the top of the next rise, you hit the brakes hard. At the bottom of this small hill is a group of ten creatures. They have encircled a horse and are trying to take it down. The frantic horse whinnies loud enough for you to hear. It runs at one beast who slashes at it, sending it scampering in the other direction. The circle closes on the terrified horse. One of the beast leaps and digs its claws into the horse's flank, then climbs to a sitting position on its back. The sight angers you. You press the pedal down and race to the rescue.

The beasts are so intent on bringing the horse down, they don't notice you until the last moment. You plow into them, sending some flying, some diving, and a few under your wheels. As you blow past, you watch the action in the mirror. The horse rears up, pitching the rider to the ground. It lifts its front legs again, knocking two creatures away, and landing on a third.

As soon as its hoofs touch down, it bolts. You feel elated you were able to free it. Now, it's on its own to stay safe. With a hoot of excitement, you speed away.

Minutes later, you turn, and a few minutes after that, you arrive at the farmhouse. You drive around back of the house, scan the area, then hop out. As you reach the back door, it is whipped open and your partner rushes into your arms.

"I was so worried!"

You reply, "I was worried about you. I had no idea where you were."

"I'm sorry. I should've…done something." She/He holds you tight and whispers, "Frank refused to let me open the door. He's not happy we're here. Feels we'll eat too much of his food." She/he releases you.

"Did you tell him we brought our own food?"

"No. I didn't think about it."

"Is he gonna let us stay?"

"My sister convinced him."

"Maybe a better question is, do you want to stay?"

"I don't know where else we can go."

"Okay. Help me get the bags in the house."

Carol comes out to help. You do not see Frank. Once inside and behind a locked door, Carol hugs you. "I'm so glad you're here."

"Are you sure it's all right?" you say.

"It'll be fine. Besides, you're not only family, but there's strength in numbers, right?"

"Yeah."

While your partner and her sister put away the supplies, you search for Frank. You find him in the second-floor bedroom overlooking the front of the house. His squat form fills the window. His hair has grown long, and he now sports a beard. You realize it's been a while since you've seen him. Not without good reason. He's usually, surly at best, and that's when he's sober. After a few beers, he gets loud and politically opinionated, daring anyone to take an opposing viewpoint.

"Hey, Frank!"

He grunts a reply.

"I want to thank you for letting us stay here."

He grunts again. "Just make sure you pull your weight. This ain't no place for freeloaders."

"Understood and not a problem. You can't watch all sides at once. I can watch the back."

He faces you. His dark beady eyes bore into you. "Yeah. That'd be good."

You nod and turn to leave.

"That was smart thinking, luring those things away from the house."

"Ah, thanks."

"How far'd you take 'em?'

"About three miles."

"Three? Huh!"

He returns to his vigil, and you realize he's done with you now. You leave, but he calls after you.

"You got any other weapons besides that knife and hatchet?"

"No."

He chuckles. "See, that's why us gun toters survive longer than you pacifists."

You bristle. You've had this discussion before. Neither you nor your partner had any interest in keeping a gun in the house. In retrospect, it's a bad decision. It's one of the things Frank hates about you.

"You'll need a gun. There's some in each room. Pick one. You do know how to use one, don't cha?"

"Yeah. I can shoot." You pace to the back bedroom. On the dresser is a shotgun and two handguns. Boxes of shells and bullets sit next to them as well as two fully loaded, extra magazines. It's obvious, this is the moment Frank has been planning for his whole life.

You pick a .40 caliber gun and the matching extra mag and stand by the window. As you stare out, you think about how life will never be the same again. Of course, none of that matters if you don't survive.

Go to Chapter 3 on page 275

2B1b) You park but leave the engine running. Scanning the grounds once more to be sure it's safe, you get out and jog to the door. Locked. You press your face against the window. You see stairs going up on the left and going down on the right. You know the right leads to the basement and the left to the kitchen. Calling your partner's name, you knock on the door. No reply. You knock louder, then walk to the other end of the house to look down the side.

No one is there. Did your partner go all the way around to the front? You move that way, looking up to see in the windows. You reach the front and go to the porch. It is a nice wraparound structure that covers the front and left sides of the house. You move from window to window, peering inside. At one point, you think a shadow flits along the far wall, but calling or knocking brings no one.

Frustrated, you lean over the porch rail and look at the barn. Could she/he have gone in there? Even so, why wouldn't she/he have come out or answered when you called? Unless...you swing your legs over the rail landing on the ground. In your haste to get to the barn, you lose balance and fall. Cursing, you get up and wipe the gravel from the scrapes on your hand.

Before you can move, a chorus of howls fills the air. You spin and gasp. Less than a hundred yards away are three creatures running toward you. You pivot, desperate to locate your partner. You call her/his name and run. The safest place to be at the moment is the car. You sprint toward it. You can hear the engine is still running.

As you turn corner, a beast comes around the opposite side of the house. You pause for an instant, judging the distance. It will be close. You yank the hatchet from your belt and run as hard as you can for the driver's door. You reach it as the beast arrives. Whipping the door open, you knock the beast off stride, but it hits the door so hard that it rebounds into your legs, staggering you backward.

Regaining balance, you shove the door open, but before you can get in, a heavy weight plows into you from behind. You are thrown into the door, your chin smacking on the frame, and you drop the hatchet. Pain erupts in your mouth. You fling an elbow back, striking the beast in the side of the head. The blow knocks it sideways. You attempt to get in the car again, but the first creature dives on you.

You hit the car and bounce off, but despite your best effort, you are dragged to the ground. You kick first one, then the other, to get maneuvering room, but even as you struggle to your feet, hope is diminished as two more creatures round the house and zero in on you.

You drive a fist into one beast and swing your cast like a club into the second. Bending, you retrieve the hatchet and raise it to strike, but the next creature arrives too fast. It tackles you and you roll, limbs entwined.

The other beasts close in, and you pray your racing heart explodes long before they start eating you. You swing the hatchet with feeble effort. Just as the mouths move toward you and a horrifying nightmare comes true, a shot cracks and one of the weights is lifted from you. A second shot knocks another one down.

Then, a flurry of legs come into view. Grunts, groans, snarls, and howls mingle in a bizarre symphony. In seconds, you are free and staring up into your partner's worried face.

"Are you all right?"

"Where the hell were you?"

A nervous glance draws your attention to a short, burly man, with black hair and beard. He is pointing a rifle at you.

"Oh. Hi, Frank. How's it going?"

In response, he says, "Check to see if he's been bit or scratched."

"And what if I am, Frank? You gonna put me down like a rabid dog?"

"Bet your ass I am. Better that than have you turn into one of them and attack us."

You partner does a quick, but thorough examination. "He's clean. The only blood is the creatures."

"What about his mouth? Looks like he bit one of them."

"Well good," you say with a hint of sarcasm. "Then maybe they'll all turn into me."

Your partner helps you up, but Frank continues to point the rifle.

"Still ain't answered my question. Where'd the blood come from?"

"I hit my face on the door when one of those things jumped on my back."

"Come on, Frank," your partner says. "Let's go inside before more of these things show up."

He motions toward the house with the barrel but does not lower it. Your partner guides you to the door and inside the house. Frank follows at a distance. Once up the stairs into the kitchen, your partner's sister, Carol, runs to embrace you. Frank stops her.

"Carol, check him out for any bites or scratches."

"Frank, seriously? I told you he didn't have any," your partner says.

"Do it, Carol."

She says, "Sorry," to you, then continues to scan you. Done, she nods to Frank. It's several seconds before he lowers the rifle. "Okay, then. You're here. Do your fair share and be useful." With that, he walks past you. Heavy footsteps announce he is going upstairs.

Carol hugs you. "I'm sorry about that. He's even more paranoid than usual. He stands watch upstairs for hours at a time."

"It's okay, Carol. I understand. I'm glad you two are all right."

Your partner hugs you next. "He wouldn't let me go out until he was sure we weren't followed. Then those things showed up, and he went crazy. If it wasn't for Carol, he might have left you out there."

*Bastard!*

Though your anger rises, you don't want to do anything to cause Frank to change his mind about letting you stay. Changing the subject, you say, "We didn't come emptyhanded. We have a car full of food and supplies."

"That's good," Carol says. "That'll go a long way to easing things with Frank."

"Let's unload, then."

Three trips each empties the car. While they sort and stock the items, you go upstairs. You find him in the front bedroom, keeping vigil out the window.

Without facing you, he says, "You got any other weapons but that knife and hatchet?"

"No."

He chuckles. "See, that's why us gun toters survive longer than you pacifists."

You bristle. You've had this discussion before. Neither you nor your partner had any interest in keeping a gun in the house. In retrospect, it was a bad decision, and one of the things Frank hates about you.

"You'll need a gun. There's some in each room. Pick one. You do know how to use one, don't cha?"

"Yeah. I can shoot." You pace to one of the back bedrooms. On the dresser is a shotgun and two handguns. Boxes of shells and bullets sit next to them as well as two fully loaded extra magazines. It's obvious that this is the moment Frank has been planning for his whole life.

You pick a .40 caliber gun and the matching extra mag and stand by the window. As you stare out the window, you think how your life will never be the same again. Of course, none of that matters if you don't survive.

Go to Chapter 3 page 275

2B1c) Puzzled, you glance from the house to the barn. If your partner went inside the house, she/he would either be standing there so you can see her/him or would've left the door open, so you'd know where she/he was. That leaves the barn.

You drive the car in a slow turn until you are in front of the large wooden barn door. You honk once but get no response. Scanning the grounds to make sure you're alone, you get out, leaving the engine running. Gripping the edge of the door, you push it along the overhead rail until it's wide enough to walk through.

You call out inside once, then again. After getting no reply, you enter. The barn is dark. The light entering through the door is limited to the distance it is open. You go back and push the door, exposing the entire interior. One side has three stalls, all empty. The right side has a work bench, assorted tools, a riding mower, and a stack of hay bales. In the middle, against the rear wall, is an old tractor. What you don't find is your partner.

Baffled, you return to the front door and stare out. The only other choice is the garage, but you would have seen her/him cross the yard. If she/he was inside the house, why wouldn't she/he let you know? Unless, of course, someone or something was inside and didn't let her/him. The thought sends a new round of panic through you. However, before you can react, a series of howls reaches your ears.

You freeze, blood turning cold. The howls come again, but you can't tell from where. You go to the car, but before you get in, you catch sight of someone looking out the window to the left of the back door. You wave, but whoever was there is gone.

You start toward the house, but before you get halfway, two beasts come from around the far side. They spy you, howl, and lope forward. You have no chance of making it to the house unless you're sure the door is open. If you get there and find it locked, you'll be trapped.

Two more come up along the near side. You pivot and bolt for the car. Opening the door, you jump in, but the first two beasts arrive before you can close it. A tug-o-war ensues with the door as the rope.

Pulling back with all your weight, you risk losing control of the door by releasing one hand to shift into drive.

It works, but the door is ripped from your grasp. You stamp down on the pedal and the car races forward. Your hands are busy fending off the beasts rather than steering. You pull away from the beasts, but the car angles toward the barn. You grip the wheel and whip it in the opposite direction but are forced to brake to avoid hitting the barn. The move swings you back toward the beasts.

Door still flopping open, one manages to leap inside and slam into you. You are knocked away from the wheel, but you press the gas pedal. The sudden increase in speed prevents the others from getting in, but you no longer have control of the wheel as you fight with the beast.

The arc of the turn brings the car into the opening of the barn. The car collides with the side of the door, knocking it off the rail. It falls, smashing one of the creatures beneath it. The car stops. Desperate to get away, you kick at the creature, driving it out of the car. You scoot over the console to the passenger seat, open the door, and hop out.

You run to the tractor and climb up. Withdrawing the hatchet, you stand poised to defend. The beast in the car crawls through. The other two climb over the top of the car. All three advance toward you, teeth snapping and drool flying. They spread out and approach.

You scan from one to the next, trying to organize a fighting sequence, but when they attack, it's as one and your plan falls apart. You kick the first one down and swing the hatchet at the second. It's a glancing blow, but still causes the beast pain. It backs away and eyes you warily.

The third one scampers up the tire and stands facing you. You raise your weapon, ready to strike, when a shot is fired, the noise echoing in the barn. The beast on the tire arcs forward. Blood splatters your face. The beast topples to the ground.

One of the survivors turns and snarls at the short, burly man holding the rifle. It charges, only to be blown off its feet by a second shot.

The third one clambers up the side of the tractor. As it reaches for you, you bring the hatchet down on its head. The blade bites deep;

blood and ooze flow out. It falls backward, taking the hatchet with it. It twitches on the ground for a minute before dying. You jump down, retrieve the hatchet, and look up to thank your brother-in-law, but he is gone.

You jog to follow. He enters the house and you run after him. By the time you arrive, the door is locked. "What? Come on, Frank."

The door opens, and your partner is there. You get an emotional hug. "I'm sorry," she/he says. "Frank wouldn't let me go to you. He's being an even bigger dick than normal."

You shut the door without response and the two of you climb the stairs into the kitchen. Inside, you find Carol. She moves to embrace you, but Frank stops her. You notice he's pointing the rifle directly at you.

"Carol, check her/him out for any bites or scratches."

"Frank, seriously? I told you she/he didn't have any," your partner says.

"Do it, Carol."

She says, "Sorry," to you, then continues to scan you. Done, she nods to Frank. It's several seconds before he lowers the rifle. "Okay, then. You're here. Do your fair share and be useful." With that, he walks out. Heavy footsteps announce he is going upstairs.

Carol hugs you. "I'm sorry about that. He's even more paranoid than usual. He stands watch upstairs for hours at a time."

"It's okay, Carol. I understand. I'm glad you two are all right."

Though your anger rises, you don't want to do anything to cause Frank to change his mind about letting you stay. Changing the subject, you say, "We didn't come empty handed. We have a car full of food and supplies."

"That's good," Carol says. "That'll go a long way to easing things with Frank."

"Let's unload, then."

Three trips each empties the car. While they sort and stock the items, you go upstairs. You find him in the front bedroom, keeping vigil out the window.

Without facing you, he says, "You got any other weapons but that knife and hatchet?"

"No."

He chuckles. "See, that's why us gun toters survive longer than you pacifists."

You bristle. You've had this discussion before. Neither you nor your partner had any interest in keeping a gun in the house. In retrospect, it was a bad decision, and one of the things Frank hates about you.

"You'll need a gun. There's some in each room. Pick one. You do know how to use one, don't cha?"

"Yeah. I can shoot." You pace to one of the back bedrooms. On the dresser is a shotgun and two handguns. Boxes of shells and bullets sit next to them, as well as two fully loaded extra magazines. It's obvious that this is the moment Frank has been planning for his whole life.

You pick a .40 caliber gun and the matching extra mag and stand by the window. As you stare out the window, you think how your life will never be the same again. Of course, none of that matters if you don't survive.

Go to Chapter 3 page 275

2B2) Not sure you can squeeze past without sliding down the steep drainage ditch, you decide to retrace your route and find another. You back up and swing the car across the road. Before you can shift into forward gear, your partner exclaims, "Oh no! Hurry!"

You glance up to see three beasts racing toward you from around the semi. You feed gas and pull away, leaving them snarling angrily. You watch in the mirror as they fade to tiny dots. "Whew! That was close."

Your partner gives no reply. You look to find her/him wringing their hands. "Are you all right?" She/He looks at you, wide-eyed and sweating. "Maybe we should just go home."

"Hey! Relax. We're okay. They didn't even get close to us."

"This time. But what happens if we do run into them?"

"I'll drive right through them."

"And if you can't?"

"We'll face that if and when it happens."

"We should turn back."

"We're almost halfway there. We need to keep going. It'll be safer when we get there."

"What if—what if they're not there?"

"They will be. Frank would never leave his fortress."

"But what if they're dead? Or worse? What if they're one of those things?"

"You're making yourself crazy. We won't know anything until we get there." She/He doesn't say anything more; however, each mile you go, she/he becomes more agitated.

You make a series of turns, working your way toward the farmhouse using back roads. Few obstacles block the path. You see a few of the creatures in the distance, but none are a threat. Twice you make a turn that leads to a dead end and are forced to go back.

In another mile, you turn down another dirt road. Though unfamiliar with the area, you are confident you'll come at the farmhouse from the opposite direction. It feels like you drive forever before reaching an intersection. You turn right. The road rises, then dips. As you come to the top of the next rise, you hit the brakes hard. At the bottom of this small hill is a group of ten creatures. They have encircled a horse and are trying to take it down. The frantic horse whinnies loud enough for you to hear. It runs at one beast, who slashes at it, sending it scampering in the other direction. The circle closes in on the terrified horse. One beast leaps and digs its claws into the horse's flank, then climbs to a sitting position on its back. The sight angers you. To your surprise, your partner says nothing.

You shift into reverse, but before the car moves, your partner places a restraining hand on your arm. "We can't leave it for those beasts to tear it apart."

You look from her/him to the horse and nod. *Yes.* It's what you would've done, had you been alone. You're glad your partner feels the same way. "Hold on. The Lone Ranger and Tonto to the rescue."

Your partner responds with, "More like the Stoned Ranger and Blotto."

Despite the danger, you laugh and begin humming The Lone Ranger's Theme. You press the pedal down and race to the rescue.

The beasts are so intent on bringing the horse down, they don't notice you until the last moment. You plow into them, sending some flying, some diving, and a few under your wheels. As you blow past, you watch the action in the mirror. The horse rears up, pitching the rider to the ground. It lifts its front legs again, knocking two creatures away, and landing on a third.

As soon as its hoofs touch down, it bolts. You feel elated that you were able to free it. Now it's on its own to stay safe. With a hoot of excitement from your partner, you speed away.

A short distance later, you come to the road you need. It is a dirt road filled with many depressions that keep you bouncing. Half a mile down the road, you turn into a long dirt driveway. The farmhouse stands tall in front of you. You come into a large clearing in front of the house and stop.

You exchange glances. The place looks deserted. Your partner opens the door, but before she/he can get out, you hear a scream coming from behind the house.

"Close the door," you say and drive before it shuts.

As you move past the farmhouse, you see a woman fending off two beasts. She has no weapon other than her hands.

"Oh my God! It's Carol."

You stomp the pedal down and aim for the closest beast. It turns while you're still ten yards away and dodges to the side. You clip it, sending it flying. The second one flees, but you quickly catch and run it down. The car bounces over the body.

Whipping the wheel, you spin around in a cloud of dust. Carol runs for the house. The first beast is rising. You accelerate. It leaps, landing on the hood. It kicks at the front windshield. You brake hard, pitching it off the car.

As it rises again, a gunshot cracks and the beast topples over. You look to see Frank standing outside the back door with a rifle. You're relieved the fight is over until he swings the rifle in your direction.

Your partner rolls down the window and leans out. "Frank, it's me. Don't shoot."

Carol runs out the rear door and yanks Frank's arms down. She has some heated words for him. He goes in house. Carol runs to you. Your partner gets out and rushes to meet her. They embrace. They talk, but you stay in the car and wait for directions.

They walk over to the car and Carol says, "I'm so glad to see you. I was worried."

"Is it okay we're here?" you ask.

"Of course. You know how Frank is. He may not show it, but he's glad you're here, too. We can use the extra support."

You doubt Frank's thrilled to see you, but as long as it's cool with Carol, you're good with staying.

"Pull up behind the house and we can unload what you brought."

You do. Three trips each later, the car is empty. You leave them to organize the items and go upstairs to find Frank. You find him in the front bedroom, keeping vigil out the window.

"Hey Frank. Thanks."

Without facing you, he says, "You got any other weapons but that knife and hatchet?"

"No."

He chuckles. "See, that's why us gun toters survive longer than you pacifists."

You bristle. You've had this discussion before. Neither you nor your partner had any interest in keeping a gun in the house. In retrospect, it's a bad decision, and one of the things Frank hates about you.

"You'll need a gun. There's some in each room. Pick one. You do know how to use one, don't cha?"

"Yeah. I can shoot." You pace to one of the back bedrooms. On the dresser is a shotgun and two handguns. Boxes of shells and bullets sit next to them as well as two fully loaded, extra magazines. It's obvious that this is the moment Frank has been planning for his whole life.

You pick a .40 caliber gun and the matching extra mag and stand by the window. As you stare out the window, you think how your life will never be the same again. Of course, none of that matters if you don't survive.

Go to Chapter 3 page 275

Chapter 2 (1A2a3c2, 1A2a3c3)

You walk for nearly a mile, checking cars as you pass. You find many of them open, but none with keys. You are tired and in pain. Your head and arm throb in competition for the most attention. You pass several bodies in various stages of consumption. Flies and crawly things roam the remains. You pass a three-car collision with two bodies splayed on the street and can only imagine the horror of their last moments.

One of the bodies has keys in its hand. That gives you a head-slap moment. You should have been checking the other corpses you passed for keys. With that in mind, you walk another half mile before coming to a woman's body. Her face is missing, as is most of her flesh, but the creatures must be discriminating about their food, because all the internal organs remain.

The sight causes you to retch several times. It's obvious the woman doesn't have keys on her, but you find a large purse near a blue Honda. You pick it up, set it on the hood and rifle through the contents. You find a pepper spray, a bottle of generic pain pills, and the key fob. *Yes!*

Excited, you squeeze into the car and adjust the seat. The engine starts, and you sit back in relief. Then, a spike of panic and you lock the doors. With a sigh, you open the pill container and swallow two. You read the label for dosage use, shrug, and swallow a third.

You are about to pull away when you catch a flash of movement in the mirror. Instinctively, you duck and push back into the seat as a small knife whistles past your head. It embeds into the seat near your head. You reach up, grab the arm attached to the blade, and yank hard. A shrill scream proceeds a female body as if flies into the front seat, impacting with the dash.

With a cry of pain and a frenzied defense, the young girl fends you off. Seeing she is not one of the creatures, you try to secure her hands and speak to her.

"Hey! Hey! Hey! I'm not going to hurt you. I'm not one of those things. Stop. Ow!" One of her wild kicks lands on your cheek. You pitch her to the side and she lands upside down on the passenger seat.

"Stop or get out. I'm not going to fight with you."

She kicks again, but this time, you snatch her foot and hold it. She struggles to get free. "Let go, asshole."

"I'll let go if you stop kicking."

"Never."

"Well, then get out and walk. I need this car."

"You get out and walk. This is my mom's car."

That causes you to stop and pale. She must not know her mother's dead. You also want to spare her the sight. You look at the girl. You estimate she's in the fourteen to sixteen age range.

Releasing her leg, you drive away to prevent her from having to see her mother's shredded body.

"Hey! You can't go. My mom's coming back. We can't leave her."

"Was your mother wearing a Steeler's sweatshirt?"

She stops kicking and looks at you. The color drains from her face. "Why?"

"I hate to tell you, but your mother's dead."

"You're lying." She scampers up the seat to look out the back window. You stop the car.

"You see that…" you search for the right word, but soon realize, there isn't one. "…that body in the street? That's your mom."

"No. Mom!" she screams and tries to open the door.

You punch the gas pedal and she falls face first into the seat. "Stop! I have to go to her. She might need help."

"She's beyond anyone's help. I'm sorry."

Her face seems to shrink in on her. Then, hard steel fills her eyes. She opens the door and readies to jump out. You screech to a stop, so she won't get hurt. As soon as you do, she leaps out and runs. You contemplate whether to drive off, but you can't do it.

You watch her progress in the mirror. She is halfway to the body when you see two hulking forms emerge from behind a house. They spot her and beeline in her direction. This equation makes you rethink driving off.

Do you:

2A) drive off? Read on.

2B) go back for her? Go to page 208

2A) You watch as the two creatures close in on her. If you don't do something right then, it'll be too late to save her. You shift into reverse but hesitate on the gas. You don't want to have to fight those creatures. She reaches her mother's body and drops to her knees. She's oblivious to the creatures coming at her. She tilts her head skyward and shrieks her grief.

You watch as the creatures swarm over her and drive off before the conclusion. Tears roll down your face and you curse yourself for being the coward you are. You try to rationalize that you wouldn't have made a difference to the outcome, but you know in your heart it's not true. You'll never know for sure.

You cry all the way home.

You park in the driveway and climb the stairs. The front door is open. Pulling the canister of pepper spray, you advance inside with caution, fearful you will discover your partner torn to shreds on the couch. However, once inside, you find the couch is empty. You call out but get no response. Slowly, you check the house. Your partner is not there.

Confused and concerned, you stand on the small porch and scan the area. Nothing. Was she/he carried away or was she/he chased? You have to find her/him. You try to decide whether to search on foot or by car, when she/he comes around the side of the house.

Your heart lightens with relief. You call out her/his name and start down the steps. The howl startles you. You freeze in your tracks and your heart sinks. The face is not looking at you with love, but like you're a meal. *Oh, no!* A sob catches in your throat. With a snarl, the creature now possessing the person you love charges at you.

You are too overwhelmed with emotion to move. As she/he reaches the porch, you back away. You lift the spray. It is as heavy as your heart. You aim and fire the spray. It releases in a stream. The initial jet catches it in the mouth, but it never slows. Its howl is hoarser than before, but otherwise is not affected. You take two more steps backward, but the porch is small. Your second step finds air, and with a scream, you fall.

Your foot lands in the flower bed and you fall on your back on top of a rose bush. The thorns gouge your skin. You barely notice as your partner catapults over the porch landing on you. All the air is driven from your lungs in a painful gasp.

Your partner claws your face. The pain is intense. You throw the worthless pepper spray into its face and kick and buck to dislodge the thing. It digs its claws into your chest and any effort to remove the beast creates longer and deeper furrows.

With all the desperation-fueled strength you can draw, you muscle the creature to the side, but as you pull away, it slashes at you. The pain in your neck is lost within that of the other wounds. You don't realize there's a problem until you try to stand and see the jet of blood drenching the beast.

In shock, you stand and press a hand to your neck. It is coated in blood in an instant. You stare down at your partner and call their name. Then, your legs buckle and your partner dives on you. You barely feel the first bite. By the third bite, blackness closes in on you. Your final thought is of the girl you left to die and understand how fitting your own death is.

End

2B) You have to save her. She is obviously unaware of the danger closing in on her. You don't want her to end up like her mother. You shift and floor the pedal, but the two beasts are so zeroed in on their target, the car doesn't register until you are almost right on them. One manages to dive aside, but the other disappears under the car, and with a satisfying bump, you know one is down.

You pull to a stop next to the girl and fling the passenger door open. She is kneeling next to her mother's corpse. "Hey! Get in. One of them's coming."

She doesn't hear you over her wailing. You honk to get her attention. She looks in your direction, but you doubt she sees you through the tears. "Hurry, or you'll end up like your mother." Not a great thing to say, but you need to shock her into motion. Still, she doesn't move.

You glance out the windshield. The one is a lump in the road, but the other approaches fast. The girl doesn't have much time. You shift and speed to intercept the beast. It dodges around you without breaking stride and continues toward the unsuspecting girl.

You reverse but arrive too late. The beast launches and drives the girl down. Her face scrapes across the pavement. You stop and leap from the car. Not sure how to attack the beast without a weapon, you run up and deliver a vicious kick to its ribs. The force is enough to lift it off the girl. She is shrieking in a blind panic.

Before the beast can regain its feet, you run closer and kick it again. It rolls several times and you follow. You miss a stomp to the head, but your second attempt results in audible cracks from the ribs. It howls and clutches its chest.

While it is incapacitated, you race to the girl. You scoop her up, but she fights you the entire way. You manage to half carry, half drag her to the car. Opening the back door, you pitch her inside, close the door, and run around the car.

The beast is getting to its feet, but slow enough to let you get safely seated. It takes a long jump at the trunk as you pull away. It misses and hits the pavement. You whoop in elation and drive off. The girl curls in a ball and sobs.

Your heart aches for her. So much trauma. How would she ever be sane? Seeing her mother like that and almost joining her is would be enough to send anyone over the edge.

You drive on, trying to blank your mind to the horrors.

When you reach the house, the girl sits up and looks around.

"Where are we?"

"My house. I have to see if my girlfriend/boyfriend is here. You want to stay here or come in?"

"I'll stay here."

You start to get out, then stop and take the keys. You climb the steps and knock on the door. No answer. You knock again and peer through the picture window. Your partner is lying down on the couch, apparently asleep. You knock again and this time, she/he stirs. Her/His face looks bruised and exhausted. An instant spike of angst pierces your heart. She/He gets up on shaky legs and staggers to the door. It takes several moments to open it, and as you step inside, you catch her/him before she/he falls.

"Oh my God! Are you all right? What happened?"

You carry her/him to the couch and lay her/him down. The face that looks back at you is of a stranger. A weak smile touches her/his face. You brush hair back from her/his face, then notice it is covered in blood. Your heart ceases its beating for an instant as your eyes go wide. "You're hurt. Where?"

You roll her/him on the side and see a circular bloody wound the size of a mouth above the waist. You gasp, jump up, and retrieve paper towels, hydrogen peroxide, bandages, and tape. Quickly, you set to work wiping away the blood, then dousing the area with the peroxide. She/he gasps.

You wipe the wound again, then press a bandage against it. You tear off two strands with your teeth and secure the bandage.

Your partner rolls over and looks at you through pained eyes.

"One got inside. I killed it and dragged it out back. It bit me, though. I thought I'd never see you again."

A lump forms in your throat. You croak, swallow hard, and say, "I'm here now. Everything's gonna be okay."

She/he places a palm on your face. "I don't think it's safe here. Can you take me to my sister's? It'll be safer there, and she can tend to me better."

"Yeah. If that's what you want." You wipe away tears. "You want me to pack some things?"

"That'd be good."

"Okay. You rest. I'll be back."

You stand and see the girl is standing at the front door. She looks from your girlfriend/boyfriend to you. "Is she/he going to be all right?"

You offer a false smile. "Yes. I think so. I'm gonna take her/him to her/his sisters. It's out in the country and should be safer. You want to go, too?"

She shrugs.

"Well, can you help me pack some things?"

"Okay." But she sounds anything but sure she wants to come further inside.

Without waiting to see what she does, you go to the bedroom and pack two suitcases with clothes. When you come back, the girl is still standing at the door. You leave the suitcases at her feet. "Can you take these outside for me?"

She doesn't reply, but again, you don't wait. In the kitchen, you fill large black garbage bags with food and medical supplies. The girl is just coming back inside when you arrive. "Here, take one of these. Careful. They're heavy."

You end up with four bags of stuff. The trunk fills fast. Only two of the three bags fit. The third one goes in the back seat. You help your partner down the stairs and put her in the back seat where she can lay down. The girl hesitates but eventually slides in the passenger seat.

"What's your name?"

She looks at you before deciding that giving her name won't hurt. "Agnes."

You tell her your name and your partner's, then back the vehicle down the driveway. The drive is about ten miles. You are forced to take alternate routes several times and dodge groups of beasts twice. Two miles from the farmhouse, you hear a wince and a series of low moans from the back seat.

"You okay?"

You get no response. You call her/his name. No answer. You glance back and see her/him writhing, curled in a ball, clutching her/his stomach.

"We're almost there. Hold on a few more minutes." You turn to Agnes. "Can you see if she's/he's okay?"

It's obvious she doesn't want to, but she unsnaps her seat belt and spins around. She speaks softly to your partner. A few seconds later, she recoils in fear. Leaning against the dash, she stares wide-eyed at your partner. The sight chills your blood.

"What?"

She shakes her head. Her mouth moves, but no sound comes out.

"What?" you say, more insistent this time.

"Something's wrong. She looks…" she pauses. "I don't know."

You turn down a dirt road less than a half mile from the farmhouse. You press the pedal down. The uneven road has you bouncing wildly. The girl goes flying with a squeak. Your partner falls to the floor.

You careen down the road and take a sharp turn up a long dirt driveway. The large farmhouse looms in the distance. You skid to a stop in a circular opening in front of the house, leaving a cloud of dust rising behind you.

You jump out and open the back door. As you lean down to check on your partner, her/his eyes open. They are not the eyes of a human.

A snarl rises from deep within her/him and you jump away. The girl opens her door and exits on the run.

You stand staring at your partner. Anguish holds you in place as she/he extricates itself from the back seat. It turns its head one way then another, cracking its neck each time. Then it looks skyward and releases a chilling howl. You back away. It howls again, this time with feral eyes locked on you. It snarls, and you turn to run. An explosion startles you. You glance back to see your partner on the ground, a bloody hole in the back of its head.

You look up to see Frank with a rifle in his hand, glaring at you. Carol, your partner's sister, sprints down the stairs and drops next to your partner. She wails her grief at the heavens.

Frank lowers the rifle, spits tobacco juice and pivots. He goes inside without a word. Agnes stands on the porch in shock. Your own matches hers.

Several minutes later, Carol stands, wipes her eyes, and says, "Go to the barn and get a couple of shovels. You hesitate. "Well, go." And you do.

You dig a grave for your partner. Carol wraps your partner in a blanket and you place it in the hole. She gives a eulogy, quotes a few Bible verses, and walks away, leaving you to finish the task.

Done, you enter the house, where Carol embraces you. She pats your back and releases you. "You know Frank isn't going to want you here."

"You want me to go?"

"Of course not. He'll get over it."

"I brought food and supplies."

"That'll help a lot."

You notice Agnes standing in the doorway. "Carol, this is Agnes."

"Welcome, Agnes." She offers a warm smile. "Why don't you drive the car around back and unload?"

You do, and while Agnes and Carol sort through it, you go upstairs to speak with Frank. You find him in the front bedroom, keeping vigil out the window. He's short and bulky. His long black hair and beard make him look like a mountain man.

"Hey, Frank. Thanks."

Without facing you, he says, "Couldn't protect her, huh?"

"I was in the hospital. By the time I made my way home, she had already been bitten."

"You got any weapons?"

"No."

He chuckles. "See, that's why us gun toters survive longer than you pacifists."

You bristle. You've had this discussion before. Neither you nor your partner had any interest in keeping a gun in the house. In retrospect, it was a bad decision, and one of the things Frank hates about you.

"You'll need a gun. There's some in each room. Pick one. You do know how to use one, don't cha?"

"Yeah. I can shoot." You pace to one of the back bedrooms. On the dresser is a shotgun and two handguns. Boxes of shells and bullets sit next to them, as well as two fully loaded extra magazines. It's obvious that this is the moment Frank has been planning for his whole life.

You pick a .40 caliber gun and the matching extra mag and stand by the window. As you stare out the window, you think how your life will never be the same again. Of course, none of that matters if you don't survive.

Go to Chapter 3 page 293

Chapter 2 (1A2b1, 1A2b3, 1A2c, 1C2b)

You take a circuitous route, but finally arrive at your house with no further encounters. Along the desolate route, the destruction reminds you of a war zone. Several bodies are strewn around. Smoke rises in the distance from a multitude of fires. The eerie silence is periodically broken by an even eerier howl.

She stops in front of your house. You study it for a minute, afraid of what you might find inside. The vinyl-sided two-story house is in an older section of town. The house and the entire street looks asleep. You scan the neighborhood, making sure none of the creatures are sneaking up on you.

"Are you going in?" she prods.

Your throat is too dry to answer, so you nod and open the door. A sudden thought stops you before you exit. "You are still going to be here when I come back, right?"

"Of course," she says. But, *of course* as soon as you reach the porch, she drives off.

You look through the windows, going from one to another. Nothing is moving inside. You try the door knob. Locked. You don't have keys. You don't risk knocking and opt for the side door.

You trot down the stairs and up the driveway, stopping at the old wooden door you'd always meant to paint but never got around to. Through the window, you see the stairs down to the basement and the short section up to the main floor. The door at the top of the stairs is closed.

A debate wages in your head whether to break the glass or pry the door. The door has two locks; the door lock and a deadbolt. Breaking the window is the easier choice, but then anyone could gain entry. Of course, that's only important if you plan on staying there.

You step back and examine the lock. There's a little give, but you don't have anything to use as a pry tool. If you ruin the lock or door frame, you'll have the same security problem. After thinking it over for a few minutes, you opt to break the window.

You go out front and pick up a decorative stone from the landscape border. Controlling the strike, you hold onto the stone rather than throw it, aiming for the bottom corner above the lock. The glass breaks and falls inside the house. The noise is amplified in your head. You glance around for any response, then realize how stupid your logic is since you're standing in the open. You reach through the jagged hole, careful not to cut yourself, and unlock the deadbolt. However, the door latch is out of reach.

You are forced to lean in as far as you can. Your fingers brush the latch. As you push beyond your limits, a shard of glass pierces you. You whine but push in farther. The latch releases and you withdraw your arm to find a trail of dripping blood. Just another thing to deal with. You enter, closing and locking the door behind you.

You climb the three steps to the closed door and press an ear to it. No sounds penetrate the wood. You close your hand around the knob and turn slowly. Pushing the door open, you step up to the kitchen. Before you can take a step, a blur flashes in front of you and pain explodes in your chest. You are propelled back down the stairs, tumbling and slamming to the floor. Only your quick reactions prevent you from falling completely down the stairs to the basement.

Through your haze, you hear, "Oh my God!" Footsteps descend, and you fear a follow up attack. Your assailant squats next to you and places an arm around you. "I'm so sorry. I thought you were one of those things."

You look up to see your girlfriend/boyfriend looking down at you, a baseball bat in hand.

You struggle to your feet. As if you didn't have enough injuries, now you have to worry about cracked ribs. You stand for a few moments to make sure you can breathe without pain, then climb the stairs. As soon as you reach the top, you are embraced. It creates more pain. You wince.

"What the hell's going on?" you ask. "What's happened since I've been out?"

"You don't know?"

"How would I?"

"From what the news said before it all went dark is that someone had been developing some sort of biological weapon. A combination of rabies and something else. I think the idea was to create some sort of super warrior. However, it went horribly wrong. The test subjects became more animal than human and broke out of the facility. I guess they were highly contagious. If you get bit and don't die, you become one of them."

"Rabies?"

"Oh, I don't know. Something like that. What does it matter? You get bit, you die."

"Must be a lot of people bit then, because I saw a lot more of those creatures then I did humans."

"That's why I'm in the house. One of the last broadcasts said to lock yourself inside. I'm sorry I didn't come back to the hospital, but we are supposed to stay off the streets."

"Is there anyone in authority handling the situation?"

"If there is, I haven't seen them. I've seen a few of those things roaming, but never any police or National Guard or anything."

You walk to the kitchen table and sit down.

"What are we going to do?" your significant other asks.

Good question. You give it some thought. What choices do you have?

Do you:

2A) stay in the house? Go to page 218

2B) leave in search of other survivors? Go to page 219

Chapter 2 (1A2b2)

You take a circuitous route but finally arrive at your house with no further encounters. Along the desolate route, the destruction reminds you of a war zone. Several bodies are strewn about. Smoke rises in the distance from a multitude of fires. The eerie silence is periodically broken by an even eerier howl.

She stops in front of your house. You study it for a minute, afraid of what you might find inside. The vinyl-sided two-story house is in an older section of town. The house and the entire street looks asleep. You scan the neighborhood, making sure none of the creatures are sneaking up on you.

"Are you going in?" she prods.

You swallow hard. "Are you coming, too?"

She shakes her head. "I'll wait here in case we have to make a fast getaway. If it's safe, motion to me."

"Okay."

You exit and walk to the front porch. You try the door. Locked. You don't have keys with you. You glance back, more to make sure she's still there than for support. Pressing your face to the window, you peer inside. No one is there. You knock and wait. After a minute with no response, you try again; this time louder.

You turn and shrug, about to walk down the steps to try the side door, when it opens and your partner is standing there. You throw yourselves at each other in an emotional embrace.

"Oh my God!" he/she says. "I was so worried about you."

"And I was worried about you. I'm so glad you're all right."

"Hurry! Let's get inside before one of those things see us."

"Wait!" You turn and motion to the woman in the car. "I came with someone else."

She limps out and jogs up the steps and into the house. Your partner shuts and locks the door and you make introductions. Jessica asks to use the bathroom, leaving you and your partner to catch up. She/he fills you in about what's happened. You are telling your story as Jessica returns.

"So, what do you want to do?" you ask.

"I got you to your house," Jessica says. "I'd like to go to mine now."

"Why can't we just stay here?" your partner asks.

"Because it's only fair. I brought your girlfriend/boyfriend here. I need to go to my home to check on my family."

You look at your partner. It's obvious he/she has no desire to leave.

Do you:

2A) apologize, but stay there? Read on.

2B) go with her, but leave your spouse behind? Go to page 219

2C) convince your spouse to go with Jessica? Go to page 237


2A) "I'm not going," your partner says. "You shouldn't, either," she says to you. "I'm sorry, but I can't see risking our lives to go to your house, only to have to come right back here. You're welcome to stay with us, but we're not leaving this house."

You realize she/he has spoken for both of you. You look sheepish as you meet Jessica's eyes.

"So, it's everyone for themselves, eh? That's bullshit. I should have left you back at the hospital."

Jessica whirls around and storms out, leaving the door open. You watch her go, feeling guilty.

"We should have gone with her."

Your partner disagrees. As Jessica drives off, you say a silent prayer for her safety as your partner closes the door.

Continue 2A on page 229

2B) "I think we should stay here," your partner says.

"That's not fair..."

"I need to go with her," you interrupt. "She gave me a ride when I needed it. I can't just let her go on her own."

"Why can't she stay here with us? It's safe."

"Because I have a family, too. I need to find out if they're safe, just like your girlfriend/boyfriend wanted to know you were okay."

She/he is angry, but you can see in his/her eyes she/he is giving in. "How will you get back?"

"If my husband is all right, I'll have him drive you back."

"And if he's not?" your partner snaps. Jessica swallows hard and her eyes water. She clears her throat. "Then there'll be no reason for me to stay. I'll bring him back, and if it's all right with you, I'll stay here."

"It'll be okay," you ensure your partner. She/he looks unconvinced. You wrap your arms around her/him. "It won't be long. I'll be right back."

"You'd better."

You kiss your partner and Jessica leads the way back to the car.

Once rolling again, she says, "Thank you. I'd have been too scared to go alone."

"But you would have."

"Yes. I don't have much choice. I have to know, just like you did."

"I understand."

Other than seeing things you wish you hadn't, the drive is uneventful. Jessica lives five miles from you in a neighborhood where the houses are twice the size of yours and four times the price.

She pulls up the driveway. The garage is attached, but the door refuses to rise. She parks in front.

You lean across the seat to scan the house and yard. It looks deserted. "Ready?" she asks.

"If you are."

She sighs and gets out. You join her at the front door. Gun shots come from one of the houses. Jessica gasps and drops the house keys. You spin around, scanning the neighborhood and cursing yourself for not thinking to bring a weapon.

Hand shaking, Jessica unlocks the door and you push inside fast, shutting the door hard. You set the locks and peer out the front window. While Jessica runs upstairs calling her husband and children's names, you search the main floor. You estimate there's more than three thousand square feet of living space. You hear Jessica's running steps above you as you clear the floor. You pause at a kitchen cabinet. What stops you isn't that the door is hanging open, but that it's empty. You rummage through each cabinet, finding the usual kitchen items but no food. The refrigerator and pantry have also been cleaned out.

Jessica returns, tears glistening on her cheeks. She carries a sheet of paper. "Todd has taken the kids to the cottage. He thinks it will be safer there."

"Isn't that a good thing?"

She nods and wipes away fresh tears.

"Then why are you crying?"

"Why couldn't he wait for me?" She sits in a kitchen chair.

"Maybe he didn't think it was safe. You don't know what was going on here at the time."

"I guess."

"How far is the cottage?"

"Almost two hours."

You understand her concern. It's a long drive to make alone.

"Why don't you look through the house for anything you want to take? I'll help you load the car. You can take me home, then go to your family."

She hesitates, giving you a sidelong glance. You get a chill. For a moment, you think she's going to refuse to take you back, but then her body sinks in on itself with the decision to take you. "Okay. Give me a few minutes to look around. She goes upstairs, and you grab a chef's knife from the kitchen and go into the attached garage in search of other weapons.

There are no vehicles, and Todd evidently stripped the garage, too. Only a riding mower and other large items remain. You return to the kitchen in time to see Jessica drag a suitcase down the steps. She seems more composed and something else, too, but what eludes you. She avoids eye contact, and you think, *Uh-oh.*

"Todd did a good job of packing. He took my clothes and things, too. There isn't much I need."

You want to get moving. You'll feel better about whatever is going on once you're on the road. You set the knife down on a counter. "Great. Here, let me put that in the car for you."

You reach for the suitcase, but Jessica backs up. You stop and look at her. To your amazement, she is pointing a gun at you. Her hand shakes so badly she releases the suitcase to hold it steady.

"My husband is so thoughtful. He left me this gun in case I needed to defend myself."

Air is in short supply, but you manage to say, "But you don't have to defend yourself against me. I'm not going to hurt you."

She shakes her head and tears fall again. "I know. This is because I'm not taking you home. I'm sorry. That's the opposite direction, and I want to get on the road before it gets dark. Please. Forgive me and try to understand."

"Not likely. You're leaving me stranded here with no way to get home."

"I'm sure you can find a car somewhere on the way." She looks down at the suitcase as she reaches for the handle. It may be the only chance you have.

Do you:

2B1) let her go? Read on.

2B2) attack her? Go to page 228

2B1) You stand still, fearful her shaky hand may pull the trigger accidentally. She backs away toward the front door. As she opens it, she says. "Please don't follow me outside. I don't want to shoot you, but I will. I have shot before, and I know how. Todd made sure of that."

Your first thought is, *screw you, Todd*. You watch with anger building as she exits, closing the door behind her. Your first thought was to let her go, then you think, *no way*. As soon as she is out of sight, you run for the garage door. You peek through a front window and see her approaching the car. She glances over her shoulder to see if you are following. Pushing a button on the fob, the trunk pops open.

She sets the gun on the ground as she squats to lift the suitcase. You reach the garage door handle and pull the automatic door release. It snaps with a loud metallic sound. Fearing Jessica heard, you bend, grab the door, and yank it upward. You duck under before it reaches full height and race for Jessica. She is staring in confusion and disbelief. She drops the suitcase and reaches for the gun. She grabs it and is standing when you reach her. You barrel her over. Both she and the gun go flying.

She lands hard, but you go for the gun and don't worry about her. You snatch it up and spin. Jessica is sprawled on the ground, not moving. You hit her at full speed, choosing to make contact rather than skewer her with the knife. You roll her over with your foot. She looks out, but you check for a pulse just in case. You find one. You're surprised by your lack of emotion that she's still alive. It'd be easy to leave her here alone. She deserves that. She didn't kill you when she had her chance. Considering the current situation, she should have.

You want to be angry; to leave her to her fate, but you can't. You try to think about how you'd have reacted to find your family gone, but no matter how you play it in your head, you'd never have left her.

Resigned that you're not a cold-blooded killer, you load the suitcase in the trunk, then Jessica in the back seat behind the passenger seat where you can see her. You pick up the key and get in the driver's seat, placing the gun and the knife on the passenger seat. As you start the car, you change your mind and place the gun in your lap.

You drive home. On the way, you notice the creatures you see are no longer solitary. Instead, they seem to hunt in packs. It was hard enough when you only had to face one. Now, there'd be no way of taking them all on without a gun. You fondle it.

You are almost home when Jessica wakes. She sits up and meets your eyes in the mirror. "What are you going to do with me?"

You want to say something horrible to make her think her life is in danger. Instead, you say, "I'm taking you to my house. Once we get there, you are free to go wherever you want."

Her head whips from side to side, looking at the street and neighborhood. "Honest?"

"It's better than you deserve, but yes."

She sits back and sobs. You arrive on your street a minute later. As you approach the house, you find two creatures trying to get inside. They stop, seeing your approach. One howls. The other leaps off the porch and races toward you.

You pick up the gun, roll down the window, and fire point-blank. The bullet tears through the creature. It takes another step before falling to the ground. The second one jumps from the porch and disappears around the back of the house.

You pull up the driveway, pick up the knife, and get out. Jessica stays inside. The front door of the house opens and your partner motions for you to enter. You call to Jessica, "Get in the driver's seat and go!"

Blind fear shows on her face. She doesn't move. From down the street come five creatures, lured by the gunshot. They haven't seen you yet but are searching.

You press the unlock button and open the back door. Jessica blinks, but otherwise doesn't respond. You grab her arm and drag her from the car. She fights you at first, until you show her the creatures, who have spotted you and coming much faster.

She screams but allows herself to be pulled from the car.

"Car or house?" you ask.

She is too shaken to reply.

"Get in the car or the house. Whichever you choose, do it now, or I'm going to leave you out here."

That gets through. She takes another look at the fast-approaching mob and the word bursts from her lips. "House!"

"Hurry!" your partner calls.

Jessica runs up the steps as you close and lock the car doors. You get behind a closed door just as the first creature pounds into it. You peer through the picture window curtains to find six creatures on your small porch. Two jump down and run around back. One leaps at the window and slams into it, causing you to jump back.

"Make sure the side door is locked. There going around the house." Your partner leaves to check. To Jessica, you say, "Check in the kitchen for anything you can use as a weapon." She gives a nervous nod and goes.

Your partner returns. "They're surrounding the house, looking for a way in."

    \* \* \*

"Find something to defend yourself with." As she goes, you drop the magazine from the gun and discover it only holds eight shots and one is gone. Seven rounds for six creatures. Doable, but only if you control the action.

They return, each carrying a large kitchen knife. You wonder how effective they will be against such wild animals.

Something pounds into the side door. You run to the basement door. It leads down four steps to the outer door. A creature peers at you through the window. An idea strikes, but it all depends if the beast is alone.

You trot down the stairs, unlock the door, and yank it open. The beast lunges, and you fire into its face. It falls over the threshold, preventing you from closing the door. Panic roils in your stomach, threatening an upheaval. You kick at the body and shut the door. Before you get it shut, a creature barrels into the door, knocking you back. Your heels catch on the lower step and you fall into a sitting position.

You fire once, miss, and shoot again. The second bullet rips through an eye. The beast falls back and tumbles down the stairs to the basement. You launch at the door and get it closed before the next beast arrives. You slide to the floor, back pressed against the door. Breathing hard, you dwell on how close you came to being killed.

You look at the gun. It's done its job, but you used three rounds for two kills. Four rounds left for four creatures. That's if no other beasts join the first group. You can't afford another miss. You hoist your body up, surprised by how heavy it feels.

Closing the basement door, you find a doorstop in the hall closet and wedge it under. It won't stop them from getting through, but it may buy you some time to react.

Your partner says, "What are we going to do?"

*Good question.* Your mind races for an answer. You can't outrun them, so staying inside is your best bet. But they will get in eventually. An idea forms as the creatures assault the front door again. The blows are hard enough to rattle the frame. You feel the vibrations through the floor.

"Grab all the furniture. We need to drag it across the hall. That way, we can control how many of them come at once."

Together, you move the sofa across the hall and the lounge chair behind it inside the hallway. You place the table on top of the sofa. It's the best you can do. Glass breaks in the kitchen.

You turn to your partner. "Once they get in, you need to climb out the bedroom window and run for the car." You hand over Jessica's keys. You don't want your partner to go out in the danger, but if you give the keys to Jessica, you fear she'll drive off and strand you. "Drive across the yard to the window and we'll climb out."

Fear registers in the wide eyes. You grip his/her hands. "You can do this. They'll all be inside." You hope. Noise and a low growl come from the kitchen. You're out of time. At least one is inside.

"Go."

Your partner disappears inside the bedroom.

"What do you want me to do?" Jessica asks.

"Stand right behind me. If one of them gets its hands on me, cut it."

She nods and grips the knife in both hands.

"We have to buy enough time for the car to get outside the window."

A beast races around the corner. It sees you and runs at the sofas, ignoring the barrier. You hope there's only one. You might be able to dispatch it without using the gun. As it jumps on the sofa, its weight throws the table off balance, and it topples into the creature. It steps aside to throw it to the floor. It is distracted, and you lunge, burying the knife into its flank. It howls and falls away, taking the knife with it.

The pounding on the door violently increases. You look from the wounded beast to the door and make a flash decision to get the knife. You climb over the top, jump down, and reach for the knife. The beast swipes a claw at you. It hooks behind your leg, knocking you off balance. You fall onto the sofa and the beast crawls on top of you.

You wrestle with it, but its teeth snap ever closer to your face. Spittle falls in heavy globs over your face. You push with all your might to force it back, but you're losing the battle. A metallic flash blurs in your periphery and the beast cries out. It swipes at the knife in Jessica's hand, knocking it away. Your hand finds the knife jutting from the beast's side. You rip it out and drive it into the creature's neck. An explosion of blood jets from the wound. The beast clutches at the wound and rolls to the floor. You jump over the sofa as the front door explodes inward and three creatures race in.

You snap a shot, but they are too fast. No score. "Go now!" you shout to your partner. The first creature hits the sofa and looms above you. You shoot, and the blast propels the beast back into the other two.

It takes a moment for them to disentangle and climb toward you. You wonder if your partner has gone for the car yet. Then, a heart-sinking sight appears. Two more beasts come in the door.

"Oh God!" Jessica says.

Trying to save the last bullets, you jam the knife into the next beast's chest. You put a hand on it and push as you pull the blade free. Jessica steps up next to you and slashes at another one. For the moment, you are holding them at bay. It's obvious you can't maintain your frenzied defense.

"Go to the bedroom," you order Jessica. She doesn't have to be told twice. She bolts, and you follow a second later. You slam the door and shove the dresser in front of it. You go for the other dresser as the beasts arrive at the door. The dresser moves under the weight. Jessica lends a hand and you manage to get the second dresser wedged between the first one and the bed.

A car horn blares outside the window. Jessica looks. "It's her/him!"

"Go," you say. You help her up and she jumps to the ground. You glance at the door. It's holding, so you follow. You land in a crouch. As you stand, a beast runs at you. You lift and fire. It's a hit, but the momentum carries it forward, driving into you.

You roll the beast off and reach the open car door as a crash signals. The creatures have broken through the barrier. You jump head first inside the back door. Jessica shouts, "Go! Go! Go!"

The car speeds away. A few minutes later as the adrenaline ebbs, your partner says, "Where are we going?"

You have no idea.

Jessica says, "We can go to my cottage. It's far enough outside the city; maybe there won't be that many of those things. Plus, with my husband there, we'll have an extra body to help with," she shrugs, "whatever."

You look at your partner, who says, "It sounds better than our other options."

Since you have no other options. You agree.


Go to Chapter 3 on page 304


2B2) You pick up the knife and throw it at her. As soon as it leaves your hand, you follow on the run. Jessica is startled by the fast movement. She flinches back as the knife strikes. It doesn't penetrate, but the weight was enough to cause pain. On reflex, her finger pulls the trigger. The explosion of the bullet is ear-shattering in the narrow space. The bullet bores into the floor at your feet. You leap in reaction to the shot, landing on her before she can fire again.

She is plowed to the floor. The gun flies from her grip. Her head smacks hard on the tile floor. She curls and wraps her arms around her head. You scramble on hands and feet to the gun. Gripping it, you roll, fearing she is after you, but when you look, she is still lying where you steamrolled her.

You get up and aim the gun at her. You are still angry, but the immobile form is defenseless.

Do you:

2B2a) shoot her? Read on.

2B2b) leave her? Go to page 234

2B2c) take her with you? Go to page 235


2B2a) Though helpless, you glare through red-misted eyes. "Why?" you shout at her. Whether because she was willing to strand you, or your constant pain, or the nagging headache, or the emotional strain of the day...or perhaps just by accident, you pull the trigger. Jessica's body jumps. You stare in horror at what you have done.

"See what you made me do?"

You drop to your knees and sob. Once you regain control, you stand. "I'm sorry." Then you leave, taking her car and the gun.

At home, you tell your partner the story and cry again. It shouldn't have happened. Jessica should have just driven you home. You place blame squarely on her, pushing aside that you didn't have to kill her.

Continue to Chapter 3

## Chapter 3 (2B2a, 2B2b, 2A)

After a long and fitful night, your partner asks, "What should we do?"

"Well," you say, "we can either stay here, or go find others. Maybe if we find enough survivors we'll be safe."

Your partner glances around the room. "Wouldn't it be better to stay here? We're safe now."

"Yeah, but for how long? What happens when we run out of food? We'll have to leave the house, and who knows how much worse it might be then?"

"Don't you think they'll get the problem under control in a few days?"

"And what if they don't? We might be trapped here and forced to leave rather than go out now when we still have a chance to get someplace."

"So, what are you suggesting? We drive around with no plan? Just see what happens? If we get attacked out there, we'll have less chance to survive than if we stay."

You sigh. He/she has a point. Then, you say, "Why don't we go to your sister's?" That gets the response you hoped for. "We can start out, and if it's too hard to get through, we'll come back. If we go there, you'll have family around you. Plus, Frank will have a ton of stuff stored in the basement. You know what a prepper he is." The word *prepper* gives you pause. "Huh! Who knew that goofy guy would actually be right about something?"

"It's ten miles. Can we make it?"

"Only one way to know for sure." You shrug. "Up to you."

"Yeah, thanks."

A few moments of silence pass, then he/she says, "Okay. Should we take stuff?"

"Yeah. Load up some clothes for each of us. I'll grab all the food, medicine, and whatever else I can find. It'll be better if we don't show up to your sister's place empty handed."

"Why? You think they won't let us in?"

"Your sister will, but if Frank has the place locked down, you know how paranoid he is. He may not let us in." What you don't say is he may shoot you both for trespassing.

You busy yourself loading a few boxes and some large garbage bags with anything you think will have some use or value. You deposit each bag at the front door. Once you have what you want, you take one last look around. A thought strikes.

You go back into the kitchen and grab the chef's knife and a steak knife. Ripping the flap from one of the cardboard boxes, you cut it in half, fold each half in half, then wrap each with layers of duct tape to create a sheath for each knife. You hand your partner the chef's knife and you slide the steak knife into your belt. Then, you go downstairs and grab the hammer and the hatchet. They're not the greatest weapons, but at least you won't leave the house unarmed. Plus, you still have the gun.

After checking the street, you load the car and climb in. However, before you can start the engine, a series of howls drifts down the street. Your partner gives you a tentative look. "Are you sure we're doing the right thing?"

*No*, you think, but force a smile to your face and pat his/her leg. "We'll be all right."

You drive away, feeling less secure than you did a few minutes ago.

The route is hampered by abandoned vehicles, but you manage to make steady progress. On another road, you see a car moving at high speed, either racing toward something or away from it. Twice, creatures make a run at the car, but you leave them behind with no problems. Another time, a herd of creatures stops and eyes you as the car goes by. They are half a block away and you're surprised they don't give pursuit. The sight of so many together is unnerving. If they organize and attack as a band, survival will be more difficult.

A few miles further, and you see another herd loping across a field.

"Maybe this isn't such a great idea," your partner says. "At least back home, we were only dealing with two or three at a time. Out here..."

"We've come this far. We might as well try to get to Carol's."

You drive on, but the herd spots the car. They angle toward you, emitting excited howls. You easily out distance them, but the sight leaves you chilled. You turn onto a hilly gravel road. As you crest on hill, you hit the brakes hard. Gravel flies and the car slides to the left. At the bottom of the hill, not more than ten yards away is a group of ten creatures.

They see you and howl in anticipation. You reverse, but in your haste, the rear end hangs over the lip of a steep drainage ditch. One wrong move, and the car will slide into it. You feed gas as you watch the fast-approaching mob with trepidation. Your partner urges for speed, but you don't want to bury the tires. You feed the gas slow and steady. The car rises, but just as it reaches more solid ground, the beasts hit the car.

They swarm over the vehicle, blocking out the sun like a fast-moving rain cloud. You drive on, even though you can't see the road. The car angles to the left as you reach the opposite side drainage ditch. Swinging the wheel, you level off, but the pounding on all sides and intensifies.

The rear passenger window shatters. Whether or not you can see, you have to get away before they get inside. You increase speed. A few of the beasts running alongside drop back, allowing patches of sun through.

The other back window is smashed. The noise motivates your foot to press down harder. Soon, only those clinging to the hood and hanging from the windows are still with you. With a good section of the windshield clear, you run the speed up to eighty. The car bounces wildly over the uneven gravel. Another is tossed from the car.

You slam on the brakes, clearing the remaining creatures from the hood. You stomp on the pedal and run over them and slam into them. The only two threats are both halfway inside the car.

Stopping fifty yards further, you brake and shift into park. You hop out, slam the body of the first beast down on the shards of glass still in the frame, then yank it out of the car by the hips. You spin and toss it like a track and field hammer. It flies and rolls down the drainage ditch.

The second one is kicking its feet in the air, more inside than out. You reach through the broken window, aim the gun, and fire into its head. It slumps. Racing around the car, you grab the legs and haul it out.

Seeing the car stopped, the herd takes up the chase. They are eating up ground faster than you thought possible. You jump in and speed away with the door still open as they get to the car. One of them runs next to the door as your speed increases. It leaps to get in but meets your fist with its face. It falls out and the car bounces over the legs.

Taking alternate routes, you reach Carol's house and drive up the long lane. You approach with caution. Nothing is moving. You continue around the house and stop near the rear door. Your partner hops out and knocks, calling out Carol's name.

No one answers. She/He turns to you as the door is ripped open and a rifle barrel appears.

"Get off this land or die," a gruff voices orders. A short, burly man with wild black hair glares down the sights.

You hop out and aim your handgun over the roof.

A voice calls from behind the man. "Oh, for God's sake, Frank. You damn well know who that is. Now, put the gun down and let them inside before I shoot you."

The man's cheek twitches, but he lowers the gun and disappears inside. Carol comes out and gives you both a hug. "Come on in where it's safe."

'I don't think Frank wants us here," you say.

"Oh, his bark's worse than his bite. You are both welcome here."

Your partner says. "We didn't come empty handed," and points at the loaded car.

"Well, let's get that inside, too."

You unload the car, and while they find places for what you've brought, you go find Frank. He's standing in the upstairs bedroom, keeping watch over the front of the house. There's no way he didn't see your approach or know who it was. He was just asserting his dominance.

"Thanks, Frank."

He grunts.

"We brought a bunch of food."

"Bring any guns or ammo?"

"Just this." You hold up the gun.

"Huh! If you're gonna stay here, you need to stand watch, and that gun won't do much good. Go pick out a rifle from one of the back bedrooms."

Continue Chapter 3 on page 275

2B2b) You get to your feet, aiming the gun at her. She is immobile on the floor, eyes closed, curled in a ball. You bend closer to check for breathing. A soft, steady moan tells you she is still alive.

"Why did you do that? Would it have been so hard to drive another thirty minutes? I don't understand. We're all survivors. We need to help each other. If you were going to do this, I could've stayed home." You stand and rub a hand over your face. The decision weighs heavy on your mind.

Coming to a decision, you say, "Since you were going to strand me, I'm leaving you. I'm taking your gun. I hope you're all right and that you rejoin your family soon. If you stay here, I'm sure your husband will come back for you."

You step over her and head for the door. As you open it, you hear a faint, "Please." You pause, then continue out, shutting the door on whatever plea came next.

You drive home and relay the story to your partner. It saddens you both. Later that night as you are trying to sleep, your thoughts wander to Jessica. You pray she is all right and that she will be reunited with her family. Your final thought before sleep claims you is of the fate of the human race if survivors can't help each other in this time of desperate need.

Go to Chapter 3 on page 229

2B2c) You stand and aim the gun at her. She is immobile on the floor, eyes closed, curled in a ball. You bend closer to check for breathing. A soft, steady moan tells you she is still alive.

"Why did you do that? Would it have been so hard to drive another thirty minutes? I don't understand. We're all survivors. We need to help each other. If you were going to do this, I could've stayed home." You stand and rub a hand over your face. The decision weighs heavy on your mind.

"I can't leave you like this, even though you were going to leave me. The only other choice is to take you with me. Lucky for you, I'm a nice person."

You tuck the gun in your belt at the small of your back and bend to lift her. The moans turn to groans. You try to get her to stand, but her legs are too shaky. You get about three steps before she bends and vomits. You hold her the best you can without letting her fall or be splashed by the residual spray.

When she's done, you walk her to the sink, press her against it to keep her from falling, and wet some paper towels. You hand them to her. She wipes her mouth and groans, then begins to sob. Her sobs abruptly end when she throws up again.

You sit her in a kitchen chair and clean her face. Her eyes are unfocused. She has a concussion. You need to get her home as fast as you can. Your partner will know what to do.

You carry her to the car, sliding her into the rear seat. You return for her suitcase and place it in the passenger seat.

The drive home is uneventful. You muscle her out of the car and carry her into the house. You lay her down in the guest bedroom and your partner bends over her. While he/she does a basic evaluation, you go out for the suitcase.

You explain what happened as your partner exchanges Jessica's soiled top for a t-shirt. "We're supposed to keep her awake for twenty-four hours," your partner says, "but I think it's already too late. We'll just have to keep checking on her. Hopefully, she'll be okay in the morning."

You go the front room, leaving the bedroom door ajar.

"So, what do we do now?" your partner asks.

"I guess we delay any plans until we see what happens with her. We need to make sure the house is secure. We can't do much about the windows, other than keep the curtains closed and stay away from them, but we can barricade the doors."

"I can't stand this sitting around, waiting for something to happen, so let's get started on that."

You move the dining room buffet against the front door, then hand cut two 2x4s and prop them between the side door and the stairs. For the moment, you feel better about security.

"Should we take turns standing watch?" your partner asks.

You think about that before saying, "No. let's try to get a good night's sleep and hope we'll be safe for tonight."

In bed, sleep comes slowly. Your mind is a swirl of thoughts running from the events of the day to the future of the human race. As sleep begins to claim you, your final thoughts are that you'll make a plan tomorrow—if there is a tomorrow.

A scream wakes you. You jump from bed, snatch the gun, and run. You burst through Jessica's bedroom door. She is sitting up screaming.

"What?" you ask, seeing no threat.

"It was at the window."

"Oh my God!" your partner yells. "There's a bunch of them. I think they're surrounding the house. You hear pounding from several points around the house at once and run into the living room. Something slams against the front door.

Not sure how much time you have before one gets inside, you start barking orders.

Go to *** on page 224

2C) "Let's go. It'll give us a chance to scout the area." She/he still looks unconvinced. "What if you follow us? That way, I'll have a ride back."

"Wait! You wouldn't be riding with me?" The flaw in your plan smacks you like a slap. "Oh! I, uh…" You look to Jessica for help, but she wants you to ride with her. "Ugh! Look, we have to come up with a solution here."

Jessica gets huffy. "Oh, just forget it." She pivots and stomps toward the door.

You feel helpless and look from her to your partner. She/he crosses her/his arms across the chest and gives you a stern look. You throw your hands up in the air in defeat. At that moment, a chorus of howls drifts down the street. You all freeze.

"Okay," your partner says, "let's get out of here."

The three of you run to the car. Jessica starts the engine as three beasts round a corner ahead and sprint toward you.

"What should I do?" Jessica asks.

"Let them get closer so they don't have time to react, then fly past."

You wait. Time seems to slow.

"Push your foot down on the gas, but don't shift," you say. "Now! Shift." The car leaps forward and out of her control. The car veers left, slamming into and over one of the creatures. The car bounces up the curb and onto a lawn. You reach over to help secure the wheel. The other two creatures race after you.

"Ease up on the gas," you say as you get the wheel under control. She manages to swing the car back on the street and you leave the beasts behind.

Twice, groups of things attack the car, but neither time proved to be a danger. Jessica blows past them, their deformed bodies bouncing off the car. You enter a neighborhood of expensive homes. It looks as deserted as your neighborhood did. She pulls up the driveway of a three-story brick house. She presses the garage door opener, but it doesn't rise.

"No electricity," you say. "You have a house key, right?"

"Yeah. Come on."

Your partner chooses to remain in the car. Jessica gets out and you follow. You join her at the front door. Gun shots come from one of the houses. Jessica gasps and drops the house keys. You spin around, scanning the neighborhood, cursing yourself for not thinking to bring a weapon.

Hand shaking, Jessica unlocks the door and you push inside fast, shutting it hard. You peer out the front window. While Jessica runs upstairs, calling her husband and children's names, you search the main floor. You estimate there's more than three thousand square feet of living space. You hear Jessica's running steps above you as you clear the floor. You pause at a kitchen cabinet. What stops you isn't that the door is open, but that it is empty. You rummage through each cabinet, finding the usual kitchen items, but no food. The refrigerator and pantry have also been cleaned out.

Jessica returns, tears glistening on her cheeks. She carries a sheet of paper. "Todd has taken the kids to the cottage. He thinks it will be safer there."

"Isn't that a good thing?"

She nods and wipes away fresh tears.

"Then why are you crying?"

"Why couldn't he wait for me?" She sits in a kitchen chair.

"Maybe he didn't think it was safe. You don't know what was going on here at the time."

"I guess."

"How far is the cottage?"

"Almost two hours."

You understand her concern. It's a long drive to make alone.

"Why don't you look through the house for anything you want to take? I'll help you load the car. You can take me home and go to your family."

She hesitates, giving you a sidelong glance. You get a chill. For a moment, you think she's going to refuse to take you back, but then, having made her decision, her body sinks in on itself. "Okay. Give me a few minutes to look around. She goes upstairs, and you grab a chef's knife from the kitchen and go into the attached garage in search of other weapons.

There are no vehicles. Todd evidently stripped the garage, too. Only a riding mower and other large items remain. You return to the kitchen in time to see Jessica drag a suitcase down the steps. She seems more composed and something else, too, but what it is eludes you. She avoids eye contact and you think *Uh-oh.*

"Todd did a good job of packing. He took my clothes and things, too. There isn't much we need."

You want to get moving. You'll feel better about whatever is going on once you're on the road. You set the knife down on a counter. "Great. Here, let me put that in the car for you."

You reach for the suitcase, but Jessica backs up. You stop and look at her. To your amazement, she is pointing a gun at you. Her hand shakes so badly that she releases the suitcase to hold it steady.

"My husband is so thoughtful. He left me this gun in case I needed to defend myself."

"Jessica! What are you doing?"

"I don't know." Tears well.

"We came with you to make sure you were safe. Is this how you reward us?"

"I don't want to drive two hours alone."

She's scared. Panic registers in her voice. You fear she will pull the trigger by accident. Then, she blows out a heavy breath and lowers the gun. "I can't do it. I'm sorry."

But you don't want to take the chance she'll change her mind. You pounce, ripping the gun from her hand. She jumps back, emitting a squeak of despair. Her hands cover her mouth and she stares with wide-eyed fear.

"I won't hurt you, but you need to drive us home."

"What if you drive me to the cottage, then you can take the car back home?"

"I don't think so."

"You can keep the car. I just want to be with my family."

"I'm sorry. I do understand, but you're not being fair. You want us to risk our lives, so you can join your family, but you have no consideration for my family."

She drops into a chair and sobs. You feel sorry for her. She's terrified of what may happen on the road, and with good reason, but she's asking too much already.

The car horn blares. You jump and run to the front window. Peeling the drape back a few inches, you see two beasts pounding on the car. Your partner looks near panic. You're afraid he/she will open the door to make a dash for the house.

You move to the door, open it, and race out. You come up behind one and place a bullet in the back of its head. It falls, and you move on. The second one snarls and comes around the car to attack you. You fire once and miss. The second shot drills through its shoulder. It spins around, keeping its balance. It releases a howl, then turns and runs away.

Running back up the stairs, you call inside. "We're leaving now."

Jessica hesitates.

"Jessica, come on. We have to go while it's still safe."

You take her suitcase outside, hoping that will spur her to move. You put it in the trunk as she comes out. She locks the door. As she comes down the stairs, you hold out your hand. "I'll drive."

She's about to protest, but then hands them over without a word.

The drive back is full of sightings of beasts running in packs. You seldom see any lone creatures now. You spot a large group on your street, two blocks from your house. You take a detour, coming in from the opposite direction. However, even there you see smaller pockets of man-things.

"I'm not sure the area is safe anymore," you say. "I think we're gonna have to move."

"Do we have time to get some things from the house?" your partner asks.

"If we make it fast."

You pull up the driveway backward, stopping near the side door. The three of you rummage through the house, taking clothes, food, beverages, and medicine. You weren't even gone five minutes, but it's already too late.

Three beasts are coming up the driveway. "Hurry!" you shout.

The other two run for the car. They toss the bags of stuff inside and jump in. You toss your bag onto Jessica's lap as the beasts arrive at the car. You fire two quick shots, dropping the nearest one, and creating some room for you to get in and close the door. The remaining two beat on the car and the window as you start the car and drive off.

In your haste, you turn the wrong way. At the end of the block, you run into the mass of creatures. They descend on you. You shove the pedal down and plow through the middle of them. Bodies fly, and the car bounces over a few, but in seconds you are clear and racing away.

"Well, that went well," you say.

"Where are we going?" your partner asks.

Jessica says, "I have a suggestion."

Go to Chapter 3 on page 304

Chapter 2 (1C2a)

Staying focused on the road and its obstacles, you pay little attention to your new friend until you hear a low moan. You glance at him. His eyes are closed and his head back against the rest.

"You okay?" you ask.

"Don't feel well." He clutches both arms around his stomach. "Feel like I'm gonna heave."

"It's the adrenaline ebbing away. You're probably going into shock," you say with confidence, but no actual knowledge. "Put the seat back. It shouldn't be much longer."

He moans in an almost constant hum for the next five minutes. You round the corner of your street and find your house under assault by several creatures. Your heart fills your throat. You brake and stare, unable to form thoughts. Your partner is in danger. You have to do something to save her/him, and you have no weapons.

But you do have a Charger.

You advance slowly, trying not to draw attention. The beasts are throwing themselves at the large picture window on your house. You increase speed, fearing the glass won't hold much longer. The car closes to thirty yards, and the window shatters. A body hangs on the ledge, legs digging into the wall for purchase. Your partner is out of time.

You slam the pedal down, and again, like a spurred horse, the car shoots forward with a squeal of tires. You angle for the driveway and bounce across the lawn. The Charger barrels into three creatures, sending them flying. You swerve, sideswiping the front of the house, scraping the hanging beast off its perch with a sickening crunch and eruption of blood.

The car jumps a bush and gets hung up. No matter what you try, you cannot get free. You turn to your passenger. "We're gonna have to make a break for it." But he is unresponsive. His head sags to the side, and for a moment, you fear he's dead. Then, he emits a soft moan.

Craning your neck, you see your partner standing in the window, baseball bat in hand. So close, yet so far. How do you get out of the car? As you struggle for a plan, something lands on the roof. You hear its claws tap against the metal; then, it is gone. Frantic to know where it is, you catch movement inside your house. The creature used the car as a springboard to jump through the broken window.

A blur of arms, legs, and bat are all you can see. You have to get inside. You spin around in the seat, searching for others as a creature launches at the driver's window. You jump backward, bumping into the other man. His body slumps against the door. He looks ghastly. You check for a heartbeat, then for air flow. Finding neither, you slide him more on his back and begin CPR. It becomes apparent quickly that he is dead.

*Now what?*

A quick scan through the broken window shows no movement. Has your partner escaped, or is he/she rolling on the floor, locked in a struggle to the death? You have to get in there now.

Climbing into the back seat, you open the rear door closest to the house. Standing on the seat, you lean out and reach for the window ledge. A sound behind you causes you to duck just as a beast slashes at your head. The wind it causes as it whips overhead stirs your hair.

The creature leans its head over the side. You duck further inside and kick at the beast. It recoils. Seconds later, it jumps into the house and out of sight. That triggers more determination. Again, you get up on the seat, lean out, and grab the window frame to avoid the jagged glass.

A shard lances your thumb. You ignore it and pull upward. With your head above the frame, you now see the two beasts hunched over something on the floor. It takes a moment to realize it's your partner. You scream. The noise causes both beasts to turn their heads toward you. Their mouths are coated with blood. The movement creates a gap, enabling you to see your partner's lifeless gaze. A low wail builds within you. The horror and the anguish leave you immobile.

Something grabs you from behind, hauling you back to the car.

Your head strikes the door frame with a solid thud. You see stars. Rough hands rip at your skin. Searing pain shoots through you. Strong hands pull you inside. You fight and kick, but your blows have little effect.

The creature crawls up your body until you are looking into the face of your new friend. His strong jaw clamps down on your forearm. The teeth dig deep, and with a loud, painful snap, your arm breaks.

You flail, but your efforts are futile. It doesn't take long for the beast to find your throat, and in a horrifying and painful end, rip it out.


End

Chapter 3 (2A1a1b2, 2A1a1b3, 2A3a2a, 2A3c1)

You drive in a trance for a good ten minutes until something runs across your path. You brake. It was a dog. You watch it speed away, tail between its legs, and realize something scared it bad. You glance the other way and see two creatures searching for it. You slink down in your seat, wondering if they'll notice the car is running.

You wait a minute before peeking. The creatures are no longer in view. You blow out a breath of relief, but too soon. One of them leaps on the hood. You startle and jump high enough to bump your head. Cursing, you stomp on the gas, throwing the creature against the windshield. You speed about a hundred yards before stepping on the brakes. The creature rolls off the front. Without waiting to see where it is, you floor the accelerator again. The SUV bounds over the beast, but you feel no second bump. It must be trapped beneath the SUV.

As the vehicle increases speed, you feel the second bump. A look in the mirror shows the mangled body rolling in the street.

You drive for the freeway ramp, trying to figure out a safe place to go. An overturned bread truck blocks the ramp. You swing around it, bouncing over the curb. You are about to pull away when a man pulls up through the driver's door and waves his arms at you.

Do you:

3A) stop? Read on.

3B) keep driving? Go to page 273

3A) You brake and study the man. Having just fought your way out of a trap, trust of your fellow survivors is not high. Still, he is human and alive. Can you turn your back on him?

He stands on the side of the truck and waves and calls to you. "Help! Please don't leave me here."

You roll down your window. "Are you hurt?"

"Just a few bruises."

Remembering what you learned at the medical center, you say, "Have you been bitten?"

"No. I've stayed inside until I heard your engine."

You debate internally, but in the end, you know you can't leave him. "Okay. Come on."

He starts to climb down, then says, "You want me to bring some bread?"

You hesitate, but only for a second. "Sure." But you decide if he comes out of the truck with anything other than bread, you're leaving him.

The man disappears for a minute. Then you see several bags of assorted breads tossed out the door. He follows moments later, gathers the bags, and jumps down. At the car, he pitches the bread into the back seat and climbs in.

As soon as he's seated, you drive.

"Man, I can't thank you enough. I've been sitting inside that truck, afraid to move for about two hours." He offers a hand. "My name's Jim."

You look from his hand to his face, then shake and introduce yourself.

"You heading anywhere in particular?"

You reply, "No. I was kinda just driving—trying to think of some place safe."

"You got a home?"

"Yeah. I was just there."

"No good?"

You think about your partner lying in a dumpster. Your eyes blur. The lump in your throat makes it unable to speak. You shake your head. Jim seems to understand. "Sorry."

You ride in silence for a few moments. Then you say, "What

about you?"

"I live two hours away. I drive this route twice a week delivering bread. It wasn't anywhere near as crazy as this where I live; at least not when I left at three this morning."

"Maybe we should go there, then?"

"It's fine by—watch out!"

You slam on the brakes and whip the wheel to avoid hitting a woman running out in front of you, waving her hands. The SUV careens off the guard rail with a metallic crunch and scrape. You gain control and stop sideways across the two-lane highway.

"Damn!" Jim says. "That was close."

You look past Jim and see the woman running as hard as she can toward you. Just coming into view are three creatures.

"Oh man, I don't think she's gonna make it," says Jim.

You've come to the same conclusion.

Do you:

3A1) wait for her? Read on.

3A2) drive to her? Go to page 262

3A3) leave her? Go to page 271

3A1) You sit and wait. The tension builds in the SUV as the distance between her and the beasts closes fast.

Jim rolls down the window and shouts, "Come on! Faster!"

Out of breath, she says what sounds like, "Wait for me."

Jim reaches over the seat and opens the back door. She is within five yards. Your chest tightens with anxiety. You have an urge to get out and help, but that would be suicidal.

She reaches for the door just as the lead beast leaps at her. It catches her feet as she leans into the car and yanks her back. Jim starts to open his door, but the second creature plows into it, slamming it against his forehead. The woman's screams fill the car and your head. You slap your palms over your ears to keep from hearing her, but her cries reverberate in your mind.

You become aware of Jim shouting at you. "Go! Go! Go!"

You look at him.

"It's too late for her. We have to go."

You press the gas and the car pulls away, but not before one of the beasts dives inside the back seat. You drive faster, as if speed will put distance between you and the beast. Jim whirls in his seat and punches at the beast. Its jaws snap with audible clacks.

Unsure of what to do, you keep driving, glancing over your shoulder at the battle. Jim yelps in pain, then, to your complete surprise, opens the door and bails out. You stare after him as the creature dives over the seat, landing in your lap. You arch back and grab it by its throat. It snarls and flails, as you increase your grip. Meanwhile, the SUV barrels down the road with your foot pinned against the pedal.

You squeeze tighter, only vaguely aware that the snarling is now coming from you. The beast's efforts slacken. You lean toward the still-open door and try to shove it out, but you can't reach far enough, as you're hampered by the seat belt. You stab at it, afraid to release its throat for fear it may revive. The belt releases and you slide across the seat. You feel the speed bleed off as your foot lifts from the gas. The beast looks unconscious. You give it a last push and it topples out.

The door hits the guard rail and shuts in your face, leaving you stunned. A loud scraping sound cuts through the haze and refocuses your brain. The vehicle lurches to a stop, throwing you into the dashboard. Pain shoots up your arm to your shoulder.

You right yourself and discover that the SUV is wedged against the guardrail. The engine is still running. You look out the rear window and see Jim limping toward you, one hand cradling the other. One beast is tearing at the now lifeless form of the woman. The beast you pitched from the car is motionless on the side of the road. The third creature, the one who bounded into the door, is nowhere in sight.

You shift into reverse and move toward Jim, angling away from the guardrail so the door can open. Jim reaches the SUV and you stop. Just as he opens the door, the third beast races up the slope on the side of the road and leaps on his back, driving him from view.

Do you:

3A1a) get out and help him? Read on.

3A1b) drive away? Go to page 252

3A1a) You slap the stick into park and jump out of the SUV. You hit the ground on the run and round the back end of the vehicle. Jim is struggling to hold off the beast. You race up and do your best field goal impersonation, kicking the creature in the side. The force lifts and rolls the beast off Jim. You bend to help him up, but the beast recovers fast. As it races toward you, you push Jim toward the SUV and swing a backhand strike with your cast. The blow connects with the creature's face, sending blood, spittle, and a couple of teeth flying. It falls at your feet, stunned. A fresh wave of sharp pain shoots up your arm. You fear you have rebroken it.

You get back in the SUV and drive off, trying to control the pain. As it subsides, you become aware of Jim's moans. You study him and notice blood seeping from several different wounds. He needs immediate help.

You search your memory for a medical facility, but your own pain makes forming thoughts difficult. You drive on subconsciously, unaware of the passing surroundings. Fifteen minutes later, the silence is as loud as the moaning. You glance at Jim and see he is either asleep, passed out, or dead. You keep driving, more focused now.

Another ten minutes, and you spy a doctor's office. You pull in and are surprised to see people moving inside. You stop in front of the door and hop out. The front door opens, and all eyes swing your way.

"Are you open for business?"

The four people inside all look at each other, but no one speaks. A woman pushes through a door and sees you.

"Can I help you?"

"My friend is hurt and needs medical attention."

"What kind of attention?" she asks.

You don't want to admit he's been bitten for fear she'll turn you away. You shrug. "Not sure. He's been moaning for a while, then he passed out."

She sucks in her lower lip as she thinks, then says, "Okay. Bring him in. I'll take a look."

Elated, you run to the passenger door and open it. Jim stirs. He looks funny. He glances around, confused. Then, as you attempt to help him from the seat, he snarls and launches at you. You fall with him on top of you. You struggle to keep him from biting you, while thinking that it's true—being bitten turns you into one of these beasts.

Determined not to become one yourself, you manage to get your cast between its teeth. It bites down hard, and you hear the cast crack. Shoving with all your might, you get free and run for the office door. The woman is standing behind it, and to your dismay, you see her flick the lock.

You slam into the door and pound on it. "Open up. Please. I haven't been bitten."

But she stares at you in fear and backs away from the door. The other four people inside are all on their feet watching, but none make a move to help you.

You can't believe they are willing to let you die and watch while it happens. Then, Jim hits you from behind, smashing you into the glass. Sharp pain comes from your neck as Jim rips a hunk of your flesh free. Warm fluids run down your neck. You see the woman inside cover her face with her hands.

You swing an elbow into Jim's head, knocking him back. As you turn to face him, you are startled to see a jet of blood hit Jim in the face. For an instant, you are confused as to where it came from.

Momentary hope fills you, thinking someone has come to your rescue, but as the truth settles in and darkness tugs at your vision, you resign yourself to your fate, knowing you won't become one of the creatures.

End

3A1b) Thinking it is already too late to help Jim and fearing to be brought down yourself, you step on the gas and drive away. As much as you want to look, you force your eyes to remain on the road ahead.

A creature leaps in your path and you run it down without hesitation. You are thirty miles down the expressway before you allow a backward look. You half expect to see a horde of beasts in hot pursuit, but nothing is following you.

You slow and try to decide where to go. In the farthest reaches of your vision, you spy another moving vehicle. Thinking it a mirage, you close your eyes, shake your head, and look again. Nothing. Sweeping your gaze forward, you see it. It's a small car and it's moving fast.

You press the pedal down and try to catch up. You are forced to slow several times to avoid stopped vehicles, but slowly you close the gap. If the lead car sees you, they show no signs. A few minutes later, the brake lights flash on. Then the car increases speed. They have seen you and are afraid.

You stay close to them and honk your horn, hoping they'll stop. A few minutes later, they slow and allow you to pull up next to them. There are four people inside, two men and two women. The men are in the front seat. They look scared. The second man is holding a handgun. You wave and lower the passenger window. You shout, "Where you heading?"

The driver looks at the other man and a brief discussion ensues. He turns and yells back. "To the National Guard base. Survivors are gathering there."

Hope fills you. You nod, excitedly. "I'll follow you."

The driver nods and pulls in front. They increase speed but keep it steady. You don't get the feeling they're trying to get away from you. The National Guard base is about twenty miles away. You begin to think everything will be all right, but that's usually when things go awry. This is no exception.

Five more miles down the road, a Hummer races up a ramp and

angles toward the car, forcing the driver to brake and angle toward the median. A gun pokes out the rear window of the Hummer and begins firing. You brake to get distance. The passenger side tires of the car are blown, and the car swerves out of control. It slides off the road and tips precariously.

The Hummer stops on the road above the car and three armed men jump out.

Do you:

3A1b1) go to their rescue? Read on.

3A1b2) drive past? Go to page 258

3A1b3) reverse and drive away? Go to page 259

3A1b1) You watch as the three men descend on the car. They show no indication of having noticed you. They shout and motion with their weapons and the doors open. The four people get out with their arms raised. One man covers them while the other two go through the car. They carry two cardboard boxes to the Hummer.

The third man motions for the four to move, and he lines them up on the side of the road. A sudden shock of horror fills you as you realize he's going to execute them. You can't let that happen. You slam the pedal down and aim for him. He doesn't see you immediately, but when he does, he spins and fires his automatic rifle at you. The shots are hasty, though a few ping off the grill. He races for the Hummer, but you reach him before he gets there and send him airborne. He hits the roof of the Hummer and rolls down the windshield. You screech to a stop and yell to the four. "Get in! Hurry!"

But the driver is too slow. The other two gunmen open fire. He takes a series of shots to the chest and goes down. They scream and duck but continue towards the SUV. The second man pulls his gun and hits one of the gunmen, driving the second one to cover.

As soon as they are inside, you move. The driver of the Hummer pushes a gun out the window and rattles off a steady stream of bullets. Several hit inside, and you hear a cry of pain. The rearview mirror shows the two uninjured men dragging their comrades into the Hummer.

You focus on the road and estimate the distance to the National Guard base. The longer the men take, the greater chance of arriving before the pursuit catches you.

"Everyone okay?" you ask.

"No," a woman says. "Paul's been hit."

"How bad?"

"It's his shoulder."

You glance in the mirror. The Hummer is now in pursuit.

"Can he still shoot?"

Paul gasps. "I don't think so."

"Well, somebody has to pick up the gun and get ready to defend us. They're coming."

Both women look out the back window. One is sobbing. The one who spoke bends down and comes up holding the gun.

"I'm going to stay on the outside, so get behind me." You pass an exit sign. Two more to go, then it's a straight shot to the base. "They don't know where we're going, which gives us a slight advantage."

The gun woman moans. "Can't you go any faster? They're gaining."

You give it all the gas it can handle, but the distance decreases anyway. With one exit to go, the Hummer closes on you. One man leans out the passenger window and shoots. A bullet punches through the rear window. A second one shatters it, sending glass shards through the car.

You need them to come up alongside you by the time you reach the next exit. You slow down. The woman with the gun yells, "What are you doing?"

"Shoot out the back window a couple of times. I need them to come alongside. The ramp is coming up fast."

The woman lifts the gun up without looking and fires twice. The Hummer swerves. Two more shots, and it swings into the center lane. You let it gain.

"Keep your heads down," you say.

The Hummer pulls right up next to you. The passenger gives a sinister smile and levels a gun at you. At the last second, you swerve toward the ramp. You almost pass it. The wheels bounce off the curb, threatening to flip the SUV. After a few quick maneuvers, you right the wheels and race down the ramp.

As planned, the Hummer was unable to stop. By the time it corrects course, you have a little lead. At the bottom of the ramp, you whip the wheel into a left turn, screeching the tires. You are under the overpass before the Hummer comes in sight. The final eight miles to the base will be a race.

You pray you are out of sight by the time they make an appearance. Perhaps they'll turn the wrong way. You are well down the road before you spot them. Seven miles to go. You try to urge the SUV faster, but it is over-matched. You count down the miles. You are down to three by the time the shots start again.

You drive down the middle of the road to prevent the Hummer from flanking you, but the driver decides to ram you instead. The sudden jolt pitches you forward. For a second, you lose control of the wheel. The SUV almost runs off the road before you gain control.

It makes a run at you again. This time, it hits and continues forward, trying to push you off the road. Two miles to go. You won't make it.

The three in the back are hunched down, staying safe. It is only a matter of time before the Hummer wins the battle.

"Someone has to fire into the Hummer. You have to make them back off, or we're all dead."

The woman's head appears. She nods at you, turns, and fires one shot after another. The bullets penetrate the windshield, and the driver is forced to back off. The passenger leans out again and returns fire. The woman continues shooting until the magazine empties.

"I'm out of bullets," she says.

Before you can tell her to get down, she cries out in pain and drops from view. Less than a mile to go. As the Hummer closes again, this time with a steady stream of rounds leading the way, you fear you'll fall just short of your goal.

You can see the fence ahead. The gate is still a distance away. The Hummer hits you again. This time, the impact propels the SUV off the road and toward the fence. You manage to avoid contact, swinging the vehicle into a parallel path. Evidently thinking you were done, the Hummer does not follow. Now, as you race along the grass, it goes off road and aims at your midsection.

Braking before the impact saves you from the full impact. The Hummer smashes into a fence post. the SUV smacks into the side of the Hummer and both come to a stop. You try to reverse, but the vehicles are locked together.

"Get out and run toward the gate," you say, knowing you can't outrun their bullets. The frightened woman helps the wounded one out. You help Paul. You hustle past the Hummer. The driver is stirring, but as you get to the other side of the Hummer, you see the passenger is lying against the dash. Obviously, he hadn't been wearing his seat belt.

Lugging two wounded people makes the going slow, but you keep moving. Behind, you hear the Hummer's door open, then a second one. Damn! They both survived. You see the gate ahead. There are people there and they are watching your progress, but no one is coming to your aid. You want to scream, "Help!' but you are too out of breath to speak.

A shot whizzes past your head. You have to keep moving and pray the shots remain off target. A second and third shoot whip past, closer each time. Fifty yards to go. So close, yet so far. The next shot tugs at your arm. A burning pain follows. You know the next shot will be the one that ends your run. Determined to make it miss, you veer to the right just in time as the next shot goes wide.

The woman falls next to you. You hesitate but can't wait. Then, Paul's weight is too much for you. He slips from your grip, falls, and trips you. You tumble to the ground twenty yards from the gate. You look up to see the gunman with the sinister smile stop over you and raise his gun. If anything, the smile is even more disturbing. Then, his smile is ripped away as a bullet tears through his face.

A second shot drops his partner, and for a moment, the world seems to stop. No sound penetrates, but then it returns with a sudden explosion as people appear all around you.

A man kneels next to you. You scramble backward.

"Relax. You're safe now. Are you hit?"

"I-I don't think so."

"Good."

"But Paul's been shot."

"Okay. Someone's taking care of him. If you can walk, let's get you inside." He helps you up. Paul and the injured woman are being loaded onto stretchers. A man and a woman help the second woman up and toward the gate.

As you pass through the gate, you relax for the first time since you woke up in the hospital and dare to believe you might actually be safe.

Congratulations! You made it.

3A1b2) As the gunmen run toward the other car, you floor it and swerve wide to the right of the Hummer. Gunfire erupts toward the car. However, one of the men swings toward you, strafing the car with a steady barrage. You flinch as the windows shatter. Sharp pain rips through your shoulder. You jerk the wheel to the right and slam into the guardrail. The airbag deploys, smacking into your face, leaving you stunned.

By the time you shake the cobwebs free, a man is standing at your window with a gun pointed at you. "Almost," he says. "Just a little too slow." He pulls the trigger.

Probably not a good idea to race past armed men.

End

3A1b3) The three men race toward the car. Apparently, they haven't seen you. As they open fire on the car, you reverse and speed away. One of the gunmen fires at you. A bullet punches through the windshield and clips the headrest, inches from your face.

You spin the wheel and turn broadside to the shooter. He is walking toward you, firing in a steady cadence. You shift and drive away. The exit ramp is close. You swing the car around and race down the ramp. The man is now running after you. Bullets pound into the body. You pray they don't damage anything important.

At the bottom of the ramp, you turn left. The shooter is on the overpass still shooting. The rear window implodes. You sink lower in the seat and try to coax more speed from the already maxed engine. You reach the first cross street and turn right, out of range and sight of the shooter. You breathe easier and plot a back roads course to the base.

Twenty minutes later, after making several detours to avoid prowling creatures, you reach the street where the base. You are three miles from safety. You make the turn as a cloud of steam pours from under the hood.

You manage another half mile before the engine coughs and quits. You look at the bags and boxes. You hate to leave them, but they will only hinder you. You've had too many close calls. You want to move as fast as you can. You get out, lock the doors, and pocket the key. It's a straight shot to the base. You start off at a jog but can't sustain it. You slow to a fast walk, wanting to save your energy in case you have to run for your life.

A mile later, you're feeling good about your chances. You stay aware, constantly scanning in all directions. Then, the hairs on the back of your neck stand up as a howl lifts above the surrounding buildings. You can't see it but fear the beast has caught your scent. You hasten your steps. When an answering howl comes, then a third, you break into an all-out sprint.

Passing an intersection, you see a beast a hundred yards away. It sees you and gives chase. You run as hard as you've ever done before. You can't help glancing behind you, even though it slows you. Two of the creatures are now after you and are closing. Fresh adrenaline jolts you into a new gear you never knew you had.

Ahead, you see the fence surrounding the base. You're close. Half a block away. Then the third beast arrives, directly in your path. Your heart sinks, but you have to keep going. It's your only hope. There is no turning back. Better to face one instead of two.

It lopes toward you. You run right at it, determined to bowl it over. As it draws near, you give a fake to the left, then break right. The beast takes the fake, but still manages to get an arm out to trip you. You fight hard to stay erect, but your balance has been thrown off. Like a running back striving for a few extra yards before hitting the turf, you put your one good arm down and keep your legs pumping. Your speed and balance are not in sync, though, and you fall.

You hit the ground, tucking a shoulder, and roll three times before you can get back to your feet. However, your lead has evaporated and the three beasts close on you. You kick at one, sending it sprawling. The others pounce though and drive you painfully to the ground.

You kick and punch in desperation, while still attempting to crawl away. You break free for an instant but are born down once again. No matter what you do, there are too many of them to beat. As they pin you down and move in for the first bites on your flesh, a gunshot sounds, blood erupts and the top most beast pitches backward.

The other two beasts look up, giving you a chance to punch one in the face. It falls back and is shot down. You have no idea who is shooting, but you are thankful to the point of tears. The last one dives at your throat. You are just able to get your cast in its mouth before its teeth sink into you.

The cast crunches. Pain comes, and you fear the bite has refractured your arm. You push hard with the cast to leverage the beast away. Above your head, a gun appears. It touches the beast's forehead and spits death. The beast goes limp and drops on you. Two sets of hands pull it off and a third pair reach for you.

You are hauled to your feet and a man scrutinizes your body for signs of bites. You are bleeding, but only from scrapes.

"It's all right," he says. "Your safe now. Let's get you inside and tended to."

"Thank you."

"No problem."

"I have a car full of stuff you can use. It's down the road."

"Let's get you inside first, then we'll send a team out to recover it."

Congratulations. You survived.

3A2) You make a quick decision and shift into reverse. You hit the gas, but instead of stopping at the woman, you race past, slamming into two of the beasts. You shift again, pull up next to the woman and Jim opens the back door. She gets in and you speed away as the third beast reaches the SUV. It leaps on the trunk but is unable to get a hand-hold and slides off. Silently, you say a "Yes!" as you watch its body bounce on the pavement.

The woman is caught between sobs and heavy breaths. She lays on the on the back seat staring at the roof. After a few moments, he gasped a "Thank you," sob, "Thank you. I thought I was ..." She breaks down in tears and you and Jim share a look.

You continue to drive with no real purpose. The woman sits up, places a hand on each seat and pulls close. "I'm Sally."

You and Jim introduce yourselves, then she asks, "Where you going?"

Jim says, "That seems to be the million-dollar question. We're not sure."

"Can I make a suggestion?"

"Sure," you say.

"Word is spreading that the National Guard base is taking people in."

"Really," you say. "How did you hear that?"

"A truck went down the street and blared a repeating message. I tried to get out in time to follow them, but some of those things came down the street and I missed my chance. That's where I was heading when you found me."

Jim asks, "Is that far?"

"Not too far from here. Maybe fifteen minutes," you say.

"It's worth a shot."

"Yep. Let's do it."

You get off the expressway two exits later and turn toward the base. It's about three miles down the road. A half mile later, you are forced to stop as herd of creatures is assaulting a car with four people in it. They have the small car surrounded. Many are on the hood, trunk, and roof, attempting to bounce their way inside. Then they begin rocking the car.

"Jesus," Jim says. "What are we going to do?"

Good question.

Do you:

3A2a) race past them? Read on.

3A2b) help them? Go to page 265

3A3c) reverse and seek an alternate route? Go to page 269

3A2a) "They're all occupied," Jim says. "Maybe we can just drive past them."

You squeeze the wheel tighter. Leaving the people in the car to die isn't right. You look in the mirror and lock eyes with Sally. "What do you think?"

Her cheeks color. She stares at the other car. "I-I don't know. I mean, what can we possibly do to help them without getting killed ourselves?"

You bite your lower lip. If you were alone, you'd go help, but Sally is right. What can you possibly do? Then an idea strikes. Perhaps you can do both.

You ease on the gas driving forward slowly, not wanting to draw attention until the last possible moment. As you increase speed, you veer toward the other car. By now, the creatures have the car rocking from two wheels to two wheels.

You position the car to sideswipe the other vehicle, although the extent to which the car is rocking makes the maneuver more dangerous. When several of the creatures notice and turn to face you, you punch the pedal. The engine whines. The SUV jumps. Now many of them see and the car's rocking lessens. The beasts howl in unison and five break away and charge you, unmindful of the danger.

You plow into them, sending bodies flying. One lands on the hood and smacks into the windshield with enough force to spider web the glass. The body and impact hinder your vision for a few seconds.

You veer right to avoid hitting the other car. A few creatures leap on the SUV. You increase speed and leave the other car behind.

"They're moving," Sally says, excitement in her voice. "No, wait! Now they're not. I think the car conked out."

You slow, thinking to go back and help, but both Jim and Sally yell at the same time, "What are you doing?"

"Going back to try again."

"No!" Sally pleads.

"Let's get to safety first," says Jim. "We can tell the National Guard. Maybe they can send a team in to rescue them. They'll be better suited to do that than we are."

Grudgingly, you agree. You make it to the front gate and are met by a cadre of armed men. They ask a series of question, the most important being, "Have any of you been bitten?" Once they finish and open the gates, you inform them about the other car. The man in charge makes a call on his radio as you drive onto the base and two military Hummers exit.

After meeting with the woman in charge of housing, you exit to unload the SUV. The two Hummers come back in. Neither the car nor the people are with them. As the first Hummer passes, you lift your arms out to the sides in a silent question. The man in the passenger seat frowns and shakes his head.

Though you're safe, your joy is hampered, thinking it came at the expense of someone else.


End

3A2b) "They're all occupied," Jim says. "Maybe we can just drive past them."

You squeeze the wheel tighter. Leaving the people in the car to die isn't right. You look in the mirror and lock eyes with Sally. "What do you think?"

Her cheeks color. She stares at the other car. "I-I don't know. I mean, what can we possibly do to help them without getting ourselves killed?"

You bite your lower lip. If you were alone, you'd go help, but Sally is right. What can you possibly do? Then an idea strikes. Perhaps you can do both.

You ease on the gas, driving forward slowly, not wanting to draw attention until the last possible moment. As you increase speed, you veer toward the other car. The creatures are now rocking the car side to side, up on two wheels each time.

You position the car to sideswipe the other vehicle, although the extent to which the car is rocking makes the maneuver more dangerous. When several of the creatures notice and turn to face you, you punch the pedal. The engine whines. The SUV jumps. Now you've gotten the attention of many, and the car's rocking lessens. The beasts howl in unison and five break away and charge you, unmindful of the danger.

You plow into them, sending bodies flying. One lands on the hood and smacks into the windshield with enough force to spider web the glass. The body and impact hinder your vision for a few seconds.

It throws off your aim and you barrel into the tail end of the car. Two of the creatures are caught between the two vehicles. Their eyes light up like you just won a prize at the "test your strength" game at the state fair.

The impact jars the three of you. Sally is pitched between the seats and lands on the console with a squeal. The mob engulfs the SUV. You reverse but can't see through them.

Jim says, "The other car is moving. Let's go."

You put the car in motion but run into the other car again. "What the hell?" you say.

"They stopped moving," Jim says. "I can hear them grinding the engine."

You reverse, then move forward again and tap the bumper. You repeat the process twice more.

"What are you doing?" Jim asks.

"Trying to get them to put the car in neutral so I can push them."

With a note of terror in her voice, Sally says, "We can't keep doing this. They're all over us. They're going to get in. We're going to die trying to save those people."

In an angry voice, you reply, "You mean, like how we could've died trying to save you?"

She quiets and sits back.

"She's right about one thing. If we can't do something to save them, there's no need to wind up dead ourselves."

You know he's right, but you refuse to give up without your best effort. You back up and try to pull alongside the other car. The creatures pinned between the two vehicles make it difficult to see. Each time you get a line of sight, you mouth the word *neutral*, but it's clear the man in the passenger seat does not comprehend.

Next you try tracing the letter N on the window. He finally gets it and retraces the N. You nod with enthusiasm, but he shrugs and turns to speak with the others. None of them understand. Your frustration grows. You repeatedly point to the steering column, mouthing and tracing the letter, but your clues are not getting through.

Finally, on the brink of rage, you lower the window an inch and scream at the top of your lungs, "Neutral! Put the damn car in neutral!"

The man's eyes widen as the light bulb flickers on. He says something to the driver, then gives you a thumbs up. However, one of the creatures now has its fingers in the window gap. You raise the window, but it will go no farther. You need to hurry. If the creature can exert enough force, the window will go down, leaving you unprotected.

You reverse again and line up behind the other car. The creature hangs on. You move forward until you tap the other car's bumper. Again, you are met with resistance, but this time, the other car moves. Slowly, you increase speed. You get up to almost ten miles an hour when the window gives way. Wind rushes in, bringing terror with it.

You accelerate faster, but the added burden of the other car keeps the building momentum to a slow increase. Hands reach for you through the busted window. You attempt to fend them off while maintaining the constant contact and speed.

You push one aside as you reach fifteen mph. It bleeds off as the other driver touches the brakes for some stupid reason. You growl like one of the beasts and blare the horn. You take a second to punch one creature in the face several times until it falls from the window. However, another is quick to fill the gap. Perhaps sensing the increased chance of a new meal, the creatures now swarm to your side of the SUV.

You can no longer go slow. You hit the car hard, and your body is jerked back into the seat. One creature dives inside across your lap. You get up to twenty and begin to leave some of the creatures behind. One stands on the rear bumper, clinging to the luggage rack. One pounds on the roof and two more manage to jump on the hood, but except for the one inside, the others are little threat.

You could shake them off the SUV by slamming on the brakes, but that would mean losing contact with the car. You keep going. Jim tries to contain the beast on your lap while you focus on the car. In seconds, you are up to thirty-five. The creatures left behind are in pursuit. The riders are still attached and holding on. In the clear now, you have time to deal with the beast inside.

While Jim keeps it occupied, you slip your arm around its neck and yank back as hard as you can. Jim punches it in the face. Blood soaks your pants. The beast on the roof leans down and reaches through the window. It snares your arm and pulls. You lose your grip on the wheel and are forced to release your choke hold to keep from veering off course.

You need to change something or become overwhelmed. Letting go of the wheel, you drive your fist into the creature's face. You fire blow after blow in rapid succession until the creature releases your other arm. One more solid shot and it topples to the ground.

You reach the fence surrounding the base. Half a block to go to the gate. You increase speed, giving the car a good last push, then drive around it. You slam on the brakes a few yards shy of the gate and send the riders flying in all directions.

You head toward the gate as the other car makes a hard turn. Its speed bleeds off fast, but it makes it to the closed gate. Behind it stand six armed men all with guns pointing at them.

"Keep this thing busy," you say to Jim. Then, you open the door and slide out. Once outside, you see the herd is fast approaching. You hope they'll let you in, but you need to deal with the intruder in your vehicle first. You grab its legs and pull backward until it flops from the interior. It hits the ground and you drag it further. Then, you run for the car, shouting, "Open the gates!"

As you reach the SUV, a gunshot makes you jump. You look behind you to see the dead body of the beast. Other gunshots follow. A minute later, the gate moves. Four of the six men rush out. A man yells, "Stay in your vehicles until I tell you to move! If you exit before then, you'll be shot."

The four men open fire on the herd, wiping them out in seconds. After a series of questions to everyone in the cars, the most important being if anyone had been bitten, you are allowed to enter the base.

After an officer interviews you and explains the rules, the man stands up, smiles, and offers his hand. "Welcome to your new home."

Congratulations. You made it.

3A2c) "We can't do anything for them," Jim says. "Let's get out of here."

Sally agrees. As much as it pains you to leave them to their fate, you back away, turn around, and drive away.

You take a circuitous route and come at the base from the opposite direction. You pull up to the gate and are met by six armed men. No one approaches for several minutes. You open the door and are instructed by a commanding voice to stay inside or be shot. You sit and wait, wondering if you're supposed to have a secret code word to gain entry.

An officer walks to the gate accompanied by two men and two women. He says something to them. They all look at the SUV. One woman points and two others nod in agreement. The officer motions for the gate to be opened, then approaches the SUV escorted by two guards.

You roll down the window and greet him, but he hushes you. "It's my understanding that you left a car full of people to die without even trying to help them. Is that right?"

Shocked by the accusation and feeling the guilt of his words, you are unable to answer. He doesn't wait for one. "On this base, we look out for other people. We never turn our backs on our fellow man. That's a crime punishable by banishment or death.

"Since no one died, death is off the table, and since you are not part of our community I can't very well banish you, but I can deny you entrance. Remember this the next time someone needs your assistance. You have until the gate closes to vacate. After that I will give the order to fire."

Sally begs, "Please. We're sorry. It won't happen again. Please don't turn us away."

The officer walks toward the gate without responding.

"We have to do something," Jim says. "We can't survive out here for long."

There's nothing you can do. You should've followed your own

instincts and helped the other car. As much as you hate being turned away, you can't blame them. It's your own fault.

As the gate begins to close, you nod at the officer and back away from the gate. As you drive off, you search your mind for someplace to go that might be safe. Jim and Sally are quiet. You don't blame them for your predicament. You were driving. You could've done something. *Never again*, you vow.

You pass a convenience store several miles down the road and see people inside. You glance at the fuel gauge and wonder if you can get a fill up. You pull up next to a pump and get out. You approach the front door and stop. The interior has been ransacked. You decide something isn't right and turn to leave. The door opens and a man shouts, "Hey!"

You turn just as the man fires. The bullet slams into you. You fall back. As blackness closes in, you hear an engine start, more gunshots, and a vehicle speeds away.

"Bastards!" you mumble as your last breath leaves your body.

End

3A3) "Man," Jim says, "she ain't gonna make it." He looks at you. "I hate to say it, but we need to leave her. We can't help her."

You look from him to her, then to the beasts chasing her. She won't last another five seconds. You could drive to her, but by the time you open the door for her, the creatures will be on her. You would risk all your lives.

Deciding he's right, you speed away, trying not to look in the mirror. Your conscious won't let you get away without a look. You see her reaching an arm out to you, as if she were close enough to grab. The desperation on her face haunts you. Then, the three beasts pounce and take her down. She is quickly lost underneath them. You avert your eyes to avoid watching her death, but your imagination plays it out in a more gruesome way than reality might have been.

*Now what?* You drive, lost in the horror of your actions. You are a coward. That woman deserved at least an honest effort. Her death will forever be on your hands.

Ten minutes later, a Hummer races up a ramp. At first, you are happy to see other living beings, but when they veer at you, the reality sinks in. They are not there to help, but to rob you.

The driver strikes you broadside, driving the SUV off the road and down the embankment. The SUV rolls over several times, tossing your body like a rag doll despite the seat belt. Sharp pain fills your brain. As the SUV stops on its roof at the bottom of the median, you try to extricate yourself from the wreckage, but the pain stops you. Your left arm is broken. Pain from your ankle informs you it might be broken, as well.

Jim moans. Blood flows from his scalp. Before you can say anything to him, men descend on the SUV. They break any windows not already busted by the collision. Hands reach in and yank your belongings out. A man crawls inside. In a cheery voice, he says, "How y'all doing today? Just sit tight and we'll be out of your hair in a few seconds."

He searches the interior and finds a few items that came loose from the bags and boxes, then disappears. A minute later, you hear the Hummer pull away. Relieved they didn't kill you, you start to take inventory of your body. Then you hear howling in the distance and the relief fades. If you can't get away and fast, you won't be able to defend yourself.

You struggle and are eventually able to snake out. Jim isn't moving or moaning. You think to help him, but the howling is much closer. You see a small copse of trees and brush fifty yards away. It may be your only hope. Limping, one arm hanging useless at your side, you head for the safety you hope the trees will offer. Halfway there, you fear it is too late.

Risking a glance, you spy several beasts closing on the SUV. Jim screams. He wasn't dead after all. You push yourself, knowing you have little chance of survival. Running footsteps pound the ground behind you. A cry of desperation escapes you, much like you imagine the woman must have done. Then, just as she had been, you are brought down and swarmed over.

The pain of their teeth ripping the flesh from your body barely registers. Your last thought is of the woman, and you pray you won't meet her in whatever afterlife you end up in.


End

3B) Fearing he may attack you, you keep driving. He screams and waves his arms, but you let him fade away in the mirror. You reach the ramp and race away. Berating yourself for not at least stopping to talk to him, you drive for another fifteen minutes, thinking next time you'll stop…if there is a next time. After all, you've seen more creatures than humans.

As if in answer to your decision, a Hummer shoots up the next ramp. At first, you are elated to see other survivors. However, when the driver aims at you, your earlier fears are realized. You are unable to outrun them and angle the SUV toward the sloping median.

The Hummer hits you on the back right quarter panel, sending you skidding sideways and you flip. The SUV rolls over several times, tossing your body like a rag doll despite of the seat belt. Sharp pain fills your brain. As the SUV stops on its roof at the bottom of the median, you try to extricate yourself from the wreckage, but the pain stops you. Your left arm is broken. Pain from your ankle informs you it, too. might be broken.

Before you can do anything else, men descend on the SUV. Any window not already busted by the collision is broken. Hands reach in and yank your belongings out. A man crawls inside. In a cheery voice, he says, "How you doing today? Just sit tight and we'll be out of your hair in a few seconds."

He searches the interior, finding a few items that came loose from the bags and boxes and then he disappears. A minute later, you hear the Hummer pull away. Relieved they hadn't killed you, you start to take inventory of your body. You hear howling in the distance and the relief fades. If you can't get away and fast, you won't be able to defend yourself.

You struggle and are eventually able to snake out. The howling is much closer. You see a small copse of trees and brush fifty yards away. It may be your only hope. Limping with one arm hanging useless at your side, you head for the safety you hope the trees will offer. Halfway there, you fear it is too late.

Risking a glance, you spy several beasts closing on the SUV. You push yourself, knowing you have little chance of survival. Running footsteps pound the ground behind you. A cry of desperation escapes you. Terror driving you to brink of madness, you are brought down and swarmed over.

The pain of their teeth ripping the flesh from your body barely registers. Your last thought is that if you had stopped for the man, you wouldn't be here at this moment. Unfortunately, you won't be alive for the lesson to be learned.

End

Chapter 3 (2B1a, 2B1b, 2B1c, 2B2,)

The night passes uneventfully. Frank sets a two-hour watch schedule and warns that if you fall asleep on duty, he'll kick you out. Your partner is given the first watch and you get the second. After taking your position, you stretch. Your body groans with several creaks and pops.

You scan the land in front of the house. It's too dark to see anything, but Frank has night vision goggles and instructs you on their use. The eerie green reminds you of being in a horror movie, which in truth, you are.

The silence gives you time to think. *What's going to happen?* Surely, the world hasn't come to an end over a few crazed animals? How widespread could whatever caused the change be? There's no doubt Frank plans on holing up in the house for the rest of his life. He's certainly stocked well enough. A rough estimate puts the food stores at a year. Frank has enough weapons and ammo to fight a small combat mission.

When Carol comes to relieve you, she's carrying a mug of hot tea.

"Everything all right?"

"Yeah. Very quiet."

"I'm glad you're here. I was worried."

"I am, too, and I was even more worried. I don't think Frank likes us being here, though."

"Oh, don't be fooled. He growls like a bear, but inside, he's glad for the extra bodies, if only so he doesn't have to keep watch all night. This is the first time he's been able to put together more than a few hours of sleep in a row. He's just nervous about what we might be facing."

"Yeah. This has all happened so fast. One day, I'm unconscious and in the hospital; the next the world has gone crazy."

"I think it was more widespread than people know. When it was first reported, the incidents were few and far between. Most thought there was an escaped wild animal from a zoo on the prowl. By the time they figured it out, it was out of control."

You lay down for a while. Sleep comes slow, but it does finally come. What feels like only minutes later, Carol is knocking on the bedroom door, announcing breakfast is on the table. You sit to eggs and pancakes and strong black coffee. Feeling revived, you go upstairs to talk to Frank.

"Hey Frank."

He grunts. "Where's your gun?"

*Damn!* You left it in the bedroom.

"You need to carry it at all times."

"Sorry. I'll have to get used to that."

He grunts again.

"So, what's the plan?"

"The plan is to survive."

"Yep. Good plan."

You stare out the window, trying to think of a conversation starter that will result in an actual discussion, when he leans forward, narrows his eyes. You do the same, trying to see what he sees. His eyes must be a lot better than yours.

He picks up binoculars. Seconds later, he slaps them into your chest and runs for the door. You peer out the window, adjust the focus, and see a horse running like it's in a race. Angling the glasses, you see why. A herd of perhaps twenty beasts is giving chase. You run to your room for your guns.

Downstairs, Frank is busy preparing for something, but you have no idea what for. You look at your partner and are miffed that he/she is already armed.

"What do you need me to do?" you ask Frank.

"You take the front window. Carol, upstairs bedroom." He points to your partner. "You watch the back door. I'm going out to save that horse. Lock the door when I leave and be ready to open it on my return. Also, watch my back in case those things get too close. No one shoot unless you have to. We don't want to draw their attention."

Everyone moves. From the front window, you see the horse approach. It has easily outdistanced its pursuers but is lathered and fading fast. Using the rifle scope, you scan the herd. It is moving at a steady pace. By the time the horse reaches the house, it is barely able to walk. Frank approaches slowly and appears to be talking to it.

It has a bridle, but no saddle. He reaches up and take the reins. Easing close to the horse, he caresses it. He is taking too long for your liking. Another look at the herd shows they have halved the distance. If they are aware of Frank, they show no signs, but it won't be long if he doesn't move. You urge him mentally, as if your thoughts will enter his mind. He leads the horse away and out of sight along the side of the house. You guess he's going to put it in the barn.

A distant howl draws your attention. More follow until the entire pack has caught the scent of prey. Their pace increases. *Come on, Frank. Hurry!* Upstairs, you hear a window being raised. Carol is preparing to fire. You wonder if you should do the same but decide not to open the window. It was safer to open a second story one, where the beasts have little chance of gaining entry.

At the back of your house, your partner says out loud what you were thinking. "Come one, Frank. Get your ass moving."

The creatures reach the edge of the property and angle toward the house. It is a frightening sight. "Yell for him to hurry. They're on the property and closing fast!" you yell to your partner." He/she opens the door and calls out to him.

The herd is getting too close. They smell blood and it's driving them harder. "They're only a hundred yards away. Where is he?"

"He's locking the barn."

"He's cutting it close."

Carol yells from upstairs. "Get ready to shoot! He needs cover."

You kneel on the sofa, flick the lock, and yank the old-fashioned wood frame window up. The screen is in the way. You try to lift it, but it sticks. You heave and the metal frame bends and falls to the porch.

You stick the rifle out and search for a target. The pillars and stone railing give you a limited line of sight. The herd reaches the house and races alongside. You wait to hear a signal or gunshot, and two things happen almost at once. Your partner screams and Carol fires.

Do you:

3A) shoot? Read on.

3B) run to help your partner? Go to page 290

3A) Carol's shot surprises you. You accidentally pull the trigger and waste a shot. You zero in on a target near the back of the herd. Your next shot spins it around. It drops for a moment, then gets back up. You fire again. Three shots later, a fine mist of blood lifts into the air and it's down for good.

Upstairs, Carol is a machine, loosing one evenly-spaced shot after another. She swears, and you hear her move from the room above you to one at the back. You have no other targets and think to move, but suddenly, three beasts burst up the front steps. Surprised, you pull back. Your bladder threatens to release. They are at the window in a flash, fighting to be the first inside.

You back away and fire. The first one's head explodes. You switch targets and blow up the next one. The remaining animal crawls inside. You cycle the bolt, and as the creature rises in front of you, you blow a hole through its chest.

Panicked, you stand gaping for valuable seconds before running to the window and shutting it.

Carol yells down. He's in the barn! The beasts are circling, trying to find a way in."

You reply. "He's safe in there, right?"

Carol hesitates. "He is unless they find the rotted boards on the far side. Frank's been meaning to replace that wood but never got around to it."

"What do you want me to do?"

"I don't know."

A quick check of the front shows no creatures, so you jog to the back. Your partner is watching at the back door. You sit at the kitchen table and peer out the window. The remaining beasts are circling the barn, howling and slamming into the doors and walls. Then a gunshot comes from outside. That can only mean they found a way in.

Do you:

3A1) start shooting? Read on.

3A2) run out to help?" Go to page 283

3A3) wait for Carol to give orders? Go to page 287

3A1) You open the kitchen window and begin shooting. A few misses hit the barn and you pray they aren't penetrating. It looks like almost half the herd has been killed. Better odds, but not for Frank. More gun shots come from inside. Carol continues to rain down death from above. She is a much better shot than you are.

After several more beasts are killed, the remaining pack moves around the barn out of sight. You have no more shots. Frank shoots rapid-fire. The beasts must all be inside. You have to do something to help him but are at a loss as to what.

Carol stomps down the stairs and falls. You race to help her. "I have to get out there. Frank needs help."

"You can't help him like this," you say. "You'll just get yourself killed." You take a deep breath, turn to your partner, and say, "Open the door."

He/she looks at you in shock. "No. You can't."

"If I don't, Frank's dead."

"But if you go out there, you'll die, too."

"I have to try."

Still, he/she doesn't move. You go to the door and put a hand out to open it, but your partner hugs you and opens it. "Be careful."

"Keep the door open."

You dart out before you change your mind. You don't need to go in the barn. You just need to draw them away from Frank. You move to get an angle at the far side of the barn but stay a distance away. You are surprised to see only two creatures still outside. Frank is no longer firing. That scares you.

You aim quickly and fire. The bullet strikes the wood above one of the creature's heads. They both duck instinctively and look around. They spy you, howl, and run at you. Your first instinct is to run, but you force yourself to stand and fire. You take down the first one and find you have spent your last round. Your inexperience shows. You forgot to check your ammo.

You panic and think about running, but fear being taken down from behind. You reverse the gun and swing it with all your might, like a baseball bat. A shot rings out mid-swing. You spin around in a circle without making contact. Stopping, you see the body in front of you and your partner standing a few feet away.

You want to run and give him/her the biggest hug ever, but the horse whinnies a cry of fear and Frank shouts, "Get away from her, you mangy bastards!"

You drop the rifle, pull the handgun, and run toward the ragged opening in the side wall. Inside is dark. It takes a moment for your vision to adjust. You enter in a stall. The gate is open. Crouching, you move forward, stopping at the gate. You peer out and see three creatures trying to climb a stall near the rear of the barn to get at the frightened horse.

Frank is above in the hayloft, laying on his stomach and jabbing down with a pitch fork. He is letting loose with a steady stream of expletives like they were bullets.

You lean out of the gate, take careful aim, and fire. Your shot strikes one in the back. It arcs backward, lets out a howl, and drops to its knees. It's not dead but is less likely to attack. The other two stop their efforts to get at the horse, looking from their packmate to you.

They rush in a flash. You back away, closing the gate. It's not much defense, but at least they'll have to climb to get at you. They hit the wooden corral at the same time. You back away firing. One falls face first inside, hit by two rounds. You switch targets but know you're too late. The beast leaps at you. You shoot in rapid succession. To your surprise, the beast never makes it to you. In fact, it appears suspended in mid-air, like time has frozen. Then you notice the pitch fork protruding from its head. Slowly, the body slides from the tines and drops on the ground.

You place a hand over your heart as if to ease its pounding. Frank calls, "Hey, can you get the ladder, so I can get down? I tossed it over there."

Minutes later, after barricading the hole, you head back to the house. Your partner and Carol come out to meet you.

"What happened?" Carol asks in a harsh tone.

"I ran out of bullets."

"Uh-huh! And where's your handgun?"

Frank looks sheepish and lowers his head and mumbles something.

"Excuse me?" Carol says. "I didn't quite hear that."

"I forgot it."

"Wait!" you say. "After all that preaching about making sure we always have guns with us, *you're* the one who forgot?"

"Well, it was a horse. I got excited. It needed my help."

You all laugh and go inside. The first thing you do is reload the rifle and handgun. Lesson learned.

Over the next three days, you have sporadic sightings of beasts, but no more confrontations. On the fourth day, a military Humvee drives up to the house. A lieutenant informs you the National Guard is doing a sweep, hunting down any creatures still roaming free.

"You're welcome to move to the base. It's locked down and safe."

You say, "Nah! We're good. We've got everything we need right here."

Frank gives you an approving nod.

"Okay. I'd stay inside for the next few days. Keep a radio on. We'll announce when it's all clear."

They drive off.

Three days later, the all-clear is broadcast.

You survived.

3A2) You run to the door and try to open it, but your partner holds it closed.

"Wh-what are you doing?" he/she asks.

"Frank needs help. There's too many of them."

"No." Fear shows on his/her face.

"I have to. If he dies because we didn't do anything to help him, we'll never be able to live with ourselves."

"If you die, how will I go on."

"Guess I better not die then." You place a hand over his/hers. "I have to do this."

"I know. But you better come back, or I'll shoot you myself."

You don't say, "If I don't come back, I'll probably turn into one of those things and you'll have to shoot me." You turn the door and step into the madness.

The creatures have swarmed the barn. Some work at opening the door. Several pound on the walls. Many howl. If you survive this ordeal, it's a sound that will haunt you the rest of your life.

For the moment, they do not notice you. A loud cracking sound tells you they broke through the rotted wood. Gunshots come from the barn. Frank needs you now. You step to a large wooden picnic table, squat behind it, and place your elbow on top for support.

You try to remember everything you've ever heard from shooters or TV shows about guns. The rifle is a bolt action. You take aim, not sure if you're supposed to squint one eye or keep both open. You opt for the squint as it seems to help you focus.

The beasts are already running to the far side of the barn by the time you take your first shot. It slams into the wood inches in front of several beasts. Three of them stop and look for the source. Standing still, they are better targets for your inexperience. The next round plows into a chest, throwing the creature back like they'd been yanked by a rope.

Carol is firing at the mob trying to get into the barn. She is a much better shot than you are. The remaining two charge at you. You wish you could shoot as fast as your heart is beating. You line up the next shot, your hands shake hard enough to throw off your aim.

You force a deep breath, aim and squeeze. The round is true and knocks one down. You recycle the bolt, but the beast is almost on you. It reaches the picnic table and you lift the barrel for a shot, but you don't get the chance. A shot from the house drops the airborne beast.

You turn to see your partner in the doorway. It makes sense coming from this family that he/she is a better shot than you, too. Thank goodness. You nod and race toward the barn. When you arrive, no beasts are outside. Three bodies are there, courtesy of Carol, but the rest are inside. *How many is that?*

Gunshots come from inside. The horse is going crazy. You hear Frank cursing at the beasts. You peer through the jagged opening. It's dark. Your eyes adjust, and you enter. You are in one of the stalls. The wooden gate is ajar.

You become aware of the lack of gunshots. With a faltering heart, you fear the worst for Frank. Then you hear, "Get away from her, you bastards."

Crouching you move forward, stopping at the gate. You peer out and see a dozen creatures. Trying to climb a stall near the rear of the barn to get at the frightened horse. It bucks wildly. A beast goes flying across the barn landing over the gate of a stall across the way. You let out a silent cheer.

Frank is above in the hayloft, laying on his stomach and jabbing down with a pitch fork. He lets loose with a steady stream of expletives like they were bullets. Obviously, he was out of the real thing.

You lean out of the gate, take careful aim and fire. Your shot strikes one in the back. It arcs backward, let's out a howl and drops to its knees. It's not dead, but less likely to attack. Two stop their efforts to get at the horse, looking from their pack-mate to you.

They rush in a flash. You back away closing the gate. It's not much defense, but at least they'll have to climb to get at you. They hit the wooden corral at the same time. You back away firing. One falls face first inside, hit by two rounds. You switch targets but know you're too late. The beast leaps at you. You shoot in rapid succession. To your surprise, the beast never makes it to you. In fact, it appears suspended in mid-air, like time has frozen. Then you notice the pitch fork protruding from its head. Slowly, the body slides from the tines and drops on the ground.

"Hey!" Frank calls. "You got an extra gun?"

"Yeah."

"Toss it up to me."

You pull out the handgun and try to determine the best way to do this. If you miss and it lands on the barn floor, you're both screwed. You have no idea how many rounds the rifle has. You should've checked in advance.

"Hurry!" he says. "They're about to get to the horse."

You reach over the gate and fling the gun upward. It lands with a thud above you. One of the creatures sees you and rushes. You are just able to level the rifle and fire point blank, before it gets you.

Above, Frank rains down death, bullets plow through the tops of the creature's heads. In less than a minute, it's over.

You place a hand over your heart as if that will ease its pounding. Frank calls, "Hey, can you get the ladder so I can get down? I tossed it over there."

Minutes later, after blocking the hole, you are heading back to the house. Your partner and Carol come out to meet you.

"What happened?" Carol asks in a harsh tone.

"I ran out of bullets."

"Uh-huh! And where's your handgun?"

Frank looks sheepish and lowers his head and mumbles something.

"Excuse me," Carol says. "I didn't quite hear that."

"I forgot it."

"Wait!" you say. "After all that preaching about making sure we always have guns with us, you're the one who forgot?"

"Well, it was a horse. I got excited. It needed my help."

You all laugh as you go inside. The first thing you do is reload the rifle and handgun. Lesson learned.

Over the next three days, you have sporadic sightings of beasts, but no more confrontations. On the fourth day, A military Humvee drives up to the house. A lieutenant informs you the National Guard is doing a sweep to hunt down any creatures still roaming free.

"You're welcome to move to the base. It's locked down and safe."

You say, "Nah! We're good. We've got everything we need right here."

Frank gives you an approving nod.

"Okay. I'd stay inside for the next few days. Keep a radio on. We'll announce when it's all clear."

They drive off.

Three days later, the all-clear is broadcast.

You survived.

3A3) You run to the front of the house and stand at your position, not sure what to do. Frank may need help, but he told you to stay in your position, no matter what. If all the action is in the back, shouldn't you be back there? But if you leave and the beasts attack the front, no one will be there to stop them. You decide to wait for instructions. Carol has a better angle on what's going on. She'll call down if Frank needs help.

Footsteps thunder down the steps. Carol runs past, saying," They got in the barn! I'm going out to help Frank."

You call after her. "What do you want us to do?" But she is already running out the back door. You go to the door and stand with your partner. "Should we help them?"

Your partner shrugs, clearly petrified.

Gunshots erupt in rapid succession. You move to the kitchen window to get a better view. Carol is standing in front of the barn firing into a group of creatures running at her. You lift the window, slide the rifle barrel out, and fire. Your shot misses. You shoot three more times, taking one down.

Carol drops another, but evidently has run out of ammo because she reverses the rifle to use as a club. It's then you decide. You run to the door, but your partner blocks you. "It's your sister. If I don't go out, she's dead."

Your partner backs up, sobbing. You burst out the door, rifle ready, and see Carol go down under the weight of three beasts. You only have seconds to help her. You run as fast as you can, afraid to fire for fear of striking her.

You reach her as one beast clamps down on her throat. You fire inches from its head and blow out its brains. One leaps from her to attack you. You jab it in the face with the barrel, knocking it off balance, then shoot through its eye.

Carol screams. You aim and fire. The last beast falls. You help Carol up and back to the house. She has blood on her arm and face, though you can't be sure if it's hers or the beast's. Your partner opens the door and takes control of Carol.

You run back to the barn and peer through the jagged boards. It's dark. You are acutely aware of the lack of gunshots. Is Frank dead, or had he run out of bullets? The horse whinnies in fear. You crawl through and find yourself in a stall. The gate is open. You crouch and walk that way. You peek out. About ten of the creatures have surrounded the horse's stall. It bucks wildly, trying to fend them off. One beast gets too close and is sent flying across the barn.

From above in the hayloft, Frank jabs down at the beasts with a pitchfork. He is bloody but still fighting. As you watch, he skewers a beast through the top of the head. The tines lodge there, and as he attempts to pull the pitchfork free, a creature leaps and grabs the handle. Its weight pulls Frank off balance. He falls from the loft and lands on his back, stunned.

You react in a flash, firing the rifle over and over until you get nothing but a click. You hit three, but there are still too many. Some go for the horse while others descend on Frank. Without hesitation, you pull the handgun and continue shooting. You stand and move into the center of the barn. You may hit Frank, but if you don't keep firing, he'll be dead anyway.

You kill two, but one has sunk its teeth into Frank's arm and is rending flesh with violent back and forth jerks of its head. Frank screams and punches at the creature's head, but the blows have little effect.

You run up close, place the muzzle against the beast's head, and pull the trigger. As you bend to help Frank up, one of the beasts attacking the horse leaps on your back. You are knocked to the ground. Before you can recover, you feel a searing pain in your shoulder. Teeth are embedded in your flesh.

You reach around your head and fire back at the beast. The explosion deafens you, but the beast is gone. You escape from its weight, push to your feet on rubbery legs, and go to the stall. The horse is down, though still alive. The beasts are tearing flesh from its haunch. You shoot both and collapse against the fence.

You don't know how long you sit there before your partner comes out. He/she gasps at the scene. He/she runs to you, tears falling in tiny rivulets. He/she helps you to your feet. The two of you help Frank up. Once inside the house, your partner works feverishly to clean and bandage everyone's wounds.

You pray that what you learned about being bitten is not true, but just in case, you grab your partner's arm and pull him/her close. "Keep a gun with you at all times. If we turn into one of those creatures, you have to kill us."

He/she starts to cry and shakes his/her head. "No. I can't. I won't."

"If you don't, you'll die. If we turn, we will no longer be ourselves. I will no longer exist. You have to."

"We'll talk about that if and when it happens."

You release him/her, knowing the end will come soon. You pray he/she will have the courage to do what needs to be done. You decide then, that if you feel the change coming, you'll do it for him/her. You hate thinking you might be the one to kill him/her.

It takes a full day for Carol to turn. You are sleeping when the gunshot comes. You look around, confused. You struggle to remember where you are, vaguely aware of who you are. A strange scent fills your nostrils. Your face twitches. You recognize the scent. It's blood. It arouses something feral within you.

You shake the sleep from your brain. A second gunshot clears your mind. You form a picture of your partner. The image, so vivid, makes you smile. The vision bursts like a balloon and a strange noise creeps up your throat. It sounds like a growl. You're confused.

You try to rise again, but a hand pushes you gently. Your partner stands over you with a sad smile. It makes you feel warm inside, but you're not sure why.

"I'm sorry," he/she says and raises the gun. The sight sends a chill through you. You try to rise, but the hand pushes firmer.

"I love you," he/she says before pulling the trigger.


End

3B) You run to the back to make sure your partner is all right. He/she is shaking but still keeps watch.

"Hey! You okay?"

"I guess."

You start to reassure him/her, but broken glass from the front room has you turning away. *Damn!* You did what Frank warned against. You left your post. You reach the dining room as a beast rises from the floor. You level your rifle and fire, blowing it onto the couch. Another one leaps in, followed by a third.

You shoot the first one point-blank, but the next one gets to you before you can recycle the bolt. It knocks you down and crawls up your body toward your throat. You get the rifle barrel between its teeth and push. It slips the impromptu bit and is about to snap at you when Carol fires from the stairs. The beast's head explodes, covering you in a fine red mist.

You sit up as another beast jumps through the window. Carol fires again, wounding it. You drive the rifle stock into its head as you rise. You jab the barrel down into its stomach and shoot.

"Watch that window," Carol says and runs back upstairs. You move to the sofa, give a quick scan, and remove the body from the sofa. With that done, you kneel on the sofa and lean out. Just as you do, hands grab the rifle and yank it from your grasp.

You jump up and reach for the handgun, but the creature leaps through the window and knocks you down again. This time, you have nothing to prevent its teeth from sinking into you.

Your partner screams and fires, but misses. The beast's attention switches, and it crawls toward your partner. Fear for him/her sparks your actions. You push the pain aside, yank the gun, and roll onto your stomach. You shoot twice, killing the beast as it launches toward your partner.

He/she runs to you, but you say, "No. Go back to your station. Watch the rear. Protect Frank."

You crawl back to the window, wishing you had heeded Frank's words. If you would've stayed there, you might have been able to prevent the beasts from getting inside. Now, you paid the price. You hear plenty of gunshots from the back of the house, but no other creatures attempt to get in through the window.

What feels like hours later, Frank comes back inside and announces they are all dead. You roll onto the couch and close your eyes. The pain is sharp from the bite. You pray what you've been told is false. You don't want to turn into one of those creatures.

Your partner kneels next to you and examines your wound. Carol and Frank stand over you with emotionless expressions. Your partner washes and bandages the wound. You swallow some pain pills, and your partner says, "Get some rest." He/she plants a kiss on your forehead, strokes your cheek, and leaves the room. You manage to doze, waking when you hear a loud sharp voice.

"Shh! You'll wake him," Carol says.

Frank says, "It has to be done. There's no choice."

You wonder what they're talking about but are afraid you already know. You drift off again. When you wake, you feel strange. Something doesn't feel right—like you're having a fever dream. Everything looks like it's in a haze.

"She's/He's awake," your partner says. He/She stands and moves aside. Carol wraps an arm around him/her and leads him/her upstairs. That confuses you.

"Hey, bud," Frank says. "How you feeling?"

"Weird."

"Yeah, I'll bet. Hey! You feel well enough to give me a hand?"

"Ah, yeah, I guess." You struggle to your feet. Frank has to grab your arm to keep you from falling.

"Where we going?"

"Just to check on the horse. After what just happened, it's not safe to go out alone."

*Just happened?* You can't seem to recall what just happened, but you go with him. You're having trouble focusing your thoughts. Bodies litter the yard. A scent of blood fills your nostrils, reviving you. You walk toward them, but Frank guides you away.

"Let's go around the back and avoid all the mess."

You allow him to guide you, but something inside screams for you to run. You have no idea what it is, but the alarm is building to a crescendo.

"Frank," you start to say, but he pushes you from behind.

"Let's not stop until we get inside the barn where it's safe."

That sounds logical to you, but you can't shake the sensation that danger is close. Your nose twitches, picking up traces of nervous sweat. It enhances the already dire warnings.

You stop, pull away, and turn. "I'm not going any further until you tell me what's going on."

"Sure thing, but you should have this." He hands you a handgun. As you reach for it, he drops it. "Oops!"

You narrow your eyes and look at him. A low growl builds in your throat. He did that on purpose, but you have no idea why. You bend to retrieve it.

"Sorry, bud, but you shoulda stayed at your post."

You look up into the muzzle. The explosion flashes before your eyes.


End

Chapter 3 (2B)

The night passes uneventful. Frank sets a three-hour watch schedule and warns that if you fall asleep on duty, he'll kick you out. You take the first watch. After taking your position you stretch. Your body groans, and your bones creak and pop.

You scan the land in front of the house. It's too dark to see anything, but Frank has night vision goggles and instructs you on their use. The eerie green reminds you of being in a horror movie, which in truth, you are.

The silence gives you time to think. Thoughts of your partner flood your mind. Great memories flow past your mind's eye like streaming video. Your eyes fill with tears. You let them fall, then wipe your face and push them aside.

*What's going to happen?* Surely, the world hasn't come to an end over a few crazed animals? How far widespread could whatever caused the change be? There's no doubt that Frank plans on holing up in the house for the rest of his life. He's certainly stocked well enough. Your rough estimate puts the food stores at a year. Frank has enough weapons and ammo to fight a small combat mission.

When Carol comes to relieve you, she's carrying a mug of hot tea.

"Everything all right?"

"Yeah. Very quiet."

"I'm glad you're here. I was worried."

"I am, too, and I was even more worried." You both avoid any talk of your partner's death. "I don't think Frank likes us being here, though."

"Oh, don't be fooled. He growls like a bear, but inside, he's glad for the extra bodies, if only so he doesn't have to keep watch all night. This is the first time he's been able to put together more than a few hours' sleep in a row. He's just nervous about what we might be facing."

"Yeah. This has all happened so fast. One day, I'm unconscious and in the hospital; the next, the world has gone crazy."

"I think it was more widespread than people know. When it was first reported, the incidents were few and far between. Most thought there was an escaped wild animal from a zoo on the prowl. By the time they figured it out, it was out of control."

You lay down for a while. Sleep comes slow but does finally come. What feels like mere minutes later, Carol is knocking on the bedroom door, announcing breakfast is on the table. You sit to eggs and pancakes and strong black coffee. Feeling revived, you go upstairs to talk to Frank.

"Hey Frank."

He grunts. "Where's your gun?"

*Damn!* You left it in the bedroom.

"You need to carry it at all times."

"Sorry. I'll have to get used to that."

He grunts again.

"So, what's the plan?"

"The plan is to survive."

"Yep. Good plan."

You stare out the window, trying to think of a conversation starter that will result in an actual discussion, when he leans forward, narrows his eyes. You do the same, trying to see what he sees. His eyes must be a lot better than yours.

He picks up binoculars. Seconds later, he slaps them into your chest and he runs for the door. You aim them out the window, adjust the focus and see a herd of twenty beasts coming toward the house. You run to your room for your guns.

Downstairs, Frank is busy preparing for something, but you have no idea what for.

"What do you need me to do?" you ask Frank.

"Carol, take the front window. I know you can shoot." He points to you. "You watch the back door. No one shoot unless you have to. We don't want to draw their attention." He races upstairs.

"Should we wake Agnes?" you ask Carol.

"Yes. We don't want her shocked awake by gunfire. I'll get her."

You move to the kitchen window and stare out. Frank and Carol's property is twenty-five acres. Only the slight stubble of a crop has sprouted. You have no idea what it is.

Carol leads Agnes into the kitchen and sits her down. "Do you like cereal?"

Agnes nods. Carol places a bowl, a spoon, a carton of milk, and four boxes of different kinds of cereal on the table. "Help yourself, honey. Oh, and no matter what you see or hear, please don't scream."

She walks out, leaving Agnes wide-eyed.

"Which do you prefer?" you ask, trying to lessen her fear. She points at the only sweet one and you pour it. She starts eating as Carol calls, "They're almost here."

You can see the back yard from the kitchen table, so you stay where you are to keep Agnes company. As you wait, you check the window. It's an old-fashioned wood frame with a half-moon lock at the top. You unlock it and slide it up. There's a screen. You depress the latches and slide it up, then close the window. The girl eyes you as she eats but does not speak.

Softly, Carol says, "They're here. At least twenty." She's in the living room, kneeling on the sofa, and staying low. "Damn!"

That didn't sound good. You are tempted to get up and see what drew the curse, but you don't want to abandon your post. An eerie silence descends over the house. It even feels colder.

Movement outside draws your attention. You hide behind a sheer curtain that allows you to watch the creature as it sniffs the air. Whatever scent it has picked up leads it to the car. You watch with curiosity. A squeak draws your focus to the living room. Carol is now lying flat on the sofa. You see why. Two creatures are on the porch. If they press their faces to the glass, they'll be able to see you and Agnes.

You stand as quietly as possible and extend a hand to Agnes. She hesitates, then takes it, and you lead her out of view. Something scrapes against the glass at the back door. You want to peek but hold back.

Agnes watches with a wide-eyed stare. You flash a reassuring smile and put a finger to your lips. Time passes slowly. *Why hasn't it gone?* Surely, they can't hear you breathing or smell you?

Something pushes against the door, testing to see if it's open. *Oh man!* You plot what to do if they get in. The rifle won't do for close quarters. You release Agnes's hand, lay the rifle on the counter, and withdraw the handgun, flipping the safety off.

Ready, you try to calm your nerves by going into a rhythmic breathing pattern. You glance down at Agnes. She leans forward to look into the living room. You are about to pull her back when she gives a sharp, "Huh!" and jumps back. Her entire body shakes. Seconds later, all hell breaks loose.

The front windows implode, sending glass shards all over the living room and on Carol. She rolls off the sofa as the first beast leaps through. You step out and fire twice. The second shot wings the creature. It spins off balance and Carol drops it with a shot.

The man-things are coming through the window, two at a time. She fires in a hurry with deadly accuracy, but there are too many.

"We have to fight our way to the stairs. We can control them there," she says.

Agnes is in steady scream mode and frozen to the spot. Leaving the rifle, you scoop her up and follow Carol. The back door crashes in. You turn and fire into the first beast's face.

Carol reaches the stairs as Frank comes down to join her. Their constant barrage keeps the beasts back long enough for you to reach the stairs. You move past them and run. They follow backwards, keeping up the rate of fire.

The lower floor is lost, and howls rise and fill the upstairs.

Frank says. "Put the kid down and drag some dressers out here."

You set Agnes on a bed. "Be brave. I won't let anything happen to you." You put the handgun in your belt, latch onto a dresser, and pull. You position it in front of the door, then get behind it and push. It scrapes against the wood floor, leaving a long scar. In the hall, Carol comes over to help. You place it in front of the top step and take up position next to Frank. For the moment, nothing happens. They may be beasts, but they're smart enough to know death awaits in the stairway.

In the lull, Frank says, "Carol, get more ammo and bring the shotguns."

She goes, and Frank turns his anger on you. "What the hell happened?"

A red veil covers your eyes. "How should I know? We didn't do anything to draw them inside." But inside, you know they must have seen Agnes.

Carol comes back with two pump-action shotguns, a box of shells, and two boxes of ammo. "You got a forty?" she asks.

"Yeah."

She gives you a box and an extra magazine. "Fill them both while we have a chance."

A strange silence breaks out as loud as the howls had been. *What the hell were they doing? They couldn't possibly be forming an attack plan, could they?* You replace the first mag and are halfway through loading the second when you hear something outside the rear of the house.

You meet Frank's eyes as you both recognize the sound. "Carol, watch the stairs," Frank shouts as you both race for the bedroom door.

Agnes screams just before the window crashes in and right before you push open the door.

One beast is on the floor, a second climbing through. You fire at the one on the floor as you reach Agnes and pull her to you. Frank finishes the second one.

Carols shotgun explodes with a sound like a hand grenade in the tight space.

"Stay here and watch the window," Frank says and darts out of the room.

You open the closet door and push Agnes inside. "Stay in here until I get you." You close the door and hear her whimper, trying hard to be brave.

You move closer to the window to see if more are coming. Something moves in the field behind the house. You spy a dozen more creatures heading your way, like someone rang a dinner bell. You edge closer and see the top of the porch roof. They've scaled the wrought iron supports to get to the roof. That surprises and worries you. It now appears the beasts are capable of thoughts beyond the hunt for food.

Glass breaks. It's the room across the hall. You lean out the window to see a leg disappear through the next one. You scream for Frank to watch his back, but you doubt he hears you through the booming of the shotguns.

Do you:

3A) stay where you are? Read on.

3B) go into the hall? Go to page 300

3C) climb out the window? Go to page 302

3A) You decide to hold your ground and protect Agnes. Surely, Frank heard the window breaking. You watch the window and wait for a creature to pop its head through.

A commotion in the hall sends a wave of panic through you. Carol screams. Frank curses. A shotgun roars and pellets pepper the bedroom door, blowing chunks out of it. Through the gaps you can see the life and death struggle.

You hesitate, then run to the door. You whip it open in time to see Frank born down by three beasts. Carol struggles with one. You shoot her assailant, then turn toward Frank's. In rapid succession, you shoot all three, but it's too late for Frank. Blood jets from his ruined throat. He covers it with his hand and turns his head toward

Carol.

She gasps and drops to her knees as two more beasts reach the top and vault over the barricade. You shoot one in mid-air. The second lands on Carol, driving her face first into her husband. You aim, but your shot is thrown off by another creature coming from the second bedroom. It plows into you. You manage to push it aside and fire.

You shoot the one, ripping flesh from Carol, then duck back into the bedroom and try to barricade the door. Another beast comes through the window. You shoot it as the door crashes in.

You fire repeatedly, thinking you need to save a bullet for you and Agnes. As they close in, unsure of how many bullets you have left, you whip the closet door open and level the gun at Agnes. Her tear-filled wide eyes meet yours. You almost can't do it, but you pull the trigger a second before they take you down.

Flailing as wild as you can, you turn the gun on yourself, only to notice the slide is locked back. You scream as the first of the teeth sink into your flesh. By the fourth bite, you feel nothing.

End

3B) You open the door just as the beasts burst from the other bedroom. You fire one shot after another until you've taken down three. Frank turns his shotgun on the next one, ripping it apart. No more are coming, but Agnes screams.

You race back through the door as a beast is dragging her from the closet. You end it fast and turn to the window. One more pokes its head through. You fire, but it pulls back. This has to end. You can't cover both windows. The only way to solve the problem is to prevent them from climbing up.

You move to the window. The beast has gone into the other room. You climb out. A creature is just rising from below. You kick it in the head, sending it falling. Moving to the other window, you see the beast about to attack Frank. You fire twice, and the beast goes down at Frank's feet. He jumps and whirls, leveling the shotgun. He spies you, nods, and turns back to the stairs.

You kneel on the porch roof and lean over. A beast is near the top. You shoot it in the face. The numbers appear to be thinning. You shoot again and the slide locks. Quickly, you exchange the magazines, remembering you didn't have a chance to fill it.

Three more shots and two more bodies, and there is nothing left to shoot. Inside, quiet settles over the battlefield. You stand your post and wait. What feels like days later, Frank pokes his head out and says, "I think we're good. While we have a break, let's reload in case more are hiding."

You go inside, retrieve the box of ammo, and reload on the porch. As darkness comes, you all go downstairs and block the various openings.

While Carol fixes food, Frank says, "You saved my life. I was wrong about you." Then he walks away. You figure that's as close to an apology and a thank you as you'll get.

Over the next three days, you have sporadic sightings of beasts, but no more confrontations. On the fourth day, A military Humvee drives up to the house. A lieutenant informs you the National Guard is hunting down any creatures still roaming free.

"You're welcome to move to the base. It's locked down and safe."

You say, "Nah! We're good. We've got everything we need right here."

Frank gives you an approving nod.

"Okay. I'd stay inside for the next few days. Keep a radio on. We'll announce when it's all clear."

They drive off.

Three days later, the all-clear is broadcast.

You survived.

3C) You step out onto the porch roof as a clawed hand grasps the edge. When the head appears, you punt it to the ground and continue to the other window. You arrive as the creature is about to attack Frank from behind. You fire three times. The creature falls at Frank's feet. He jumps, spins, and levels the shotgun at you. You have a flashing of your life, but he nods and turns back to the stairs.

You turn in time to fend off an attack. You never heard the beast crawl up. It pushes you back. You side step and shove, and the beast goes airborne. Another one rises, and you shoot it. Moving to the edge, you peer over the side. More are coming.

You kneel for better balance. A beast nears the top. You shoot it in the face. The numbers appear to be thinning. You shoot again and the slide locks. Quickly, you exchange the magazines, remembering you didn't have a chance to fill it.

Three more shots and two more bodies, and there is nothing left to shoot. Inside, quiet settles over the battlefield. You stand your post and wait. What feels like days later, Frank pokes his head out and says, "I think we're good. While we have a break, reload in case more are hiding."

You go inside, retrieve the box of ammo, and reload on the porch. As darkness comes, you all go downstairs and block the various openings.

While Carol fixes food, Frank says, "You saved my life. I was wrong about you." Then he walks away. You figure that's as close to an apology and a thank you as you'll to get.

Over the next three days, you have sporadic sightings of beasts, but no more confrontations. On the fourth day, A military Humvee drives up to the house. A lieutenant informs you the National Guard is hunting down any creatures still roaming free.

"You're welcome to move to the base. It's locked down and safe."

You say, "Nah! We're good. We've got everything we need right here."

Frank gives you an approving nod.

"Okay. I'd stay inside for the next few days. Keep a radio on. We'll announce when it's all clear."

They drive off.

Three days later, the all-clear is broadcast.

You survived.

End

Chapter 3 (2B1, 2C)

You follow Jessica's directions, and in a short time, you are on the coastal road along the lake shore. The drive takes longer than anticipated. Even without traffic or having to worry about cops, you are forced to detour around clogged roads and bands of creatures.

You enter a road that stops at a gated lakefront community. It's obvious that those who live there have an exorbitant amount of money. You come to a stop. You see a man in the guard booth, but he doesn't make a move to get out.

"What do we do?" you ask.

"The guard will check the car to see if it's on the list. Then, he'll check to see who's inside. When he sees me, he'll open the gate."

The guard takes a long time. You're beginning to think he's not going to let you in. Then, Jessica says, "Oh, he must have called Todd. There he is."

A tall, good-looking man arrives at the gate and stares at the car. He looks perplexed.

"I think you should poke your head out, so he can see you," you say.

She does. "Todd, it's me. Let us in."

He looks relieved and speaks to the guard. The gate rolls back and you move inside, stopping where the guard tells you. Jessica jumps out and runs into her husband's arms.

"I don't like this," your partner says. "Why aren't they just letting us in?"

*Good question.* You open the door and step out, but the guard moves your way with one hand up in a *stop* signal and the other one resting on his sidearm.

"Get back in the car, sir," he says, leaving no doubt by his tone that it's an order, not a request.

"But ..."

"Now, sir."

You look at Jessica, but she averts her gaze. You get in and roll the window down. You can't hear everything, but you catch enough to know you're in trouble.

"But Todd, they saved me. I gave my word."

"I understand, Jessica, and that would be fine during normal times, but these aren't normal times. If we take them in, it lessens the amount of food we have for our family. We have no idea how long this crisis will go on."

Todd looks at you, sees the open window, and guides Jessica away. The next words are out of earshot.

"Jessica wants to let us in. Todd doesn't think they have enough food for us and his family."

"What should we do?"

Do you:

3A) continue to wait for the decision? Read on.

3B) get out and try to negotiate? Go to page 319

3C) drive away? Go to page 322

3A) "Let's see what happens," you say.

You don't have much longer to wait. Todd speaks to the guard, then the two men approach the car. The guard comes to your partner's side, and Todd to yours.

"I'm sorry, but there's no room for you here."

"You've got to be kidding me."

"No," he says, his voice hard as steel. "I appreciate what you did for my wife, but you need to find somewhere else to go."

You glance across to the guard. His gun is halfway out of the holster.

"And," Todd continues, "we're going to need you to get out of the car."

"What?" the word explodes from your mouth. You see red as you open the door to confront him.

Before you get the chance, the guard is right there, weapon aimed at you. "Back away now, sir. Don't make me shoot you. I don't want to, but I will."

You yell at Jessica's retreating form, "Is this how you repay us? I saved your life—twice."

She lowers her head but never falters.

"This is wrong."

"Tell your friend to get out of the car, or Carl will be forced to remove her/him."

You're so angry that if you ever get your hands on the man, you'll strangle him. The gun is in the belt at your back. You wouldn't have a chance to draw it before Carl shoots you.

"You're sending us out there to die," you plead.

"I am sorry. But when it comes to a choice between my family and someone else, well, better you than us."

You glare at Todd, thinking of all sorts of things you'd like to do to the man. Your partner gets out of the car, spitting mad. "This is how one human treats another? You're no better than the beasts."

He/She gives a sarcastic growl and gets into the driver's seat. With Carl moving to the other side of the car, you bend quickly and jab the knife into the tire. You turn and take your partner's hand. The car makes it about thirty feet before the tire deflates. Todd gets out and shouts at you. You flip him off.

"Now, what do we do?" your partner asks.

You give it some thought.

Do you:

3A1) keep walking until something comes up? Read on.

3A2) try to find a car? Go to page 312

3A3) find someplace to stay? Go to page 316


3A1) You keep walking, but your anger grows by the step. You begin looking in cars until a mile later you find one, a minivan. Searching, you find an unopened bag of pretzels. You start the engine and grab the tire tool. It's too short for your purpose. You scan the ground until you find a stick that will work.

You drive back toward the gated community and stop a hundred yards away. "You need to get out here," you tell your partner.

"What?"

"It's payback time," you say.

Whether he/she agrees or is just afraid of the tone of your voice, he/she gets out.

You press the pedal down and drive closer. Removing your foot, you wedge the stick between the accelerator and the seat, then roll out. The pain jars you. It's not like in the movies where the hero gets up and walks away. This hurts.

Carl sees the car coming and jumps in front of it and starts shooting. He leaps to the side as the minivan crashes into the gate, ripping it away. To your surprise, however, it keeps going. Carl gets up, shakes a fist at you, and gives pursuit.

You walk back to your partner and continue your stroll.

"You realize we have to find another car now, right?"

"Yeah, but it was totally worth it."

From behind, you hear a collision. It brings a smile to your face.

You walk for miles without seeing anyone or finding a vehicle, but at least you haven't seen any creatures.

You reach a main road. Unfamiliar with the area, you aren't sure which way to go. You're still trying to decide when a car comes barreling down the road. You hope it will be someone nice enough to give you a ride, but as it gets closer, you see a red-faced Carl and another man in a guard uniform.

"Run!" you say. Taking your partner's hand, you lead toward some woods off the road.

The car screeches to a stop and doors open. You reach the woods, release your partner and say, "Keep going. I'll call your name when it's clear."

You move laterally for several yards and duck behind a tree. The men in pursuit are not quiet about it. Carl says, "When I catch that asshole, I'm gonna kill him."

That tells you the ground rules. You take out the gun.

The man with Carl says, "There."

They set out toward your partner. You go around the tree and stalk them. They make so much noise that they never hear your approach.

Carl slows and puts up a hand. "That's one. Where's the other one?"

They scan around, and you step out, gun leveled. "Don't move. Don't force me to shoot you. I don't want to, but I will," you say, repeating Carl's words.

The other man goes for his gun and you fire. The bullet slams into his shoulder and spins him to the ground. You weren't aiming for the shoulder, but they don't know that.

"That's your only warning. I'm an excellent shot. Next one goes through your eye." You're either out or have one round left. You can't remember.

You call your partner's name. "You can come back now."

"I'm gonna kill you," Carl rages.

"Says the man with the gun aimed at him. If you're gonna kill me, I might as well shoot you."

That brings a fearful look to Carl's face.

"Take out your gun and toss it over here." He moves too fast and you shout, "Slowly, or I'll be forced to kill you." Carl tosses the gun off to the side. You smile at Carl's move.

You hear rustling and glance to see your partner coming back. "Stay wide. Come around behind me. You motion with your gun toward the wounded man. "Take out your gun and toss it over here."

"Why don't you come over here and get it?"

"Sure, I can take it from your cold, dead body." You take a more careful aim.

The man reaches across his body and withdraws the gun. You can see he's thinking about trying something, but a glance at your face convinces him otherwise. He tosses it.

"Go get the guns." Your partner returns with both. You take one. It is larger and will have more stopping power than the one you took from Jessica. "Now, the car keys." Neither man moves. You tell your partner, "You aim at the one on the ground. If we don't get the keys in five seconds, fire."

Your partner raises the gun and it goes off. The shot startles him/her as much as it does the two men. Carl is all motion now. He takes out the keys and tosses them to you.

"Last thing. Take off your boots. Don't give me that look. Just do it." You tell your partner to get in the driver's seat of the car.

When the boots are off, you tell them to toss them to you. You pick up Carl's and take off running. Before you exit the woods, you pitch them to the side. You're driving away by the time the two men appear.

"See, told you I'd get us another ride."

"Yeah. Right."

It's dark by the time you reach the city. Ahead, you see headlights. You tell your partner to slow, not wanting to run into anyone else who may want to rob you. "Pull off here and turn off the headlights." Once out of sight, you search for someplace to hide.

There," you point. "Pull up that driveway as far as you can. Turn off the engine and get down."

A few minutes later, a slow-moving vehicle appears on the road. You watch over the seat. It drives past, stops, and backs up. It's blocking the driveway. A spotlight swings your way, then a megaphone barks out, "You, in the car. We are not here to hurt you. Come out so we can talk."

"Not a chance," you mumble.

"We know you're in there. We have night vision goggles. We can see your heat signatures, as well as the cars. I'm Sergeant Mathews of the National Guard. We're rounding up survivors and taking them to our base. It's safe there. If you're interested, follow us. If not, we won't bother you again."

"You think that's true?" you partner says.

"I don't know. It's hard to trust anyone after everything we've been through."

"If they leave, we can follow them at a distance. If they try to get too close, we run."

The spotlight goes off. As they drive away, you think you see a shape standing in the back of what might be a jeep.

"Okay. Let's try it."

But even as the car reverses, you are readying the guns for a battle.

You follow at what you think to be a safe distance. The lead vehicle is at least going in the right direction. When it turns on the main road running in front of the base, you become more confident in your decision. Then a second vehicle falls in behind you.

You rotate in your seat to see what it is, but it sits higher than the car, placing the headlights directly in your eyes.

"What do you want me to do?"

You have to make a quick decision. "If the lead vehicle turns up the driveway, stop and see if the gate opens. If so, we drive up. If not, speed away as fast as you can."

The lead vehicle does turn, but it sits at the gate and waits. The one behind stops and waits for you. Spotlights on the fence flare to life and aim inside your car.

"We've been here before. Go!" you shout, fearing you are being targeted.

The car races away, but the trail vehicle does not follow.

"Whoa! Slow down."

As you watch, the second vehicle drives up and they both go onto the base. Now you're not so sure it was a trap.

"Turn around and let's drive past again."

As you draw even with the gate, you see it is open. Someone is motioning you to enter. "Well?"

"I'm thinking," you say. After much mental coin tossing, you say, "Okay. Let's try it. But this time, I'll be prepared. If they try anything, get out of there fast."

Your partner pulls up alongside a man in a uniform. He is smiling. "I thought you might come back. All are welcome here. Drive to that second building there and go inside. Someone there will help get you settled in."

"This is for real?" your partner says.

"Absolutely. We've got close to three hundred people here already."

"I can't believe it."

"Believe it. You're safe now."

"Thank God," you say.


End

3A2) You are too angry to speak. You should have shot the bitch when you had the chance. You keep walking before realizing your partner is no longer next to you. You stop and look back.

"I think the keys are in the ignition."

You go back. Sure enough, the keys are hanging there. Finally, a break. You get in and start the engine. It's low on gas but should be enough to get you someplace safe. You drive for almost an hour before your partner says, "I've been thinking. Why don't we head to Carol's house?"

Carol is your partner's sister. She lives on a farm with survivalist husband, Frank. Frank does not like you, but if anywhere was safe, it'd be their farmhouse. "Good idea…if Frank lets us stay."

"Carol will make him."

You get on the freeway and head toward the farm. A few miles later, a Hummer shoots up a ramp and angles at you. You brake and swerve to the left to avoid the collision. The sudden move and speed sends you down the sloping median. The Hummer gives pursuit.

The car bounces along the uneven ground. You swing it back up the slope, but the Hummer cuts you off, forcing you to the bottom again. This time, you climb up the opposite side. You reach the pavement and drive in the wrong direction. The Hummer follows. A man leans out the passenger side window and fires at you. You swerve side to side. As far as you can tell, the bullets have all missed so far.

The Hummer pulls alongside of you. Another man opens the rear window and takes aim. Before he can shoot, you turn for the ramp. The driver of the Hummer was unprepared for the move and zooms past. You have a slight lead and need to make the best of it. Turning away from the freeway, you floor the accelerator. You turn into a shopping center where there are still plenty of parked cars. You park between a pickup and an SUV and turn off the engine.

"Stay down," you say and get out of the car. You lock the doors and hide in front of the pickup, gun in hand. You can see the street. The Hummer comes into view moving slowly. You think it's going to pass you, but as it reaches the intersection, it reverses and pulls into the parking lot. You watch as it patrols up and down the aisles. In the row before yours, two men get out and begin searching cars. In a few minutes, one says, "Hey! This one is full of groceries."

The driver stops next to the man. He gets out and tells the third man to keep searching, then moves to help the first man load the bags of food into the Hummer.

The man closest to you finishes the row and comes down yours. In the distance, a series of howls announce new arrivals.

The man searching your row stops to look. The driver says, "Come help so we don't have to waste bullets putting those things down." The searcher turns into the lane next to your car and your partner chooses that moment to lift his/her head to see what's going on.

"Hey, I found our missing car." He taps on the window. "Open up or I'll shoot through the glass."

The driver calls over. "Do they have anything worth taking?"

"No, unless they've got stuff in the trunk."

"Kill them and check."

Before the man can pull his trigger, you step from your hiding place and fire. The small caliber bullet smacks into the man's chest, leaving him stunned and confused, but still standing. He looks up at you and his face flushes with rage.

You fire once more into his eye, putting him down.

The driver runs toward you, firing on the move. You duck and slide to the rear of the car. Your partner opens the door and gets out. You take off to draw him away from your partner.

The man gives chase and lines up a killing shot, but the muzzle flash does not come from him, but from the right. Blood and matter fill the air and he falls. Your partner stands there, holding the dead man's gun. The man still by the Hummer opens up on you. One bullet grazes your partner's shoulder. You call out. He/she answers, "I'm okay," but the pain in his/her voice says otherwise.

"Get back in the car," you say. You retrieve the second man's gun, return fire, and get in.

You start the engine as the man steps away from the Hummer and fires. The bullets punch through the windshield. Several rows behind the man, you see two beasts coming. You back away fast, smashing into a parked car behind you. The man runs forward, unaware of what pursues him. You drive away as bullets chase you.

In the mirror, you see the beasts jump on the man and take him down. You turn up the next aisle and stop behind the Hummer. "Time to switch rides," you say. You both jump out and take over the Hummer. The keys are in the ignition. The rear of the vehicle is full of food, supplies, and weapons.

You speed away and soon are on the dirt road leading to Carol and Frank's place. Pulling up the driveway, you see Frank standing watch in the second-floor bedroom window. You stop behind the house out of sight from the road.

Your partner knocks. No one answers for several minutes, then Carol comes to the door. She wraps your partner in a hug and motions you inside. Frank stands there with a hunting rifle. The angle is somewhere between being aimed at you and being secured.

"What do you want?" Frank says.

Carol says, "Frank. Stop it."

"We don't have enough food for four mouths." To you he says, "You need to move on."

"They're staying, Frank," Carol says.

"That's all right, Carol. If we're not wanted, we'll take our food and weapons someplace else."

Frank's mouth hangs open, looking like he's in pain, which meant he's thinking.

"Hold on, now. If you brought your own stuff, that's different. How many guns you got?"

"Haven't counted. More than twenty."

"Ammo?"

"Some."

"Well, what you standing there for? Let's get you unloaded and moved in.

The next day, Frank is happy he allowed you to stay. Six beasts catch him outside. You and Carol step out with AR15s and mow them down.

Over the next three days, you have sporadic sightings of beasts, but no more confrontations. On the fourth day, A military Humvee drives up to the house. A lieutenant informs you the National Guard is hunting down any creatures still roaming free.

"You're welcome to move to the base. It's locked down and safe."

You say, "Nah! We're good. We've got everything we need right here."

Frank gives you an approving nod.

"Okay. I'd stay inside for the next few days. Keep a radio on. We'll announce when it's all clear."

They drive off.

Three days later, the all-clear is broadcast.

You survived.

3A3) You walk at least a mile before finding another house. It's dark and shows no signs of life.

"Let's try there," you say. "We can stay there for the night."

You walk up the path to the front door and knock. No one answers. You make a circle around the house, looking in the windows and trying the doors. You don't see anyone, and all the windows and doors are locked.

You break out the door window with the butt of the gun, reach through, and unlock it. You enter with caution. It's not only dark, but someone might be hiding. You enter the kitchen and your partner goes through the cupboards, finding several cans of soup, fruit, and vegetables.

You empty them into pots and go outside to cook them on the propane grill. On your way back in, you hear a loud bang followed by a heavy thud. You set the pots down on the kitchen table and pull out the gun. You call your partner's name. No answer.

You creep toward the kitchen door, but the old floor creaks, making stealth all but impossible. You can't see a thing. A low moan comes from the front room. Had he/she fallen or been attacked? You decide not to call out again. If someone is there, they know exactly where you are by now.

Ducking, you step into the front room. You move toward where you heard the moan, keeping your head up. Another moan guides you. Your foot touches a body. You bend to check it, then something explodes in your head. Complete darkness engulfs you.

When you wake, your hands are bound behind you. Your head is pounding. A flashlight comes to life, the spotlight shining in your face. Your head hurts even more. Your partner is next to you, head lolling to the side.

"What do you want?" you ask.

"That depends on what you want." The voice is female and husky.

"We were just looking for a safe place to stay the night, that's all. Someone stole our car at gunpoint. We've been walking for a long time. We were tired and hungry. We don't mean you any harm."

"Huh! Easy to say now that you're all tied up."

"How would we know anyone was staying here? Just untie us and we'll leave."

"I think I'll just leave you where you are 'til morning."

"My head hurts. What'd you hit me with?"

"Baseball bat. I think I hit two consecutive home runs, eh?" She laughs. "Sleep it off. You'll feel better in the morning." She leaves, closing the door with a clack as the lock engages. You must be in one of the bedrooms. If that's the case, why is there a lock on the outside? Who had she been locking in here?

The morning arrives and to your surprise, you slept. Your partner is still out, and you fear he/she died during the night, but you see slow and shallow breaths. You try to stand, but a wave a nausea passes through you. You must have a concussion.

As the sunlight filters through the curtains, the room is revealed. It is small; perhaps a child's room. You are on the floor leaning against a bed. A chest of drawers is across from you. There is a net strung in one corner holding a pile of assorted stuffed animals.

Extending your hands behind you and under the bed, you feel along the metal frame until you reach the end. You find a burr and a rough edge. You begin scraping the rope against it. A few minutes later, you hear the lock and the door swings in.

"So," she says, "you made it through the night. Good for you."

"What are you going to do with us?"

"Well, that's a good question. I'm not sure."

"Just let us go."

"So you can come back and attack me later? I don't think so."

"I'm making some tea. Would you like a cup?"

You shake your head. She leaves, reengaging the lock.

You go back to work. The process is too slow. Then, you discover you can catch a portion of the top loop over the corner of the frame and pull. It works. The first loop opens. You are working the second one when the door opens again.

The stocky older woman kneels next to your partner and checks for a pulse. She moves the hair back to reveal a large knot.

"He's/she's not looking too good. I'm taking him/her into the next room to see what I can do. Don't worry, I'm not going to hurt your friend. I'm not a killer. Well, at least not intentionally." She laughs. "Never intentionally."

She drags your partner out of the room and locks the door. You immediately go back to work on the rope. The second loop is tighter and harder to get started, but once you do, it too falls open. Now the rope is loose enough to snake out of.

You stand and search. The only weapon you find is a hardbound Bible. You wait behind the door. When she comes back in, you slam the book into her surprised face, staggering her back. She recovers quicker than you would've thought possible, but you don't give her a chance to shut the door. You pull it from her grasp and punch her in the face. She drops in a heap.

You relieve her of the gun she took from you and go find your partner. He/she is still unconscious. You put him/her in a fireman's carry and start to leave. You stop as you pass a bowl with two sets of car keys. You grab them both.

Outside, you press the fob and see the lights flash on a car parked in the street. You slide your partner in the back seat and drive home. There, you barricade every window and door and stay in for the duration of the emergency.

Five days later, your partner is alert and recovering as the TV squawks to life and a National Guard officer announces the crisis is over.

A week later, you are back at the hospital to get your arm checked. On the way home, you spy a familiar woman pumping gas. You pull over and walk up. You tap her on the shoulder and as she turns, you punch her in the face. *Damn Jessica.*

You walk away feeling vindicated. You survived her treachery and the deadly ordeal. You whistle a happy tune as you drive home.

3B) You get out, but as soon as you do, the guard crouches, ready to draw on you, and shouts, "Sir, you need to get back in the car!"

Your eyes narrow. Your hand opens and closes, itching to reach for the gun at the small of your back. You swing your gaze toward Jessica and Todd. He has her wrapped in his arms and pushed slightly behind his large body. She peeks out, catches your eyes, and quickly averts them. However, the glimpse you caught was enough to tell you something is wrong.

"What's going on? Jessica?"

"Don't talk to my wife," Todd says.

"All right, then maybe you can explain it to me. We brought your wife here in good faith. After saving her life, I might add. Did you forget that, Jessica?"

"I told you, don't talk to her."

To the side, the guard fidgets with the holster, ready to draw. He makes you nervous.

Todd continues. "Thank you for what you did, but there is no place here for you."

"What are you talking about? There's nothing *but* room here. If you don't want to put us up in your house, we'll stay in a basement or garage. We just need someplace safe."

Jessica whispers something to him. Todd replies, then says, "Carl, they're leaving. Oh, and the car stays. It is ours, after all."

"That's bullshit." You take a step forward and Carl has the gun out, hands shaking, and screaming at you to move on. You hold your ground and fire bullets at him with your eyes.

"I don't want to shoot you, but I will. Walk out the gate and be on your way."

Todd leads Jessica away. She glances back, a look of regret on her face.

You move next to the car out of a direct line of fire and slide the gun out. As Carl moves to the driver's door and motions for your partner to get out, you lift the gun over the roof and fire before you mean to.

The bullet rips into Carl's shoulder. He spins and falls, sending the gun goes flying. "Get his gun!" you say and race after Todd and Jessica. They paused in shock at the gunshot, but seeing you coming at them with a gun, they turn and run. You catch Jessica in seconds, her big, brave husband having left her behind. She calls for him, but he ignores her.

"Looks like you picked a real stand-up guy. You should've just let us in. It shouldn't matter that we're not in the same financial situation as you. We're all still human and trying to survive."

"I'm sorry. Please don't hurt me. It was all Todd. He didn't want to let you in."

"Lady, you two are meant for each other."

You let her go and she falls crying to the ground. "At least have the decency to get poor Carl some medical attention." You walk back to the car. A bullet whistles past you, striking the windshield. You whirl around and see Todd running toward you with a hunting rifle. He fires again, and you duck. From a crouch, you take aim and fire your last round. Todd runs two more steps, slows, and tumbles to the ground. You're not sure where you hit him, but he's not moving.

You stand and move to Carl. He tries to crawl away, afraid of being killed.

"Hold up. I'm not going to hurt you. I doubt these people care enough to get you help. Come with us. We'll take you to a medical facility."

It takes some convincing, but Carl lets you load him in the back seat.

"Sorry. I'm getting blood all over the car."

"That's okay. It's not ours. You're more familiar with the area than we are. Any suggestions?"

"I think the hospital is still open."

He gives directions and you take him there. Inside, no one asks questions. They just take him into a back room. You sit, too exhausted to move. No one asks you to leave, so you stay, happy to have someplace safe, if only for a few minutes. The hospital is open, but appears understaffed, so when someone else staggers in with a head wound, you guide him into the back where a nurse takes him.

Later, the nurse comes out and says, "Your friend is out of surgery and in recovery. You can go see him in a bit." Then, a look a fear fills her face. She puts her hands to her face and screams.

You follow her gaze and see two beasts coming through the emergency room door. You jump to your feet and fire at the two creatures, killing them both. You drag them outside to the opposite side of the parking lot. When you return, the blood has been cleaned up. When the nurse appears again, she is carrying a tray with a pot of coffee and two cups, and two cold egg sandwiches.

"Thank you," you say.

"As long as you're here waiting for your friend, would you mind watching over the emergency room? As you can see, we're very shorthanded."

"No problem."

She gives you a quick tour, showing you where you can sleep and shower. You settle in to your new home and stay for the duration.

Five days later, the National Guard shows up to offer security and announce the danger is almost over.

You have survived.

3C) "Let's get out of here before they decide to take the car, too."

"You sure?"

"Better to make the decision for ourselves rather than have it made for us."

Your partner shifts and floors the pedal. You shoot backward out of the driveway, bouncing wildly on the street. The guard gives chase, gun now in hand. Before he can set up for a shot, your partner switches gears and aims for him. He is forced to dive out of the way.

A few quick moves with the steering wheel and you are racing away.

"Now what?"

You say, "I haven't a clue. But we need to find someplace safe to stay."

"Should we go back home?"

"I think we should find something around here. There doesn't seem to be nearly the number of beasts out here as in the city."

You drive for thirty minutes before seeing a car fly past on the adjoining road. You follow, hoping they'll lead you to a safe haven.

The car speeds for another few minutes, before taking a turn on two wheels and bouncing up the drive of a small hospital. It appears to be open. As you glide up behind the first car, you see a harried man emerge carrying a small girl. Her body is limp in his arms. He runs into the emergency room and is met by a nurse.

A head moves in the back seat of the car. You get out to ask some questions and find a woman leaning against the door, covered in blood.

Do you:

3C1) help her? Read on.

3C2) go back to the car? Go to page

3C3) go inside the hospital? Go to page 326

3C1) You open the door and catch the body before it falls out. "Can you hear me?" No response. She's unconscious but appears to be breathing. You have no idea the extent of her injuries but manage to get both arms under her and carry her toward the emergency room door.

As you arrive, the frantic man meets you. At first, he displays panic, seeing his wife carried by a stranger, but you say, "Help me." He steps forward and the two of you get her inside where the nurse instructs where to place her.

"Thanks," the man said. "We were attacked a few miles out, trying to get home."

That brings a feeling of fear and sorrow. If those are bite wounds, you know the end result. You wish him luck and go back to the car. While you sit trying to decide what to do, two beasts come out of nowhere and enter the hospital.

You reach for the door, but your partner stops you. "What are you going to do?"

"I have to at least warn them. No one's guarding the door."

You exit on the run and burst through the door. The beasts reach the inner door. You raise the gun but are too late to get off a shot. You run after them.

As you go through the door, you hear a scream, a crash, and commotion ahead. You run in that direction and find the nurse trying to keep the bed with the injured woman on it between her and one beast, while the man wrestles with the second.

You step close to the first one and shoot it in the back of the head. The man grunts and falls back with the beast on top. You step over, place the muzzle near the side of the beast's head, and kill it. The man collapses from exertion. You help him up and see his arm has a jagged wound.

"Thank you," the nurse says. "We are very shorthanded. Would you mind watching the emergency room until I can get these people where they need to be?"

"Sure. No problem."

The man says, "Thanks for your help," and offers his left hand. You grip it, trying not to show the sadness you feel for him and his family.

You motion your partner inside and the two of you protect the room. You help two others with minor injuries inside over the course of the night. Later, the nurse brings a tray of coffee and cold egg sandwiches.

Two days later, the entire family is dead. The doctor makes sure they never reanimate as beasts.

Three days later, the National Guard arrives to defend the hospital. Two days after that, the threat is considered to be over. You drive home to start your new life.

You survived.

3C2) You go back to the car and report your findings. The man comes out and runs to the car. He opens the door and drags the woman's body out. He's trying to lift her when the beast leaps on his back. The man is already ripped open by the time you get out to help. You level the gun and shoot. The beast falls. You move to check on the woman as a second one tackles you.

You hit the ground hard, and the gun goes flying. Getting both hands under its chest, you heave, but can't toss it free. A searing pain races up your arm. You turn to see a chunk of your flesh torn from your arm. *Damn!* You know what that means. Your fate is now sealed, but you can't quit. There might be something they can do in the hospital.

You partner jabs a knife into its neck. The dead weight lands on you. You get up and your partner helps you inside. The nurse takes you back. If she realizes you're a dead man walking, she gives no indication. She cleans and dresses the wound. As the infection takes hold, you slip in and out of consciousness.

You wake, seeing your partner next to you. You ache. Sweat pours from you. Your face and arms hurt, like something is trying to tear its way out of your flesh. A doctor enters with a syringe. You see pity in his eyes.

Your partner leans over the bed and says. "I'm so sorry." He/she plants a kiss on your forehead and steps away for the doctor. He injects you. "It'll be fine now. You can rest in eternal peace."

His words are comforting. You become drowsy. You feel warm inside. As your consciousness slips away for the last time a distant thought rises to the surface. *Did he say eternal peace?*


End

3C3) You step away and enter the emergency room. The man runs past you and out to the car. A few minutes later, he returns with the woman in his arms. You step forward and help the man carry her into the back room. The nurse instructs where to place her, then starts the examination.

While she works and without looking up, she says, "Are you together?"

"No," he says.'

"Are you here for a medical reason?" she asks you.

"No."

"Would you mind watching the emergency room? We're so shorthanded that I can't do both."

"Ah, yeah, I guess."

"Thanks."

After motioning for your partner to join you, the two of you sit and wait. A short time later, you hear a wail rise up from inside. The man sobs, telling you what happened to the woman or the girl; you can't tell which.

He comes out and collapses in a waiting room chair. Covering his face with his hands, he cries.

A short time later, you hear a snarl and a scream from inside. You jump up, gun in hand, and run through the door. There you see the woman, now a beast, trying to get at the nurse. She is using the bed that the injured girl is on to keep the creature away.

You step up behind the woman and fire a shot into her skull. The head explodes, sending blood, bone, and matter over the nurse and girl.

No sooner has the body fallen then gunshots come from the waiting room. You run back out to see your partner battling two beasts. The man is hand to hand with one of them. The second has a red spot growing on its shoulder but is still pressing forward on your partner. It swipes, knocking the gun from your partner's hand, then jumps on him/her.

You fear you can only save one.

"Do you:

3C3a) save your partner? Read on.

3C3b) save the man? Go to page 328

3C3a) You aim and fire at the beast on your partner, killing it. By the time you swing the gun toward the second beast, it has bitten into him/her. You are out of bullets, but you cut its throat with the knife.

Later that night, the girl dies. A doctor injects her with something to prevent her from rising again. You stay to lend a hand, helping people in the emergency room and guarding the door. That night, the man slips into a coma, and the doctor ends his life as well.

You stay, becoming a part of the staff. Five days later, the National Guard arrives to add security. Two days after they arrive, the crisis is over. You have survived. You drive home to start again.

End

3C3b) The man is closest. You think you have enough time to shoot both before anyone gets bit. You move in for a sure kill, but the beast sees you and swings a clawed hand. It strikes your hand, dislodging the gun. You scramble after it, pick it up, aim and fire. It takes two rounds to put it down—the last two bullets you have. You pull the knife, but the cry of pain tells you it's already too late.

You cut the creature's throat as it swallows flesh from your partner's neck.

Blood jets from the wound. You call for the nurse and crawl to help him/her. Pulling off your shirt, you press it to the wound and shout again. The nurse comes at a run, sees the injury, and bites her lower lip. You help carry him/her to a bed, and immediately, the nurse attaches wires and tubes while you keep up pressure. The doctor arrives two minutes later, dressed in scrubs, fresh from whatever surgery he's just performed.

A minute later, the steady beep indicating no heartbeat sounds. The doctor nods to the nurse and she shuts it off. He says a quick, "I'm sorry for your loss," and hustles off to handle the next crisis.

You stare at the lifeless body, unaware of what the nurse is doing. When she injects the body, you realize it's to prevent her/him from becoming one of the creatures. Your tears flow.

You sit in the waiting room almost comatose, until the nurse comes out and asks for your help. You stay and assist for the next three days until the National Guard arrives and announces the crisis is over. You drive home in a trance. You survived, but nothing will ever be the same.

End

# Other titles by Ray Wenck


The Danny Roth Mystery/Suspense Series
*Teammates*
*Teamwork*
*Home Team*
*Stealing Home*
*Group Therapy*
*Double Play* (coming soon)


*Random Survival* Post-Apocalyptic Series
*Random Survival*
*The Long Search for Home*
*The Endless Struggle*
*Hanging On*
Book 5 currently untitled (coming soon)


The Dead Series
*Tower of the Dead*
*Island of the Dead*


Standalone Titles
*Warriors of the Court*--young adult fantasy
*Live to Die Again*–suspense thriller
*Ghost of a Chance*–paranormal
*Pick-A-Path: Apocalypse Book 1*

## Author's Notes

I wrote the first Pick-A-Path because at most shows, people came up to the table to ask if *Random Survival* was a "choose your own adventure." The book's tagline is *If the world as you know it ended today, how would you survive?* I shortened that for the banner created by the very talented Ren McKenzie, who also did the cover of *Tower of the Dead*, to *How will you survive?* Those passing by came to the conclusion that they were like the favorite books of their youth.

With so many interested, I decided to try my hand at writing one. I mean, how hard could it be?

The answer came lightning fast. It was &^#*&%$ hard. It was easy to lose track of where I was. I started with a single storyline and ended up with so many, it was too difficult to know who did what in each option. In one, the main character is in an SUV; the next, in a van. Still, another has the MC alone, and another, with someone. Or in one, there's a weapon and another, nothing. I passed it to my editor, the incomparable Jodi McDermitt, who had a breakdown and took to drinking. (Well, that is her current excuse.)

In the end, after a lot of hard work and rewriting, we managed to get it finished. I remember putting the first copies on the table on Saturday during the Columbus comic con and telling fellow author Addie King that the books had either better not sell at all so I never have to go through this again, or sell so well that going through the mind-numbing process is at least worthwhile.

It sold out in a matter of hours.

Addie turned to me and said in a *haha hahaha* voice, "Looks like you'll be writing another one." (crap)

So, here is Book Two (groan), but having learned from the mistakes of the first book, this one was easier.

I want to thank all of you who have had that nostalgic look in your eyes when you stopped by the table at the various shows I've done since its release and picked up a copy. It has easily become my best seller.

Thanks again to Jodi for the editing and to Tyler Bertrand for the cover.

Thanks to Scott at Cajun Cafe for allowing me to drink his coffee, eat his spectacular food, and hang out and write when I'm in the Columbus area.

And thanks again to all of you who have enjoyed the first book. However, even though it was easier, I'm only tackling Book Three if you make me.

So, read on. I'll write more.